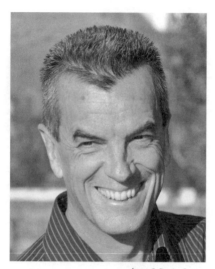

photo © Dario Cespa

Mark Davies went to school in south-west London, mid-Wales and Puerto de la Cruz in Tenerife. In between writing song lyrics, magazine articles and comedy sketches - and in the interest of a varied existence - he has played in a band, worked in wildlife conservation, got involved in sports events marketing, was a karaoke presenter, ghost writer, guide, film & TV extra, stand-up comedian, kindergarten teaching assistant, toy demonstrator and counter espionage agent. That last one was a lie.

A Table In Berlin is his first novel.

He lives in Fuerteventura with his wife and two children. And a cat.

A TABLE IN
BERLIN
MARK DAVIES

MACKEREL

A TABLE IN BERLIN

A CIP catalogue record for this book
is available from the British Library.

ISBN 978-0-9928238-0-1

Printed and bound by CPI Group (UK) Ltd, Croydon CR0 4YY

Editor Oleguer Sarsanedas
Cover Illustration Philip Bannister
www.philip-bannister.co.uk

First published in Great Britain in 2014 by Mackerel Books
www.mackerelbooks.co.uk

For Mum and Dad, with love and thanks

ACKNOWLEDGEMENTS

My wife, Jacqueline, who has had much to put up with. She waited patiently, and occasionally impatiently, for the weekly instalments as they came out of my head. I suppose I wrote this for her entertainment.

Claire Elizabeth Terry, whose innocently posted photograph started the whole thing off and without whom, therefore, this book would literally never have been written. For her positive energy and unfailing support I cannot thank her enough.

Brian Levine, who also never wavered in his support and encouragement.

My editor Oleguer Sarsanedas for making the process so painless - such is trust.

Elinor Perry-Smith for proof reading with such vigour.

Philip Bannister, an artist with an uncanny eye.

Also, thanks to Julia Rawlins of the British Council in Berlin; Tara Finn of the Foreign & Commonwealth Office; Steve Hughes; Lucy V Hay; Chris Jones; Marian Reeves; Elaine Janice Terry; Dario Cespa.

And finally to my two little girls, Neva and Cerys, who are not allowed to read the book but think I'm wonderful anyway; my brothers Tom and Nick, my sister Tamara, and my parents, who made me what I am and never doubted me for a minute.

Mark Davies

A TABLE IN BERLIN

E Minor

It all began, as it ended, at a table in Berlin.

It was a Greek restaurant. I only went in because it was the nearest open door. I was striding along, hunched forward, trying to make it back to the apartment ahead of some really ugly weather. The cloudburst, when it came, caught me as I drew up alongside. I instinctively swung the guitar case over my head in a futile attempt at shelter. Deafened by the boom-a-boom-boom of the rain on my case, half-blinded by the veil of water across my eyes, I sprinted towards the open doorway and, as I tried to clear the threshold, dropped the slippery case loudly onto the floor, tripping headlong over it immediately afterwards.

There may have been a more embarrassing entrance in the restaurant's history, but I very much doubt it.

Of course, I do occasionally think about how differently my life might have turned out.

What if the door had not been left open?

What if I hadn't gone in?

But it had, and I did.

My name is Charlie Stokes. If only I had been then, the man I am now. I was young, and I thought I knew women.

1961

Hamburg, West Germany, Thursday, March 16th

Manfred thought he had done everything there was to do in Hamburg, but he was wrong. He had never left anyone to die before.

"I'm fine. I'm fine. I'm fine. Just go, pal. Go!"

"You're crazy. You've been hit. You're bleeding."

"I'll be fine."

"Jesus Christ!"

"I'll tell them it was me. Get out of here."

There was sweat on his brow, beads trickling down and welling up across his thick eyebrows. The breathing short, snappy and something else. Rattling. He was looking across to the wall on the left, from where the man had fallen to the tracks below. There were shouts from a distance. Witnesses. What a mess.

"He's dead, isn't he?"

"Hold this against the wound. Press as hard as you can. I'm going to get help."

A hand gripped his wrist tightly. The injured man's voice was tight and insistent.

"Pal, you know who that was. You know what it means. Now, please, Christ, bugger off and leave me. Police will be here soon, don't you worry. You can't get involved."

Can't get involved? He was responsible!

A siren leached onto the scene.

"Manfred... you stupid Kraut!" he spat the words out with an exasperated smile. "You've got to get out of here!"

The tall man scanned the embankment. The siren drifted away. Another fight in another part of the city. But it would only be a matter of time. His friend was right. He had to get out of there.

"Don't fall asleep," he said.

And he left. He didn't run, he walked. Incredibly quickly. He looked at his watch and, as he made his way along the shadows to the office above the bar, he had already worked out what he was going to do.

"This way. Move. Now!"

There was a hard urgency to Manfred's voice that she'd never heard before. It frightened her. It was very early, barely dawn. She stumbled along the hallway. He gripped her hand. When they passed Hanne's door, she was puzzled to see it open, and tried to stop. But he was in no mood to wait and she was practically dragged down the stairs.

"Darling, wait. Stop please, I'm going to be sick!" she cried weakly.

"No, you're not. Don't be dramatic."

They were outside. She tensed against the dawn chill but was glad of the fresh air against her cheeks. Or as fresh as the air got, this close to the Reeperbahn. Suddenly, they stopped and he turned to face her. His face was flushed, making him look more handsome than ever.

"Here's the car," he said. "Get in."

It wasn't his car, she noted. Not the Mercedes. He yanked open the driver's side and began to bundle her into the little Volkswagen.

"You want me to drive?" she asked incredulously. He never let her drive them anywhere. Not because he didn't think she was any good, he just couldn't let someone else take control of anything. Not even a simple little car journey.

"You must hurry. The boat leaves in an hour. A woman - her name is Helga - will meet you at the gates and drive with you onto the ferry. She has the tickets."

"What?"

"You really need to leave now."

"Leave where? Why? What have you done?"

"When you get to Harwich you must drive to London and call this man."

He handed her a plain white postcard. On it was written: Brian Levine Management, 9 Orme Court, London W2. On the passenger seat was a blue airline bag, with BOAC on the side. He made her look at it.

"Your passport's in there, and five thousand US dollars. The money's yours but Brian will deal with it for you." He knew it was over now and he just wanted it to be done. "I can't explain. But, please. Go. Now."

"Five thousand dollars? I can't go to England! Not now. And what about you? What about us?"

"I'm driving home to Berlin. As soon as I know you're on the ferry."

"Berlin? What in God's name will you do there?"

"Ingrid," he began, "something's happened. You can't stay with me. Not here."

Ingrid could only repeat the question he hadn't answered.

"What about us?"

"It ends here."

"I'm pregnant."

She knew it would be a surprise. But she expected a response. There was none.

"I'm going to have your baby. And I really am going to be sick now." She leant out of the car and threw up over his shoes. She slumped back in the seat, eyes closed, and reached into her handbag for a tissue. The words had stopped. The urgency had gone. But the silence was every bit as chaotic.

It did not, however, last very long.

"I'm going back to the apartment," said Ingrid, "this is, really, just ridiculous. And what about the rehearsals?" It was as if she had flicked a switch. Immediately, he was back in control. He put the keys in the ignition, stood back to slam shut the door and looked anxiously back up the street. He seemed to relax. Ingrid had opened the window. She spoke in a quiet, calm voice.

"What have you done, Manfred?"

"I'll call Brian. I'll come and find you. At the end of the month. Until then you won't hear from me. Do you understand?"

It seemed to make her feel better. She had a date. An appointment. These were things she could understand. And if he promised to come and find her, then he would come and find her. Yes, all right, she would leave. She

4

started the car and turned to look into his dazzling blue eyes. He said he'd come and find her.

"Promise?" She asked.

He didn't answer.

She put the car in gear and shook her head sadly. With a last glance, weighed down with meaning, she meant to say 'Goodbye'. Instead, the words slipped out:

"What have you done?"

The tyres gripped the cobbles and the car was gone. He watched it leave and sighed.

"I killed a man." He slipped into the shadows. "Maybe two."

1987

West Berlin, Thursday, October 15th

A fat blanket of soft drizzle had broken the early promise of a beautiful day. It choked the light out of Berlin, and sent the population about their business, chin down against the damp.

On Kantstrasse, off the Ku'damm, as a strengthening breeze brought with it some proper rain, the door of the Athena Restaurant was being wedged open with a folded beer mat stolen from the Armenian bar four doors down. Dimitrios checked whether it would hold the heavily-sprung door open. He stepped out onto the pavement and, after a squint up at the sky, quickly scanned the street. He noticed a man approaching purposefully, one hand clutching at his collar to keep the rain from his neck, the other holding a guitar case. Probably one of those street buskers. As he went back inside, a chill wind followed him. Briefly, he considered removing the wedge and closing the door.

He shrugged, and left it open.

As the heavens finally opened, Dimitrios watched the rain bounce up off the street outside as if the entire road had come to the boil. He had turned his attention to the middle-aged couple on table three, when the flat crack of something falling made him start, and the dark, sodden body of a young man skidded across the floor, hit a table leg, and came to an untidy stop at his feet.

There was an uncomfortable, heavy pause. The young man lay still, the heat of self-consciousness raising his pulse. The theme from Zorba the Greek was playing in the background. What he most wanted to do right then was curse like a sewer rat. What he actually did was squeeze a few hoarse words through tense lips.

"Table for one. Please."

Outside, a grey Audi 5000 had pulled up and was idling. It remained there, partly on the kerb, for fifteen or twenty minutes, and then slowly drove away.

It may not have been one of those grim grey buildings that are Croydon's gift to England, but the British consular office on Uhlandstrasse, knocked up quickly and efficiently atop the rubble of war, was a study in ruthless architectural understatement. It was well-built, practical, uninspiring, yet self-assured enough not to flirt with its more traditional neighbours.

Of course if Beth had wanted the exterior of her office to lift her spirits when she went to work in the morning, she was in the wrong job. But she already knew that. She had been in a succession of them since she graduated from Cambridge. After three years of studious mediocrity, she hadn't even been given a nickname. If she had, it would have been *Go-getter*, but only in a strictly ironic sense. Her time at Downing College was marked with such indelible invisibility that even the boy who absconded with her virginity failed to remember her in his roll call of conquests. Not out of spite, he just failed to remember.

Unlike her exuberant younger sister Isabelle, Beth didn't need the attention. She didn't go looking for it and none ever came looking for her. She was resigned to take life as it took her. But, as her friends would often say, if you were looking for unflappable, look no further.

Beth finished with her phone conversation, having taken notes, and surveyed the glistening street as the rain lashed the browning leaves of the young lime tree in front of the building. She began to worry about whether she had left the window of her bathroom open. It was the kind of thing she worried about a lot, if not for long.

She phoned her sister at the British Council to tell her where they should try for lunch, as she now had a location. It didn't sound like the kind of place where you needed to book, but she'd leave that for Isabelle to decide. Once or twice a month they all went out for lunch. Alexandra paid, and none of them ever questioned it. It was Alex who had the well-paid job with an expense account. She was the one who swam in the mineral-rich waters of the private sector.

"Isabelle," Beth began, "I'm leaving now. Here's the address, have you got a pen? It's not far, you can walk."

A t the offices of the British Council on Hardenbergstrasse, a street running off from her sister Beth's place of work, Isabelle shook her head as if someone had sent a short burst of electrical current across her earlobes.

"I'm not going to walk there, am I? To practically Savigny Platz, for God's sake. In these shoes? In this weather?" Every follicle of her being shuddered in mock indignation. "You'll split a taxi with me, won't you, sweetie?" This she directed at her colleague, Joanna, who smiled indulgently.

"Is it that far, Izzy?"

"Far enough, Jo." She gave a short flick of her face to clear some renegade strands of wavy blonde hair. She passed over a scrap of paper. "Could you call Alex and tell her where she's taking us? I have to take these upstairs." She picked up a well-worn, manilla folder and initialled the corner. She flashed a smile and a sly wink.

Joanna shook her head.

"You do know he's married, don't you?"

"Not to me." She skipped out of the office, trailing a gentle haze of Chanel No. 5 in her wake. Even her perfume belonged to somebody's wife.

Joanna was drawn to the window to watch the rain hammer down. Hardenbergstrasse was not a street that took kindly to rain. She looked at her watch then dialled an internal number on the phone.

"Hi Anja, it's Jo. Can I borrow your umbrella? You did say you were working through lunch, didn't you?" Joanna knew that Isabelle would agree to walk in the end.

"Yes, I am. Of course you can."

"Thanks."

"Hey, Joanna, you'd know this one," said Anja.

"Oh?"

"Yes. Elvis Presley. Would you say he's definitely dead?"

"Sorry?"

"You remember that girl, Michelle, from the Canadian Embassy? She was at the opening last Thursday? The abstract paintings?"

"Oh. Yes?"

"She says there's a file going round, very secret. She says there are people in Montreal who run a department, called The Graceland Project, from the Consulate." Joanna guessed, from the type of the silence, that there was a punch line on the way. "People are saying Elvis is in Canada."

Joanna glanced at her watch. Was that the time?

"Have you ever been to Canada, Anja?" she asked.

"Yes. Twice."

"If money were no object, and you could live anywhere in the whole world, anywhere at all, where would you go?"

There was a squeal from the other end of the line.

"Oh, I like this kind of game! Let me think. Acapulco. No, wait. Tahiti. Honolulu!"

"Right," said Joanna, "not Canada, then?"

After a short but significant pause, Anja said: "The umbrella's hanging behind my door."

Joanna put down the phone and smiled to herself. She was still new enough to West Berlin to find the constant webs of rumour, misinformation - intentional or otherwise - conspiracy theories, and outright lies, amusing. She looked more closely at her new watch, which had stopped. She lifted the receiver and called Anja again.

"Anja. Hi, sorry, my watch is on the blink, what do you make the time? Really? It can't be… no, I mean the time here now, in Berlin."

Dimitrios Fanariotis was a man named and built to run a Greek restaurant or, at a push, a small family hotel. His restaurant, which he had named The Athena, was average in every way. The food was good without being exceptional, and neither the décor nor the prices had been excessively updated. It was honest. And in Berlin that was something to be valued for its own sake.

His wife Alikaki did the cooking, a task which she undertook with silent relish. Fortunately for the restaurant's stability and well-being, she also took care of most of the finances. Dimitrios's understanding of the mechanics of money was basic at best. But he was a natural and effortless host. His reaction to the sudden, loud, and unconventional arrival of a damp young Englishman and his guitar was a practised smile and defensive footwork.

"Would you like a towel?"

Charlie Stokes was still rubbing the side of his head and had not heard clearly. He assumed it was a food-related statement. He had never eaten in a Greek restaurant before and knew nothing of the cuisine other than a vague notion of something called moussaka.

"Excuse me?"

"For your hair. A towel?" Dimitrios helpfully mimed a drying action.

"Ah, right. A towel," said Charlie, "yes, I see. No, thanks, I'm fine. Just bumped my head a bit. My fault." He laughed unconvincingly and stood up, rather too quickly.

That might have been a bit of a mistake.

E Minor

There were four of us in the band. I didn't count Troy, the saxophonist, who only played occasionally and was an American. I was the one in charge and Luke, who was a couple of years older and also played the guitar, was my number two. Jake the drummer and Ritchie the bassist made up the foursome. Luke was in England, and had been for a few weeks. We'd had a bit of a falling-out. A kid called Daniel was kind of standing in for him in the meantime.

We were an odd bunch, held together by a common bond.

We were all skint.

Ritchie was practically a doctor before walking out of his medical degree to "live a little." So, we were never short of a prognosis, and it was he who informed me that I was prone to orthostatic hypotension. He said I could also use the term postural hypotension. But if, after having stood up too quickly somewhere and finding myself swaying like a drunk in a hammock, I told anyone I felt dizzy, he would disown me and join a blues band. He didn't have much time for head rush, either.

"Girls love a bloke with a syndrome," he'd said to me. "It sounds stupid, but there you go. Girls love a bloke with a baby, too. That's just life. If you tell a girl you're having a dizzy spell, they'll think you're a gay boy living at home with your mum. Give them a bit of Latin and you're laughing."

Bumping my head on the table leg hadn't helped, but I got up much too eagerly in the restaurant, and as everything swirled around me, I only just made it to my table before I was ready to pass out. I held on to the edge, and clenched my jaw, while pretending to gaze out onto the joys of Kantstrasse.

This was hard to do realistically as my eyes were closed.

"Everything fine?" I heard a deep voice behind me ask.

I nodded.

"Menu or would you like to hear Special of the Day?"

I nodded.

You can never have too much nodding. When I opened my eyes again I saw a car partly mounted on the kerb outside, and a pigeon shaking its feathers under the shelter provided by a now-bulging awning. There were holes all over it - the awning, not the pigeon - allowing the water to escape in an irregular line of pulsing streams. It wouldn't have looked any different had a group of drunken lads taken to the roof to have a piss.

The waiter had placed my guitar case in a tiny alcove that could have been especially built for the purpose. The water ran off it and pooled onto the floor. In the gloom, it reminded me of those old black-and-white police photographs of Mafia murders, where a newly-minted corpse gently rests on a bed of fresh blood. Travelling from that image to opting for the Special of the Day - moussaka, no less - took no time at all.

Strange choice of dish for a vegetarian to order.

They made their way along Uhlandstrasse like a trio of cool female TV detectives, with plenty of flapping gaberdine and bouncing hair. Coincidentally, Beth was passing the entrance to the British Council's offices just as Isabelle and Joanna stepped out. There was a short pantomime moment when the umbrella wouldn't open, but otherwise the three of them barely broke step.

Isabelle had taken Joanna's arm so that she was tight up against her and benefiting from the umbrella's cover, though the rain had eased off to the point of inconsequence. She bounced as she walked, as if her personality could be distilled into a single action. She used her walk, and her heels, to extract every last vertical inch of her being. Joanna, in contrast, glided along the wide pavement with a grace both effortless and unintentional. Beth clutched at her coat collar with both hands and couldn't have cared less how she walked.

They turned right onto Kantstrasse and began to look for Alex.

"There she is! Good, she found it, then. Thank God, my feet are killing me."

"Izzy, for God's sake, it's hardly been ten minutes."

"It's not pizza is it, Beth? I couldn't bear pizza again."

"It's Greek."

"Oh darling, not more cheese." Isabelle spoke quickly, usually because whatever she was saying was already out of date before it had even left her mouth and she needed to make space for something else. "Alex, sweetie, you look amazing."

Alexandra was tall and fair and immaculately turned-out. She was often teased about how alike she was to Meryl Streep, but in truth she was much better-looking. She wore a long flowing coat, a beautifully cut white blazer, and a tired smile. The spark had gone from her blue-grey eyes and the others all saw it leave. Nothing a bottle of ouzo wouldn't fix. They stood in front of the doorway, as if doubting they should enter. Dark skies still threatened.

"Shall we?" said Beth, bundling them in.

It was a tiny restaurant, by some people's standards. It couldn't have taken more than thirty at a push. But there'd be no pushing today. Apart from an elderly man alone, there were two couples and a table of six at the far end. Alex, remembering her role as the group's leader-in-residence, took off her coat and looked around.

"All right, then. Where shall we sit?" she asked.

"Over there," said Isabelle impishly. "That table over there, by the wall. The one with the man underneath it."

E Minor

When the dish arrived, I ate it quite quickly, chivvying every second mouthful down with a heavy draught of mineral water. I had no idea what moussaka was, or what it would look like. I had seen a lasagne up close before, and I could see a family resemblance immediately. I had given up red meat quite a few years before and, despite it having become fashionable since, and therefore hopelessly uncool in my eyes, I was still this vague version of a vegetarian. It wasn't as if I were allergic to meat, so there was no chance that my hair would fall out as a result of putting the moussaka away.

I discovered the owner's name was Dimitrios, and he'd spent seven years in London's Palmers Green. We exchanged short, erratic bursts of repartee on the Holy Trinity of gentlemen's conversation: music, football and women. He enjoyed Nana Mouskouri, Arsenal and dependable women, where I was into Elvis, Spurs and girls loose enough to rattle.

I thought it best to give the moussaka a chance to digest before risking any prolonged exercise, so I fished out my Walkman to listen to a bit of the morning's rehearsal, as we'd had a first go at my new song, *"Later ('Cos It's Much Too Early Now)"*. I don't know how it happened, probably pulling it out of the coat pocket, but the volume control ended up at maximum so, when I'd stuck the earphones on and pressed play, I actually shocked myself. I knocked my pen off the table in the scramble to adjust the level, and I watched the navy blue Parker skid across the floor and under table seven.

I thought nothing at all about crawling on all fours to retrieve it, but I couldn't see it in the sudden gloom and I suddenly got distracted by the lyrics in the song and closed my eyes to concentrate better. Had I really rhymed *"renewal"* with *"you all"* in the double chorus? Accepting that I had, an odd sensation came over me. It had nothing to do with the lyrics. It was that primeval instinct that senses shadows in the dark. I opened my eyes and was aware that a pair of extremely feminine and immaculately polished high-heeled leather boots had appeared inches from my face. Worse still, a flap of tablecloth lifted to reveal an amused face with cheeky green eyes and a pretty upturned nose saying something to me, not one word of which I could hear over the music.

So I reversed out into public view, stood up as slowly as I could and switched off the tape. I was aware of an ensemble accumulating around me, spearheaded by the girl who had flushed me out. She may have had some light freckles either side of the pretty nose I'd mentioned before, but it was the slightly raised eyebrows that gave me the impression that she might have asked me a question and was waiting for an answer.

"Essen Sie dort unter dem Tisch?" she said.

I had been in Berlin for six months or so, but the German language and I remained strangers. My standard response on such occasions was the classic, if overused, *sorry, I'm English*, but I was held up from launching it by the arrival of my blue Parker pen. It was attached to an arm dressed in red.

"Dieser Tisch ist frei, oder?" said the cheeky one again, but I was now listening to another voice, a warm, comforting one, belonging to the pen-returner.

"Was suchen Sie hier?"

"Thank you," I said, a phrase I hoped would cover everything outstanding on the discussion front.

"Oh, you're *English*!" said the first voice. "Is this table taken?"

"Not by me," I replied, for honesty is a virtue and all that.

"Shame," she said and I could swear I heard one of the group groan.

"Well..." I lifted the pen in the general direction of the girl who'd given it back to me, "thanks." I edged back to my table. Dimitrios had left me a coffee, so I arranged myself around it with as much poetic nonchalance as I could and, assuming a glassy-eyed vagueness to complement my pantomime of pretending I was writing, made several visual sweeps of table seven. There were four women in all, each of them attractive. Give or take a handful of years, they'd have all been around my age, too, so the only pimple on this particular nose was that I was outnumbered four-to-one. If only the rest of the lads were here.

I had to be back at the apartment for when Luke called at three o'clock. Or was it four o'clock? And was that our time or London time? I tried to blank out the restaurant so I could frisk my memory and that's when it came back to me that I'd left my wallet in the apartment. That's why I was walking back in the rain and not taking the bus. And now I had a meal to pay for.

I considered making a bolt for it. I reckoned there was enough Kantstrasse to go around to give this particular stretch of it a miss for a month or so, and I didn't think my face was that memorable. On the other hand, I was a 26-year-old and a bit past it for that kind of thing, surely. I'd think of something. I might even consider telling the truth. In the meantime I decided to stay put and gaze from afar at a pretty girl in a restaurant, pretty much my full-time occupation lately. If it was better to have loved and lost than never to have loved at all, it was much safer to do so from a distance.

I would like to have overheard more than I did, but the table of six at the far end were Greek and, in keeping with the traditions of all Mediterranean peoples, conversation was passionate, rowdy and happily shared.

There were four of them, clearly friends. There was the attention-seeking effervescent blonde, a black wide-necked sweater exposing a shoulder now and then; the well-dressed one, looking a bit like Meryl Streep without the pointy bits, who probably had more attention than she knew what to do with; the brown-eyed girl in the red sweater who had found my pen; and the shorter one with shoulder-length, slightly unkempt hair who cupped her chin in her hand in an ambivalent gesture of simultaneous boredom and interest, a look not many people can pull off.

Despite all my best efforts, my attention was drifting towards just the one. Annoyingly, it was the grumpy, unkempt one who kept firing surreptitious glances in my direction.

You know, as if you're being judged for no particular reason you can imagine.

"Beer I think, don't you?"

"Not for me, not at lunch time. Some sparkling water and a bottle of red."

"White."

"One red, one white and a beer."

"We're having lunch, it's not a hen night."

"You decide, Alex, you're the boss. Alex?"

"Hmm? Yes all right."

Alexandra Gagnon, Alex to her friends, allowed a delicate smile to play safely across her mouth while she kept her chin high and regal. It was lovely to be with her friends again, but she would have to work at the bonhomie today. And pay attention, too.

"You look fab as always, darling," said Isabelle, "I love that jacket, you lucky thing. It's not Alexander McQueen, is it?"

"No, Izzy, it's from a new designer called Matthew Goulding."

"It's very you. "

Izzy was Isabelle's pet name. It rhymed with dizzy which, by nature, should have been her middle name. She wore a loose-fitting black knit open neck sweater, and had rolled the sleeves up to her elbows in readiness for some action.

"Thank you," said Alex.

"Is it comfy?"

"Not at all." And they all laughed.

Charlie Stokes noticed that the women were at ease with one another, in much the same way that the band were, at least before Luke left. Women were so good at that sort of thing. They bonded easily. Boys bonded superficially on hot air, bravado and beer.

In a few short minutes the restaurant's ambience had settled into one of comfortable, relaxed, family-run restaurant. Not too loud, not too quiet, just right. Maybe one day Charlie would come back with the lads. The table of Greeks tucked into their plates with no lessening of tumult, the girls giggled and mock-argued, the other couples raised their own murmurs to be heard above the babble, and so the zither muzak was finally drowned out. And that, as far as Charlie Stokes was concerned, was a result.

Joanna was a listener. Of course she did her share of speaking, but at listening she excelled.

And being still.

And enigmatic.

And Charlie Stokes was a sucker for still, enigmatic girls. When they came packaged with brown eyes, full lips and a head of lustrous brown hair, he was Lord Sucker of Suckertown Manor. Isabelle spoke tirelessly, animating her chat with sudden and potentially hazardous hand movements. Beth, with her studied air of resignation, did what she could to counter her sister's outpourings with a steady diet of put-downs, while Alexandra presided over the whole affair with the elegance becoming of a glossy fashion magazine's advertising manager. But Joanna's role was one of sparkling glances, understanding nods and indulgent smiles. Occasionally, she contributed something in a calm, velvety voice.

Charlie Stokes was single and, unless he could see proof to the contrary in front of him with his own eyes, assumed that any girl he took a shine to in public would be equally unattached. Clearly, this was ludicrous. During his saner, more mature, moments he knew it was ludicrous. It was just unfortunate such a moment could not have troubled itself to come to his aid now. Instead, rational thought got up and left the premises.

And so Charlie sat there, sadly intent on further inflaming the cataclysmic rage that the reintroduction of meat had unleashed within his bowels by the continued sipping of Dimitrios's ferociously-strong coffee. He was allowing an image to develop in his mind.

He and the dusky-haired princess are strolling hand in hand down Oranienstrasse en route to Moritzplatz and the myriad bars and cafes beyond. While the breeze plays with her hair they continue, achingly slowly, towards his apartment where the reality of his frankly pestilent existence in the murky netherworld of the east Kreuzberg district of West Berlin comes as something of a jolt.

He could always move.

Joanna, who was not a dusky-haired princess in real life, sensed that Alex was not quite herself today but held back from enquiring. Beth was also mildly distrait, though with her it was less obvious as she had a tendency to dip in and out of a conversation as if she had to get up and answer an imaginary knock on her front door. Isabelle was Isabelle, and particularly so today.

"Sweetie, you said you were giving up," said Isabelle.

"I am," said Alex. "I am giving up. I just haven't given up yet. Tch!" Her lighter wasn't working. Click. Click. Click.

At this point, Charlie Stokes missed his opportunity.

In one suave movement he could have made his way to table seven, arm outstretched and, with his lacquered Dunhill lighter, ignited Alex's cigarette. He wasn't interested in Alex, but it would have given him an excuse to gatecrash the party. If only he hadn't realised, ten years ago when he was sixteen years old, that smoking was a futile, disgusting habit he might actually have had a lighter on him. But he didn't. So the opportunity was lost. Isabelle lit Alex's cigarette. Charlie looked at his watch.

And this time it did register with him that it still showed ten minutes to twelve. And it could not possibly be.

E Minor

One should never look a gift horse in the mouth, they say. So I didn't. I leaned as far forward as the chair allowed and tried to interject at a point where I had the most chance of being heard without having to raise my voice.

"Excuse me, do you have the time?" I aimlessly patted my wrist. "My watch has stopped." I aimed the question at the brown-eyed girl, of course, but it landed right in the middle of the table and the chatterbox blonde reached it first, something any man with half a brain would have known would happen.

"Oh, that's funny, so has yours, eh, sweetie?" she said, not at me but at the brown-eyed girl. It was a rhetorical question, clearly, as she didn't wait for a reply. "It's half-one."

"Thanks."

I had to go. I would be pushed to get back in time for Luke's call, and I didn't want to give him any more reasons to be narked. I got up, gathered my stuff and went to the counter to explain the bill payment issue to Dimitrios *sotto voce*. I don't know why I didn't just explain it simply and truthfully. But living in West Berlin where, if you didn't have a story more convoluted than the next man you were an unworthy resident, I had to stretch my excuse out a yard or two. Dimitrios accepted my promise to return. The offer to leave my guitar behind as a deposit may or may not have swayed him. He clearly didn't want it clogging up his little alcove, but I think the gesture was appreciated.

I waited while he wrote the restaurant's phone number down, as I had promised to return *en masse* with the band. I was feeling more myself then and perhaps should have known better than to turn and toss out a couple of surplus glances towards table seven again, because the brown-eyed girl chose that very moment to look up, and caught one of them full in the face.

And what a face.

She seemed to have an aura. Was that the right word? Dangerous things, auras. If you get too close to one it'll suck you into its vortex and, by the time you come out the other side, you're not the man you were. Then again, if there were any sucking to be had, would you care?

Our eyes locked for probably no time at all, a couple of seconds, but it was long enough for a celestial choir to start warming up, and for my entire central nervous system to shut down. A large basket of Speckled Wood butterflies were released in the very pit of my stomach as one thought limped across my mind, albeit through metaphorically gritted teeth.

"Smile, for Christ's sake, smile."

She looked back down and across her table as one of the others offered her a top-up. So she missed my attempt at a smile. I think my lips might have moved slightly upward, but only on one side. Was that a smile, or had I just had a stroke? Either way, the spell was broken. I turned on my heel, exchanged a couple of practically incomprehensible pleasantries with Dimitrios and, bending down to pick up my guitar, left the restaurant with a fluidity sadly missing from my entrance.

I paused outside to adjust my collar, and to buy some time. I allowed the passing rumble of a bus to bring me back to the real world. It was a bloody long walk from here back to the apartment, but at least it had stopped raining. I turned left and headed home. Even then, I allowed my eyes to send a couple of darting glances through the window, because you never know.

The brown-eyed girl had looked at me.

It could have been ten minutes, it could have been five.

I was faintly aware of the syncopated rhythm of my steps as I hurried along the Ku'damm, the occasional *ker-scuff* interrupting the *clack-clack-clacky clack-clack-clack*. It didn't help having the guitar case in my right hand, or being in a hurry. That wasn't the main problem.

The main problem was that my mind was still in the restaurant.

And I wasn't.

A strange affliction affects those who, as Luke would say, "need to get laid and don't hang around." The eyes lose a sense of perspective. It's like Jake, the drummer: he drinks and the girls he's trying to chat up become more and more ravishing with every downed pint of Krombacher. With others, the same happens with every passing month of celibacy. You take a shine to a girl and you convince yourself that she is the most beautiful woman that ever lived.

I realised that straight away. My eyes were too desperate to be allowed out unaccompanied. So I gave myself an imaginary slap and shrugged off my high opinion of this brown-eyed stranger, whose only claim to greatness was an overrated ability to bend down and pick up a ballpoint pen.

I say shrugged off, it would probably be more accurate to say that I gently peeled it off. And folded it in half. And placed it carefully in my pocket, just in case. And as I stood waiting patiently and foolishly to cross over Joachimstaler Strasse, I determined to do three things. One was to stop thinking about that girl. And so were the other two.

So, I went back towards the restaurant.

I sort of had a plan.

Alexandra had drunk a little too much for a weekday lunchtime. Or perhaps she had drunk it a little too quickly. She felt worn and faded, like a photograph left in a shop window. The conversation she was trying to follow acted as a backing track to the monologue playing out within her own mind. And when the two inevitably absorbed each other, she gave an involuntary start, a sudden jolt in her left leg. Had anyone noticed? She brushed some imaginary crumbs of pita bread off her lap, and was about to brush some more, when she became aware of the others watching her with what she could only describe as expectation. She had just enough energy for the kind of smile worthy of the Mona Lisa.

"Yes, or no, then?" Isabelle was asking from close range.

"Yes, obviously," she replied, blindly but correctly. And to ensure continuity, she drank some more wine.

"Outnumbered again, Jo," teased Isabelle.

"I thought Alexandra would have been with me, at least. You're all hopeless. Pass the cheese."

They all dissolved into schoolgirl giggles, Alexandra too, despite having no idea at all what she had missed. She blinked and stretched her back. Time to get herself together. She would ring London in the morning. Sell the bloody shares. All of them. Get the money back to the bank and kiss the sorry enterprise goodbye. Good riddance. Anyway, Tony was sure to ring her soon. He could handle it all. Bloody Tony. Husband, entrepreneur, and complete useless prick! In fact, she wouldn't wait until tomorrow. She'd do it as soon as she got back to the office. Or perhaps she would be too pissed to make sense? Tomorrow then. Whenever. Enjoy this lovely company, and keep a lid on it. No one needs to know.

She was drifting off again, and was brought back by something Joanna was saying.

"Izzy, it's that boy again, with the marvellous hair."

"Perfect. I'll get him to take the picture, then."

"Wonder what he wants?"

"Perhaps he left his pen behind?"

Another round of giggles.

Charlie Stokes had not left his pen behind but, if he had, it would have been a better ploy than the one that had persuaded him to turn back. The restaurant had live music at the weekends, if the little posters were anything to go by. Now, a man in traditional costume giving it some on a bouzouki is a whole different story to a four or five piece, electrically-powered outfit - but for Charlie it was enough of an excuse to offer Dimitrios his band's details, in case he ever felt the need for a bit of a party. That giving a business card to Dimitrios would do nothing to produce an introduction to the girl was the blatantly obvious flaw in the scheme.

This realisation only took hold once Charlie, after having danced safely across the traffic, found himself standing alone by the counter, with the eyes of the diners upon him. He was mildly floundering when, very much to his surprise, he noticed that the vivacious blonde was gesturing for him to go over. He put his case down where he stood, and went over.

Things quickly became muddled around table seven. Charlie arrived just as someone, whom he couldn't see clearly, temporarily blocked his path by standing up to remove a jacket. Dimitrios, with his large arms concealed by an intricate terracing of colourful dishes, had also materialized into this space, creating a small social gathering. Mindful of the ceramics, Charlie froze mid-movement to allow Dimitrios's natural flow to continue, but had less luck with the over-dressed diner. Poking his head around the obstruction, he found himself looking at a small black camera. It was a Minolta AF-DL. His drummer Jake had one practically the same. It appeared to be heading his way.

"Would you mind?" Isabelle asked, pulling a fake apologetic face in the process. "A couple of quick, casual snaps." The twinkle in her eye was the one she kept for the vulnerable men, and Charlie was one of those. She could tell. He had a great mass of thick, dark hair and eyes that were both intense and sensitive. She wondered what it would be like to grip that hair and pull him towards her lips. Not now, of course, just generally.

"Sure."

"Only Dimitrios, that's the owner's name you know, happened to mention that you were an artist. I was going to ask him to take it, but when I saw you were back I thought it best to take advantage."

Charlie Stokes had no idea what she was talking about.

"Okay."

"Though yours isn't a camera case, is it?"

"No," said Charlie. He looked back towards his guitar and wondered if it was all right to leave it so close to the open doorway.

"He's not that kind of an artist, Izzy, not a visual artist, right?" said Joanna.

The shock of hearing her voice again, warm, sweet, and calming, forced Charlie to look at her, something he had steadfastly avoided since his return. He was close enough to notice the length and natural thickness of her eyelashes, and the steady, unblinking gaze of her brown eyes. He was close enough to smell her perfume. Had he been more of a gigolo he would probably have been able to identify the scent. He wasn't, so he couldn't. But it was nice. For her part, Joanna was taking in the young man's features. An interesting face. Probably a nice man. Seemed a bit uncomfortable, right now. Probably not sure how to handle Isabelle. She can be quite full-on, but she always gets the guy in the end. Poor lamb, perhaps she should guide him away to safety? Oh, did he just say something incomprehensible?

Now that he had a second chance, and with the conversation presenting him with the perfect opportunity, Charlie Stokes fully intended to introduce himself with a suitably memorable opening line. Instead, and probably a result of his nervous system shutting down in the vicinity of the girl's aura, he simply stammered out a random selection of short words.

"Then, it's yes, well."

Joanna inclined her head ever so slightly to one side in an evident expectation of greater clarity. Charlie Stokes wondered if any of the Great Romances of History had ever been launched on the back of four scrawnier words, five if he removed the apostrophe. The hiatus that followed lasted only two and a half seconds, but that was two and a quarter seconds longer than was comfortable. He put himself out of his misery.

"Okay, here goes!" he said briskly, raising the camera to his eyes and pressing the shutter. Click. Someone, thinking it would be funny, made a half-hearted attempt to get into the photograph from an adjoining table, which seemed to amuse everyone, particularly Isabelle. Charlie thought it best to have another crack at it, certain that an arm or shoulder had got in the way. But that was the last frame on the roll.

"Won't you join us for a drink? Sorry, what's your name?" It was Alexandra speaking now, a static presence at the table till now. She had an imperceptible smile, thought Charlie, or barely perceptible, at least.

"Charlie," he answered, "Charlie Stokes."

"Ah, that's a nice name. Charlie Stokes. Sweet."

Sweet was a word that hit a man's radar right in the connector cables. The lads had always vehemently assured Charlie that if a woman ever calls a man sweet, he may as well cash in his chips and call for a taxi. That it had been Joanna who said this, however, only proved that the lads were a pack of simple inbred halfwits who knew less than nothing about anything.

"I don't mean you, Charlie. Just your name," said Joanna. "Men would rather die than be called sweet, wouldn't they?"

"Not at all," said he, wrapping a gaze of adoration around her shoulders, and tying the ends in a bow. "I've been called worse."

"Worse than sweet?"

"No. Never."

He smiled. She smiled. The moon and stars, heaven and earth smiled. Then Beth said: "Someone's just run off with your guitar."

As a mood breaker, it worked.

Charlie Stokes spun around on his heels. There was already no sign of anyone, or his guitar. He froze. Trying to put into words the untold agony of a beautiful moment being throttled because the most important inanimate object in his life was heading in the opposite direction, he explored the far reaches of his considerable vocabulary, just to articulate the complexity of his feelings.

"Fuck! For fucking fuck's sake!"

He bolted out onto the street, followed by Dimitrios, whose customers were left fluttering slightly from the sudden commotion. Beth, Joanna, Isabelle and Alexandra watched him leave and shared a range of bemused expressions. It was Beth who spoke first.

"I must say, it's a rare treat to hear a man express such a wide range of raw emotion, don't you think? And only using one word."

"I agree," said Alexandra. She lifted an empty glass. "A toast to Charlie Stokes. Here's hoping we meet again."

"Yes," said Isabelle, suddenly serious. She briskly moved some of the detritus around the table, looked down by her feet and even, ludicrously, stood up to check her seat. She was sobering up quickly now. "He's got my camera," she sighed, more to herself than to the others.

Shit. He's got my camera.

E Minor

I don't mind running far. And I don't mind running fast. But I do not like running both far and fast. And that is exactly what I was doing. I had no idea that Dimitrios had joined me, or that he had feigned injury within seconds of realizing the anticipated level of athletic ability being demanded.

I was moving like a demon. In those days my body was, if not a temple, certainly a place of quiet reflection. But it was neither fitness levels nor clean living that was driving me on, it was unmitigated fury at having lost my guitar and at leaving the restaurant, again, with unfinished business.

The other blot on the escapade was an adrenaline-fuelled inability to think rationally. Although I was hitting the speedometer impressively, it should have occurred to me that I didn't have a target in sight. This was a concern. In Hollywood it doesn't matter how far ahead the target is, or whether he has turned into an alley or side street unseen by the hero. The hero always knows which alley or side street to turn into. He just knows. I, on the other hand, once I had broken the world record for running the quarter mile in civvies, wondered why I had not noticed any fast-moving person with a guitar case up ahead. I had assumed that Beth's exclamation was in real time and not something she had previously recorded. The door to the restaurant was at one end, and there were windows along its full length: if the thief had headed due West, he would never have cleared sight of the windows before I had looked round. Not even if he had been the Olympic sprint champion. So, I assumed he must have headed due East. And perhaps has already executed his turn into a side street?

On the other hand, had I thought through which procedures I had in place for the type of scenario that immediately followed the catching up of a thief? Hot and sweaty and slightly desperate as he would inevitably be. It occurred to me that an understanding smile, a shrug of the shoulders and a polite "I think that belongs to me" might not necessarily bring the story to a happy conclusion. Now, despite being in a band that had played in many highly dubious locations, and despite even occasionally entering, unaccompanied, unknown public houses where sawdust was still sprinkled on the floors, I was a studiously violence-free zone. I was proud to have lived that long without ever hitting, or being hit by another human being. But West Berlin was not a city for the faint-hearted. Anyone brazen enough to steal a guitar from a busy restaurant in broad daylight must be pretty sure of himself.

I was starting to lose some of the indignant righteousness that would have boosted my self-worth in a physical confrontation. What if the thief was one of those big fat wallahs who are wider than they are tall? I had been practically a vegetarian for years. This had sharpened my mind, and brought peace and poetry to my art, but it was not going to be any good to me in a brawl. And a single dose of moussaka was not going to tip the scales in my favour.

I stopped running.

I just stopped. My heart was pumping, both from the physical exertion and the perceived threat of violence. I still scanned the street. After all, it was no ordinary cheap guitar. And the thief might just have been a kid. I could handle a kid. And, if not, then I could threaten him with this rock, I thought, idly conscious of an object in my hand. It was not a rock, of course, it was a little black camera. Not mine. And then, an interesting thing happened.

A bus trundled past, splashing across the wet tarmac. It was the death rattle of its diesel engine that made me glance up, but something else altogether that caught my attention. Taking pride of place on a window seat, clearly visible through the rain-splattered glass, was my guitar case.

Time to run again.

B eth wore contact lenses. Her eyes were bothering her. She got up.
"I'm going to take my lenses out."

"Beth I'm sorry, is it the cigarette?" asked Alex.

"No, no," lied Beth, "just feel like putting my glasses on instead."

"You're a martyr to your irises," said Isabelle.

"Back in a tick."

Beth made her way to the rest room. A tired face reflected in the spotless mirror. She was glad to put the glasses on, they helped to camouflage a puffiness around her eyes. She would have an early night tonight. She wondered whether she had taken the bedclothes out of the washing machine. Why could she never remember these things?

Beth could see that Isabelle was still grumbling about the camera. Even though they were only half-sisters, Beth and Isabelle were so extraordinarily different. Isabelle had had a nice time. She at least could always be relied upon to treat Thursday lunchtime in a Greek restaurant as if it were a Saturday night at the Metropol. If only she would calm it all down sometimes, for her own sake.

"I'm staying until he comes back with the camera," said Isabelle, as Beth returned to the table. Surly just about covered it.

"He'll come back," said Beth. "The poor boy's had his guitar stolen. He won't be thinking about the camera. I bet he doesn't even realize he's got it. And when he does, he'll bring it back."

"Beth's right, Izzy" added Joanna, "We'll leave a phone number with the restaurant and they can ring you."

"All right, then, do that," agreed Isabelle. She stood up. "Is the loo serviceable?"

"It's very nice, and very clean," said Beth, correct on both counts. The glasses made her look frumpy. They had large frames, larger than they needed to be, but in keeping with the fashion of the moment. That was the expression Beth's optician had used wasn't it, the fashion of the moment? Strange choice of words, she had thought.

"You always look so intellectual in your glasses, Beth," smiled Joanna.

"So how's it going with the Laura Farey visit?" Beth asked, skipping around the issue of her glasses. Laura Farey was the glamour queen of the ballet world and the London-based prima ballerina was performing in East Berlin's Staatsoper in November. Isabelle and Joanna were part of the British Council team behind the trip.

"Fine. Everything going like clockwork so far." And then she added: "touch wood." Joanna was enjoying the project, particularly as it meant she would be spending a few days in London next week. Whilst West Berlin was uniquely fascinating, the intense isolation often left her feeling as if she were living in a pressure cooker. She smiled and said: "I'll leave him a phone number, for when Charlie Stokes brings the camera back."

"Do you think he'll bring it back?" asked Beth.

"Oh yes. Definitely. You can tell straight away, can't you?"

"Not always, Jo." said Beth, though she also thought he'd bring it back. As she watched Joanna move silently to the counter, she turned to Alexandra:

"Are you okay, Alex? You don't seem yourself today."

"Really?" Alex feigned benign surprise. "I'm fine. A bit busy, you know, like always, but fine. Everything's fine."

"Good."

Dimitrios used a new pencil to write the number down. Joanna had barely begun to explain when Dimitrios interjected:

"Oh yes, don't worry. He'll be back. He still has to pay for his meal." Dimitrios leaned forward and tried to lower his voice. "It's a long story. Very sad."

"I see," said Joanna.

"Maybe you should write the number down?"

Joanna wrote down Isabelle's phone numbers, one for the apartment she shared with Beth, and the other for the office. Above them she added "Isabelle", and "camera" for good measure. She pushed the sheet of paper back across the counter.

"There you go. And could we have the bill, please?"

"Separate or all together?"

"All together. It's for the lady in the white jacket."

Jake Harrison, drummer, student of life and one quarter of the population of Charlie Stokes' apartment, was amused and surprised to catch a glimpse of Charlie. He knew that Charlie had left his wallet in the apartment and had nothing on him. He also knew that he had planned to be back in time to catch a call from Luke. So it didn't add up that he would be goofing about in a Greek restaurant in Kantstrasse.

He considered it nothing more than his duty to swipe the guitar as he passed the open doorway, just for the comedy in wondering what Charlie's reaction would be. There was a bus discharging passengers barely ten steps into his getaway and he barged into it to wait for Charlie.

But Charlie flew past like an antelope on heat. Jake pressed his face against a window to try and get a better view, but he had already lost sight of him. Well, they would meet up soon enough. The bus drove along and Jake wondered whether it was going in a direction that suited him or whether he should hop off at the next possible stop. He became distracted at the sight of two young women jogging along the pavement in agreeably unsuitable sportswear. He was idly speculating about the heavy one, when he heard a hoarse and surprised voice blurt out his name. He turned to see the familiar face of Charlie Stokes staring at him with an expression that was not one of his regular ones.

"All right, Charlie?" he beamed.

Charlie Stokes, with his mouth still trying to extract as much oxygen as he could from the air available to him, threw darting looks at his case and at Jake and up and down the bus. He looked confused and perplexed.

"Have a seat, Charlie, you look knackered, mate." Charlie Stokes steadied himself on the seat rails and became aware that he had been shaking his head slightly from side to side in that classic tic of incomprehension.

"Are you alright, Charlie? Only, I don't know, you don't seem pleased to see me." For the first time, Jake began to feel that his good deed might have fallen on fallow ground.

"Was it you?" gasped Charlie, after what was really a very dramatically timed pause, "Was it you that took my guitar?" He made no effort to squeeze the incredulity out of his voice. In fact, he soaked it in some more and added, "Did you, Jake?"

"Don't need to thank me, mate."

"What?"

"Although we are probably going to miss the phone call now, so best get off and find a bus that's going the right way, eh?"

"I thought someone had nicked my guitar."

"Yeah," nodded Jake, with a goofy grin. "I know."

"I just blasted out of a restaurant. I left people in there, they must be thinking I'm a complete wanker."

"That was the general plan. Listen, it's happened to me before, so I know how you were feeling."

"Sorry?"

"Stuffed your face, knowing full well you can't pay for the meal, then you sit there thinking: now what?" Jake cast his head back a bit to give the impression he was delving into a catalogue of similar incidents he had experienced during his own impoverished upbringing in Sevenoaks. In fact, he had never eaten in a restaurant in the knowledge that he could not pay for the meal. "All you needed was a great way to leave in a hurry. I gave it to you. Bet you got a pat on the back as you left, too. Bit of encouragement?"

Charlie had to admit that, had he actually been in the position that Jake had thought he was in, it was a perfect plan. It had worked. On the other hand, Operation Overlord had been a great plan too. It might not have been so well received, however, had France not needed liberating at the time.

27

"I wasn't having trouble paying the bill, Jake," began Charlie. "I wasn't having trouble with anything. Until now."

"Good."

"I need to go back, Jake, you take the guitar home, okay?"

"Eh? Back where?"

"The restaurant. I was in the middle of something!"

The bus was pulling up at a stop. Jake manhandled the guitar towards the door, and Charlie Stokes followed. "Suit yourself, Charlie, but by the time you find your way back, they'll probably be gone."

Charlie thought about this, and conceded that Jake was probably right. He relaxed his muscles. He still had the camera. That was all the excuse he needed to make contact, at least with someone from the group. All was not lost. They stepped onto Liestenburgerstrasse, and Charlie watched as the bus pulled away.

He was conscious of a sharp, unpleasant pain in the back of his heels, and a sensation of blood sticking his socks to his blistered skin. There'd be no more running today. It was only as he watched the bus juddering on its way that he noticed the number. The bus was going to Kreuzberg! Jake had noticed. The bus was still in sight. But there'd be no more running today.

"We should have stayed on that one, Charlie."

"That's right, Jake."

Guildford, England

Luke McCallister's walk up North Street had not gone unnoticed. He was just passing the Civic Hall when he heard her calling out to him. It was the redhead. The name escaped him for the moment, but it would come. He tried to push on, by pretending he hadn't heard her, but she gave it another go. It was a shrill voice and it carried. Luke stopped and turned to embrace it. But he made sure anyone watching could see he was looking at his watch first.

"Where are you off to in such a hurry?" she asked pointedly.

"Got to see my cousin. Bit late."

"Where does he live?"

"Epsom Road."

"Epsom Road? Where?"

"By the vet."

"Going the wrong way," she admonished, and immediately a note of suspicion joined the conversation.

"Well, I know. I like to go this way and turn right a bit later on." His response did less than little to ameliorate.

"You're not going to see your cousin, are you? You haven't even got a cousin." The girl's tone of voice had changed now. The rest of the monologue was delivered with a face thrust forward, and arms locked to the side: "You're going to the Leisure Centre to swim with Rachel. And don't deny it, because she told me, you lying bastard. Don't think I care, either, because I couldn't give a shit." She had put the full force of the consonant into that last word. "And Rachel can go to hell and all. You're only interested in her tits. That's all she's got, you know, great tits. That's why she's always in the pool, so she can show them to all the blokes. You make me sick, all of you. Wouldn't even cross the road if I saw you again."

And with that, she left. She wouldn't cross the road but she'd walk up the entire length of North Street. Luke knew nothing of any Rachel and had no intention of going to the Leisure Centre, although he did feel mildly curious about these tits that were being brandished about so freely. Girls were strange. Maybe Charlie had been right all along and Luke just never knew what he was doing after three pints. Roz. That was her name, Roz the redhead. At least that was one thing he remembered from last night. He shrugged, and continued towards his cousin's house on the Epsom Road, by the vet.

Luke's cousin Judy didn't have a phone, or rather it had been disconnected after a misunderstanding that buying shares in the privatised British Telecom didn't absolve her from continuing to pay for the service. So, Luke would have to call Charlie from a phone box. There was one on the corner of the Park, but he decided to get to Judy's for a cuppa first. He had reddish brown, shoulder length, hair and wore wire-rimmed glasses. His hunched appearance might have given him away as a guitarist to those in the know but, if you had asked ten people what they imagined he did for a living, nine would surely have said: "nothing". At the house he made a brew, and scavenged for biscuits and unused phone cards.

At three o'clock he walked to the phone box. There was no answer.

Typical.

He left a message.

29

West Berlin

E Minor

I can't remember exactly which way we ended up going home.

Jake had the great good sense not to talk to me at all until we reached the apartment. He had the even greater good sense not to start once we'd arrived. He put the kettle on and began counting out the tea bags. He may eventually have said something along the lines of how it was a good job Luke was back soon with more Hobnobs and PG Tips because we just barely had enough to last. I don't know, because I had removed my shoes and was peeling off my socks as one would a putrid plaster. As I was wondering whether we had been too late to catch Luke's call, I saw the answer phone was flashing and I pressed the play button.

We had been too late.

"Oi, oi, saveloy! Pick up the phone you bastards, I know you're in there… come out, come out, wherever you are! Right, listen. My flight's Saturday afternoon, not tomorrow, okay? Anyway, Charlie, I've got something for you. Not sure exactly, probably nothing but you never know. If you want anything else bringing back, make a list. I'm crashing at Judy's tonight and she's not on the phone, so I'll call you from a box, probably late. Be in, though, yeah? All right. Laters, ladies."

There were no other messages. I put the camera down on the mantelpiece and sat on the sofa to check the raw patches on the back of my heels. I decided against putting a plaster on, to let the air get to work. I wasn't planning on going anywhere. Berlin could rock without me this Thursday. Jake brought the tea. The last of the Hobnobs had long since been eaten, and not by me. I sat in silence, my lower back tight from the unaccustomed exercise, and drank. Jake, like most drummers, was bonkers. But he knew how to make a cup of tea. That he ate all the biscuits was another issue.

I was looking forward to seeing Luke on Saturday. I wondered whether it would be awkward. The falling out was the first I'd ever experienced. I've drifted apart from friends, of course. You change, they change, we all move around, and nature takes its course. Yes, it would be good to see him again. I could tell him all about that girl.

The one whose name I didn't know.

Guildford

L uke had been back at Judy's more than an hour. He had returned from his long dinner appointment and been dropped off outside her door at eleven. He had fallen asleep within seconds of sitting himself down in the living room, and only the crash of a plant pot outside woke him. It was already gone midnight, but he was determined to call Charlie, if only to wake them up. He was just drunk enough to think that would be funny. He could hear the wind moving another loose pot around the patio. He'd borrow Judy's bike. It wouldn't take long, he thought. He went out the back way. The bike seat was much too low for him, and he cut a comical figure as he pedalled across the short gravel path that cut across the back lawn and straight out of the open gate.

He was more conscious of the wind here. There were twigs and leaves and even small branches scattered on the road, though the houses and trees on either side were affording some shelter. His quads were already aching from trying to ride such a small bike. He turned towards the park.

He was thrown to the ground instantly.

"Jesus Christ!" It was the wind that had knocked him over. Not a car, or a horse, or a runaway dog. A monstrous gust of wind literally lifted him and the bike sideways and onto the pavement. And for a few seconds more he could not even get himself to his feet. Then there was a lull and he rose and pushed the bike the rest of the way to the pay phone. He should have gone back to Judy's there and then, really, he thought, but now that he was here, he may as well wake those sods up in Germany.

"Charlie!" he shouted, once he got through.

"Luke?"

"Hello, mate!" It was more shouting than talking. In truth, Luke could hear nothing at all over the howling sound that the gaps in the phone box helped to create with the wind.

"You in a night club?"

"What?"

"I said, are you in a night club?"

"Ha-ha. I wish. It's blowing a gale here, mate! I'm in a phone box!"

"Why? It's one in the morning."

"Eh?"

"Can you hear me, Luke?"

"Listen, forget it! Did you get my message? My flight's in at ten to six on Saturday, not tomorrow. Dan-Air from Gatwick. Okay? Ten to six!"

"Okay. Ten to six from Gatwick. Dan-Air."

"I'll tell you all about it then!"

"What's happened?"

"It'll be a laugh. Listen, mate, this is pointless," he shouted, "I'll see you on Saturday! Not tomorrow!"

Luke replaced the receiver. He shook his head. Well, that was a waste of time, then. But he couldn't help smiling. He was looking forward to Berlin again. But he was looking forward to getting into bed more. I'll push the bike back, this time, he thought.

He sensed a new shadow somewhere behind him. There was a shattering crunch. He was still smiling when the uprooted elm crashed through the phone box. Luke was dead before he hit the ground.

West Berlin, Friday, October 16th

From her very first day in the city, Joanna had found Berlin fascinating. The British Council - cultural flag wavers for the nation of Shakespeare, Chaucer, Elgar, Hockney and, as Charlie Stokes would most certainly have added, Lennon & McCartney - was an employer that suited her. She enjoyed meeting people. She did not at all find the many evenings taken up at receptions or openings or presentations in any way tiresome. Not yet, anyway. And she had even discovered a sense of national pride that she never even realised she had. She had no interest in patriotism for patriotism's sake, but she felt happy to see the enthusiasm with which much of what she worked on was being received.

There was a certain irony, she thought, having taken herself off the market, so to speak, that since her arrival in Berlin she received such a great deal of polite and enthusiastic attention from a continuous stream of earnest gentlemen with achingly good manners. She occasionally accepted a dinner date, or a trip to the opera - which she loved - but had handled all such events with the warm, unhurried neutrality of the gifted diplomat. She had begun to suspect that some of her dinner dates were not all they appeared, and that some of the better-looking men who sat across the dinner table were spooks sounding her out. There were so many secret services around, all of them calling Berlin home to some degree. There were the Germans themselves, both sides; the Americans; the Brits; the French; and, of course, the Russians. But she'd never had a drink with a Russian.

Not yet.

Not that she was aware of.

But if men would continue falling into her dreamy brown eyes, what on earth could she do about it? So, she shook Damian Smith's hand, allowing him to hold it just that little bit too long, before saying: "I'd love to, really, but I'm working tonight. It's a reception at the Nierendorf Gallery," she added, as she could see that he hadn't taken it well. "But why don't you come, anyway, it's for a very worthwhile cause? And just a few doors down the street, too."

Of course she knew that he would not go. She knew because Damian Smith was married, his wife being one of the many worthy women who would be at the reception that evening.

"You have to swat them off like flies, darling," said Isabelle. "It would be so tiresome if it weren't so much fun to watch."

"Hardly like flies, Izzy," she retorted.

"Come on, Jo, I don't think there's a man in this building, or the next, that hasn't had a go. I mean, don't get me wrong, if I were a man I'd have a go."

"Thanks, Izzy, I'll remember that."

"Anyway, there was a phone call earlier. Someone asking for you."

"Oh?"

"Asked a few personal questions about you, then changed the subject when Helga pressed him on some details."

"Him?"

"Always a man, darling. What did I just say? Flies." Isabelle made a soft swatting movement and then remembered something else. "Oh, have you rung anyone back home this morning? London area?"

"No. Why?"

"Loads of phone lines are down. There was a bloody great storm last night. Trees down, people dead, worse storm in a hundred years or more. Maybe you should check your Mum?"

"She's in Scotland. I'll bet it was worse up there. Always is." Joanna frowned.

Not this time. It was only in the South, so don't worry."

So Joanna didn't worry.

Alexandra, on the other hand, was worrying enough for both of them. At her desk, she was gripping her telephone tightly as she listened. If anyone had looked closely enough, they would have seen the slight fluttering of her skin around her temples, as she fought to contain her irritation. Her jaw line also betrayed her black mood, and if anyone needed another sign to warn them to keep away, then the pursed lips ought to have done it. It was unfortunate for Lester Grunwald that he was blind to such details. He sat himself down at the empty chair in front of Alex's desk and grinned goofily by way of an alternative to clearing his throat. There is always a time and place for short round men and this wasn't it. She put the receiver down, and then she snapped.

"What?"

Lester Grunwald spent his weekends playing the glockenspiel at his Church's Youth Orchestra (he was one of a number of permitted over-age members). He could read music, but he could not read women. He was probably the only member of staff in the entire building who would not have stood up at that point and beaten a retreat. Instead, he just grinned that little bit wider, and raised his eyebrows. There might also have been the smallest hint of an impish shrug of the rounded shoulders.

"Lester, what do you want, for goodness sake?" she spat. She sounded shrill and tight and not at all like Alexandra Gagnon. "Why are you sitting there, grinning and wobbling at me like some castrated gnome?" Lester was a small man, and playing the glockenspiel was his only exercise. Cheeks he had, and plenty to spare. "I'm very busy, now just go. Go!"

Impervious, he leaned forward. "Maurice wanted me to tell you that there are some problems in London. He noticed you've been trying to call London." It was a voice that suited him in every possible way. If one had to imagine what sound air forcibly extruded through the gaps of a garden gnome's face would make, it was the voice of Lester Grunwald.

"I beg your pardon?"

"Telephones are down. Not everywhere, but" he thought how best to describe it, "nearly everywhere. There are big power cuts in London." It was important to stress the gravity of the situation. "Big," he insisted. She didn't appear to be a good listener this morning. "The markets are closed."

The markets are closed? What was the man talking about? Billingsgate? Smithfield? Camden?

"Which market? Why do I need to know?"

"The stock exchange, you know. 'The markets."

"Is Maurice listening to my telephone calls?

"You asked his secretary for Jeremiah Warrender's phone number and you said it was urgent."

Jeremiah Warrender was a broker. He handled share transactions for the Managing Editor of *Berlin Now* magazine, who sat two floors above Alex. He also handled transactions for Alex's husband, Tony. Tony had gone to London for a two-day meeting exactly a week ago and she had not heard from him since. Yesterday, amongst an otherwise indifferent selection of post, was a letter from the bank, dripping with ruinous portent. Alex needed money, or her husband, fast.

She didn't need Lester Grunwald.

"I suppose I can still send a telex?" she asked.

"Shall I go and find out?"

"Yes. Why don't you do that?"

B eth stayed in the car as she always did when she was meeting him. She thought she was coming down with a cold, the first of the new season. When she got home she was going to blast it with a massive vitamin C overdose, and to hell with the consequences. She might give the evening's reception at the Nierendorf a miss. There was only so much diplomatic revelry a girl could take. She'd loaf on the sofa and watch a video instead, perhaps. Or perhaps not, of course. She really ought to support her sister. She was consular staff after all, it wouldn't look good if she weren't there. On the other hand, if she was sick?

She began picking off rogue cat hairs from her skirt, listening to the army's radio station. They played a surprising amount of Wham these days. It didn't seem appropriate somehow, but then again it was probably used for coded messages.

He was late today.

And when she finally saw him coming along the path, he was not alone.

She sat up and suddenly tensed. He had his arm around the shoulder of a woman with wild blonde hair. She had her left arm around his waist and was holding him tightly. He was also walking a Labrador on the end of one of those long retractable dog leads, a happy couple taking their dog for a walk by the lake. They walked straight past the car and he didn't pay Beth the slightest attention. Well, of course he wasn't going to stop. Beth waited until he was out of sight. She opened the car door and got out. She walked to a bench by the water's edge and began to throw crumbs of bread from a small brown paper bag, feeding the ducks.

When the bag was empty she returned to the car and drove away.

There were no ducks.

E Minor

I was having no luck finding the phone number of that bloody Greek restaurant. Naturally, I'd lost the little leaflet Dimitrios had given me and I'd had the Yellow Pages on my lap for an hour, scanning up and down every entry in the restaurant section and stopping at every single one of them with an address on Kantstrasse. My job was made needlessly difficult by a complete inability to remember the restaurant's name. I had seen it, it just hadn't sunk in. It began with 'H' or 'A'. I was pretty sure it was 'A'. Andromeda? Acropolis? I tossed the directory to one side and looked at my watch. Restless. Odd. I needed to get outside.

Checking that the plasters were not peeling off my abused heels, I rummaged around amongst the unpleasant ecosystems under my bed to pull out something softly suitable from a collection of broken-in running shoes. I made sure I had my wallet, and some change for the bus, and then wasted a bit of time trying to find the camera. I was sure I'd left it on the mantelpiece. No, there it was. With that safely in my jacket pocket, I made for the door. I caught a glimpse of myself in the hallway mirror and thought: shall I do something with my hair? Yes, nothing. I left a brief note for the guys. It said: *You arseholes.* They wouldn't question it.

I didn't wait long for a bus, but long enough to realize, as I looked down at my shoes and brushed off the last of the thick carpet fluff, that I had put on a Nike Pegasus on the left, and a Brooks Trilogy on the right. I had to admit, they really didn't look alike. Bollocks. I boarded the bus anyway.

I spent the first half of the journey trying to remember the name of the restaurant, just for the mental exercise. Having more or less settled on The Aegean, I passed a clothes shop sporting the Hermes logo and suddenly began to lean more towards it starting with 'H'. I spent the second half of the journey wondering why I was so confident that the brown-eyed girl would not be married, or engaged, or living in sin, or at the very least, dating?

No, not this one. Not this time.

Dimitrios was standing back from the windows to check that a little notice he had put up was straight. A bit more up on the left side, perhaps?

"A bit more up on the left."

It was a quiet, almost uncertain voice. Dimitrios turned round and momentarily narrowed his eyes a touch, to help jog his memory. It did not need much jogging.

"Ah, my friend! How are you? And where did you go? Everyone was so worried. Come inside. And the guitar? Tell me you found the guitar? Alikaki, look who it is!" Dimitrios put his arm around Charlie Stokes and manoeuvred him into the restaurant.

Athena, thought Charlie, of course.

Alikaki appeared, and seeing the empty-handed young man gave a philosophical Grecian shrug of the kind Charlie Stokes imagined were commonplace in Plato's time. But he nipped the tragedy in the bud.

"I found my guitar. Everything turned out fine. All a misunderstanding, really." He smiled. Charlie Stokes had a nice smile, when he could be bothered, and knew when to employ it. "Same as this," he added, pulling Isabelle's little camera out from his jacket pocket. "I ran out with it. I didn't even realize it was in my hand, to be honest."

"Ah, yes, the young lady asked me to ring her if you brought it back. You leave it here?"

"Yes, I think so."

"You eat here today?"

"No," said Charlie, "Here. This is for yesterday." He pulled out a ten Deutschmark note from his wallet. He took a breath to steady himself. "Dimitrios, I was wondering. Maybe, when you ring her, you could ask the girl with the camera...well there was a girl at the table, remember? She was sitting just about, let me see, about there," Charlie stopped talking, if talking was what he had been doing, because Dimitrios had started to laugh. It can throw a man off his trail, having laughter intercede.

"Do you think I do not remember what it is like to be young?" said Dimitrios, his eyes now twinkling with the effort of wondering whether he did actually remember what it was like. "I can see that look on your face, my friend. You are about to start a journey, are you not? Your heart, it must travel. It must live!" Charlie reckoned that was about the drift of it. But Dimitrios was not done. "Your heart must crack and break. And, when it has healed, rise up again twice as strong as before!"

Although Charlie Stokes did not go a bundle on the cracking and breaking, as a lyricist he did appreciate that there was little in life more likely to make a song fly than a heart well and truly crushed.

This was not a song, though.

"Maybe you can tell the girl that I could bring it to her apartment?" These were the childish words that wriggled pitifully out of his mouth just as he remembered that his girl wasn't the one the camera belonged to in any case. Although, now he gave the entire episode his full attention, the camera could have been anyone's.

"What I meant was…"

"You want me to fix you up, is that so? You just have to ask, my friend. Perhaps you would prefer for me to give you the telephone number?" Charlie Stokes thought at first that that would be by far the simplest solution. And yet he could not avoid the inevitable over-complication that he brought to so many of his dealings with women and said:

"Look, why don't you call her and tell her you have the camera. Then, just suggest that they all come over for lunch again. Then, you call me and tell me when they're coming, and I can arrange to be here. What could be more natural?" Dimitrios shrugged. He went behind the counter and out of the till took a scrap of paper.

"The girl you want, the one with the brown eyes and the hair, yes? She gave me this number. You call her, no problem." Charlie Stokes took the paper and noted the name. It was a lovely name, just the right sort of name for that sort of girl. He handed the paper back to Dimitrios.

"Okay, what about this. You ring her, but don't tell her that I brought the camera back, just tell her that I rang you to say that I had it. And ask where and when should I meet her to give it back?" He could barely keep the triumph out of his voice, though he feared some of the words had probably tumbled clumsily over Dimitrios's head. They hadn't.

"Stay there, my friend," Dimitrios said, "let me sort it all out. I will be with you in a short moment, sir." He said that to a customer who had walked in, a tall man in a dark suit, with a charcoal hound's-tooth overcoat that might have come out a month earlier than necessary. The tall man appeared to have stopped behind Charlie, closer than was comfortable, making him feel as if he had become the head of a short but important queue. Charlie watched Dimitrios dial the number, carefully checking it against the paper.

Charlie waited, doing his absolute best not to fidget, and failing. But finally someone answered. Dimitrios's voice boomed. "Ah, yes, this is

Dimitrios from the restaurant. I have news about your camera."

During the conversation that followed, the tall man backed away and let the corner of the table closest to the door take his weight. Charlie Stokes paid little attention to him as he was desperately willing Dimitrios not to ruin everything by saying something wholly inappropriate.

"And a very charming young man he was too, I remember," said Dimitrios wholly inappropriately. "But that is a different story. If you let me know when you can pass by the restaurant I can see to it that the boy comes in with it. Yes, I have his phone number, of course." Dimitrios listened intently and then frowned slightly. "You want me to give you his phone number?" Charlie nodded his head so violently he almost set off a dizzy spell. "No, my dear, I cannot do that. I have to respect his privacy, you understand?"

No! What did you say that for, you idiot? Charlie Stokes raised his hands in despair. Dimitrios shrugged the response away. There was evidently plenty of chat coming from the other end of the line and it was agony missing it, but Charlie was doing his best to hold firm.

"Tomorrow evening? That would be perfect, my dear." *Yes! Bingo!* "The restaurant is at its best on a Saturday night." *No, wait! Saturday night? I'm picking Luke up! Bollocks.* Charlie Stokes shook his head urgently and flapped his hands about as Greek-like as he could. Dimitrios caught on. "But Sunday would be better, because tomorrow night is always a difficult evening, you understand?" She's going to hang up in a minute, he's talking cobblers, now. "Yes. Yes. Exactly, right." *What? What is exactly right?* "One o'clock and Sunday lunch for two, as you say. I shall pass on the message. And if he is not free, then a quick drink instead." *Not free? Watch me!*

Dimitrios set down the receiver and turned both his palms upwards. It was a gesture that said: *et voilà.* Just in Greek. As Dimitrios turned his attention to the man in the overcoat, Charlie Stokes nodded his approval and slipped out into the delights of Kantstrasse again, quite literally bumping into a different tall man but in an identical overcoat. The man took a single deliberate pace to the side but, as Charlie carried on walking, the man joined up alongside and firmly guided him by the arm to a large grey Audi saloon. It took Charlie Stokes three strides before he was sure what was happening was actually happening, and that's when he resisted and stood his ground. From right behind him a voice whispered calmly into his left ear.

"Just get in the car, Charlie. Don't make a fuss and there won't be any problems."

E Minor

It was a nice car, the Audi. New, with the leather seats still giving off that unique aroma. Car phone installed, I couldn't help but notice. The unmistakeable scent of Marlboro Lights, too, but that might have come from the overcoats rather than the car.

He'd shown me his identification on the pavement. A postcard-sized white paper inside a plastic-covered black cover, folded in half; a cropped passport photograph of a man who could have been anyone, really. If I'd had a Dad it could just as easily have been a picture of him. He'd held it in front of me for barely a second, which is never enough really, is it? I felt I had had to make a small stand on the point of the photographic likeness.

"Not sure that really looks like you," I started.

"That's what we keep telling him." It was the man holding open the door. "He won't listen. In you go, Charlie." It had all been so frightfully polite. I had noticed some kind of official-looking crest, too, like the sort I used to notice on Kellogg's Corn Flakes' packets as a nipper. There was nothing foreign about the accent, Queen's English through and through. At least it wasn't going to be something about German taxes or the like. No, this was a prank by the lads.

Then again, this was a very nice car.

There was a third man, sitting behind the driver. I got in the car, and slid towards the centre, once it became clear that the man holding the door was joining us. A snug fit it was, there being something of a run on overcoats in the back seat. The tall man sat up front and closed the door. I was expecting him to start but it was a voice to my left.

"Lift home, Charlie?" It was a friendly voice, utterly at odds with the face that delivered it. I imagined that a tug at a door handle and swift exit would have been my first instinct, but there was a man on every door and probably a dog in the boot. I allowed myself to get scared.

"You're obviously not expecting me to just scream my head off, then?" I said, though why I said it was beyond me. The driver was pulling into the traffic, focusing on his wing mirror with conscientious vigour. He spoke with a voice that would make ordering a pizza sound like a declaration of war, and had one of those mangled, East End accents that can rarely be acquired without persistent trauma to the nasal region. On another occasion I might even have found it amusing.

"This is an Audi 5000, Charlie," he said, enunciating his dropped

41

consonants. "It's not a 2CV. You could sing the chorus from Beethoven's Ode to Joy with a full choir and no one would hear a fucking word."

He made it sound like poetry.

"Did anyone show Charlie some identification, Lewis? He seems perturbed."

"Yes, someone's shown Charlie some identification, Sir."

"We're on your side, Charlie. There's nothing to worry about. As long as you're on our side, of course."

All this talk of sides, and not having anything to worry about, had begun to warm up the inside of my head and I could feel my chest banging around a bit.

"I don't feel well."

There was the smallest hint of a whirr and a window opened a few inches. The sudden cool of the wind helped.

"Drink, Charlie?"

I wondered where they kept the drinks. I shook my head slightly. Any more and I'd probably have passed out. I ran an open palm across my forehead, feeling the dampness. We drove along in silence. We were running parallel to an S-Bahn line. The atmosphere was so calm and normal as to be surreal. It certainly was for me. The man to my left spoke again.

"Lewis?"

The tall man in the front passenger seat turned to face me and passed back a large envelope. The man on my right took it from him and pulled out a number of enlarged photographs, all in black and white and of varying quality. Outdoor shots, all of them in Berlin, I recognised most of the backgrounds.

"I want you to look at these photographs, Charlie. Take your time. Tell me anyone you recognise. Then we just need to ask you some questions. All right?"

If there's one thing I guarantee is not a good thing for me to do in the back of a car is to read or look at a map. But I had these men down as the type you don't bother discussing dizziness with, so I looked at the photos with as little focus as possible. Then I looked at them again, one by one until no one could have accused me of not giving them my full attention. I handed them back with a shake of the head.

"Nothing, Charlie?"

"No." I said. "I'm a musician. I play in a band most weekends. I meet lots of people. I mean, I might have met one of these people sometime but…"

42

"I understand, Charlie. But take another look. See if anything jogs your memory."

Again? I took another look, and you know, he was right. Sometimes you just have to concentrate a bit more. The woman in the third photograph. I handed them back.

"Well, Charlie?"

"Nothing," I said.

The man to my left reached into the inside pocket of his coat and pulled out a business card. It only had a phone number on it.

"Remember, Charlie, we're on your side. I want you to ring that number if you suddenly realise that someone on one of these photos turns out to be your cousin. I also want you to call us if someone else suddenly starts asking you funny questions about these same people. Do you understand, Charlie?"

At this point, I felt obligated to open up a bit.

"No, I don't, actually. I don't understand at all. Why would somebody ask me about some strangers I've never met? In fact, why are *you* asking me? You can't go around snatching people off the streets. This might be Berlin, it's not Beirut." And I meant it to sting.

"We're just giving you a lift home." The car pulled over. We were outside my apartment building.

They knew where I lived.

East Kreuzberg. For them, it would be a dump. Hell, for *me* it was a dump. The man on my right got out and stood waiting for me outside. Completely out of the blue, the driver suddenly asked: "Do you like Chas 'n' Dave, Charlie?" *Chas 'n' Dave? Dear oh dear, well he would, wouldn't he? Where would I put them in my personal music chart? Did it even go down far enough? I thought Chas 'n' Dave were complete shit. Well, I would, wouldn't I?*

"I think they're great." I got out.

"They're fucking shit, Charlie," he shouted.

The man called Lewis was suddenly at my side, as his colleague got back into the car. He offered his hand and we shook on something.

"Thank you for your help, Charlie," he said, adding in a voice that confirmed he wasn't: "Sorry for any inconvenience. We didn't frighten you?"

"Yes."

"Good."

And they drove away.

I loitered outside the front door for a while, acutely aware that I was out of tea bags. It's a funny thing about memory and photographs taken out of context. It had only been yesterday, yet I still hadn't really recognised her. But the woman in that third photograph was the serious, gloomy one at the restaurant who'd kept giving me a bit of eye.

Very bloody odd.

"That's a lovely perfume, Joanna, what is it?"

Joanna had no idea. "I don't know."

"Don't know?" repeated Isabelle with a giggle. "How can you not know?"

"I used something from one of those little samples. I gave it a dab and liked it, but I don't remember looking. Ysatis, maybe?"

"No."

"I'll try and remember to check when I get home."

They were in Isabelle's car because she had the boot full of brochures. They drove past their offices and the gallery, which was practically next door in Hardenbergstrasse. Joanna groaned.

"Oh God, Isabelle, it's that dreadful Damian Smith. I can't believe he actually showed up. Do take him on, Izzy, or I'm staying in the car."

"What, am I only good for your leftovers now?"

"He's not a left-over, he's a left-alone. Go on. He's married."

"Well, why didn't you say? He can carry the boxes in for us." Isabelle drove past, searching for a spot to park. She eventually found one. Even for a VW Polo it was going to be a tight fit. She looked back over her shoulder and reversed. Joanna put her hand on the door.

"I don't think there's room, Izzy, shall I go out and guide?"

"Darling, you could stick a bus in here." There was a solid crunch, as she hit the car behind. "There," she said.

Turning the wheel full-lock, Isabelle stabbed at the accelerator, and the car lurched forward the few inches of space available, until it hit the car in front, smashing its offside rear brake light. She continued in the same vein, bouncing back and forth between the two adjacent cars until she had worked her way up alongside the kerb. Without a word, she got out and kicked a few visible pieces of brake light underneath the car in front.

Joanna couldn't help but notice, with a sense of embarrassment, how new and shiny the grey car in front looked as she followed Isabelle to the gallery. It was the way Isabelle always parked, and the reason few were prepared to lend her a car.

It was crowded that evening, but pleasant enough. Joanna floated around the room with unhurried grace, exchanging smiles and nods and occasional air kisses. She became embroiled in one or two conversations that went on longer than she might have liked, but nothing onerous. She noticed that neither Beth nor Alexandra had made it by ten o'clock, but she had not attached too much significance. Isabelle was having plenty of fun. She worked a room far more energetically than Joanna did, rather like a bee in a summer meadow. By eleven everyone had left, some heading home, others on to the nightspots to rev up their weekends.

Isabelle leaned back against the doorjamb to the ladies' room and lit her second cigarette of the day. She toyed with the idea of going out with some of her friends from the gym, but was beginning to feel like she'd rather smoke a little joint at home and listen to some Lionel Ritchie.

"Shall I drop you off, Jo?"

"Yes, go on then."

"Wonder what happened to Beth and Alex. Are you doing anything on Sunday?"

"Don't think so."

"Meet me for lunch."

Saturday October 17th

Beth was tired, as expected after a practically sleepless night. She and the rest of the team had met in the nondescript apartment in Charlottenberg, one of three different locations available, and steadfastly followed procedure for twenty-four hours, just like the last time a breach had been flagged up. So Beth missed the reception at the gallery anyway, just not because she was feeling iffy with a tickly nose.

It was not that Beth had missed the gallery reception, it was that Beth had not come home at all, therefore leaving Isabelle alone in the apartment. She was not good at being alone. Beth had not bothered to ring Isabelle until mid-morning. A little grumpy banter had been exchanged, gratitude missing on both sides, before Isabelle moved to a safe topic of harmless lunch dates, by informing Beth that she and Joanna would be at the Greek off the Ku'damm for a bite on Sunday lunchtime.

"Yes, fine," said Beth, wondering whether or not to take her friend along. "If I finish here on time."

"I don't understand why you're working at the weekend, Beth."

"Well, you know, sometimes we have to."

"News to me. The Embassy's a morgue at the weekend."

"Not always, Izzy, and it's not an Embassy, it's a Consulate," corrected

46

Beth, not for the first time.

"Well, why aren't you coming home tonight, then?"

"Well, we'll see. Maybe I will. It depends."

There was a silence. Beth imagined Isabelle probably pulling a face.

"So... I'll see you Sunday, then?"

"Yes, I expect so. Yes."

Isabelle didn't much approve of Beth's excruciatingly dull gentleman friend. He was a red-haired accountant called Derek, already three negatives as far as Isabelle was concerned.

"Girls only, remember," she added.

East Berlin

East Berlin was having a bad air day. Its citizens may have been prevented from crossing freely into the West, but the Wall did nothing to impede its industrial effluence from making the journey.

Christian Bauer would not be accompanying the pungent clouds across any time soon. Not through official channels, anyway. He was idly strolling down Friedrichstasse, people-watching with his best friend Max. There was a mixture of tourists disgorged from Bahnhofstrasse, and students from the nearby Humboldt Universität. It was always so easy to spot the *Wessies*. The bright, chatty English girls that he had seen going in and out of the British Embassy on Unter Den Linden reminded him of his only visit to London, before that luxury had been ripped out of his life by the Party's petty vindictiveness. It would be nice to stop and chat. But that wouldn't be possible, they would intervene. Someone was watching him right now. Who? He didn't know. Did it matter any more?

He looked away into the distance, without focusing on anything, letting his thoughts loose. An idea had formed which needed an environment where it could grow, and develop into a plan, and thence to a future. Christian needed to feel, with full and total conviction, that there was indeed a future.

And, this time, he felt it.

"Max?"

"Uh-huh?"

"It's my birthday in three weeks."

"Yes. Are you expecting a present?"

"I shall be twenty-eight."

"It's a great age, Christian."

"Now, listen to me: when I wake up on my thirtieth birthday, I will be living as a free man in a democracy. On my mother's honour, with you as my witness, I swear to that."

"You know full well that nothing will change here in a year, Christian, so don't say such things. It is cheap to throw your mother's honour around in that way."

"I do swear to that, Maximilian," said the tall, angular man, his intense, deep-set eyes still gazing into the distance. "I shall have a very happy birthday indeed, or I shall not have a birthday at all." He left the words hanging in the autumn air.

"Come, Christian. Let us go."

"Will you come with me, Max?"

"What are you saying?" Max hissed the words under his breath, as if anyone could hear. They had stopped outside a bar packed with people who were not put off their excellent coffee by the rancid décor. Not a place to be caught with loose talk.

"I am going to break out."

Max shook his head.

"You have been away from Leipzig too long."

"No, Max, just long enough."

"You're not planning on taking me away before the ballet arrives, I hope?" asked Max with a cheeky smile. "You know how impossible it was for me to get the tickets."

Christian placed a long arm across his friend's shoulder. He smiled, too.

"There's no rush, Max, we have to make a plan, and one that works."

They turned their backs on the distant siren call of the West and walked steadily back to reality. In fact, Christian already had a plan.

"So, we're still going to the ballet, right?" asked Max.

"Of course. Come on, let's have a beer."

West Berlin

The Dan-Air flight from London Gatwick to Berlin's Tegel Airport was the customary forty-five minutes late arriving, as indeed was Charlie Stokes. Troy had given him the use of someone's car. Charlie assumed it had probably been forcibly removed from one of Troy's former army pals as it handled like an armoured truck. But it was better for the luggage than pissing about with buses.

Charlie was sure it was a dodgy motor and decided not to attract attention by parking up on the kerb in front of the exits, and headed for the official car park instead. Still thinking he was late, he jogged into the terminal. Having duly noted the delay on the arrivals' board, he passed the time by walking in and out of the terminal building, thinking first about Luke, and then about the girl, depending on whether he was inside or outside.

He'd been practising saying 'Isabelle' a lot since last night. Charlie was a man who did a lot of his conversing in his head, where the outcome was easier to control. He'd imagined a lot of conversations in his short life, and he was now adding 'Isabelle' to the list of names. The men in the Audi had shaken him, undoubtedly. He was probably going to have to give that incident a bit of thought. Nice name, Isabelle. She had already stated that Charlie was a sweet name so, as far as he was concerned, he was in clover.

By about quarter past seven, Charlie began to wonder whether Luke might have slipped past him. He couldn't imagine how, or indeed why, but the possibility was there. At quarter to eight he imagined that perhaps Luke had dropped something nefarious into his luggage and was having to explain it to a customs officer. But by quarter past eight, as the passengers being disgorged through the automatic doors all spoke Italian, he concluded that Luke must have missed his flight.

On the way out he picked up a worn copy of the Telegraph that must have fallen out of someone's bag. There were pictures of the storm back home, all very apocalyptic in places. On the way back to the car he noticed a grey Audi 5000 that looked exactly like the one in which he'd been so kindly driven home the day before. That would have been a disturbing thought had he not noticed that it couldn't be the same car.

This one had its rear offside brake light broken.

He walked on through the car park, mulling over Luke's non-appearance, and hoping he wasn't going to be expected suddenly to pick him up tomorrow lunchtime, when he stopped abruptly and looked around. He had no idea where he'd left the car. In his rush to get to the terminal, he hadn't paid attention. But if that wasn't bad enough, he couldn't even remember what car he was driving. Troy had walked him to it, opened the door, and sent him on his way. All he could remember was that it was a medium-sized pile of scrap metal on wheels but, looking around him, that wasn't going to narrow it down all that much. Well, it must have been a Citroen because he had the keys in his hand and they were on a Citroen leather key fob. Blue? Red? Brown? Definitely darkish, he was sure. He began to trudge up and down, looking at each car carefully as he passed, hoping for a sign. How long before someone noted how suspicious he was looking? Headlights shone on him as a car pulled up.

Not very long at all.

"Are you lost, Charlie?" That unmistakable voice. "You look lost."

"No."

"It happens sometimes, Charlie. You rent a car, pick it up, stop at the supermarket, one of those with a big car park, and then you come out and you've got no fucking idea what you were driving."

"Yeah," Charlie spoke quietly. He decided to tell them the truth about the photograph, because this sort of thing was not fun at all.

"I suppose that's why they put the registration numbers on the key rings. Don't you think that's why they put the registration numbers on the key rings, Charlie?"

Charlie looked down at his key fob and wondered why no one had had the foresight to attach the registration number to it.

"You're in the wrong row, Charlie. Two rows down that way. Your car is the fifth one from the end. It's a maroon Opel Kadett, and if you had any self-respect at all you wouldn't be seen dead in it. But then, it's not your fucking car, is it, Charlie?"

Charlie Stokes wasn't listening. He'd already set off. The big Audi followed, and slowed to a walking pace. Charlie heard the window wind down again. This time it was a voice from the back.

"We're not here following you, Charlie, by the way, just a coincidence." That reassured Charlie, despite not believing a word of it. "Thought you ought to know. Have a nice weekend." They drove away.

Charlie trudged off. Just in case they were still watching him - perhaps they had access to their own personal satellite - he went towards where they claimed he'd left his car. They were wrong, of course, just trying to take the piss. It's always easy when there are four against one. But Charlie went two rows down and walked to the fifth car from the end anyway, even though he knew he was looking for a Citroen.

There was a maroon Opel Kadett exactly where they said one would be. As there was something mildly familiar about the location of the rust, and for that reason only, Charlie tried the key in the door. But it was only when he sat himself in the seat and turned the ignition on that he accepted that this was the right car. So, they weren't following him. They just knew which car he'd been driving and where he'd parked it. They knew where he lived and they knew where he went.

It was a slow drive back. It was raining again and the car's wipers were so worn they merely redirected the water on the windscreen with every pass. This might have been why he found himself driving along Gorlitzer Strasse when he patently wanted to be on Kopenicker. Saturday night in West Berlin and the electricity was already in the air. He was lucky to find a spot near the apartment, and left the key inside the exhaust pipe, as per Troy's instructions. He was feeling a bit stiff in the shoulders from the tension of the wasted evening, but Charlie Stokes' Saturday evening was about to get worse. No Luke, no PG Tips.

The living room was deserted. Charlie immediately checked the phone and, although there was nothing to indicate a new message, he pressed the play button. Luke's sister!

"Are you there? (a pause), *Charlie?* (another pause). *It's about Luke,* (one more, then something that could have been a sigh). *Call me when you get this message. Five-oh-four-two-one-eight."*

Click. Charlie was about to lift the receiver when he heard the bathroom door. Jake was in then, he must have been first to listen to the message. Charlie dropped himself and the newspaper he'd picked up at the airport onto the sofa and carefully began to remove his shoes. He called out: "Jake?" He flipped through some more pages from the storm and read that six of the seven great oak trees that had given Sevenoaks its name had been knocked over. Perhaps they'd have to call it something else now.

Oak?

"Jake, I suppose you rang back, then? Missed his flight, right? What's the excuse, and when is he coming?" Charlie couldn't see the bathroom from where he was sitting, so he could only sense that there was someone there. He twisted round.

"Jake?"

The continuing silence was beginning to disconcert him. He got up, and as he did so he heard the bathroom door close again. He tapped at the door.

"Jake? What is it? Open the door, mate, it's me." He had his hand on the door handle. "Jake!" And then it suddenly hit Charlie that maybe it wasn't Jake.

And if it wasn't Jake, then who was in his bathroom? A wave of neurosis rolled over him as he began to think of his new friends from the Audi. No, surely not? Had his life become like one of those film thrillers from the Seventies full of shadows in hallways and whispers in the bath?

Charlie glanced around the living room and couldn't see any signs of disarray, or at least added disarray. It was hard to keep a place tidy when it was shared by three single men and used as a halfway house for waifs and strays. The door twitched and Charlie stepped back and hurriedly looked for a suitable weapon.

"All right, Charlie?" said Jake, in a barely audible cracked voice, as he stepped ashen-faced out of the bathroom. "What's the dustpan for?"

Charlie Stokes had seen Jake drunk, hung-over, stoned, in love, angry, surprised, disappointed, even hysterical. But he had never seen him with the look he was wearing now. It was a haunted look, a frightened look, a look that did not fit him very well at all. Jake walked towards the windows and looked out, more to avoid eye contact with Charlie than to look at the view, because there wasn't one.

Just the Wall.

"What is it, Jake? What's wrong? Did you ring back about Luke, then? Not coming today obviously?" Still with his back to the room, Jake shook his head.

"Don't worry, mate, we'll find some more tea bags somewhere. There's probably a couple dropped behind the cooker." Charlie was just trying to think of something stupid to say to break the atmosphere. It wasn't working. Jake cleared his throat softly and tried to speak, but nothing came out. Slowly, Charlie sat down again on the sofa. He was conscious of needing the toilet. Jake half-turned but could still not bring himself to face Charlie, who could just about see that Jake's eyes seemed unable to settle on anything. Very quietly, Jake mouthed something. Charlie leaned forward.

"I can't hear you, mate," said Charlie, beginning now to feel uncomfortable. He even regretted the tea bags comment. Jake turned to face Charlie and immediately turned away again. This time he directed his gaze at the telephone. He was nodding at it when he whispered the words.

"Luke's dead."

E Minor

I don't remember how long it was.

It might have been a minute. It might have been three seconds. There might not have been a pause at all. Perhaps the earth just stood still for a bit.

"What?" I said.

"Luke's dead," he repeated.

"No, he's not."

"Yeah. He is, Charlie."

"Leave it out."

The door opened, and Ritchie and Dan burst in breathlessly.

"Jake," said Ritchie. "This better not be a fucking wind-up."

"All right," I said, nodding. "You got me. Ha bloody ha. Very funny. Where's Luke then, behind the curtains? You can come out now, mate, and don't think I won't get you back."

But there was no laughter. Luke did not appear dramatically from behind the curtain.

Nothing happened that was remotely funny.

They sat around the room, each far enough apart from the other as to allow their own personal grief to be without interference. Jake felt the weight of obligation to explain, but it was Charlie Stokes' band and it was he who spoke first.

"You rang back, then?" said Charlie.

Jake nodded and bit his lower lip. He had a wide, freckled face and he suddenly looked like a very young boy indeed.

"Who did you speak to?"

"Lucy."

"Go on."

Jake let out a long, slow sigh and swallowed.

"The fire brigade were out, she said. Lots of people calling 999 about telephone wires down over their roofs, trees on their greenhouses, that kind of thing. An engine was driving back to base and they passed the phone box on the corner of Stoke Park. This bloody great tree had smashed it down. But then the guys…" Jake stopped and searched for a face in the room. He settled on Ritchie's, the Doctor. "The guys noticed there was a body under the tree."

The air in the room contracted.

"It was Luke."

"What?" They all mouthed it at once, in whispered disbelief.

"That's what she said. Luke's fucking dead, mate."

"Jesus Christ," said Dan, Luke's stand-in, the only one who seemed able to speak. He had never met Luke, and was now never going to. He thought about piercing the asphyxiating atmosphere in the room with a little uncalled-for levity. If he had thought about it twice, he might not have considered saying:

"Does this mean I get to stay in the band full-time?"

"Piss off, Dan."

"Just trying to…"

"Well don't."

"When did it happen? Did she say? Christ, I mean how long before they found him?" Ritchie had switched into sensible medical student mode, his face a canvas of earnest inquisition. Jake said nothing. He stared at Charlie with a wild-eyed desperation that Ritchie picked up on immediately.

"What? What is it, why are you looking like that?"

"Tell him, Charlie."

"Tell him what?"

"Tell him why Luke was in the fucking phone box in the middle of the night! Go on."

"Shut up Jake." Charlie snapped. "Everybody. Shut up. Just… just…" he struggled for the words, "shut the fuck up, will you?"

E Minor

A quarter to four in the morning is the worst time that exists. No good ever came of being awake then. Even when we'd had a long gig, four sets and starting late, we'd be home asleep unless any of us had pulled. If you hadn't gone to bed by then, you were just desperate. And, God knows, I have been desperate. But this was different. This was lying in my bed, hours after having given up on the day. This was half an hour after the last time I had woken up, and maybe the twentieth time in all. This was it. This was my mind being slowly microwaved by guilt. Guilt and horror. Guilt that because of me not being here when Luke called as planned in the afternoon, he had decided - for some stupid reason - to go out and try again at a time he should have just been in bed. And horror, because unless he had stayed in the phone box and rung loads of other people, I must have heard his last spoken words on this earth. Horror and guilt.

These are not the words for quarter to four in the morning.

I turned over, and found a new comfortable position. I slowed my breathing. I allowed my body to feel heavy, and I emptied what remained of my mind. I might as well have just jumped into the Baltic, for all the difference it made. Snippets of the phone conversation I'd had with Luke's sister kept flitting in and out. Despair.

And then, the practical issues like the funeral arrangements.

And a mother's anguish - Luke's mother had never taken to me.

And I'd never been to a funeral. Not ever. I couldn't believe that my first was going to be for one of my friends. I couldn't face it. Everyone would understand. I'm abroad: it's difficult, the flights, and the money.

Jake had left his door open. I could hear him snoring. It was the only time in my life I had ever not minded. He even snored in time. Drummers.

Please, if there is a God, I just want to sleep! Tomorrow is another day – another day without tea.

West Berlin, Sunday, October 18th

Charlie Stokes was not in the mood for love and wanted to let someone, anyone, know that he would not be at the restaurant. Of course, he had lost the leaflet that Dimitrios had given to him, and was once again up to his elbows in the telephone directory. It made no difference that this time he had a name to look for, for it did not exist. But then, what very few people realised was that Dimitrios's beloved little establishment was not actually called Restaurant Athena.

His customers, regular or infrequent, generally referred to it as *the Greek on Kantstrasse*. When Dimitrios had taken it over, in late September back in '72, it still went by the name *Die Verlorene Ehre*, under which moniker the place had laboured relentlessly for decades as an unreconstructed flag bearer for sauerkraut and schnapps. The owner was Hans Zimmer, a one-eyed reprobate from Leipzig who had washed up in Berlin just as the combined might of Stalin, Churchill and Eisenhower had finished carving up the rubble of the once great city amongst themselves. Herr Zimmer finished up as the surprised owner of an undistinguished eatery, and with the help of his new wife, built up a small but faithful band of regulars, happy to wallow in the stodgy sentimentality of his food.

When his wife left him, he moved on to Kantstrasse and continued bravely until the summer of 1972 when, hearing of the energetic Greek immigrant's own search for premises, Zimmer practically threw the establishment at him.

For reasons he never acceptably explained, Dimitrios changed the name on the window to something more culturally relevant, but left the entire official trail to function under its old title. So it was little wonder that Charlie Stokes found it impossible to track down the restaurant's number through official channels.

No, his wasn't the mood for pursuing women. It was a tired and gutted mood. It was a black, bilious fog of a mood. It was a mood that should have been retired from public life, but which he crept out with anyway.

Charlie Stokes took the ridiculous farce of not being able to trace a simple phone number as a sign that he had to go.

So, go he did.

Isabelle had persuaded Joanna to join her, of course, and the pair of them picked at a small plate of feta cheese and olives that Dimitrios had invited them to try as they waited. He had also prepared them an ouzo aperitif, which Isabelle at least thought helped in the transition from Saturday night excess to Sunday afternoon sobriety.

"Beth might come," she said, "threatened not to come alone, but she won't bring Desmond. I know she won't."

"It's Derek," corrected Joanna. "Did she say why she didn't come to the reception?"

"Said she was out. She's still out, actually. Haven't seen her since Friday morning."

"Really?"

"Probably having an affair. Wouldn't blame her, I know I would. God, darling, she's got such a dull life! Boring office job in the Embassy, boring Douglas to go out with, and if she didn't have you and Alex, boring friends." Isabelle popped an olive into her mouth. "She does have the most amazing little sister, though." She laughed.

Joanna shook her head.

"I think she's happy enough. His name is Derek. And technically it's only a Consulate, not an Embassy."

"That just makes it even duller. And, if she was *happy enough*, she'd smile and laugh a lot," she added, "like me. Don't you think Alex wasn't herself the other day?"

"Crossed my mind, yes. Busy at work, I expect." Joanna was trying to rub off a certain stickiness from her fingers with a napkin.

"Are you flying to Heathrow or Gatwick?" asked Isabelle.

"Gatwick, why?"

"Clinique!"

"Don't they sell that in Heathrow?"

"Oh, it's a much nicer shopping experience in Gatwick. I'm only thinking of you."

"I'm just going to wash my hands."

"She's got lovely soap in there, darling."

Joanna had barely gone into the bathroom when the door of the restaurant opened, and in walked Charlie Stokes. Isabelle flashed him a smile, but it didn't get the reaction she might have expected or hoped for. He looked like a man who realised he had walked into the ladies' by mistake. She tried again.

"Hello, Charlie Stokes!" She said brightly. She was nothing if not persistent. "Come over and have an olive." And she smiled some more.

E Minor

I walked all the way to the restaurant. Well, why not? I didn't want to sit down. Not in a bus, or a train, or on a bike, come to that. I did have a bike. It was in the bottom of the Landwehrkanal.

I wore running shoes, the Brooks Trilogy model, on both feet. Of course I wasn't going to run there, it was just to look after my heels. I don't know exactly when I left the apartment, but I'd given myself plenty of time. I didn't want to get lost, or be late.

Obviously I did, and I was.

It was dry and bright, and one of those Sundays where humans are reminded of their utter insignificance. Yes, the world would keep turning. It was hard to think of a more trite cliché than *life goes on*, but it does. Not always your own life perhaps, but someone's, somewhere. I suppose I was expecting some sense of contemplation and remembrance, an acknowledgment of a great tragedy.

But life just went on.

And in that moment, so did I.

Once I got onto the Ku'damm, I drifted again to thoughts of the girl and was glad I hadn't backed out. I knew she would be the listening type. You can always tell. Perhaps, with someone I didn't know, I could talk about Luke, because I certainly needed to. Though what I needed the most was a bloody cup of tea. Breakfast had been a boiled egg, and toast made from last week's wholemeal bread with the mouldy bits cut out. Marmite alone could not rescue such a meal. So, once I approached the now familiar façade of Restaurant Athena, my stomach began to tighten and ache, and this time not just because of the girl. The door was closed and, for a brief instant, I thought the restaurant might not be open. It was just enough of a thought to distract me.

As I already knew I was late, having asked a tourist and two separate police officers for the time, I fully expected her to be there already. I expected her fingers casually twisting around her dark brown hair, or perhaps softly drumming on the table, or idly caressing the stem of her glass. I didn't really know what I was expecting when I opened the door and walked in.

But I wasn't expecting to see the blonde girl grinning at me. What was going on? Dimitrios had described *Isabelle* to me, and this was not she. This girl here was the one who had handed me the camera in the first place, yes. But that doesn't mean it was hers? Does it? What had I done?

Okay, calm down, here's the plan.

Take a deep breath.

Be polite.

Go home.

And peel the startled cod expression from your face. She's saying something about…olives?

She was bright and cheery, I'd give her that, but it was wasted on me. I broke the spell by raising my hand and twitching a few fingers in acknowledgment. I noticed the small plate of olives and was pulled it towards it by the same inexorable force that draws a dog towards another dog's poo. I don't like olives. I had a bad experience with one as a child and I held a grudge.

"No thanks," I said.

"Suit yourself," she said. "They're scrummy." To prove this she placed one deliberately between her lips and held it there just long enough so that I would notice, then sucked it gently into her mouth. But it was wasted on me. There were two little side plates, and a seat pulled a little way from the table. Clearly I had been expected to stay for a while. I had expected no less myself, but not now. This wasn't what I had in mind. There was a small, yet significant, break in the proceedings as a low-lying depression settled in from the North, and tumbleweed scuttled across the dusty recesses of my brain.

"So…" I said, by way of filling the void. But it was a small word, and a big void.

"Have a seat, Charlie," she chirped.

I sat down. It didn't look smooth, and she noticed.

"Late night?"

"Something like that."

"Same here," she said. "I never learn."

And then we ran out of words to waste.

I caught sight of Dimitrios. Up to then I hadn't noticed another living soul, such was my blinkered view. He was beaming knowingly at me. Beaming! Looking for all the world like the proud winner of *Matchmaker Of The Year 1987*, instead of the bungling buffoon that I had him down as right there and then. I could have peppered him with olive pips.

It's not that the blonde wasn't a catch. It's not that I'm so bloody gorgeous I can pick and choose. It's just that I was expecting the brown-eyed girl and I got the blonde. Sometimes you could kill for a fried egg sandwich. If someone says they'll run you one up, but then give you a chicken roast with all the trimmings instead, you still want the bloody fried egg sandwich, all right?

It wasn't the blonde that Dimitrios had been beaming about.

"Hello, Charlie? You made it, then?"

A different voice, soft, dusky, uplifting. It came from somewhere behind me. I knew who it was before I even turned around. But I still turned around, just to be sure. And there she was. The fried egg sandwich, so to speak. There was a mixture of emotions: nervous anticipation, excitement, curiosity - and guilt. Guilt for not thinking about Luke, and guilt for having wanted to pepper Dimitrios with olive pips.

Inside the dented Volvo, Beth changed the channels on the radio again. Out of habit, she confirmed the car clock was telling the same time as her wristwatch. Another four minutes until the news on the BFBS. So, it was another four minutes of Bryan Adams or U2. If she got what she wanted in this next bulletin, she'd try and catch Isabelle and Joanna at the restaurant. She was in the car park of the sports hall, and she'd probably leave the car there and walk. But it all depended on the news.

Derek had been early, which was a relief. After driving round during the midday bulletin, she had decided to be parked up for the next one. Now that he was gone, she could try and pick her own music. She managed to trawl through every station and had hooked herself some Duran Duran, Madonna, Sting, and the new Michael Jackson track, which she hated but listened to anyway, like millions of other suckers. She'd even stayed on one of the bloody awful Berlin stations, so she could listen to the end of Trio's *Da Da Da*, which always made her smile.

She scanned the car park again. Nice enough day, a bit sharp, but bright. It would be nice to get back to her apartment again, though. Isabelle would start asking awkward questions soon. A posse of art students filed past in ubiquitous black. The one at the back wore a long vintage dress over scuffed denim drainpipes, and Beth wondered why she could not try something that ludicrous just once in her life. Berlin would be the ideal venue for such a stab at the avant-garde.

Here we go, time for the news. First, the syndicated stuff from the BBC's World Service. That's two minutes of cramming in as many soul-crushing stories as possible, so that we may all better appreciate our own lives. Back to the BFBS now and the birthday requests. Pay attention now, Beth.

It was the fourth of five announcements. *"Happy Birthday Eleanor Rigby from everyone at the store. Now's the time to let your hair down, and looking forward to seeing you all tonight at Casey's and Nine."*

"Finally," she muttered to herself. She switched off the radio, once the opening chords of *Summer of '69* confirmed the message, and stepped out of the olive green Volvo. She locked the door and dropped the key into her pocket. As she walked towards the S-Bahn on Charlottenburg she took off the gloves she'd been wearing in the car. It was fresh, but not cold enough for gloves. Of course she hadn't been wearing them to keep her hands warm.

Not at all.

C harlie Stokes stood up.
"Hi," he said. And, as if standing for a lady was not formal enough, he extended a hand. He felt both actions lifted him well out of his age bracket, and social standing, but having committed himself, he stayed the course.

Joanna noted the awkwardness, but took Charlie's hand and allowed it to softly squeeze a greeting onto hers.

"Yes, we didn't really introduce ourselves the other day. I'm Joanna," said

Joanna.

Joanna.

"Me too," said Charlie, inexplicably.

Joanna pulled out another chair and sat down quickly, as she had an idea that Charlie might otherwise continue the chivalry by holding the chair, and tucking her under the table

Joanna.

"You look tired, Charlie," she said.

"He had something like a late night, Jo. He was just filling me in."

Joanna looked at Charlie. He was a tousled young man, handsome despite all efforts to the contrary. He had clumps of dark, very thick hair. It would be quite a comb to get that mop into some kind of shape, probably a brush actually. He clearly hadn't bothered today. She noted the puffiness around his eyes and clamminess about his skin, as if he had slept all night at a bus shelter somewhere.

Shambolic.

But still cute. Or was it vulnerable?

Then, who is Isabelle?

Joanna smiled across at Isabelle and was about to say 'So, here we are again', when a tune from her childhood popped into her head. It was the words that arrived first, the tune slinking by just behind. It was Charlie who broke the spell.

"Um," he began, forcing himself to look at Isabelle rather than Jo, "So the camera, is it yours?"

"Yes. I thought you'd nicked it."

"God, no. I just didn't realise I still had it in my hand when I, you know, ran off."

"That's exactly what Jo said."

"Is it?"

"Practically word for word."

This one must be Isabelle, then.

"Well, she was right," said Charlie, and he turned to look at Joanna. "It was all a bit of a mad panic."

"Such a shame about your guitar," said Joanna. "What happened?"

"Oh, nothing. I mean, I found it. Yeah. Caught the guy who took it. All's well and that kind of thing."

"Was there a fight?" asked Isabelle with a disconcerting twinkle.

"I'd rather not talk about it" said Charlie vaguely. "I got it back and that's all that matters really. Let's leave it at that."

"I bet he pulverised the thief, Jo!" squealed Isabelle.

Joanna bet he did no such thing. She knew in an instant he was not that type of man.

"So how long have you been here, Charlie?" asked Joanna.

"Oh, no time," said Charlie, "Literally just walked in before you came in."

"I mean in Berlin."

"Oh. Right."

Isabelle popped another olive into her mouth, not holding back on the suggestiveness the second time around. Joanna admired her relentless persistence when it came to flirting.

"So, where were you before you came to Berlin?"

"Here and there," was all he could come up with.

"Here and there?" smiled Isabelle. "Is that near Haslemere?"

"Probably."

"Shall I take the camera now?" asked Isabelle. "You never know. Something might suddenly spring up."

Charlie Stokes reached into his pocket before remembering that the camera was already at the restaurant. He wafted a finger in the air by way of a pause, and went to collect it. Joanna was sifting through words and notes in her head to piece together this song that had come back to her.

"The camera was here all the time?" queried Isabelle, watching as Dimitrios handed it over to Charlie. "I thought Charlie had it. I thought you had it, Charlie?"

She took the camera from him and dropped it into her red leather handbag, without so much as a cursory glance. She could relax now.

"Right then," she went on. "Who's eating? Charlie? Jo? Anyone?"

It seemed they were all eating.

E Minor

The bread was nice and I was picking away at the glistening white goat's cheese. It was light, fresh, and squeaked when I chewed on it. I had no idea if that was customary or a sign of defiance from the cheese.

I didn't care. I was only interested in Joanna.

Whether or not by a trick of the light, there seemed to be flecks of gold in her brown eyes, as if she'd been painting the ceiling with honey. And when she spoke, the movement of her lips was hypnotic. They were sculpted onto her face like a work of art, and the voice that came out of them was mellow as velvet.

Isabelle was pushing for more on the captured guitar front.

"What did you say to the guy when you caught up with him?"

"It could have been a girl," pointed out Joanna.

"Oh my God, Charlie, no…you didn't hit a girl did you? *Would* you? Could you?"

Maybe, Isabelle. Maybe.

"No, of course not," I said. "It wasn't a girl. It was a guy. I ran around for a bit, didn't see anything, then a bus went past, and there was the guitar up against a window."

"Against a window?"

"Yup. So, I just hared after it, really."

"Hared after it?"

We had arrived, as is so often the case when a guy is telling vaguely exciting stories to a female audience, where every statement was reflected back to me as a question.

"Yes. The guy was just sitting on the seat with it."

"Sitting on the seat with it?"

"Yes."

"What did he say when you caught him?"

"He said, 'Alright, Charlie?' "

I left a bit of room for the pause to work its way across the table and out the door, then carried on. "It was one of the band that took it, for a prank."

"For a prank?" This time it was Joanna, at least. I'd have happily let her question me all day, and night. Only Isabelle never gave her the chance.

"Yeah. They like a prank. He thought I could use it as an excuse to run out of the restaurant without paying, and no-one would notice."

"That's quite a good idea, actually. I can't believe I've never thought of it before."

"It was a mad idea," I said. "But there you go, he's a drummer."

But that wasn't all.

"And he's from Sevenoaks.

I was about to joke about them having to rename the place, now that six of the oaks in question had been laid out. And that was when it all came back to me: trees, storms and deaths. Other people had died last week. Other people's friends would be feeling this. I stared at my fingers, tapped them against the tabletop. I felt a gentle prickling sensation about my eyes. Not from tiredness and lack of sleep alone, but from the need to cry. Isabelle had chosen that of all moments to stop talking and the silence pushed me over the edge. The tapping had become more blatant.

"Are you all right, Charlie?" said Joanna.

I looked up and nodded in that frantic, staccato way people do when they've accidentally stepped onto a threshing machine. The pursed lips and raised eyebrows didn't seem to be the answer she was looking for.

"What's wrong?"

"Is there something wrong?" added Isabelle. "Charlie? Was it the cheese?"

I stood up. The chair kicked back a fraction, the noise of which brought Dimitrios over.

"You not leaving already, Charlie? Sit down." He said.

I sat down. I broke down. I cried.

It wasn't the opening verse of a pop song, it was just an awkward moment. I didn't know these people. I had an irrational little crush on one of them, and I couldn't see where blubbing in public was going to help on that score. I placed my elbows on the table, hid my face in the palms of my hands and waited for everyone to leave.

No one left.

In the darkness I'd created for myself, I saw images of the original *Rolled Oatz* line up.

> I was at the wheel of the red VW camper van. Luke and Jake sat next to me, along the front bench seat. They were both huddled in their overcoats. That was Berlin, back in February, it was bitterly cold and the heating had stopped working in the van back in 1979, the same day the Shah of Iran got his marching orders. I saw Luke's indignant face, and Jake's conciliatory eyebrows wordlessly mediating and pretending that everything was fine.

"Are you all right, Charlie?" Joanna's voice again. I opened my eyes.

"No." I said quickly.

Joanna and Isabelle exchanged glances. If it were scientifically possible, I would have exchanged a glance with myself because I'd intended to say yes.

"No, I'm not. Last night I went to the airport to collect a friend. My best friend. I arrived late. So did the flight. I waited, and waited but he didn't show up. I gave up and went home. Alone. It's not much of an anecdote, eh?" I began to flounder. Joanna seemed to notice, and guided me back on track.

"So what happened?"

"What happened next was that I got back and discovered that Luke was dead. That's why he wasn't on the flight, you see," my voice began to lose some of its control again, "because he was dead. Dead, you see, and they won't let you get on a plane dead, will they?" I hunched forward and rested my elbows on the table again. "I haven't really slept, and I'm really not sure what to feel. Here I am with you two - nice, lovely people - I don't even know you, but would like to know you, and I can't think straight..."

"Charlie, I'm so sorry," said Joanna in just exactly the tone of voice required.

"How did he die? What happened?" asked Isabelle.

"He was killed in Thursday night's storm. The one in England. He was hit by a tree in Guildford." I hadn't gone for the dramatic, it had just come out that way. There were two audible intakes of breath. Joanna put her hand to her mouth.

"That's terrible," gasped Isabelle, "Guildford!"

"Izzy!" hissed Joanna in a hushed tone of admonishment.

"Well, darling, have you been to Guildford?"

"And it's all my fault he's dead," I stood up. I needed to escape, "My fault."

I lurched out of the restaurant without a word, leaving table seven to mull over a second consecutive unexpected exit.

I couldn't decide which way to go. The little patch of Kantstrasse outside the restaurant was becoming familiar to me, and with familiarity came non-appreciation, so I stood on it non-appreciatively. It didn't help me decide which way to go, but I made up my mind at least to cross the street. As I waited on the kerb, a short gust blew a chill through my body and that's when I realized that I'd left my coat in the restaurant. Of course.

So, I just stood there, gazing across the street as the traffic flicked past, aware of pedestrians shuffling along behind me. And then I closed my eyes. I can't imagine how disturbed I must have appeared, tottering on the edge of a busy kerb, but it was nice to be in the dark where nobody could see me.

"Charlie?"

It was beyond heavenly the way she made my name sound. I opened my eyes and turned around. Joanna stood there, holding my coat.

"Do you want this, or will you come back inside?"

I didn't want to go back inside. I didn't want to look foolish in front of Joanna again. I didn't want to look foolish in front of anyone, come to that. And I was convinced that I would. It seemed to be one of those places where the fates have it in for you. *No, I will not come back inside.*

"Maybe you just need to talk about it?" She said.

We went back inside.

A pleasant calmness enfolded table seven, like one of those agreeable high pressure zones that have a long nap over England every fifth summer or so.

Charlie Stokes had washed down the bread and cheese with at least a pint of sparkling water. Purified and bloated in equal measures, he estimated his chance of breaking wind shortly as fair to middling.

Isabelle, her lightly freckled cheeks now set off with the subtlest hint of a glow, was working herself towards the centre of a bottle of retsina for no good reason that she could think of. Joanna absorbed Charlie's sad news with a genuine sincerity that surprised her, being as he was someone she had only just met. That song was coming back to her again.

What they had all settled upon was that Luke's death was a tragic accident for which Charlie could not hold himself in the slightest responsible. They had allowed Charlie to speak a little about Luke, about the band's arrival in Berlin, about their falling out, and about his imminent return. Small finger snacks of easily digested dialogue.

"Your lips are moving," said Charlie, right out of the blue. "Are you reading an invisible book to yourself?" He smiled, despite himself.

"Oh, my God, you didn't notice?" she blurted out and started to blush.

"What is it? What?" asked Isabelle. "What?"

"I just remembered a song I used to hear when I was little. My Mum played it all the time, and it just came back to me because of what we're doing now, here."

"We're doing something now, here?"

Joanna began to sing. To show it was all a bit of fun, she used a quiet, breathy voice and bobbed her head from side to side in time to the beat. She made the effort to make it sound like something the Beverly Sisters would have recorded, and the snippet she pulled out from her memory went:

"Dum-di something, something, something,
It was Lord and Lady Harris,
When in Amsterdam or Paris,
That they celebrate her win.

It's a funny little feeling,
When your heart is on the ceiling,

But it's just another evening
At a table in Berlin."

When she'd finished, she sat there with her mouth open in puzzled amazement. Whatever, if anything, she had expected as a response, it was certainly not seeing Charlie join in the last two lines.

"You can't possibly know that song, Charlie!" she said.

"Why not? You do."

"How could you know it?"

"I know lots of songs. I'm in a band."

"Here's Beth," said Isabelle suddenly, having felt uncomfortably left out. "Good, she isn't bringing what's-his-name, I told you."

E Minor

I never doubted we would have something in common, I just didn't think it would be a novelty record that was a throwback to the forties. It seemed to rattle her that I recognised the song as much as it rattled me to hear her sing it. We would have had quite a discussion about it, but for Beth's arrival and the subsequent fifteen minutes of sibling banter between her and Isabelle. Away from the chatter, Joanna spoke to me again.

"When is the funeral, Charlie?"

Oh God. The funeral.

"Not sure yet," I said. "I shan't be going." This seemed to shock her. "I can't."

"Why not?"

Why not, indeed?

"It's complicated."

"You have to go, Charlie."

"I know."

Beth seemed to take an interest in me then, gently flipping a crumb of bread from the corner of her mouth.

"Where do you have to go?" she said, barely opening her lips lest anything should escape.

"A funeral."

"Oh dear." She sounded sad.

"It's not mine."

"Still."

"It's his best friend. So young." Isabelle at least sounded understanding. "Oh, I'm sorry to hear that, Charlie." Said Beth, though she managed to sound as if she was anything but. "Your best friend? Oh dear. But then surely you must go? Derek has a black tie in the cupboard." She added.

"I don't think the lack of a black tie is holding him back, Beth!" It was Isabelle raising her voice.

As it happened, she was right. I had three knitted silk ties, any one of which would have done the job, as they were all black. I tried to draw Joanna back into the conversation.

"I've never been to a funeral. I just…" *Just what, exactly?* "I just don't think I could handle it."

Looking round at their faces, it sounded a bit soft. Beth certainly seemed unconvinced anyway, though I already had her down as someone who generally lived life unconvinced. I could sense that Isabelle was going to say 'Bless' or something bloody close, but Joanna got in ahead of her.

"You'll probably regret it if you don't go, Charlie."

I just knew she would be the sensible one. I knew I'd have to go for my own sake, not Luke's. Why would Luke care? He wouldn't know. Funerals are for the left behind.

"I'll be off to England next weekend," said Joanna.

"Oh," I replied, crushed. I only just met her, and now she's leaving? Thanks.

"We have a ballet gala over in East Berlin coming up, and I have some work to do on it in London for a few days." I brightened up. She was coming back. "If the timings work out and it's not too far… I'll go to the funeral with you, if you like. Moral support."

I brightened up rather a lot more.

"Really?"

"Oh, Jo, you're such a sweetie! Isn't she a sweetie, Beth?"

The general consensus was that she was a sweetie. For my part, I was trying to work out whether I had just been asked out on a date, and I decided that yes, I bloody well had. It still seemed a strange offer to make to someone she didn't know. I wondered what the catch would be. I didn't care. I'd happily go to my own funeral if I knew Joanna would be there.

"I'm going to use Dimitrios's phone and see where Alex is," said Isabelle.

Joanna watched her bob across the floor, and I watched Joanna. Beth watched me watching.

Alexandra, like Beth before her, had not felt one hundred per cent on Friday. Her throat had been dry, and the occasional irritating tingle in her nostrils confirmed the telltale signs of an impending cold. But she was also prone to flare up under stress, and it was down to that that she had put the symptoms. By Saturday evening she had begun to feel rancid, so she had wisely bypassed any thoughts of dropping into the Greek place on Kantstrasse.

She boiled the kettle and dropped a rooibos tea bag into her largest mug. She enjoyed experimenting with different infusions, and had been taken in by the alleged health properties of this South African beverage, smuggled in by a colleague from work, despite its exotic taste. Just as she had placed herself in a self-indulgently comfortable position on the sofa, the phone rang. Finally - Tony. Even the timing of his phone calls could be annoying. Not so that she wouldn't pick up, though. She got up and snatched at the receiver. Not Tony. Isabelle.

"Oh, darling, you sound like an alien, what have you got up your nose?"

"Feeling rotten, head cold or something. I'm staying on the sofa. Probably end up going to bed. You having lunch in the end? Got your camera back?"

"Yes. We're just having a drink and a pick. Beth's here, too. Anyway, I take it you're not coming. We're fixing up a dinner for when Jo's back, okay?"

"That'd be great, Izzy."

A few hours later, she was throwing up violently. Clammy and fuzzy-headed from assorted medication, she did what she could for herself under a very long, lukewarm shower and went to bed. She was asleep at eight-thirty and by quarter to nine was snoring so loudly that her neighbour actually banged on the wall. She didn't wake up until nine-thirty Monday morning.

By which time she had become effectively penniless.

Joanna struggled again with her front door key. The key and the lock of her front door were once again at loggerheads and she audibly implored herself not to forget to ask the landlord to look into it. She hung her dark grey camelhair coat on a hanger in the hallway and dropped the keys and her handbag onto the kitchen table. She had walked as far as the S-Bahn station with Charlie and the girls before going their separate ways. It hadn't surprised her that he lived in the East Kreuzberg district. If there were a part of West Berlin that drew life's artistic flotsam and jetsam like a giant magnet, then the SO36 district was it. He had written down his telephone number on a packet of sugar. "So you'll remember it's my number," he had said. "The sweet boy."

The song was in her head again, of course. She couldn't remember the name of it anymore, but the LP was called *So Much World, So Little Time*. It had been years. She almost asked Charlie how he had come to know it, but the moment had passed.

She had watched him as he walked away, noting the tension in his shoulders pulling at him.

E Minor

M any of the bars and cafes in East Kreuzberg, certainly all the ones I frequented, seethed with anarchy and studied rebellion. Whenever anything kicked off in West Berlin, it likely as not kicked off here. Every strain of Berlin society, admittedly more some than others, was absorbed into this kaleidoscope of restless humanity, bounded on no fewer than three sides by the hulking nonsense of the Wall. Revolutionary thoughts hang heavy in these kinds of surroundings and, once the spoons come out, it's never just the coffee that gets stirred.

A bit grim.

We were at *Die Rote Harfe* on Oranienstrasse, a café where the band often accumulated amongst the rabid left-wing ideologists there, because it was hard to find cheaper beer anywhere else in the city. Jake, Ritchie, Daniel and Troy were jostling around a table when I arrived. I shuffled towards them. Jake saw me first.

"Alright, Charlie?"

"Jake."

"Charlie."

"Dan, Richie."

"Dude."

"Troy."

That about settled the accounts on the conversation side of things. After that, it went quiet for a bit.

I recognised the girl at the table next to the guys. She had flame-red hair and unfeasibly large spectacles casting an enormous shadow across her freckles. She seemed to be berating two identically dressed men on the subject of Gorbachev, splitting her vitriol between German and English. She was pretty, behind all the glazing, but she had fiery opinions and no volume control. Dan had taken her home after a gig once, and was traumatised for a week.

"Drink, Charlie?" asked Ritchie.

"Yeah, go on."

"There's a message for you," said Jake. "The funeral's arranged for Friday."

"Right." I wasn't expecting that. "Am I supposed to confirm or something?"

"Don't know. It didn't say. I expect so. You are going, aren't you?"

"Are you?"

"Thought it best left to you, Charlie."

"Why him?" asked Ritchie, who hadn't made much progress in fetching me a drink yet. "They all hate Charlie."

This was true, and a valid point.

"Do me a favour, no they don't." Jake brushed Ritchie's comments away. "Nobody hates Charlie."

"Luke's Mum does," continued Ritchie.

"Yes, but apart from her?"

I got up and left.

"Don't forget the tea bags, Charlie."

London, Monday, October 19th

L oudly and harshly, telephones were ringing everywhere.

If such a thing were possible, it sounded like telephones had declared war on other telephones. But there was something else. You couldn't hear it, the inaudible tenor of panic and self-delusion that primed the only other sound you could hear: men shouting. They were yelling instructions, barking orders and orchestrating the end of their professional careers. It was the great 'c' word that the media saves for moments like these.

Carnage.

At one point, Jeremiah Warrender actually sat back in his chair and rested the fingers of both hands against the side of his head, in a theatrical expression of bewilderment. He was powerless, overwhelmed in a helter-skelter of uncontrollable sell orders, the system incapable of coping. The market was in meltdown. He had clients who were haemorrhaging money to a life-threatening extent, and there was nothing he seemed to be able to do to stop it. Four different phones sat on his desk. He stood up and began using them all, simultaneously. It involved impressive digital dexterity, but mainly shouting. His eyeballs were on stalks, the vein in his neck was engorged. His blood pressure went up to 142.

But he didn't drop dead for another seven years.

It wasn't his money, after all.

West Berlin

Jake loved snapping pictures. He had a very good camera once. He'd sold it, in a purge of his hobbies, to raise the cash for most of his new drum kit. He'd found the initial naffness of having a compact model wore off as he became less obsessed by artistic composition and more interested in collecting a simple visual record of his routine.

They knew him at the shop where he got his photos developed. Not to the extent of conversing, but they acknowledged his regular if unspectacular business. He'd dropped off the cartridge on Friday morning. Standing at the counter, having handed over his slip, he noted a level of interest in him that had never been shown before. It was as if he were the last person in the room to have got the joke. Only he wasn't, because he still hadn't got it. There was a lot of Teutonic smirking going on before they handed him the envelope, making what Jake thought to be rather a show of checking the serial numbers. Jake left, with the most perfunctory *danke* he could muster, and scuttled home. He was a good scuttler.

Charlie and Dan were in the living room when Jake returned. They were sitting with their guitars, jamming. Charlie was playing the Gibson acoustic, his fingers effortlessly caressing the fretboard, while Dan overlay riffs on his old hollow-bodied Hofner electric, plugged into a tiny practice amp. The sound filled the room. Something had to.

"All right, Charlie? Dan?" said Jake. "How's it going?" He walked into his room and tossed the pack of photos onto the bed, while simultaneously removing his coat. "Hey, Charlie!" he called out.

"Yeah?"

"Did you hear back about the Suzy Quatro thing?"

"No."

"Think we'll get it?"

"Yeah. But May's a long way ahead. A lot can happen. But hope for the best, expect the worst. Usual thing."

"Just be nice to get something big soon, you know, Charlie? Sooner or later. Been a while, hasn't it?"

"I know. I'm working on it, Jake." Was that the slightest whiff of mutiny in the air?

"I know you are, Charlie. Just saying."

"I still say we should be getting *her* to support *us*!" said Dan, grinning.

Jake filled a large tumbler to the rim with Coke and downed it in one. Charlie and Dan paused in polite expectation. Jake immediately tried to belch the entire introductory *Bop bopa-a-lupa a-whop bam boo* of Little Richard's *Tutti Frutti* in a single exhalation. He got as far as *whop*.

"Good effort, Jake," said Charlie.

"Nice one, mate," concurred Dan.

Jake went back into his room and sat on the bed after kicking off his shoes. He had been considering some more bar work. His money was drying up and so, it appeared, were the gigs. Idly weighing up his hazy memories of the female bar staff at the Irish pub on Ku'damm, and that freaky place around the corner with the psychedelic basement, Jake took out the photos and began looking through them. He didn't get further than the third.

"Jesus *Christ!*"

Beth and Isabelle had spent Sunday evening discussing the relative merits of their respective hair salons as only sisters could, making innocuous conversation sound like an argument.

Isabelle was surprised at the level of discomfort she had begun to feel not having her sister at home - it was so unlike Beth, regardless of the telephone updates. Everything had got back to normal about eighteen seconds after Beth had walked into the restaurant, but Isabelle had felt a surge of happy relief the moment her big sister had reappeared.

And Monday had been a tedious day at work. Half the office had gone to East Berlin to prepare for the London Ballet's visit, and the remaining half were the committed I Hate Mondays Brigade who embalmed the building with layers of melancholy. Add to that the filling that had broken on her last bite of a Twix bar, she was relieved to get home and anaesthetise some of the gloom with a bottle of that hideous Liebfraumilch that she had inadvertently brought home from the reception before last. She'd had time, during an elongated lunch break, to buy another film cartridge. She decided to reload the camera and put the used film somewhere secure.

When she opened the back of her camera, it certainly did not lift her prevailing mood to discover that the compartment was empty. At first, a wild wave of Liebfraumilch-fuelled hysteria bathed her in panic, for she had absolutely no recollection of having taken the film out. And yet she must have done. Otherwise, where was it?

Charlie Stokes.

"You naughty, naughty boy," she whispered to herself.

Jake was nonplussed. Although this was practically a default setting for him, this time he was what he would call "really nonplussed." He had his camera on the bed and he could see quite clearly that the used film cartridge was still there. Considering that it couldn't be, as he'd removed it and taken it to the photo shop to have developed, he sat and stared for a time. He then flipped open the back and took out the cartridge. Again.

Nonplussed.

E Minor

"Charlie?"

I looked up and saw Jake leaning against the doorframe of his bedroom. He had a small stack of cards, or maybe photographs, in his hands and he was directing a goofy gaze at them.

"Yes."

"You got a sec?"

I had been sitting cross-legged on the one solitary rug that gave our wooden floor a bit of barefoot comfort. I unfolded myself carefully to my feet and sauntered into his room.

Jake was wearing one of his seriously confused expressions. Holding the photographs - I could tell now that's what they were - he used them to punctuate his words, emphasising what he was saying and acting much like a man wafting a series of unpredictable cobwebs away from his path.

"On Friday morning, after I got back, I took a film to be developed. I remember thinking 'what's the camera doing there on the table?' Anyway, so I took the film out. And I got the pictures done." He illustrated this by lifting the hand that held the photos, and giving them a little shake.

"Okay," I said. I assumed there was more.

"So, I just passed by the place now and collected them."

"Okay," I said again.

"So, the thing is, Charlie," he began, "how come the film I took out of the camera on Friday is back in the camera now?"

How come indeed?

"Well," I said, "I expect you put it back without realising. You know, when your mind was on something else?" I stopped short of adding "like it very often is", as I sensed he was not in the mood for it.

"In that case," he said, handing over the photographs, "whose are these?"

I took the pictures and glanced down at the first one. Yes. I had been right enough, there was an elbow in the frame. Shame. It was a nice enough snap, it caught the mood of the moment. Isabelle's naked mischievousness was there for all to see; Beth, forcing a smile; Alexandra's unconvincing grin; Joanna's warm, soft, delicious... Hang on, these were the photos from Isabelle's camera!

Although Jake was clearly bemused, I could see what had happened. Jake had taken the film out of Isabelle's camera without realising. I was about to explain this to him, as I continued shuffling through the photographs, but found myself saying something completely different.

"Jesus *Christ*."

Lots, and I mean lots, of very dodgy photos.

"That's what I said."

Thinking quickly on my feet, which had become a speciality of mine in recent months, I scooped up the pack with the negatives, stuffed the photos back inside, and shoved the lot into the outer envelope. I used it to tap Jake's shoulder as I left his room.

"Not to worry. Obviously a mistake at the shop. I'll sort it."

"Eh? At the shop? How? And what about this?" He lifted his camera, with the film still inside. "I took this film out and left it at the shop yet here it is back again, remember? That's spooky, that is. And why are *you* going to sort it out? They're my pictures."

"I think not."

I had meant to tell him that he'd simply taken the film out of Isabelle's camera - which I had then returned to the restaurant - and not his own practically identical one. I was going to explain that they were Isabelle's photos he'd had developed. But I didn't. I just said:

"Put the kettle on."

"There's no tea."

Tuesday, October 20th

Charlie Stokes had had a dream. Although it was about the past, Joanna was in it. Sometimes as herself, and sometimes not.

In the café on Tottenham Court Road, Charlie and Luke drank coffees that Joanna (as the waitress) had brought to them.

"Luke, I've had this great idea."

"Not another one of your hare-brained schemes, is it, Charlie?"

"Is there any other kind?"

"What is it this time?"

"Germany."

"Oh yeah?"

"Rock 'n' roll, Lukester. They're gagging for it."

"The Germans?"

"Not just the Germans. Even the people who are not the Germans, just living in Germany. They catch it. Like a disease."

"I never thought rock 'n' roll was contagious, Charlie."

"It's like the plague, mate."

They were all on a plane now, chatting up the stewardesses as they sailed across the North Sea in the grip of a big swell. Joanna (as the stewardess) was complaining about all the vomit she had to clean up.

Where are we going, again, Charlie? Everyone was asking. Can you buy Hobnobs in Germany? Do you they have proper milk or that piss they have in France? They were in a red VW camper van. Charlie was convinced that Joanna (now no longer a stewardess) was cuddling someone inside a sleeping bag. Stop it! You can't do that.

"So much great rock and pop history, Luke" said Charlie. "The Beatles went to Germany as boys, and came back as men; as demigods."
"I'd rather be a man than a demigod, Charlie."
"Why's that, Jake?"
"Less responsibility."
"There's the strip clubs, and dock workers and proper working people needing to let off steam at the weekend. And we'll be 'special'. We'll be the 'English band'. We can be outrageous and controversial and no one will mind."
"The strip clubs are fab," said Joanna, launching into a burlesque pose while dressed from top to toe as a stripper. "I can't wait to get back to work. The money's great." She was shaking her breasts, bare but for garish silver tassels. They were her dream breasts, at least three cup sizes up from her real ones.
"Dock workers? Do they still have them?" went a voice.
"Hamburg is bursting."

They were in Hamburg and the port was heaving with pirate ships and tall ships and sheep? The Beatles. Fame. Eight- hour sets. Discipline. Poverty. Sex. Life.
Joanna kissed Charlie. No, Charlie kissed Joanna, but she let him. Heat. Lips. Softness.
Charlie bathed in the warm fragrance of the subconscious, their bodies pressed together. His face nestled in her cheeks and her thick silky hair brushed against his eyelashes.

Now it was Berlin. February. An easterly wind diced the Englishmen as they assembled in a heap of grey misery in a Godforsaken corner of a Godforsaken frontier of capitalism. The boys were trying to pronounce Kreuzberg, and all they could say was Krapberg. Charlie was shouting: "I forgot! I said Berlin to the agency and left them to it! I don't know why the word Berlin came out. It's

Len Deighton's fault."

Joanna (as an East Berliner) was running towards them from the Wall, trying to escape. Guns were firing.

"Play in the footsteps of The Beatles, you said," screamed Luke. "You promised us the Reeperbahn and gave us a fucking Wall!"

Charlie was holding Joanna in his arms. She was dead, but still talking. Dream dead. He looked down at his bloodstained t-shirt. It read: "I Went To Berlin But I Meant To Go To Hamburg And All I Got Was This Lousy T-Shirt."

Charlie Stokes had never been so happy to wake up. The phone was ringing. He answered. It was Isabelle.

Awkward.

Yes, she could come round and collect some photographs.

E Minor

The knock, when it came, was a little bit cheeky, with a hint of insecurity. Understandable under the circumstances, I thought. I picked up the envelope of photographs and tried to construct myself a suitably non-judgmental face with which to open the door. It was harder than I thought. The more I tried, the more self-conscious I felt. Eventually I seized on the firmly neutral look I was after, locked it into position, and swung the door open.

"What happened to your face, Charlie, been to the dentist?"

With a twitch, the expression of blank insouciance that I had been trying to fabricate changed to one of mild incomprehension as I registered the tall, sombre-suited shape of Lewis. While I couldn't say I was looking forward to seeing Isabelle, I'd have taken her over Lewis any time. Only his name didn't seem to be Lewis today. Not according to the identification he was holding up. It was his face in the photo, though. He looked good for his age, I had to give him that. What else did it have written there? Bloody small print. Was that something about a Bureau 9? I just caught myself squinting, ever so slightly.

"Do you need a torch, Charlie?"

It was the type of tinder-dry sarcasm that leaked at will from experienced British coppers. I guessed he had been one once. I waited for the invitation. It wasn't long coming.

"I wonder if you'd like to pop down for a moment, Charlie?"

"Actually," I began, "I was expecting someone."

"That's nice, Charlie. So are we." He pulled out a smile, and tried it on for size.

"I'll just get my coat."

I had the feeling I was going for another little ride in the Audi, and wouldn't need my coat, but I wanted a reason to go inside and dump the photo package. Lewis wouldn't follow me in without invitation. It's not like I was going to escape from a third floor window or anything.

So, it did make me jump a bit when, after placing the photos in my sock drawer, I turned to find him four inches behind me, uninvited so to speak. But there was no malice in either his demeanour or actions. It was just that he was so, well, unrequired in my life. I couldn't be sure if he'd been watching where I'd put the photos, or just generally watching, but he gave the gaff a polite once-over.

"Nice place, Charlie."

I hate to be disloyal, but my apartment was a small dump in the armpit of Berlin.

"You like your irony, don't you?" I suggested.

"Everything in moderation, Charlie. Shall we?" He helpfully indicated the way out and had this to say as we entered the hallway: "You might think about a better lock, Charlie. The big bad wolf could blow this door down. Should the need arise."

Why would the need arise?

Joanna waited for Isabelle a few minutes longer and then set off alone. Isabelle knew where the meeting was. Not like her to be late for a work appointment. Then again, as Joanna thought back over the past months, not altogether unlike her, either.

She walked briskly. That morning, drying herself after her shower, she felt her body was changing. In the wrong direction. She had always been an absolutely normal female shape. She went in and out in all the right places. She'd never been slim or toned, but she'd always been just right, really. She was wearing now a pair of dark grey, woollen trousers that she adored, but hadn't worn since before the summer, and they were definitely tighter than they needed to be. She wouldn't let it become an issue, but she'd decided on putting a bit more exercise and a bit less eating into her immediate way of life. There was no danger she'd fall prey to the affliction that was aerobics, and was no more likely to encase her femininity in stretch lycra and ludicrous sweat bands than she was to put a kitten in a microwave. No, she wouldn't let it become an issue. She would simply adapt slightly. She might buy herself a bicycle, and use that to commute about the place. Walking would be the best, but one couldn't always afford the time it took.

"Hey, Jo, how's it going?" It was a man's voice. Dobson, from the travel agents, wasn't it? Yes, it was. Never mind.

"Oh, hello. Fine. And you?" She didn't want to stop and chat because, of course, having waited longer than necessary for Isabelle to come back, she was on a tight schedule. So she kept on walking.

"Super, thanks. I was just coming with your ticket," he said, oozing smarm from every pore.

"Great." She waved apologetically and flashed her wristwatch. "In a rush. Bye."

"Ah." It is difficult to express crushing disappointment in a single syllable, but Dobson, from the travel agents, made a commendable effort.

As Joanna hurried on, she was aware of her reflection in the windows of the shops as she sped past. It was true what Isabelle said, however embarrassing and surprising. Men did seem always to fawn around her. Not the sort of thing one should complain about, but still.

"These trousers are definitely tighter around the bum than they need to be," she mumbled to herself as she strode away. A car horn shrieked. Isabelle.

"You're not walking there are you, darling? Come on, get in. We don't want to be late!"

"I thought you'd been abducted."

"No such luck. Mind your head, sweetie!" Joanna's attention had been caught by something on the other side of the street and she'd almost clipped the door frame with her forehead. Isabelle stabbed the accelerator and they lurched off, back up to normal traffic speed in the time it took to nudge a man off his bike.

"Everything all right, Izzy?"

"Couldn't be better," lied Isabelle. "Nice lunch?"

"Yes," said Joanna, equalising with a lie of her own.

"Lovely."

With that, they continued in an unusual but comfortable silence all the way to their meeting. A meeting through which Isabelle's concentration was tested by the gnawing distraction of having stood in the hallway knocking forlornly at Charlie Stokes' unanswered door for the entire duration of her lunch break. Weren't men funny little things.

"So, what's the food like in that Greek restaurant you are always visiting these days, Charlie? Any good? I'm not sure that I'm a fan of Greek food."

"It grows on you," said Charlie.

"So does mould, doesn't make it any the more appetising."

"No, I suppose not."

They had already fixed the broken rear light on the Audi. Charlie had noticed straight away. Perhaps the police were hot on that sort of thing in West Berlin. It was only Lewis and the driver in the car this time, accentuating the car's spacious interior. And although he was sharing this space with a group of highly professional, mysterious men who may or may not have been who they claimed, Charlie was surprisingly relaxed. Relaxed enough to ask some questions of his own.

"Is it legal?" he asked conversationally, "taking people from their homes and driving them around Berlin for no reason?" He hung a small smile on the end, just to be sure the intent was clear.

"Legal, Charlie? Are you lodging an official complaint? We wouldn't like that, would we, Sid?"

"I certainly wouldn't," said the driver, his first words of the journey. The atmosphere had changed completely in an instant. Edith Piaf may have never had any regrets, but Charlie Stokes certainly wished he'd kept his mouth shut. Still, when you're in a hole, keep digging.

"It's just that not everyone would just, you know, come along with you without asking a lot of awkward questions."

"I didn't know you had a lot of awkward questions, Charlie."

"I might."

"I'm all ears."

"Right."

Charlie glanced across and saw that Lewis was watching the street as the car drove along. His was a face that lived in a different world to Charlie's, a face that could not care less about any question, awkward or otherwise, that Charlie might have had - and Charlie knew immediately that this conversation was over. So he sat gloomily, staring at the upholstery of the seat in front of him. It was a nice car, but he sure as shit was never going to buy one for himself, should the resources to do so ever present themselves.

Beth didn't like the way her nails had been done. She didn't like to appear as interested in her own appearance as her sister, but now and again she'd treat herself to a manicure, rather than do it herself. And here she was wishing that she'd done it herself.

And what was in that salad she'd just snatched at? Salad in this weather, how pitiful was that? A nice bowl of spaghetti bolognese would have hit the spot.

Goodness, could she be any grumpier? She picked at a loose thread on her cardigan. There must be more to life. She was checking her watch when the Audi pulled up in the courtyard. She waited, listening to the engine idling. Then she threw a grey pashmina over her shoulders and picked up her handbag. The engine had stopped. She peered into the courtyard again. Lewis was in the back with the boy. Sid was walking over to open the front passenger seat. She still didn't really know how she was going to handle this, but something would come to her. She hoped she hadn't misjudged this Charlie Stokes.

E Minor

Time was hanging a bit on the heavy side. To help pass it, I snatched views of Sid, the driver, in the rear view mirror. Whereas Lewis and the two other suited men who had formed part of the Audi entourage in the past had a certain Establishment air about them, Sid was altogether more antediluvian. He looked as if he had been fished out of a primeval swamp still warm, been dropped on his face in the process, and then reassembled by a class of infants. What was left of his nose, serving little practical purpose as far as inhaling and exhaling were concerned, gave his voice its distinct glottal patois. Oddly enough, though, he didn't look out of place in a suit and tie, but if he was employed for his driving skills alone then I was a scotch egg.

With neither a hint of indicator nor a glance in his mirrors, Sid threw the car right, into a side street and, almost immediately, right again into a small courtyard. The Audi pulled up. I wasn't expecting that. Constant movement was comforting. Being in public surrounded by other cars and people, that was fine. But two sudden right turns, and a deserted courtyard was altogether not my cup of tea. From the depths of my Neanderthal past, a tightening and shrinking of my scrotum introduced me to the concept of real fear for the first time. When Sid switched off the engine, all I could hear was a high-pitched whistling in my ears.

He got out and began to walk around to my side of the car. Yes, he was a big man. I briefly considered making a run for it when I looked out of the windscreen and saw Beth walking towards me.

Isabelle's Beth.

Beth from the restaurant.

Beth?

"Hello, Charlie," she said, a bit awkwardly, "shall we…go inside?"

Beth led Charlie along a short corridor and through a door on the left into what looked like a storage room. One wall was lined with warehouse shelving on which were packed boxes of industrial cleaning products. A line of chairs, each different from the other, formed a polite queue along the opposite wall, and at the far end stood a mahogany writing desk with a green shaded banker's lamp atop. It was difficult to imagine anything more incongruous.

Beth did not sit behind the desk, but on one of the chairs lining the wall. She patted the one next to her to indicate to Charlie that he should sit on it. As he did so, she noticed Sid hovering at the threshold. She made him leave with the subtlest shake of her head. She looked across at the shelving, at all the one litre plastic bottles of unbranded toilet cleaner, and wondered whether it worked as well as the Domestos she always had at home. One day she'd really have to take a bottle and see.

"I was surprised to see you," said Charlie. Surprised was an understatement.

"Really?"

"Yeah, I mean, well I didn't expect," he paused and looked around the room, "this." He smiled through pursed lips.

"Right," said Beth. "What do you mean?"

"I thought you worked at the Embassy?"

"The Consulate, yes. It's not the Embassy. The British Embassy is in Bonn."

"Oh."

"Yes."

"That would be a bloody long commute."

"Yes it would," she said, smiling insincerely.

There was another pause, for which Charlie's world was well known. Beth considered one of two options as to how to proceed and chose the first.

"Can you keep a secret, Charlie?"

"If you like."

"Would you do me a favour?"

"Sure."

"My job at the Consulate," she began, "it's…"

"I know all about it," said Charlie. "Isabelle told me everything." Beth tensed involuntarily. This was not turning out well. "It's dull and boring, and all you do is type out forms, process birth certificates, and make tea for someone called Derek." Beth relaxed. "But a job's a job." Beth smiled again.

"Why didn't you tell them the other day that you knew me, when they showed you the photographs?" Charlie shrugged, but only with his lips. "But you recognised me, didn't you?"

"Yes. I suppose so."

"What about Troy?" she asked. And then it was Charlie's turn to tense. "You didn't tell them you knew him, either. Why?"

Silence.

"How long have you known him for, by the way?" Beth's voice was bright and airy and indifferent. Charlie pulled another face. He thought it might buy him a few more seconds of thinking time. It didn't.

"Do you know what else he does, apart from playing with you?"

"No," said Charlie finally, having run out of serviceable silences. "He's never said, and I don't ask, I suppose. He used to be a Marine, or something. He came here with the Army, anyway. He's not in it anymore."

"Is that what he told you?"

"Yes. Well, I mean, it's not like he told me in one dramatic sentence. Just in the odd chat here and there."

"So would you say you knew him well?"

"He plays with us. Not always, just when he can fit it in. We all hang out and goof around together sometimes. Just normal band stuff, you know."

"He doesn't play with you all the time?"

"No. It's better when he does, it's a nice extra sound having the sax, but he can't always make the gigs."

"How does that work out with the money, then?"

"What do you mean?"

"Well, you pay him the same as the others? Wouldn't they be better off if he didn't play?"

"Oh," said Charlie, "he doesn't get paid. He doesn't need the money. He just wants the fun. And the girls, if there are any going." He had relaxed now. He knew this was some elaborate prank. He couldn't be certain, but his guess was that there was a video camera tucked away behind the bleach. He'd go along, but make sure he didn't say anything that would make him look stupid, particularly after some clever editing.

"If you don't pay him and he's not in the Army any more, Charlie, where does he get his money from?"

Where indeed?

"Perhaps he's one of the Rockefellers and can do as he pleases?"

"Perhaps not."

"Why do you want to know about Troy, anyway?"

Beth looked into Charlie's eyes then, which made him feel slightly uncomfortable. She reckoned it was time to get things going. She was comfortable with her hunch, so she decided to go ahead.

"I just want you to do something for me. It's a job. You can say no, of course. But first you have to understand that this is between you and me. That's very important, Charlie. If you tell anyone about anything we talk about now, I shall deny it. In return, I shan't talk about it to anyone, either. Except for my work colleagues, because it's work." Beth stood up and, from the top of the desk, picked up a large white envelope. "This is for you. Okay?"

Charlie took the envelope, waiting for the big reveal, or something similar, or anything at all really. He looked up from the corner of his eyes, towards the spot on the shelving where he imagined the video camera to be hiding.

"We believe that Troy Cafarella is helping in the transfer of confidential material between West and East Berlin. It's only low-grade, but it's my responsibility to track this kind of thing down and, well, fix it.

Fix it?

Charlie still said nothing. He decided to open the envelope and have done with it. Beth continued.

"I think you can find out what he's been up to, Charlie. That's all. Just let me know, and, we'll take it from there."

Charlie pulled out five twenty-pound notes and an airline ticket. Puzzled to stretching point, he opened it. It was in his name and it was a return flight to London's Gatwick airport, leaving on Thursday, the day before the funeral. The atmosphere in the room changed entirely, and Charlie began to flush.

E Minor

"Sorry, Beth, but what's this all about?" I said, because I had reached the point where I thought that enough was enough, and this was enough. "Seriously. Are you saying you don't have a little boring job at the, whatever, consulate?"

"I have an office at the consulate, yes. I just don't do visas and passports and lost travel documents."

"Okay, what do you do, exactly?"

"I have a small bureau and I help sort out any intelligence leaks."

"Okay," I said, no closer yet, "I want you to speak to me in Hollywood language now."

"I'm a spycatcher, I suppose."

Obviously.

"Finally, the punchline," I drawled. "Nice one." I handed back the envelope, after returning both the money and the ticket. "Here." I got up to leave.

"Charlie?" she seemed not quite to understand that the game was up.

"Leave it out," I said, meaning more or less every word, "my friend has just died and I'm not in the mood, alright? And I don't need a lift, thanks."

I headed for the door, which was the first time I'd noticed Lewis filling so much of it. There was something about his expression. I stopped, as he gave no indication that he was going to move out of the way, and there was a lot more of him than I felt comfortable pushing to one side. I stared down at his shoes and found myself smiling and shaking my head at the same time.

"This is not a joke, is it?" I said grimly.

When I looked back at Beth she wore the expression of a Princess who had just lowered herself to ask the gardener out to tea, and been turned down. She was looking at the envelope in her hand like it was a dog turd someone had just asked her to mind. I took a breath and returned to the chair. I relieved Beth of the envelope while I was at it.

"Nobody can know what I do, Charlie. Not even Isabelle knows."

"Right." I thought I'd get to the important business. "Will there be fast cars?"

"No."

"Will there be gorgeous girls?"

"No."

"Will anyone be punching me in the face?"

"No."

"Sounds boring."

"It is boring, Charlie. It's extremely boring. But sometimes it's also important."

"Right."

"I thought you might appreciate the flight ticket. Better than taking the coach trip."

"Oh yes."

"Joanna will be on the flight with you. I thought you could do with the company."

Oh, I thought. I make that *yes* to the gorgeous girls, then.

"Ask Troy to give you a lift to the airport. You can make a start on him."

It was hard to imagine Beth believed I would actually spy on my own friend, but clearly she did. I took the money anyway.

She didn't ask for a receipt.

Wednesday, October 21st

Troy Cafarella had left the Marines but his hair was still cut in their honour. A sandy shade of custard, he let it grow long enough to be visible every autumn, as the nights drew in and the temperature dropped. He slipped the car into second and swerved noisily into the Tiergarten. He was chewing gum, Charlie noticed. Charlie was noticing lots of things. He saw Isabelle up ahead.

"Whoah, there she is. Anywhere here, mate."

"That's about as quick as I could have made it, Dude."

"No, that's great. Cheers." Charlie leaped out and tried to catch Isabelle's attention so that she would know at least that he'd arrived.

"Tomorrow at eleven, then."

"Yeah. See you, Troy. Thanks for the lift."

Troy sped off in what was probably the seventh different vehicle Charlie had seen him drive.

Isabelle was wearing a long black coat and had done something with her face. Charlie guessed it was probably make-up related but he couldn't be sure.

"Hi," he said. Seemed like the right word.

"Charlie." She said.

There was a predictable awkward silence. It was Charlie who broke it, albeit inadvertently, by dropping the bag of photographs on the floor and, in hurriedly picking it up, ramming his head against the base of a lamppost.

"Careful Charlie! Shall we just walk?"

"I can do that," said Charlie, and they ambled along like a couple on the early stages of a blind date. "Oh, here, these are, you know, yours." He handed over the pack of photographs, without breaking step. Isabelle took them without a word and they continued. It was more a walk than an amble now.

"I suppose you had a bit of a giggle looking through these."

"No one else has seen them," he lied, "just me. And only a couple, enough to realize what had happened."

"Funny coincidence about the cameras," said Isabelle. "But your friend, Jack did you say? He must have seen them."

"Jake? No. I collected the photos for him. He asked me to pick them up because he knew I was passing the shop."

"I suppose you're a bit curious, then?"

"Not at all, really, I hadn't given it a second's thought." Charlie was surpassing himself, the lies tripping off the tongue with such natural fluidity. They stopped at a kerb. Taking advantage of the pause, Isabelle turned to look at the tousle-haired young man standing next to her.

"Can you keep a secret, Charlie?" she asked.

"Yes," he replied instantly.

Can you keep a secret, Charlie? Blimey, second time this week I've been asked that, he thought. They crossed the street and continued walking.

"Have you ever been stuck for a date, Charlie? Been somewhere by yourself, fancied an evening out, but not alone?" Charlie thought about it, but apparently it was a rhetorical question. Isabelle carried on: "It happens a lot here in Berlin. People passing through all the time: businessmen, diplomats, soldiers. There are night clubs, restaurants, and bars - lots of fun places, but you wouldn't necessarily want to go there alone. And you wouldn't necessarily want to spend an evening trying to pick someone up, if you could just pick the phone up instead. Right, Charlie?"

"Right."

"Normally, it doesn't go any further than that. Actually, it never goes any further than that, this was the only time. But it was extra, you understand, so it doesn't count."

Clearly Isabelle must have been under the impression that Charlie knew what she was talking about, an impression he felt he should exfoliate and quickly.

"Listen, I have no idea what you're talking about." he said, clearly enough.

Isabelle stopped dead in her tracks. It took Charlie several steps to realize he had overshot the runway. He stopped, too, and then made his way back to an Isabelle who appeared to have slipped into something more caustic.

"I thought better of you, Charlie."

"You and me, both," he replied.

"What do you want? You after money? A few marks to keep your mouth shut?"

It was obvious that Charlie was missing something.

"Eh? Money? What are you talking about?"

"Why do you keep saying 'what are you talking about' for Christ's sake?" The conversation was rising in volume and pitch. "You can overdo the little-boy-lost routine, you know?"

This was news to Charlie. Luke had always assured him that a man could never overdo the little-boy-lost routine. But then, Luke was dead. And so, clearly, was all his advice.

"What little-boy-lost routine?" he asked, buying himself a bit of time.

"Have you not been listening to me?"

"Yes."

"Yes, what? Yes, you've not been listening?"

"No. Yes, I have been listening. I just thought you hadn't finished."

"I thought you could fill in the fucking blanks!" Isabelle hadn't expected to swear. The word seemed to escape unexpectedly, like a Pope's fart.

"Now you made me swear. I never swear."

"You should. It suits you."

Isabelle almost laughed. She started again, but this time she spoke only in facts. And short, simple sentences.

"I sometimes go out for dinner. With gentlemen. They have a nice time. We laugh. We eat. We drink. Then I go home." Facts. Short sentences.

"Right-oh."

"And they pay me."

"Oh?" said Charlie. "Oh!" said Charlie.

"I work for a very nice lady. She has an agency, and everything's very nicely done. The money is very good, and I always need the money because - and you can ask Beth to back me up here - I'm shit with money and I never have enough of hers."

"Oh."

"And will you stop bloody saying 'Oh'?"

Charlie stopped bloody saying 'oh'.

"It's not whoring, Charlie. If that's what you're thinking. It's escorting."

Charlie was milliseconds away from saying "oh" but replaced it with a weighted silence instead.

"Some of the girls take it further. That's down to them and the client. I'm just wining and dining, that's all. But if I was to fancy some guy, then there's nothing untoward about taking it a step further, if I wanted. That's after-hours, so to speak. It'd be the same if I'd just met him at a club and hit it off."

"So, who is the bloke in the photos?"

"What photos?"

Charlie smiled. Fair enough.

"No one knows about this, Charlie, just you. It has to stay that way."

"Yeah. No problem." He felt privileged to join her inner circle. "What do the others think about it?"

"I just told you. No one knows about this. Not even the girls. I'd just die. I work for the British Council. God, imagine the reaction."

"Why? I mean, it's just dinner dates, and you make a bit on it."

"Do me a favour, darling! I'm an escort. That's practically like being a prostitute in my eyes."

"It wasn't a minute ago."

"Well, I didn't know how you'd react a minute ago."

"How did I react?"

"All right."

"Look, I'm going to head off. Make sure I find my passport and everything."

"Come on, Charlie, have a drink with me," said Isabelle. "There's no charge."

She laughed. He laughed. But he didn't want a drink. He wanted to pack.

"No, thanks, really. I need to go and pack. My passport could be anywhere."

Isabelle looked at him.

"Be careful with Joanna, Charlie," she said softly. "She's a candle. She flickers. Don't be her moth. "

Thursday, October 22nd

E Minor

I only found my passport about eleven minutes before Troy pulled up, in a red convertible Mk1 VW Golf with its faded fabric roof criss-crossed with strips of gaffer tape. I had told him we had to leave by eleven, because I estimated he'd be half an hour late. He was. But he drove with the cool self-confidence of a man for whom the term unfazed was invented. I was stupid enough to actually tell him out loud that I was pushing it a bit for time and his innate military competitiveness did the rest. It seemed like we left half an hour too late, and arrived half an hour too early.

"Dude, get out, buddy, I can't park here." Troy had pulled up and was hustling me out of the car. Behind us another driver was sounding his horn sharply.

"Cheers, Troy. Tuesday, then, yeah?"

"Sure thing. Good luck tomorrow. Do what you have to do, then forget it forever." He winked, something I'd never seen him do before. I nodded, nabbed a trolley, and headed off into the concourse. I hadn't wasted much time asking Troy whether he was involved in any acts of treason, but promised myself, as soon as my long weekend was over, that I would grill him relentlessly on the way home.

I was just thinking how much of a laugh that could be when, quite literally, I bumped into Joanna. The front left wheel on my trolley pulled to the right, and I was looking up at the departure information rather than on where I was going.

"Hello, Charlie."

"Hey. Hello. Sorry. Dodgy front wheel."

"I was expecting you to be late," she said. "You assured me you'd be late," she added with a smile. It was true, I had.

"I won't let it happen again."

"I've already checked in," said Joanna.

"Of course you have," I replied, "lead on."

"Don't you need to check in?" She seemed more inclined to continue through passport control than accompany me to the check-in procedure. Not going to be sitting together then, I thought.

"Yes. I'll see you at the gate," I said as I stood and watched her heading towards passport control. I'd have stood and watched her heading towards anywhere.

I probably stood watching too long, because by the time I reached the check-in desk for my flight, I was stuck behind a sizeable group that had just disgorged unsteadily from a minibus. I never sit at the back, or take a middle seat and I don't smoke. Being one of the last to check in ensured that I was allocated a seat that covered all three. The only reason I didn't burst into tears as I poured myself into the middle back seat of the Smokers section - as far back as a man can get on a plane without sitting on the toilet - was that the passenger on the window seat turned out to be Joanna.

"I didn't know you smoked," I said, making an effort to keep any sense of disapproval out of my tone.

"I didn't know you smoked," she replied, not making quite as much effort. "I don't."

"I hardly ever. Sometimes to unwind, if I've been really busy. And, of course, on a plane because I hate flying."

"Really?"

"Really. So I'm afraid you'll have to put up with some of my puff."

"I'll manage," I said, more or less smiling.

"And I'm also going to have to grab hold of your hand on take-off and landing, too."

"Again. I'll manage."

Thank Christ I didn't say *you can grab hold of anything you like, darling*, which were the actual words originally lined up, before my brain remembered I had started to walk upright and make tools out of flint. As inevitably as night follows day, the passenger I had drawn as a neighbour on the aisle side was a mountainous specimen who required the annexation of my armrest to accommodate the spread of his existence. I did what I could to find a position that was bearable. The moment the aircraft pulled away from the gate, in a mildly juddering backward movement, the colour seemed to drain from Joanna's cheeks. Not even the reassurance of perfect flying conditions contained in the chirpy sing-along announcement made by the stewardess seemed to help.

I like flying. So far, I haven't had any bad experiences. Turbulence is another issue, but that's not because I think we're going to crash. It's because I think I'm going to throw up. As a grown man, you forfeit any of the sympathy that children and the elderly get. Going pale and clammy and vomiting in public when you're in that tricky period between childhood and retirement marks you out as an alcoholic, or a drug addict. Neither of which gets you a damp cloth and a cuddle.

She was looking out of the window and I pretended to do the same as I watched her beautiful profile. Well, all of her was beautiful to me. I started wondering, again, about her looks. Is it just me? I imagined myself asking the heap to my right what he thought of her. What would he say? Lovely? Gorgeous? Nice? Perhaps, only okay?

The engines began to rev up, and we paused briefly at the end of the runway. With a hunted look on her face, Joanna shifted her position so that she looked straight ahead, and made an inelegant but committed grab for my left hand. I let it go limp, as I didn't know what she had in mind. She placed it on the armrest and squeezed hard as the plane accelerated away. I squeezed back and gently caressed her hand with my thumb. I didn't know if this was suitable hand-holding etiquette for the situation, but it usually worked for me at the cinema.

I wanted to fly all the way to England with my hand in hers but, annoyingly, the part of the journey known as *the take-off* was over with a ping of the tannoy. Joanna, visibly relaxed, transferred her attention from me to her handbag, from which she pulled out a packet of Silk Cut and somehow managed to make popping a cigarette into her mouth an act of wanton eroticism. She was kind enough to blow her first plume straight up into the air, an act of kindness not afforded me by the other smoker on my row.

"Well, I have to say, Jo," I began flippantly, "it's a good job I was sitting next to you otherwise who'd hand would you grab?" *Whose hand would she grab? His?* I looked across at the large, imposing man next to me and shuddered. "I can't believe we ended up sitting next to each other, when you think of all the seats there are on this plane."

"Well, I told them at check-in that we were travelling together, so you were always going to sit next to me," said Joanna. "I wouldn't want to be holding just anybody's hand, would I? Oh, go on, let me see your picture."

She said this as I was transferring my passport from the breast pocket of my shirt to somewhere more secure.

"No, you're all right."

"Go on!"

I opened the passport.

"Oh my God," she went. Now, my passport photo, perhaps uniquely, is not in any way humorous or shocking, so I was a bit taken aback. But it wasn't the photo that had caught her attention. "Charlie, you have the same birthday as me!"

"Really? You're 16th of September?"

"I'm the 16th of September *1961*. We were born on the same day. How funny."

They were at cruising altitude, according to the co-pilot, and that was good enough for Joanna. Once a plane was at cruising altitude, in the quiet air, away from trouble, she always relaxed. She was thinking about her mother, which reminded her of her childhood, which brought her back to that record.

"So, Charlie, seriously: how do you know that old song from the other day? It's just some old record my Mum used to have years ago. She said you couldn't even buy it in England, and it's never been on the radio. There's no way you can know it."

Charlie gave it some thought. It was the least he could do, being as she was clearly after an answer.

"My grandparents had it. They didn't have many, and that was one of them. But I haven't heard it for, I don't know, fifteen years or so."

Joanna was genuinely surprised, shocked even.

"They must have played it a lot, you remembered the lines." She smiled. "Were you at their house all the time?"

"I was brought up by my grandparents. I'm an orphan."

"Really?"

"Really." Charlie smiled. "Does it still count as an orphan if you have grandparents?"

"Not sure. It's not quite like being a Barnardo's boy. What happened to your parents? Do you remember them?"

"No. My Dad was abroad, National Service. He never saw me. He died probably six months before I was born." Charlie raised his eyebrows. "It was a car accident."

"That's a shame."

"Yup."

"What about your Mum?"

"I only know that she died a few days after I was born. There were complications, and she wasn't well anyway…"

"Oh Charlie, that's terrible."

"It gets worse." Charlie smiled. "I was born on a bloody bus! A double-decker, and not upstairs either."

"Charlie?"

"It's true. By some miracle, there was a midwife on the bus, just done a shift at the hospital. So, there you go. You'd think that would be enough for a free bus pass for life, eh?"

Joanna already knew what it was like growing up without a father, it was something she took for granted, but also not to have a mother would have seemed altogether harsher.

"I grew up without a father, too," she said.

"Yeah?"

"He didn't die. He just left, when Mum got pregnant."

"Oh." Charlie fought, and failed, to say something deeper. "Nice."

"Money sometimes arrived, Mum said, but he never did." She laughed as she spoke. "For a while I thought he'd been one of the great train robbers, and run off to Brazil. Mum always changed the subject when I brought it up."

"That would have been pretty cool, though, if it had been true," said Charlie.

The stewardesses were approaching with the trolley service and Charlie put himself into holiday mode. "Are you going to have a drink?"

"Are you?"

"Maybe a Coke. Anything much stronger, and I can't pronounce my own name."

The trees, hundreds of them, lay flat upon the ground, like discarded matchsticks. From the air, as the plane descended over Sussex, Joanna began to see the extent of the devastation. She had seen trees that had fallen after storms before, but always just the odd one here or there. But on top of that exposed hill, there was not a single tree left standing. She wondered whether they had all toppled over together, as one, or whether they had succumbed individually, each in their own private hell. She just managed to stop herself showing Charlie.

West Berlin

The plush, lightly worn leather chair squeaked as Alex sat down, and was no less talkative as she adjusted herself for comfort. Perhaps it would encourage her not to fidget. Herr Reiseneder, whose imposing existence was being propped up by an identical chair across the desk, had a line of letters and papers set out which he was glancing at in a show of earnest concentration. Alex duly noted both the earnestness, and that his seat did not make a sound.

She had entered the office - her expensive perfume carving her a path through the stale air - expecting the worse, and her expectations were being met. So she sat still on her chair, her hands resting on her lap, her back straight and her expensively made-up face radiating the kind of impassive beauty one would expect from a Bond Street mannequin. She looked a million dollars.

And, apparently, she owed almost as much.

Reiseneder was not what Alex would have described as a typical solicitor type. He was tall and forcefully built under incongruous slicked back hair that went considerably beyond the collar line. A pair of disarming blue-grey eyes distracted the casual viewer away from a broken nose, and his sensual, wide full lips were redolent of some comic-strip mob leader. That he was encased in an immaculate, understated, navy-blue suit did nothing to dispel the image. Alex, stressed and flustered despite her outward calm, had opened proceedings in English and he had responded instantly and effortlessly in kind. His English was impeccable

"Mrs. Gagnon?"

"Hmm?"

"Yes, or no?"

Yes or no, indeed. Alex had drifted. Again. The man on the other side of the desk had the air of one who had seen it all before, and although he would never permit the enormity of another's problems ever to pierce his own professional cloak of indifference, he exuded courteous sympathy.

"Do you have a job, Mrs Gagnon? A regular income of your own?" He asked.

Alex bristled and was only prevented from drawing herself to something akin to righteous indignation by the certainty that such a move would have been undermined by the squeaking chair.

"Yes, I have a job," she replied, with a terse stillness. "I actually work, you know, and I can take care of myself. But not all *this*!" She leaned forward and elegantly waved her hand across the letters and bills and final demands. The chair squeaked in punctuation. Her Reiseneder smiled, as was his right. It was his office.

"Is my husband dead?" Alex said suddenly, surprising herself in the process.

"Why would he be dead?" he replied.

"Perhaps he died." Alex spat politely. "Then that would be why."

"No."

"Do you think this is fair, though, really? I mean, none of this…" she searched for the right word, "none of this *shit* is anything to do with me."

"It's all in your name."

"That's because Tony put it all in my name. You know that. *You* did it for him. You take care of all his…*stuff.*"

"And you haven't heard from him?"

"No." Alex was inwardly furious, and not just because of Tony, but because she was actually thinking what a lovely tie Herr Reiseneder was wearing. This was not the time for fashion! "Do you know where he is, then?"

"In what way do you mean?" he asked.

"Is there more than one way?"

Herr Reiseneder bought himself some time by making some slight adjustment to his cuffs. He banked a few more seconds by adjusting the distance between the last of the final demands and the left side edge of his desk. Satisfied, he continued.

"Your husband appears to be in Toronto."

Well, this was progress, thought Alex.

"Toronto," she said. "Toronto, Canada?"

"Yes."

"He told me he was going to a meeting in Milan. I expected him back for dinner."

Alex had given up on the faux stillness, so the room bristled with squeaking leather as her agitation expanded. She felt her cheeks flush, but seemed less aware of the erratic fluttering of her eyes. Tony Gagnon, her husband, was Canadian. From Toronto. That he would be there would not, under different circumstances, be particularly untoward. But under these circumstances, it was very toward indeed.

"When you say 'appears to be' in Toronto, is that legal language for 'he is' in Toronto?"

Herr Reiseneder smiled again. It was a smile as genuine as it was insincere, the smile of the consummate professional. The smile of a man who had to say:

"Your husband appears to be in jail. In Toronto."

Alex sat immobile, listening to the words but not hearing. Or perhaps she was hearing the words but not listening.

Woking, England, Friday October 23rd

E Minor

Everyone has an opinion on what kind of weather is preferable for a funeral. Should it reflect your mood, or should it divert it? Is it worse to sit under a relentless downpour of rain, or inappropriate bright sunshine? Dark, billowing clouds, or a beautiful cloudless day full of disrespectful chirpy birdsong, lacking all sense of reverence? How would you like your unbearable grief packaged? What would you order with your brass handle and mahogany casket package?

I had never given it a moment's thought until I stepped out of that taxi, and stood at the side of Hermitage Road, looking across at the redbrick Woking Crematorium in all its miserable glory. It was, of course, simply a grey day. Not raining or overtly tempestuous, just a typical, shitty, grey day the like of which scar the eyeballs of an Englishman practically every day of his life until he can stand it no more and emigrates to somewhere South.

I remember having been to the track in Woking, years before, not to run or train, but to collect a girl called Stephanie. She was a hurdler and I had fallen in love with her bum, because frankly it would have been rude not to. But I had got so lost that both the bum, and the Stephanie attached to it, had long since been collected by someone else. This time I had taken a taxi from the station.

I hadn't seen Joanna since I had cocked up taking advantage of what I thought was a golden opportunity to leave a soft kiss on her cheek. We were on the train platform at Gatwick airport. There was a bit of a misunderstanding with the luggage. I don't know what it is with large bags and me. Anyway, we took our separate trains and confirmed our rendezvous at the crematorium.

Raynes Park was very much as I had left it. I walked up Pepys Road feeling I'd only walked down it days before, rather than years.

I didn't sleep well, thinking about Joanna. Sometimes I thought about holding her hand on the plane, the softness of her skin and how I'd tried not to let her feel the callouses on the end of my fingertips. And the other times I thought about how I'd cocked up the opportunity to give her a kiss on the cheek. Occasionally I thought of all the real problems there were in the world that could have kept me awake instead, but always returned to mine.

"Charlie?" It was a quizzical tone. "Charlie Stokes?"

I turned round and gave a short, round-faced man a blank expression straight out of Jake's collection. That he knew me was clear from his smile and bright-eyed sense of wonderment at the re-discovery of a long-lost pal. I had no idea who he was.

"Hi," I began, leaving pretty much the rest of my sentence in a pending file.

"God, you haven't changed a bit! Just, even taller," he said.

Even taller? How far back were we going?

"Yeah."

"Oh, my girlfriend's waving me over, wait till I tell her I've seen you! Shame it's taken this for us to meet up again."

"This what?"

"Luke." He fidgeted about a bit. The pull of his girlfriend was strong, but he withstood it for a little while longer. As for me, I suddenly felt sick.

Barely three elephants' lengths away and pointedly ignored by everyone, was an upturned beech. It lay on its side, with its great roots exposed, looking a lot thicker and more monstrous lying down than upright. I imagined being underneath it. I imagined Luke underneath it. I managed to force myself to look away, and the first thing I saw was Joanna.

"Charlie?"

I tried to say something, but found I couldn't. She walked up to me and opened her arms and we hugged. She held me tight but didn't say anything. What could she say?

There was a good turnout. Charlie Stokes looked around the nondescript interior of the crematorium and tried to pick out the recognisable faces from the crowd. Seven out of the sixty, and that included Joanna. Few enough to suddenly make him wonder if he was at the right service. A brief spasm of irrational angst chewed at his insides at the thought that he had gone to the wrong place, but it passed, like a burst of trapped wind.

"You okay?" asked Joanna. She spoke in a husky low whisper that was practically engineered for such occasions. She gave the back of Charlie's right hand a short gentle caress.

"Don't know any of these people," he replied, having to force the words out of an arid throat. He was starting to feel a bit not quite right. "Do you think half of these people are professional congregation fillers? Pad the room out a bit?"

"No, Charlie."

"There's hardly anyone here Luke's age. They can't all be uncles and parents. How many parents can one person have?"

Joanna didn't answer. She didn't think Charlie wanted one. He was just letting words come out. Funerals were funny like that.

"Do you know what happens?" asked Charlie. "How do these things work?"

"Depends on the service. There'll be prayers, some singing and people will talk about Luke."

"Sounds like a band rehearsal, without the prayers unless you count saying *Jesus Christ*." He was mumbling by now, almost slurring his speech, as if he were not prepared to put in the effort. Joanna noticed he had begun to tap his foot in short, twitchy bursts. "I ought to say something - about Luke. I want to say something. Who do you think is in charge, Luke's Mum? She never liked me much. Bad influence."

"I don't know, Charlie. Let's just wait and see how it goes, shall we?" Joanna just wanted the thing to start, and more than anything else finish. She didn't think Charlie was quite synchronised with the world, and was certain he should not be encouraged to say anything. She wondered whether anyone knew that Luke had been speaking to Charlie when the accident happened. She hoped not.

Joanna was seated at the end of a row, with Charlie just inside. Charlie remembered how, years earlier, an older work colleague had chided him for having walked alongside a girl without ensuring he took the car side of the pavement. He looked at Joanna, and stood up.

"Here, I'll go there," he said, confusingly. "You shouldn't sit at the end."

"Why not?" But she stood up anyway, and changed places.

Charlie began scanning the big intimidating space again, like a man expecting a surprise at any moment, and growing ever more frustrated by the delay. It was a trait of his that Joanna had picked up on at the restaurant in Berlin: his restless eyes. Not restless like those of a hunted man, but they rarely sat still. Butterfly eyes. Good title for a novel, perhaps, but not the sign of a settled mind.

The elephant in the room was the aching rectangle of empty space hovering above the raised dais in the right-hand corner. Charlie Stokes noticed it the second he walked into the room, and then immediately airbrushed it out of his head. He turned and faced the front, ramrod stiff in a chair barely worthy of the title. His view of the front of the room was blocked by a short, bald, incredibly dapper man with hazel eyes that twinkled unexpectedly under a pair of severe dark eyebrows. He'd stopped alongside Charlie and raised his eyebrows enquiringly at the empty spaces next to Joanna.

"May I?" he'd said.

It was a statement of intent dressed up, albeit smartly, as a question. An advance party of subtle and expensive aftershave led the way, the well-cut, dark charcoal suit of reckless broad pinstripe, following. He wore incredibly small and unfeasibly shiny black shoes, and seemed to hover in front of the empty chair next to Joanna. Charlie assumed he was arriving early for the next funeral, so unlike a Luke mourner was he, and was surprised when the man addressed him directly.

"You must be?" It was a quaintly old-fashioned voice. For a second or two Charlie didn't see the hand that was extended towards him. He took it.

"Charlie."

"Brian."

The man was still holding Charlie's hand.

"Charlie Stokes."

"Brian Levine."

"Okay."

"Marvellous."

Smiles, of all sizes and degrees of sincerity, cascaded about the place as people arrived. And then, from the back of the room there was a movement and, as one, the mourners turned to watch four stern-faced men, with skin the colour of bleached marble, carry the casket in. A hushed silence was broken by a single loud sob.

Luke's Mum.

Reality had arrived. Charlie turned to jelly. Without making a sound, he mouthed three words up to the ceiling, despite being a man who believed in God as much as he believed in Father Christmas.

"Oh. God. No."

He stared ahead, trying to appear dignified and respectful, but an insurmountable weight poured into his body as the dark, blurry embrace of unconsciousness dropped him gently to the ground. The last sensation he recalled was the smell of shoe polish.

E Minor

"Charlie? You can't sleep here."

Sleep? Me? I wasn't sleeping, I was… what was I doing? Lying down for a bit? There was a hand doing something with my trousers. Undoing the button and loosening the waist I'd have called it. There was more than the one voice, male and female. I kept my eyes shut. My feet were caught under the chair, but I was comfortable lying there, out of the way. I kept my eyes shut so that no one would see me. Soft fingers were undoing the top button of my shirt. I hoped they were Joanna's and not Brian's.

"We ought to get him outside and into clean air," I heard Levine say, as if I were already dead. "You need to give him room to breathe."

"Are you a Doctor?" I heard an elderly female voice ask, with a hint of hopeful expectation.

"Would you like me to be, dear?"

I kept my eyes shut.

A number of those mourners who had arrived by car left their vehicles at the crematorium and walked to the nearby hotel. The rest of them drove, save for the handful that called it a day, satisfied that respects had been paid and that tea and canapés would add little to the occasion.

Charlie Stokes sat in the front passenger seat of a shiny new Austin Maestro, a car as dull as it was inappropriately named. Furthermore it was beige, something Charlie had taken to being a joke. Joanna had borrowed it from a friend of her mother's. Joanna herself was poised behind the steering wheel, trying to decide what to do next. She turned to Charlie, who was staring indecisively at some invisible spot in the middle distance.

"Probably not the best funeral you've ever attended, Charlie."

"Well, it's the only one," he mumbled in reply. "Safe to say that the bar has been set low." His frame of mind was that of an unauthorised overdraft and he sensibly decided to cut his losses. "Anyway, that's enough for me, I think. I'll quit while I'm behind. Can you drop me off at the station?"

"Are you sure?"

"Oh, yes."

"Oi! oi!," a sudden shout from somewhere over to the left, on Charlie's side of the world. He craned his neck and saw a couple of the lads from way back when.

"Saveloy!" he shouted back. "All right?"

One of the lads wore the widest, shiniest black tie Joanna had ever seen in her entire life. He was also almost getting away with wearing a suit that clearly belonged to a dead predecessor, and grinned wolfishly under the weight of thick longish straw-coloured hair that had been hijacked by a tub of gel and told to keep still with its hands in the air.

"Charlie fucking Stokes!"

Charlie was always pleased to be addressed by his full name and Joanna bit her tongue so as not to giggle out loud and spoil the mood. Boys.

"We're only here for the beer," came back the voice, loudly from across the marshes. "It's what Luke would have wanted. You got room in there for two more?"

Charlie shrugged and turned to Joanna. She already saw the colour returning to his cheeks. He shuffled slightly in his seat. They looked at each other. What the hell, why not?

"Perhaps I'll just stick around for a little tiny while," he said. Joanna nodded. She watched as Charlie loitered while reaching for the door handle and the two lads began approaching the car.

"Do you want me to come with you for a bit?" she asked.

Charlie just smiled, which Joanna took to mean yes.

The small function room, grafted on to the hotel's bar area by way of an extension, required that guests at any well-attended event be comfortable rubbing shoulders. Joanna was happy enough to watch from a distance. Naturally, she didn't know anyone there, other than Brian Levine of course, but she grazed amongst the snacks, and sipped mineral water with some of Surrey's finest whilst keeping half an eye on Charlie.

She noted early on that Levine was a loyal Tom Collins drinker and she watched him, standing in the centre of the room as the party orbited around him, sipping with the steady insouciance of a man who knew there was another on the way. Charlie, on the other hand, seemed to be drinking a little bit of everything and making short work of it. Joanna had forgotten that Charlie had no immunity to booze, or she might have intervened and prevented the inevitable carnage that lay ahead.

Of all the women present, whatever age, there were two that caught her attention, and one of them was a member of staff. It was irrelevant now that she was back in England, but she liked to be aware of her feelings. She stepped aside to allow the waitress to pass, oblivious to her gentle smile, and waited patiently for Levine to settle up alongside.

"You really do look radiant, my dear," he said, instinctively raising his glass in a subtle toast. Joanna smiled in thanks but said nothing. She looked across at Charlie and Levine followed it. "Just a friend, your Charlie?" he asked.

"Charlie's a funny one," said Joanna after an age. "There's something about him that's just… I don't know."

Charlie was wedged in an unsteady huddle of lost souls, each trying to leach their inner sadness out with alcohol and masculine bravado. Four of them had just taken on a variant of the *depth charge* - a shot glass, filled with Bailey's, had been dropped into a pint of Theakston's Peculiar, the concoction swallowed in a single, sting-in-the-tail draft. Charlie Stokes had thus given himself the gift of instant Armageddon by breaking two cast-iron laws of the novice drinker in a single time-saving action - never mix your drinks or drink them quickly.

"So," began Levine, "is Berlin still working out for you?"

"Yes," she replied, smiling gratefully. "Yes, it is."

"A young lady can very much lose herself in Berlin," he mused, "if she so wished. It's what I always said."

"You were right. You are right. It's nice to get out for a few days, though."

"You make it sound as if you were in prison," laughed Levine.

"I know," smiled Joanna. "But, you know, sometimes that's how I feel. It's how a lot of us feel. As if *we're* the ones who can't escape. All we have to do is buy a ticket, and yet…" her voice trailed away.

Levine glanced around the room for the waitress. He was down a Tom

Collins. It seemed he could draw serving staff to him with the will of his mind, for one appeared immediately from behind an aspidistra plant.

"I'm looking forward to tomorrow night, by the way. Your mother is still coming, I hope?"

"She hasn't spoken about anything else for days," said Joanna.

"Did you tell her I was coming?" asked Levine.

Joanna laughed.

"No, she'll just accuse me of matchmaking. Can you imagine?"

Levine allowed a chuckle to escape.

"I'm not the kind of man that someone like your mother would need, my dear. I'm more than certain she knows that, too."

They each absorbed the moment awhile.

"Do you think we'll ever track down my Dad? Or would we have done it by now?" Joanna hadn't meant to bring it up again, but it was inevitable, with Levine there.

He took the enquiry in his stride, as he took all in life.

"I don't know."

Levine did know, he just couldn't say. Or wouldn't say.

"Are you all right for money, Joanna?"

"Yes, why? No, I'm fine."

"The boy, Charlie," said Levine suddenly. "He tends to look over at you a lot, wouldn't you say? Fond of you, is he?"

"He's just drunk, Brian."

"Is that what you call it these days?" He looked at Joanna with a keen eye, like a man who'd just found the light switch for the basement. "You *have* told him, haven't you? Only he looks like a man with hope."

"I think he looks like a man with a drink problem, Brian," said Joanna quickly.

But she hadn't told him, no.

Outside the hotel, on a gravel drive flanked by rows of empty terracotta pots, Charlie Stokes was taking long, crunching steps to nowhere. His brain, having left the muffled claustrophobia of the function room, was suddenly bathed in breezy fresh autumnal air, and promptly unravelled. He had apparently lost the ability to direct either his legs or his arms and was marching around the pots saying "well, this is very strange" in a loud voice when a small dog, no bigger than a large cat, shot out of one and gave his left ankle a nip.

"Oi! What's your bloody problem?"

Charlie yelped in a voice that gave each word its own key change. He noticed Brian Levine in front of him.

"Oh, hello. It's you, isn't it?" he said, putting some enunciation into things. "That ducking fog just bit me. Bit me! What's that all about, then? It's not against the law to walk on gravel in Surrey, is it, Ryan?"

"Brian."

"Charlie."

"I expect you were making too many sudden movements."

"Too many sudden movements? Ah." He gave that possibility some thought, but not too much. "How many is too many, Brian? Seven? Twelve?" The incredulity in Charlie's fermented voice was matched only by the eagerness of its volume. "I need to drink something, don't I? Feel a bit odd, as it goes. I need some water, let's track down a waiter. Watch out, Brian, it's that dog again, run for it! Save yourself, man, I'm done for."

There was little more than a half-arsed attempt at a yap from the miserable excuse of a dog as it scampered, stiff-legged, back towards the open door to the reception. But it was enough to panic Charlie.

Brian Levine made a theatrical but controlled gesture with his right arm and guided the affronted young man back towards the sanctity of the hotel. When they reached the threshold, Levine had a better view of Charlie Stokes. It was quite some battle that was being raged within the young man, as his pupils tried desperately to hold focus on something. Anything.

"Have you seen Joanna?" Charlie blurted out. "She's fucking gorgeous, she is," he muttered, immediately stopping to sway a bit. "Did I just say that out loud? Hmm? I had a thought and it came outside by mistake." There was a shadow emerging in the corner of his eye.

"Charlie bloody Stokes! Get out of here! You've got a fucking nerve." It was delivered through a clenched jaw. Charlie had to squint slightly to get a better idea of the shape from which the unfriendly banter was emanating, but unfortunately he was beyond the stage where squinting would help. It was a woman doing the talking, albeit having borrowed the vocabulary of a man, and this is what had thrown Charlie.

"Is there something I can do to help, madam?" Levine wasn't someone who needed to turn the charm on and off, it seemed to slosh effortlessly out of him at the slightest movement, like an overfilled bucket, but he had infused his question with the maximum dose. The tone, and the dapper man's general demeanour, threw the aggressor off balance long enough for a grim-faced doorman, in a cheap spray-on tuxedo, to reach the scene.

"Is there a problem?"

The lady stood in silence, a club's length from the wobbling Charlie, with only the erratic blinking of her eyelashes belying the raging volcano beneath the sombre suburban attire. She didn't want to speak to anyone, just the unbearable Charlie Stokes, and now she was being bombarded with questions.

"There was a misunderstanding," said Levine gently. "Perhaps Charlie, we should find Joanna and be on our way?"

"I haven't finished the party," interjected Charlie. "Oh, and I still haven't done my speech. Best hang around for that, eh?"

At that point, Charlie was slapped across the cheek, and the sharp clap drew gasps from behind the reception. There were often altercations at weddings, but funerals never pulled in the excitement so much. The lady was gently, but forcefully, guided away from the shell-shocked Charlie Stokes, but she lay a heavy broadside as she went.

"You killed him, Stokes, and you never had the nerve to tell me it was you. You're a coward and a shit."

There was more of the same, just quieter, as she was led off to another part of the hotel. Charlie felt the need to keep moving and considered going outside again, where he had been perfectly happy striding amongst the plant pots. Standing still made him aware that he was missing all the fun, as everything else on the planet seemed to be moving in circles. Joanna was standing alongside Levine. She had appeared from nowhere, and was having a quiet but intense conversation with the older man. Charlie would normally have felt incredibly left out, had he not surmised that the conversation was very much about him. Which made it all right.

Levine left Joanna with Charlie.

"Is my face red, Jo? Think it might be, you know. Bit stingy."

"It's fine, Charlie. Perhaps we should slow down, for a bit."

"That was Luke's Mum. Have you met her? Nice woman."

"What have you been drinking, Charlie?"

"No thanks, Jo. I don't drink. I'm just going to have a dance." He moved towards the function room again but allowed Joanna to intercept and guide him towards the foot of the staircase next to the lifts. She stood there with him for no more than a minute, trying to think of something practical to say, when Levine returned.

"I have taken a room, my dear. Apparently, by the hour is very much frowned upon, so you are here for the night if you so wish. Here," Levine pressed a key into Joanna's hand. "Perhaps a lie down would be the safest thing?"

And so Charlie Stokes had insisted on marching up the stairs, to show Joanna how very much in the pink he felt, singing nursery rhymes in the style of football terrace chants as he went. Joanna followed him up, ready to catch him, shaking her head in disbelief. At the landing he stopped and turned very suddenly on the thick, well-worn quasi-Axminster pile and raised a dramatic index finger in the air. What he wanted to say remained a mystery as he toppled backwards and slid all the way back down the stairs, on his back and with the finger still raised, until crumpling to a carpeted halt at the feet of the fat lady who owned the dog that had bitten him. Joanna rushed down to check.

"Charlie! My God, are you okay?"

Of course, he was.

"What is the *point* of Woking, for fuck's sake?" he said, having looked disconsolately around.

West Berlin

There was barely enough coffee left in the cup to warrant another sip, but Isabelle sipped it anyway. If it helped give her something tangible to do, she would continue sipping air.

"Do we go onto somewhere from here?" he said.

"It depends," she replied, with a smile.

He smiled back. She hoped he didn't ask her what it depended on.

"Depends on what?" he asked.

He was an insurance analyst, lived in Inverness, and was in Berlin for two days and a night. This was the evening of the night in question, and it was to Isabelle that the agency had bestowed Scotland's most boring man. But set any man in front of her and Isabelle, for all her extravagant self-absorption, would happily eke out whatever nuggets of gold lay buried in the most unprepossessing of exteriors. And if not, she would move swiftly and brutally on. When one is being paid for one's time and company, however, the moving-swiftly-on option had a minimum time built in, and this evening it couldn't come quickly enough. The one thing in his favour was that he wasn't called Derek. He was called Duncan.

Ever since Charlie Stokes had discovered her secret, Isabelle was feeling soiled. She had convinced herself that her time was hers to do with as she pleased and, as two of her favourite things in life were male company and eating out, she had seen her sideline as practically a gift from the gods. She had made it quite clear at her first meeting with Frau Grunwald that she was good for the company, but under no circumstances was anyone to consider her body as being up for rent. Frau Grunwald was a purveyor of refined, educated ladies for supper engagements with visiting and equally refined and educated gentlemen. Instant dismissal awaited any of her ladies who indulged in the promise of sexual favours for cash. But Claudette, the girl who had introduced Isabelle to the life, made it perfectly clear that men would offer to take things further, and that it was up to the girls what they did with their 'bonus' time, and how much they would charge for it. Isabelle had pulled an anguished face and dismissed the very idea instantly, assuming that all the men she would be accompanying would be lonely, old, fat and uninteresting. But hearing herself tell Charlie about it had felt like undressing. And, left naked, she had begun to have doubts.

The night of the photographs was just one of those occasions when things had got out of hand, but in a nice way. Anton was a Belgian who owned a chocolate company, and Isabelle had naturally lost control of her senses as a result. He was good-looking in a cocoa-loving kind of way and had a funny accent that she found incapable of not teasing. It was Isabelle who had invited Gaston back to her place, knowing that Beth had gone to Derek's cousin's wedding in Slough, and by the time they had begun to kiss, they had both assumed the roles of consenting adults on a one-night stand. A bottle of ridiculously expensive brandy that Gaston had bought at the restaurant flushed away any remaining decorum they each possessed, and the outrageous photo session was just one of a range of mildly inappropriate activities that ensued. Unsurprisingly, none of these was looked back on with the same degree of fondness the following morning. Indeed, such had been the ferocity of her hangover, and so fragmented her memory, that Isabelle's nude photo shoot had fully slipped her mind for over a fortnight.

"I usually finish at eleven," said Isabelle.

"You said twelve."

"That's right, twelve. Eleven or twelve."

"It's only half ten now," he began.

"Really?"

This genuinely surprised Isabelle. It felt like she'd been there so long that she had missed Christmas. How true that time flies when you're having fun.

"Was it a night club you were after? They don't tend to crank up until closer to midnight. Not the good ones, anyway."

"No. I'm not a loud-music or dancing-about kind of man."

"You don't say? You surprise me, Derek."

"Duncan."

"Sorry. Somewhere quiet for a night cap, then."

"There's a nice, cosy bar at my hotel."

"I don't go back to clients' hotels, Duncan, sorry. It's not permitted."

"Oh."

"Let's stay here, instead. It's a lovely restaurant, don't you think? You chose well. Congratulations." She lifted her empty cup in a mock toast and gave a cheeky grin, lest she had overcooked the mock in the toast.

"It's a little bright, that's all."

"I think darkness is overrated, Duncan, unless you are propositioning someone. Neither of us is, are we? You know, I bet they do a lovely brandy here."

She smiled. He smiled. And the carousel went round again.

Beth watched the second half of the video she had borrowed from the Ambassador's niece and surprised herself by staying awake through it. The phone rang. She listened briefly to the sound of a girl sobbing uncontrollably and trying to speak. Isabelle.

"Izzy? What is it? Isabelle?"

More heaving sobs, then some barely comprehensible words. Beth tensed and squinted in concentration.

"Isabelle, say that again."

"Someone's tried to rape me!"

"Where are you?"

"I don't know."

"Isabelle!"

"Café Lutz."

"Are you hurt?" Silence. Sobbing. "Are you hurt?"

"No!"

"Stay where you are. I'm coming to get you. Do you understand? Stay where you are."

The journey back was tense. Beth had driven with ruthless precision to the Café and Isabelle had run out across the pavement and into the car, her arms tightly folded against her chest. The car was moving again before it had even come to a complete standstill.

Isabelle sat in the passenger seat, incapable of speaking to her sister. When she had phoned she had felt raw, desperate and humiliated. But now she was already trying to recover the initiative, play down what had happened, and deflect the truth. She had allowed Duncan to take her back to his hotel for a nightcap. But things had swiftly taken an unexpected course, and she had found herself literally beating the man's clumsy unwanted hands off her breasts. She had said no. No was no. But he wouldn't stop. He tried to pull her towards his face by grabbing the back of her neck like a coarse and oafish impression of a stage embrace. She could still hear him panting.

"Was it someone you were out with?" asked Beth. "Did someone just grab you? Where did it happen? Should we call the police?"

Beth was becoming confused by her emotions, and ashamed, too, because she was already searching for signs that this would all have been Isabelle's fault. How could she think that of her own little sister? Where was that outpouring of panic and love as she raced out of the apartment just a few moments ago? Isabelle didn't answer. She sat, her arms still folded tightly across her chest in lieu of a seat belt, staring out of her window like a teenager who'd been collected from a friend's house just as the party was about to start.

Just before they arrived home, she spoke.

"I was tired. I panicked. Someone tried it on. I said I wasn't interested. He wouldn't stop, so I ran. Who's going to call that rape?"

"For God's sake, Izzy..."

"It's not always my fault, you know."

"Are you sure you're all right?"

"Yes."

They drove past at least two parking spaces into which Isabelle would have tried to bounce the car, before Beth pulled up and switched off the ignition.

"We need to report the man," said Beth.

"Just leave it, darling. Really, it's not worth it."

Woking

"Is it Christmas?"
"Not yet."
"I fell down the stairs."
"I know."
"Is it bedtime already?"
"I think it might be. For you."

"Do you think there's a Corby trouser press in this room? Or a Gideon's Bible? Why am I talking so loudly, Jo, have you been fiddling with the remote?"

It seemed that the alcohol had burnt away all of Charlie Stokes' punctuation. His words escaped untrammelled. Joanna found it rather cute.

"They all hate me now. Did you hear that before? Must have done. That was Luke's Mum, you know. Hey, who's that funny man with the funky suit? I forget. Is that my Uncle?"

"No, Charlie."

"Did you take my trousers off?"

"No, Charlie."

"Where are they, then?"

"You're wearing them, Charlie."

"*These?* These are my trousers? They're horrible. Why didn't you tell me? Are these my shoes?"

"No, Charlie, they're your socks. Your shoes are over there. I took them off."

"Good for you, Jo. Are you taking yours off, or do you want me to?"

It had been going on like this since Joanna had coaxed Charlie into Levine's room. She had guided him towards the bed in the hopeful expectation of depositing him quietly on it, and achieved only to set him on a rambling counter-clockwise hike around Room 17. He seemed to like walking as much as he liked drinking and talking nonsense. Occasionally, he sat on the bed to remove an item of clothing. First his jacket, then his tie. At one point, he had flopped back onto the mattress, his arms stretched to the side, his eyes closed. That was when Joanna had taken his shoes off. She sat on the edge of the bed and looked down at his face, softly brushing skeins of unruly hair away from his forehead, and trying to imagine what he was feeling. How much of his confused mind was still functioning underneath all that booze.

She wondered how long he would sleep for, which is the very moment he sat up and said:

"Fucking hell, don't much like lying down. Shall we go for a run?"

"Do you want some more water, Charlie?"

"Why do you always call me Charlie?"

"That's your name, Charlie."

"No, I mean that. What you did just now. Whenever you say something to me, you always put Charlie on the end. *'All right, Charlie?' 'That's just the way it is, Charlie.' 'Half past nine, Charlie.'*"

"I didn't realise," said Joanna. "I suppose I just like the name. I'll try and stop doing it, Charlie."

"I feel funny."

"You look funny."

"I'm just going to lie down for a bit."

Charlie dived onto the bed. He turned onto his back and covered his eyes with the crook of his right arm.

"If I die now, will you be my angel?" he mumbled. "Don't go, Joanna, I don't want to be alone."

"I won't," she replied. "Try and relax."

"The bed's moving."

"No, it's not, Charlie." She smiled.

"Gonna fall off the bed," he moaned.

Joanna took Charlie's left hand and held it, just as he had held hers on the plane.

"If you have to take my trousers off, I think I left my nice underpants in Raynes Park. These have got a hole in them. So don't look, all right?"

"All right, Charlie."

"I love you, Joanna whatever-your-surname-is."

"Go to sleep, Charlie."

"You're doing it again, aren't you?" he said, his voice now a barely discernible drawl.

"Goodnight, Charlie."

"Don't go. They might come after me."

Joanna realised that he was crying. It hadn't been a very good day, really. She gave his hand a little squeeze, but said nothing. Charlie hid his face under his arm, but she could feel and hear his sobs. She waited for them to stop and, when they didn't, she began to stroke his hair softly. Eventually, he simply ran out of grief.

"I'm tired," he slurred, his voice now calm once more. "I think my underpants have a hole in them. My nice pair is in…"

He was asleep.

"In Raynes Park, Charlie. I know."

E Minor

The smell woke me up, I think. I couldn't say for certain, but the lasting memory has always been that of the smell. But it might have been Joanna tapping my shoulder. I had been dreaming a little, too - Beth, the counter-espionage agent, telling me to help her out with Troy - but there were no fuzzy, confused moments between the unconscious state and the awake. I was asleep, then I was awake. Before I had even opened my eyes, I half opened my mouth. What for? Oh, yes.

To vomit.

I was on my right side, facing out, and Joanna was on the other side because her hand was on my shoulder. I was throwing up with my head still on my pillow. If one could accuse a man of throwing up and being lazy simultaneously, then I was that man. The fingers on my shoulder were prompting me nearer the edge of the bed.

"You can't be sick on the bed, Charlie," she said.

Obviously I can, I thought to myself, because here I am doing it. But I got her point. So, I dragged myself across a short expanse of toxic bed sheet, and dropped anchor over the side - exactly as I had done one summer on a small rowing boat in Sandgate, about seven and a half lifetimes ago. It was humiliating. I was dying of some infectious disease, of course, probably something picked up from that bloody Greek moussaka thing and it'd been lying dormant ever since.

Is that Joanna I can hear laughing?

"Oh, Charlie. Look at this mess. Come on, into the shower."

Even the prospect of being in a shower with Joanna made not the slightest scratch on my iron cloak of misery. I wasn't sure the soft laughter was helping much. I didn't know where the bathroom was, as I didn't know where I was, so I slithered - face first - out of the bed in much the same way alligators slip off riverbanks into the water. I managed to get along with crawling, but that was about as high as I could get my head. Gravity has its uses. I didn't get that airy sensation that anything was hanging down amidships, so I assumed the underpants had held firm. I had wondered, because I wasn't otherwise wearing any clothes. I couldn't have cared less.

I heard a shower running, set my bearings for that and kept my eyes firmly closed to help in the pretence that none of this was actually happening. Some soft hands tried to pick me up. I opened my eyes briefly, an act that improved nothing whatsoever about my general wellbeing. Quite the opposite. What I saw of Joanna was quite enough leg to be going on with, with a long white shirt acting as a replacement nightshirt, in a reproduction of the film cliché where the young lady's morning-after attire is the gentleman's shirt from the night before. It dawned on me that I must have had rampant sex with the girl of my dreams, and did not have even the slightest recollection of having done so. And then, just to ensure that it would be a night she would never forget, as a waking up gift, she got a bedful of sick.

My head hit the bathtub.

"Get in, Charlie."

"No." I said. "I can't. I'm ill. I need a Doctor."

"Just put your head over the bath then."

I did what I was told and hung over the bath. Jets of cold water hit my head. If I'd had any functioning nerve impulses, I would probably have leapt into the air with a yelp. But I just kind of flopped there like an old discarded mop, having its detritus rinsed down the drain in a steady flow of watery unpleasantness. But then the water heated up, and there were soft fingers at work. A luxurious froth of shampoo or soap or shower gel, I couldn't care which, presaged a brief moment of bliss. Once that passed, I threw up again, this time in the bath.

"Oh, Charlie!"

Some ten minutes later, I was lying across the sofa under a spare blanket Joanna had found in the wardrobe. She was stripping the bed, bending down, reaching forward, doing things in a gentleman's shirt that were worthy of a standing ovation. But I was dying, and therefore it was wasted on me.

"I've saved the mattress, Charlie," she said.

And me, I thought.

"I'm dying, Jo."

"No, you're not, Charlie. You're hungover."

"The room is spinning, and I'm already lying down. I've got some kind of illness. Did you call for a Doctor?"

"You've got a hangover, Charlie."

"Bollocks."

"Come on, Charlie, you know what a hangover feels like. It's not like you've never had one before."

"Of course I've never had one before. I don't drink. I feel like shit. If this were a hangover why would any sane person ever drink?"

I immediately wished I hadn't spoken, because I felt hot around the gills again but I didn't have the heart to puke again after all the hard work Joanna had put in. I closed my eyes and kept my head still and breathed steadily through my nose. Panic abated.

"Have you really never been drunk before, Charlie?"

"I don't drink. Can't stand the taste. I try the odd glass of something, just to fit in, you know. It's bad enough that I don't eat meat."

"You practically poisoned yourself back there, no wonder you think you're dying."

She looked glorious. I wish I could have remembered what the sex had been like. Perhaps it would all come back to me if I fell asleep and woke up again. She went into the bathroom and returned with a glass of water.

"Drink this, Charlie. I'm putting this little bin here. If you think you're going to be sick again…"

I had no idea what the time was, or if I was ever going to be able to stand up again, or what it was the Levine man was all about. I only knew that Joanna and I had crossed a line and were about to begin an epic journey of romantic discovery, just as soon as she'd finished clearing up a trail of vomit. I couldn't wait to tell the lads back in Berlin.

"I'm sure you'll all have a laugh about this when you get back to Berlin," she began, as she bent down to pick up the empty glass and cruelly exposed more than a hint of cleavage.

"Nobody's business but ours."

"You tell them everything, Charlie, don't you? Here, drink some more." She'd been in and out of the bathroom for a top-up.

"Nah. I don't like anyone to know everything about me. Sometimes you need to keep things to yourself." I hoped this conversation was on its last legs because I certainly was. I calculated I had three good sentences left in me.

"We talk about everything." She said. "The girls, we share everything. It's not fun to have secrets. It's nice to have friends you can trust. Talk about anything, you know? No secrets. It's a bit of a girl thing."

I could have set her straight there and then on that score, knowing as I did about Beth's real job, and Isabelle's exotic sideline. But I was sworn to secrecy. And that was a boy thing.

I was wrong. I didn't even have three good sentences left in me. I fell asleep. The last thing I remember, apart from feeling cold and self-pitying, was a slight nagging sensation that I might not actually have slept with her after all. Maybe, it just didn't actually happen.

And then again, maybe it did.

Saturday, October 24th

"Are you always this miserable in the mornings, poppet?" said the waitress.

"I haven't had my tea," he forced himself to say.

"Well, it wouldn't hurt to smile."

"I bet it would."

"Will you be wanting anything to eat?"

"Just toast. But I need tea first."

Charlie Stokes was miserable in every existing shade. He no longer felt nauseated but poisoned, which was not much of an improvement. He had been thinking that if someone were to cut his body in half, they would have found a vibrant green core of some sort of radioactive offal rather than the more expected snails and puppy dogs' tails. It was this admittedly pointless thought that the bustling, good-natured waitress was repeatedly interrupting. Charlie, in that difficult period that preceded the day's first cup of tea, preferred his bonhomie spread thinly. This lady had been laying it on with a trowel and his equanimity had been destabilised.

He had tried to look like he wasn't still wearing yesterday's clothes by ignoring the existence of his suit's jacket and of course, not bothering with the tie. This left him at least a layer short of what was comfortable for the time of year, but by one of those occasional miracles that are bestowed on the wretched, he had chosen a window table at the precise half hour during which sunshine had been allocated for the day, and he used this magnified warmth to keep his toxic blood circulating.

Charlie had no idea what time Joanna had left. The last time he had woken up, a large Spanish woman was vacuuming around the sofa, having already returned the bed to a crisp new freshness and collated, into a neat septic pile, all his clothes bar the underpants he was fortunate enough still to be wearing. Rolled up and tucked into the waistband of these had been a small sheet of hotel notepaper with the words *"Didn't want to wake you. Call me if you're bored. J x."* Well, he was planning to be very bored indeed.

The tea arrived on his table accompanied by an uninvited middle-aged woman in a twinset. If anyone had asked him, Charlie would have guessed that there were between fifteen and twenty empty tables at the dining room. He was the only remaining customer.

"This seat isn't taken, is it?"

"No," said Charlie, cursing the porridge in place of his brain when, clearly, *yes* had been the word required.

"You don't mind if I join you?"

Such a sweet lady. But Charlie would rather dip his head in a bucket of cold custard than share his misanthropy.

"No, I don't."

"You look like you need the company."

"No, I bloody well don't," he managed not to say out loud.

E Minor

Some people think I'm overly precious about tea. My painstaking addition of two extra drops of milk to a cup, to get the shade just so, once caused such a torrent of hysterical giggling from a girl who I hadn't even fancied, that she began to choke on the last of her walnut whip and had to be rescued by a complete stranger performing the Heimlich on her.

So, as I gently cajoled inside the teapot with an inquisitive spoon, checking depth of body and thickness of soul, I couldn't help but sense the potential for something similar to reignite here now with this woman who had attached herself to my table. But she made no comment. When I finally raised the cup to my lips, I actually had my eyes closed in anticipation. After the first mouthful, I felt almost subhuman again.

"I remember when I first came to the country. All the tea drinking, I never understood it."

She smiled after she said this, which I took to mean she was joking, or insane. A conversation was threatening to break out, despite all my efforts to the contrary, and I could see the arrival of my toast being the subject of more sparkling repartee. I was right.

"Is that all you're going to have for breakfast?"

"Yes."

I got busy with the knife, and the butter, and the spreading of this and that.

"Marmite."

"Yes."

"I never understood that, either."

It seemed futile to continue the pretence that I was breakfasting alone.

"So," I began, cautiously, "where in the country do you live?"

I was curious why she had imagined there was more tea drinking in rural districts.

"London."

"I thought you said you lived in the country? You mentioned about the tea, that it was when you first moved to the country?"

"Yes. England. When I first came to England."

Perhaps I was now detecting the merest suggestion of an accent. "Sorry, I misunderstood," I said. "So, when did you first come to England?"

"Twenty? No, more than twenty years ago. Sometimes it seems like forever."

"Yes," I said, rather too quickly.

The woman turned to look out of the window. She had neatly-cut, shoulder length hair dyed a henna brown colour that she could still just about get away with. Experience had shown me to be practically inept at guessing a woman's age, having been trained since childhood by my grandfather that to enter such a field was fraught with more danger than a boy could imagine. I could imagine a lot, so I avoided the topic.

"Where were you living before you came to England, then?" I asked, busying myself with a refill.

"The continent, mainly. France and Germany, you know."

"I'm living in Berlin at the moment."

"Berlin?" It seemed to pique her interest. "Really? And how are you finding it?"

"Well, different. Yes"

I chewed on some toast, bringing on a headache.

"Did you go there for work?"

"I have a band."

"Oh," she said. "Not for work, then."

She looked out of the window suddenly. I don't know if she'd seen something or just wanted a break from looking at me. I can't have been a pretty sight. My eyes were stinging so much, I presumed I'd put them on inside out. I rubbed them. When I stopped and opened them again the woman was still there.

"What instrument do you play?"

"Guitar," I began "and mandolin, believe it or not."

Mandolin? Why did I say mandolin? When did I ever play a mandolin?

"I played the piano when I was a young girl. And I sang. We all sang. But that was all a long time ago."

She seemed wistful then, and wistful is hard to deal with even when you're feeling on top of your game. I caught a glimpse of her profile, and something about it made me think of someone. Perhaps a newsreader or some such.

"Are you back here visiting family?"

"No." I busied myself with toasty things. That wasn't really an answer. "My best friend died last week. He was killed actually, during the storm. The funeral was here, round the corner, yesterday. I came over for that. It didn't go very well. But in the end I was saved by a girl."

"Oh? There's always a girl, isn't there?"

"Not always enough," I joked, if joke it was. "And I got very drunk, I'm afraid. It was a right old night in the end."

"I see," she said, and I think she meant it. I might have opened the door for her to slip out of my life. "I hope you took precautions? Young people shouldn't go around taking chances these days."

I just sort of smiled that stupid laddish smile that you do when you're speaking to someone you've never seen before and will never see again.

"Well, you know, rock and roll and all that."

"Do you smoke?"

"Only on Tuesdays and Thursdays."

I was on a roll now. She didn't laugh, or anything similar, but her attention had evidently been caught by someone behind me. She waved and made to get herself to her feet.

"Ah, there you are, darling." That was not directed at me.

"Hi, Mum," said a voice I recognized immediately without having to crane my neck round for a visual.

Joanna.

Which made the lady sitting in front of me, listening to my laddish flapdoodle, Joanna's Mum, for fuck's *sake*.

Toast, butter, Marmite. Toast, butter, Marmite. Toast, butter, Marmite.

"Hello, Charlie!" It was almost a squeal. "You're up. I thought you were dead," she added, helpfully.

I could see there was a struggle for comprehension being played across her Mum's face that, on another day and under different circumstances, I might have found amusing. But not today.

"I see you've met."

"Actually, no," corrected her Mum. She was still smiling but her eyes flitted twixt the radiance of her beautiful offspring and my own battered countenance.

"Well, allow me. Mum, this is Charlie. Charlie, this is Mum."

I did what I could with a handshake, hoping that having a table between us was excuse enough not to have to stand up and hike across for a kiss exchange. At least I knew there wouldn't be a Dad coming over the horizon any time soon.

"I thought you'd left," I said to Joanna.

"I'm going now. Do you want a lift? You're staying right close by to where Mum lives. I'll drop you off."

"No, I'm all right," I lied. "I'm going to Guildford. I'm supposed to see Judy, Luke's cousin. Ten minutes on the train."

"I'll drop you at the station, then."

"Okay, yeah. Now?" I asked.

"Finish your toast." She said.

"Thanks." I said.

"Okay." She said.

"Great." I said.

Not the greatest piece of dialogue in history. Other people's mothers can do that to me. Then, a man with a face like a shovel of shit, wearing a deliberately funereal suit of tarmac grey, burst in and sliced the dining room into great shards with his eyes. If I hadn't already known to the contrary, I'd have sworn it was Joanna's father looking to right some wrongs, starting with me.

"Is that your car outside, blocking me in? No one in this bloody hotel seems to know." The voice matched the face. "Only, if it is, please move it. I need to go and bury my bloody Uncle," he continued, harrumphing. "I am, needless to say, late."

He was a man who enjoyed consonants and enunciation in equal measure.

"As is your Uncle now," I heard myself actually say out loud.

I received a kick in the shins from Joanna for that, which I took as a term of endearment, though that didn't stop it hurting.

"I beg your pardon?"

"It's my car," said Joanna in her emollient voice, interceding. "We're just leaving."

She drowned the man-monster with her smile, removing his power of speech. He grunted, made some fish-like movements with his lips, and finally turned sharply and left, for which the room, I'm sure, would have been grateful. I know I was.

We left.

"Tell me you didn't sleep with him?"

She pitched her voice low and quiet, after Charlie had gone to reception on a paracetamol hunt. Joanna just shook her head and rolled her eyes. She held the door open.

"Out we go, Mum," she sighed.

They walked briskly to the car, which sat proudly in front of a maroon-coloured BMW belonging to the stranded and grieving nephew.

"Come on, Charlie!" She called out in mock exasperation as she saw him bundle his frame through the front doors.

He looked up. In the harsh light of day, the ravages of the night before had left their mark, and his face was probably as tousled as his hair.

"Why aren't you wearing your coat, Charlie?"

Charlie Stokes stood gaping like someone who had had his brain removed for a service, and was waiting for the replacement.

"Where's your coat, Charlie?" Joanna repeated. The BMW gave a sharp honk. "Go and get your coat, I'm going to move the car."

She dropped herself into the driver's seat and reversed, to allow the BMW to shoot off towards the crematorium in a hail of orange gravel. Her mother busied herself with the seatbelt, humming an excerpt from the *Nutcracker* while she did so. Joanna was taking her to see Laura Farey perform it that evening, and it was a close-run thing as to whether Laura

Farey's dancing or Joanna's mother's efforts with the seatbelt would be the bigger performance.

"You're pulling it too hard, Mum."

"I don't know why you didn't borrow a German car, dear."

"Right, here comes Charlie. Try and be nice. He's not well."

"I know. He had a rough night."

"Is that what he told you?"

"Amongst other things."

"He's very sweet, Mum."

"Yes. Of course."

Charlie Stokes let himself into the back of the car and tried not to slump in the corner. The tea and toast had kept him alive without moving him noticeably closer to feeling human. He regretted accepting the lift the moment Joanna swung the car out of the short drive and into the road. Long walk to the station in the bracing air might have been a better choice. He let his head fall back against the headrest and closed his eyes. They were too frayed to focus.

"You all right, Charlie?" asked Joanna, having caught sight of him in the rear view mirror.

"Never better."

"Charlie, is that a plaster on your forehead?"

"Yes, it is."

"Where did you get it from?"

"The First Aid box in reception."

"Why what happened? Did you hit your head?"

"Yes. On the First Aid box in reception."

Joanna pulled out to give a cyclist a wide berth and immediately veered back as there was a blue transit coming the other way. Charlie was seriously considering bailing out and going on foot. It was that, or ask Joanna's mother to change places.

"Mum and I are going to the *Nutcracker* tonight. Do you know Laura Farey? She's coming to Berlin in a few weeks. Are you into ballet?"

Charlie Stokes was not at all into ballet. But he knew who Laura Farey was because she was a bit of a stunner and her fame lapped beyond the world of ballet. She had a huge, dazzling white smile, and stone-piercing blue eyes. Along with the rest of the band, when they were discussing her appearance in a magazine that featured some controversially raunchy poses, he had declared her to be a five-star horn bucket.

"The name rings a bell."

"Mum's a big fan, aren't you?"

She turned to her mother as she said this, allowing both her concentration, and the car, to wander. Joanna avoided the Heathrow-bound National Express coach with a neat flick of the wrists, but it was a sudden movement too far for the clotted inner workings of Charlie Stokes. He leant forward, his hand already on the door handle.

"You can just leave me here, Jo. I need to get out. Quick."

"Good Lord, he's not going to be sick is he, dear? Not in here, surely."

"No, he's not! Charlie, it's fine, look we're nearly there. Open your window."

Charlie opened the window. The car filled with noise and cold air. It seemed he could not have one without the other. He practically lolled out of the window like an inquisitive Labrador, just without the inquisitiveness. Joanna was right, they had been nearly there. He barely allowed the car to stop before getting out.

"Expect I'll see you on the plane if you don't call before. I'll be a bit busy, though."

"Yeah. Sure." Charlie loitered. "Seriously, though. We must do it again," he repeated, pointedly. He bent down as low as he dared in order to direct some words at her mother: "Nice to meet you. I'm not normally like this."

He gave a final unassertive wave and headed into the station.

Joanna leaned into the back of the car to wind the rear window back up.

"He is very sweet really, Mum."

Her mother didn't answer. Her face was a picture. And if a picture paints a thousand words, Joanna was getting an earful.

E Minor

I remembered to get off the train at Guildford's London Road station, only a short walk away from Judy's house off the Epsom Road. I knocked. I knocked a second time, and then a third. The door opened, but it was an elderly man who stood at the threshold, not Judy.

"Charlie?" He asked.

"Yes." No sense lying. "Judy?"

"No, I'm Rodney."

"I meant, is Judy in?"

"No. She left yesterday."

"I see."

"If you wait there, I'll get the envelope."

With that he disappeared, as did all sense of comprehension on my part. *I'll get the envelope?* I only had a few seconds of metaphorical head scratching before he filled the doorway again with his grizzled presence. He held out a large brown envelope, to which I responded with one of my puzzled looks. I hadn't come for any envelope. By way of an answer, I received a combination nod and smile, followed by the door closing politely.

It was an unused envelope, in that there was no stamp or writing on either side, but it had been resealed with a strip of sellotape. It felt like it contained smaller envelopes inside, or maybe letters and cards, but definitely not ten grand in used fivers, which would have perked me up no end. I didn't open it.

I went back to Raynes Park.

I didn't go straight back, mind, because I fell asleep and didn't wake up until the train terminated at London Waterloo. But I caught up with most of the missed landscape on the return journey. I was on the verge of falling asleep again when the train pulled up at my station.

The house was empty, but my aunt had left a note. *Jake rang. Do you know where Troy is, or has he moved? He's missing.*

I returned the call. No answer, of course. I had no doubt at all it was just Jake having a flap, and that Troy would be at the airport on Tuesday to pick me up.

Well, almost no doubt.

I went upstairs and straight into a long and almost effeminate shower, leaving no stone unturned. Dressed in a fresh pair of admittedly non-ironed cream chinos, and finally no longer feeling in need of an autopsy, I raided the bread bin and started to stock up on the carbohydrates. I flushed down another couple of paracetamol tablets with a tumbler of fresh water and felt I had earned the right to get back on the tea.

I then opened the envelope and pulled out an assortment of old letters, papers and photos. I noticed straight away they were my Grandad's. There was his Union card, NHS card, various odd IDs from this and that, a couple of postcards and assorted miscellanea. He died a year ago. What they were doing in an envelope in Judy's house was slightly beyond me, other than he and Luke's great Uncle were pals. It was only on the Monday night, when I was packing and about to leave the envelope with my aunt, that I looked through everything again, with time and a clear head. And that's when I found out that my Dad had been shot, all those years ago.

And that he was not dead, after all.

Joanna was still getting accustomed to driving again. Although she occasionally risked a drive in Isabelle's fender-bent Peugeot, she used public transport to get around West Berlin. With it being a Saturday, traffic was easier, and she navigated her mother back to Merton Park with minimal fuss under leaden skies, after stopping once, briefly, for a loaf of fresh bread.

The house had been home to Joanna since her ninth birthday, and was comfortable and familiar in the way a favourite sweater might be. It had been paid for with a lump of money that her father had left for her mother, in lieu of writing a Will and dying.

"Do you think my father knows I'm in Berlin?" asked Joanna, as she put the finishing touches to a couple of ham sandwiches.

"Is that what Brian's trying to tell you?"

Joanna had long ago noticed that her mother was peerless when it came to responding to questions with other questions. The one constant in Joanna's life had been the void left by her missing father. She had met a number of other children over the years whose homes lacked a father, but hers was the only household never to have replaced the missing patriarch with some kind of substitute. She might have better accepted the situation if her father had simply died, like Charlie's. The finality of that took away all the uncertainty. Now that she had friends with children of their own, Joanna became ever more curious as to her father's motives in leaving her. It never helped that her own mother refused to discuss it.

"Why don't you want me to find him, Mum?"

"Do you think he doesn't know where we live?"

It was another question for an answer. Joanna took a nibble out of a sandwich, and drifted. She hadn't seen her mother for months and had no interest in wasting what time they had together now on taboo subjects. Once she had outgrown her childish notion that her father had absconded to Brazil with the loot of a heinous robbery, Joanna had imagined a man living a life either of reckless, selfish debauchery in Edinburgh or one of anguished, poetic solitude in the bitter wilds of north Cornwall. In truth, she could not have been more wrong, but her father had always believed that what she did not know could not hurt her.

The phone was ringing.

"Get that for me, would you, darling?" Joanna's mother asked her.

So she did. And the call was for her. She instinctively lowered her voice and moved into the hall.

"What is it, is something the matter?"

Joanna hadn't wanted to be called at her mother's house. She had mentioned that before she left. She shouldn't be rung unless there was something important, and not just to chat, or to check up on her, or because she was being missed, or anything else that brought her Berlin world back into her mother's living room in Merton Park.

"It's just for a few days," Joanna said, listening some more. "I can't. I just can't," she was practically whispering now. "You have to let me decide when."

She walked about in the kitchen and opened a couple of drawers so that her mother would not think she had left the room for the sake of the phone call, though that was exactly what she had done. This was getting more and more difficult.

"All right, yes. Yes, I will. Bye. Me, too."

As soon as the call was over, and as a distraction, she called out to her mother.

"Where's the salt, Mum?"

Overdressed for the tube, they both alighted a few hours later at Tottenham Court Road station, to double back on themselves on foot towards Covent Garden by way of the bookshops of Charing Cross Road. That was more for Joanna's benefit, of course. Unforecast drizzle caressed them every step of the way.

"I bet it doesn't rain all the time in Berlin."

"It doesn't rain all the time here, Mum, it just feels like it does."

As they walked past Denmark Street, where London's music shops huddled together in Britain's version of Tin Pan Alley, she thought about Charlie. He had told her that once, at Andy's guitar shop, he had inadvertently pushed Eric Clapton down half a flight of stairs.

"It's all electronic these days," said her mother, noting the plethora of keyboards and samplers and buttons and sliders. "They think anyone can be a musician now."

Joanna said nothing and they continued their slow walk.

"How long did you say you've known that boy Charlie?"

Joanna found her mother's tone perhaps a shade or two overly patronising.

"He's not a boy, Mum, he's exactly the same age as me."

"Men mature so much later," her mother said, highly distracted as if she had just found the sentence in an old cupboard and was airing it. "You'll find dinner with a forty-year-old man much more bearable and stimulating, sweetheart."

"I know. I do."

"Oh?"

"Lots of dinners, and lots of forty-year-old men. I met Charlie a few days ago, as I already told you twice before."

"I just want you to meet somebody nice."

"Lots of people are nice."

"That's not what I mean, darling. Why are we crossing the road?"

Joanna had taken her mother by the elbow and guided her to the kerb.

"I want to look in Foyles."

"Oh."

Perhaps only the parent of a grown-up child can infuse such a tiny word with the stench of such disappointment. Joanna was well aware that her mother never entered, unaccompanied, the labyrinth that was the country's biggest bookshop since the day she bizarrely denounced it as "that place where they sell peculiar books." Joanna, on the other hand, had probably never spent a day in central London without paying it a visit.

"But what time is Brian expecting us?" asked her mother.

"Not for ages, Mum."

"That's what I was worried about, dear."

West Berlin, Monday, October 26th

They were walking to the station together, lost among the Uhlandstrasse commuters in the late afternoon gloom as they headed to the U-Bahn. Isabelle had disengaged her mind from her recent trauma by simply ignoring it. It was how she dealt with almost everything in her life. Her vivacity tank was full to the brim again, and she was keen to throw it about a bit. Beth was not thinking at all about Isabelle nor, surprisingly, about work. She was thinking about her shoes and how bloody uncomfortable they were. She couldn't wait to get home.

"Is Jo back today?" asked Isabelle.

"Tomorrow."

"So, is it tomorrow we're all having lunch, then?"

"No, it's Wednesday. And we're having dinner. Much less of a rush."

"Shall we invite Charlie?'

"If you like."

Beth was thinking, while taking a mental snapshot of her kitchen cupboards.

"I've got nothing in the flat, shall we order pizza?"

"Beth, I'm sure someone's following me."

They were waiting at a crossing, Isabelle craning her neck, Beth bored and waiting for the red man to turn green.

"Nobody's following you, Izzy."

"I'm absolutely sure, darling," insisted Isabelle.

"Pizza. Yes, or no?"

"Yes. More health food, why not."

"You could always try cooking, you know." Beth thought that might be a nice thing to witness.

"But then we'd both be slaving in the kitchen," Isabelle pointed out. "I like it how it is now."

The lights changed and they continued briskly, Beth's sensible shoes affording her no comfort, and Isabelle's brazen heels marking the tempo. They slipped into the U-Bahn and a train was pulling up as the stepped on to the platform.

"There's a man following me, Beth, but it doesn't matter because you're clearly not interested." Isabelle despaired of ever injecting any excitement into her sister's life.

Beth sighed wearily. "There's a seat over there. Go on."

The journey home revolved around a discussion about pizza toppings.

Beth already knew there was a man following Isabelle, because she had arranged it. Suspicion and paranoia came as standard in her line of business, and Beth had wanted to assure herself that Isabelle's whatever-it-was the other night wasn't anything more intricate than it seemed. The man doing the following was due a spell in prison, but for the intervention of the British consulate. He had paid for his freedom by being at the Bureau's beck and call should anything come up that he could sort out on the quiet. Beth had asked him to shadow her sister for a couple of days without arousing suspicion, a job for which she could now see he was hopelessly inadequate. She would call him off in the morning.

In the end they shared a calzone, a bottle of Rioja, and not a single argument.

Tuesday, October 27th

A lex fumbled for the bedside lamp, and then stole a glance at the little clock. She had been deeply asleep and the phone, loud and shrill, was cutting her head into little ragged pieces. Half past three in the morning. As far as phone calls went, that was bad news o'clock.

She felt completely disorientated, and lay on the bed partly propped up on one elbow, looking for all the world like someone who had just partaken of one of Mike Tyson's finest. She reached for the receiver and fell back onto her pillow.

"Hello?" she croaked.

"Hi honey."

"Tony."

"Hey. I guess I woke you." Alex's heart was thumping. Wildly. Whether out of relief and joy, or anger and confusion, or just shock, she couldn't be sure.

"Where are you?" she asked, unnecessarily.

"Don't worry, I'm fine."

"You're fine? How can you be fine? I'm not fine," she added.

"Why, what's happened?"

What's happened!

"Are you okay, Tony, are you well?" Alex was confused and couldn't decide which train of thought to board.

"You spoke to Reiseneder?"

"Yes. Lucky for me that I did, otherwise I wouldn't know that I'm in complete financial meltdown, thanks to you."

"He doesn't know about all the other stuff, honey. He does, you know, some Berlin and Swiss things. Relax, everything's taken care of."

Alex had rehearsed this conversation many times in her head, but now that it was real she seemed to have developed rampant stage fright and nothing came. She began to realize that it was relief that had knocked her thoughts out of focus. Relief that her husband, for whom she harboured barely a single positive feeling, was alive and talking, and not dead in all the manner of unpleasant ways that she had been wishing upon him recently.

"What other stuff does he not know about? So you're going to pay all these bills, then? When, tomorrow?"

"I'm not really, you know, I don't need these companies any more. I'm not really taking care of that side of, er, things right now. No one can lay a thing on me for that."

"You're leaving it all for me?"

"You sold all the stocks."

"Yes?"

"Shouldn't have done that, babe."

"Your lawyer's telling me I'm basically bankrupt."

"I told you, babe, he doesn't know everything. You know it's… come on, it's -"

"So, where are you, Tony? You're not in jail in Toronto?"

There was a short, single-shot laugh down the phone, as if someone had burst a balloon full of snorts.

"Christ, babe, who have *you* been talking to?"

"Where are you, Tony?" She tried to keep the desperation out of her voice.

"Okay, I have to go. Everything else okay over there? The girls okay? How's work?"

How's work?

"Tony…"

"Listen to me. Don't worry about a thing and, seriously. Just keep on keeping on, babe, everything's like it couldn't be simpler."

"Oh, Tony. No. That's just it. I don't…I don't understand what you mean."

"I really gotta go now. Get some sleep. I'll call you."

"Tony?"

He had hung up. She lay on the pillow with the phone still pressed to her ear. Just before she hung up she thought she heard a click.

Raynes Park, England

E Minor

Joanna rang as I was literally heading out of the door. I hadn't spoken to her over the weekend, though it transpired that she'd called me around lunchtime yesterday, when I had been out and the house had been empty.

"They've had to change my flight, Charlie," she said, after a bit of fluff regarding the missed calls. "Something came up. Now I'm flying from Heathrow, this afternoon."

"Really?" I said, and disappointment didn't even begin to describe it. "Who's going to hold my hand?" I said, but it wasn't *my* hand I was thinking about.

"You'll find someone."

"I wanted to tell you something I just found out about my Dad."

"That's okay, I'll see you tomorrow. We're all going to eat at the Greek place. You're invited, you can tell me then."

She had to hang up, someone was waiting. So, the Greek place. Again. Nice and normal this time, perhaps. I swung my bag over my shoulder and hoped all the tea and Hobnobs would survive the journey intact. I had enough to last beyond Christmas, as long as I stashed them somewhere Jake would never find them.

The laundry basket perhaps.

Tegel Airport, West Berlin

E Minor

I couldn't remember the last time I'd sat in a limo.

Oh, yes I could. Never.

It was an improvement on all the other cars Troy had given me lifts in since we'd known each other, though it wouldn't have needed much of an upgrade to achieve that. One thing that didn't change was the music. Troy

138

seemed always to carry with him a cassette of his personal favourites. There was a dirty bluesy number filling the interior when he switched on the ignition. He turned the volume down, but not much, to make chit-chat less of a chore.

"So, how did it go, buddy? Crappy day, huh?"

"It was very..." Very what was it, actually? "Interesting," was all I could think of adding.

I sensed him looking at me, so I turned to face him. For some reason we both burst into, if not laughter, then something very much like it. He smiled while he nodded along with the beat.

"Did you get laid?"

"It was a funeral, not a bloody wedding."

"Dude, you can't let that stop you. Wait, listen to this."

He pointed a finger at the cassette player, but whatever it was I was supposed to be listening to evidently didn't arrive on cue, because he waved his finger away.

"I got laid three times at funerals I've been to."

Sadly, that didn't surprise me.

"Bloody hell, how many funerals have you been to?"

"Two."

What I had pieced together about Troy to date was that he had been born and brought up in Idaho, or some such similarly put-upon State, where he was probably left out in the wind as a baby. On his eighteenth birthday he had joined the Army, and when he ended up in Berlin, he married a local girl, so that he could stay in Germany and she could go and live in Vegas. The first time the happy couple had met in person was at the wedding itself.

He didn't seem to fret about money ever, unlike the rest of us for whom it was habitual. I had assumed he had accumulated it nefariously like the bastard child of Sergeant Bilko, or was a long-lost Rothschild.

"Here we go..."

He reached forward for the volume and yanked it up to the point where your ears flap. It was a saxophone solo, one of his probably. He turned to me with a scrunched-up face, nodding in appreciation.

"Yeah, man!" he drawled, if it can be called a drawl when it's so loud. "You *did* get laid!" He was laughing. "I can see it in your eyes."

We drove on through to the end of the saxophone solo, whereupon he finally turned the volume down just as the leather upholstery was beginning to crack.

"We ought to do that number some time. That solo will blow a dress clean off a woman at forty yards," he said. "Guaranteed."

"You never played over the Wall yet, right Charlie?"

Interesting question, I felt, under the circumstances.

"No," I replied, "but I bet the money's good."

We laughed.

"I could fix it up for us to play, if you like."

"You can fix anything, can't you?" I asked.

"Hell, yes!"

"Can you get me a ticket to the ballet at the Opera House at the end of next week?"

"East Berlin?"

"Yes."

"Ballet?"

He seemed incredulous, like I'd owned up to a murder.

"Yes. Friday, fifth of November. It's not far off, I know."

"Dude, if you want dancers, there's a burlesque show right near the base every Thursday."

"Cheers, mate," I said. "Not quite the same thing."

"Girls is girls, buddy."

"A ticket would be a problem, then?"

"For Thursday?"

"The ballet, for fuck's sake!"

Troy laughed. "I love that expression!" He tried it a couple of times using the same accent that Dick Van Dyke had mastered for *Mary Poppins*.

"Yeah, a ticket to the ballet would be a problem, but nothing I couldn't fix. But listen, let's go over and do a gig there. It'd be cool."

It had occurred to me already, of course - the idea of playing over the other side. Any *Wessies* I'd ever mentioned the idea to, had simply said: Why? Then I said: Why not? And then someone would get a round in.

"So," Troy began, "you got laid. English girl, I'm guessing. Worth the wait?"

What was it with all my mates having the idea I hadn't had any action in months?

"Well, I was a bit pissed, as it goes," I admitted.

"Why, what did she do?"

"Pissed, not pissed off," I corrected. "I was drunk."

"Well, obviously you were drunk," he said, apparently shocked that anyone would countenance sex while sober.

"I can't actually remember anything about it."

"Okay. So, you mean really drunk."

"I threw up in the bed in my sleep. Drunk enough for you?"

He nodded wildly in appreciation, still in time to the music. He managed to fit in a leery grin at the same time.

"Rock and roll, dude! Still, at least you'll never have to see her again."

"Right."

"Small mercies."

We drove on. It began to rain. It was going to be a long, uncomfortable wait until Spring. I'd only been away less than a week but it seemed longer. I looked at Berlin anew. I still didn't know what I was doing here. But each time I felt I'd reached the point where I wanted to leave, something changed my mind. It was Joanna this time.

"Did you see Jake while I was gone?"

"No."

"He rang me and left a message. He thinks you're missing."

"Missing what?"

"Just missing. Have you moved?"

"Yeah."

"You didn't say."

"It was sudden."

"What was?"

"Moving."

I had the slightest impression that he was paying more attention to the rear view and side mirrors than he ever normally bothered.

"Do you like Greek food, Troy?"

"It sucks."

"No, then?"

I just wanted some tips on what to order tomorrow night without showing myself up. Suddenly I had a vague déjà vu.

"Have we just gone round in a circle?"

"Yes we have, Dude. We're being followed."

"Give it a rest."

"We are. Grey Audi."

"Whose limo is this?" I said. And then, by way of deviation: "Listen, are you doing anything later? Just for a chat about something. Coffee, or whatever, at the usual place."

East Berlin

It was the smell of cabbage, loitering like a lethargic teenager on the ground floor hallway, which welcomed Christian Bauer. It wasn't the sound his feet made on the cracked lino, or the thick stale stillness of the air, or the way the smile on his face melted away like a skulking alley cat. No, it was Frau Gruber's eternal boiled cabbage that told him he was home sweet home.

To avoid any senseless waiting around for the lift, he took the stairs, as was his wont, two at a time, his long stride eating up the steps as he raced to the fourth floor. Helga was home, but she was due out in an hour, and he and Max could then talk safely. She looked up from the sink in the kitchen as he entered, and he could tell immediately that she had been crying again. He took off his coat and only after he'd hung it up did he notice the suitcase. Just to check she hadn't just been tidying up and forgotten to put it away, he picked it up. He could barely lift it. Why did women pack so senselessly when trying to make a point? If she was really leaving this time, who was going to carry her bag down? He went into the kitchen. She wouldn't look at him. Everything was very clean. It didn't sparkle, because nothing could make this apartment sparkle, but it was very, very clean. She must be really unhappy to have made it all so pristine. No sign of anything having been cooked but, with all the cleaning and the packing, who'd have the time?

"Max will be here in an hour," he said. She always cooked for them on the evenings Max came. It wasn't that he expected her to, she just always did.

"I know."

"What shall I tell him?"

"Goodbye?"

West Berlin

Although it was far too early, even for West Berlin, the place was heaving with squaddies celebrating their boredom, and the bar was therefore little more than a misplaced eyebrow away from a full-scale brawl. Such details were lost on Troy, whose life was drawn in broader, more ragged strokes than Charlie's. Many of the bars and cafes on the

Ku'damm were characterless places where unambitious tourists and off-duty soldiers willingly over-paid for beer and TV overdosing on the rise of MTV. Charlie, on his third day in West Berlin, had been in one once, and once was enough.

Charlie was drinking Coke. He aimed it into a glass tumbler from as high as he could without a spill, filling it with a hissing brown froth. Once that settled to reveal an inch of liquid, he repeated the process. By the time he had a drinkable quantity, Troy was half way through his beer. The American shook a wistful head.

"You're weird, buddy."

"I can't be arsed to wait for it to go flat."

Troy smiled, took another swig and unwrapped a stick of American gum, shooting out two glances as he did so, one at his battered Breitling, the other at the doorway. He already had a date, which was why Charlie had to agree to the location change. Troy was immune to his surroundings and with his Southern self-confidence could lay his hat anywhere, but his English musician friends preferred the comfortable, dark eccentricity of East Kreuzberg's eclectic maze of bars.

A sudden, rasping shout cut through the raucous babble and made Charlie start. Troy's eyes instinctively searched for the source, Charlie's instinctively not. Laddish guffaws signalled all was still under control, and Troy settled on Charlie again.

"Why are you so jumpy, Dude? It's just a bunch of jarheads."

"We're not all ninja warriors like you." Charlie juggled a few words around his head, something to get the ball rolling, but was distracted by a sight of the Bee Gees on a TV screen in the corner. "Bee Gees just got to number one in the UK, by the way," he said pointlessly. "Does no one have any shame?"

"Listen, Charlie," and Charlie listened, because Troy never, but never called him by his name. "Ritchie wants to quit the band. He's gonna quit the band. He just can't bring himself to tell you. I guess he thinks you're gonna stop soon anyway, I don't know. I just thought you should know." Troy had always played it straight with Charlie.

"Ritchie?" said Charlie. But he wasn't really surprised.

Ritchie had been laid low by an outbreak of sensibleness over the past few months. Charlie wondered whether Ritchie could even salvage anything out of the wreckage of his abandoned medical education.

"Is he going back to his medical degree? Can you do that when you've already pulled out?"

Troy nodded.

"In January. Back home for Christmas, I guess. I think his Ma and Pa have got some pull."

That much Charlie already knew. Ritchie's family was ferociously well connected, so Charlie put Ritchie's chances on the probable side of possible. Charlie would miss all the free consultations.

"The good news is that I got you a gig at the one and only Ground Zero!" Troy announced. "If you want it. November 21st."

"The Ground Zero? Blimey. Bit off-the-wall for us, though, isn't it?"

"Maybe, but it's the coolest dive in town, Dude."

Charlie wouldn't argue on that score.

"And obviously I'm going to play with you."

Charlie raised his glass.

"To Mr Cafarella," he said, "soldier, saxophonist, playboy, spy, car thief and master theatrical agent."

"Hallelujah, son," came the reply, along with a restrained clinking of glasses.

Charlie had found his opening.

"Is *Cafarella* actually your name? Or is it a nickname, or something?"

"It's real. Why? Does it offend you, boy?" Troy cranked up his Southern accent to plantation owner level.

"The other day, in England, I found some of my grandad's papers and stuff. There was a telegram, an army telegram. It was sent to my Mum, obviously before I was even born. I've always been told that my Dad was killed in a car crash, right? He didn't die in a car crash. He was shot. Shot and badly wounded. But he didn't die. Why wasn't I told?"

He let the words brew. This had been very big news for him. It didn't seem to be making Troy hold his front page, though. He went on:

"There was a letter, too. Again, written to my Mum. It's not from the Army, it's from a friend - a friend of my Dad's, that is. It's on that airmail paper, and the second page is lost, but it clearly tells her about what happened, I think, and how my Dad was being sent to Berlin…"

"Whoah there, cowboy," Troy had to pile in there. "What a crock. A letter about your old man being shot and badly wounded, and then being sent to Berlin? Why would anyone send a Brit National Serviceman to Berlin? He'd stay where he was and get sent back home. And I thought you told me he was in Cyprus?"

Charlie bristled. He hadn't expected such a sudden interruption.

"Nobody ever talked properly about it. My Grandad said my Dad was a worthless chancer and blamed him for what happened to Mum. If someone tells you your Dad died in a car crash, on national service, and you understand the posting was to Cyprus, then why would you believe anything different? The telegram was from Rhineland. That's bloody Germany."

"No shit, Einstein."

"The thing is, Troy, what if my Dad is still alive somewhere?"

"Dude, please, come on."

"He didn't die in a car crash though, did he?"

"Says who?"

"I've just told you. He was shot. And wounded. That's all."

"Charlie, man, don't do this to yourself. He could still have died in a car crash. When was he supposed to have died, eh? Do you even know exactly?"

Troy leaned forward. Charlie had never seen him so fizzed up. He was normally horizontally laid-back.

"So he was once shot in some accident. Big deal. He gets better. He still dies in a car crash. Period."

He sat back in his chair and, again, glanced over towards the door. Charlie stalled, and then began to feel slightly ridiculous and deflated. What had he been thinking all last night and today? Troy was right: he may have been unaware that his Dad had been involved in a shooting incident, but what did that have to do with his death in a car crash? Nothing.

No. Hang on. Keep on track, Charlie. Remember what you came here to say.

"I haven't finished, yet. There's one other thing I thought was funny."

"Good, you could do with a laugh, buddy."

"The man who wrote the letter to my Mum was called Chad."

"Okay. Sounds like an American."

"Chad Cafarella."

There wasn't much time to saviour any sense of dramatic pause because there was another sudden shout from the squaddies and a fight broke out, or at least a chair-scattering ugly wrestle. Charlie's fight-or-flight mechanism kicked in, and he was outside and walking away on the Ku'damm before Troy had time to drain his glass.

E Minor

Iwas aiming for the zoo more or less, I don't know why, but had barely made it across the other side of the Ku'damm before Troy had caught up with me.

"Why do they always seem to want to fight all the time?" I said, a bit pointlessly.

"They're soldiers, dude. You might be glad of it one day."

"I suppose."

"Let's go back. They'll have finished by now."

"Can't we just walk and talk a bit?"

I could see that he wasn't that keen but, after a long hard look back over at the bar, he nodded. So, we began to walk but not talk. I'd lost my rhythm and couldn't get the conversation going again. I'd gone into the bar believing that my father was alive and living who knows where, perhaps oblivious of my existence. Troy had instantly realigned my planets. And yet, there was still the Cafarella business. That could be something to be getting on with.

"Look," I began, "this letter. What about it, eh? Chad Cafarella? You wouldn't by any chance think there was any connection with you?"

"It's certainly some coincidence, I'll say that," conceded Troy.

"Not your Dad, then?" I asked, less than half-heartedly.

"Why would it be my Dad? His name is William and he's never set foot outside of Oklahoma. We can't be the only family in the world called Cafarella."

He may well have been right, where would I look to find out anyway? But it still seemed so odd, I had to keep going.

"My Dad and I, twenty plus years apart, both friends with people called Cafarella, and there's no connection?"

I stopped outside a *Kneipe* on the corner of Fasanenstrasse with Lietzenburgerstrasse, and briefly considered diving in. Troy was buckling under the weight of a shrug.

"Dude, what can I say? That's premium, twenty-four carat weird, but what's it got to do with me? Hmm? Give me a week and I'll get you a list of a hundred Cafarellas. There's probably a dozen living in Berlin."

"There isn't. I already checked the phone directory. There isn't one. Not even you."

I didn't know what I wanted him to say. I had just been hoping that he'd say something. I slumped, and puffed out my cheeks, because that's just about where I was with things. Troy was right. I decided to drop it. And pick up the other prickly subject of the day. Beth.

"There's one other thing, Troy."

"Shoot. But follow me, I'm heading back."

We walked more or less the same way we came, and as we waited at a pedestrian crossing, like good citizens, I just hit him with it all in one go.

"I got picked up the other day by a woman who kind of works for the embassy. She knew we were friends. She was basically accusing you of being a traitor, a spy or some such thing. She wanted to know what I thought about that. I think she's expecting me to follow you around for a bit and see what you're up to. That okay with you?"

I didn't realise that he was laughing at first, because the green man had come on and we crossed the road. But when I looked at him, as we walked, he was chuckling his head off.

"What did you say again?" He asked.

"Yeah, I know. You can laugh. I felt the same."

"Why the hell would anyone say something like that?"

"I was hoping you could tell *me*."

We turned left and strode at some pace back towards the bar.

"That Audi you said was following us earlier today. That was them."

"Them?" I'd never seen Troy smile so much. "And you're supposed to do what exactly?"

"I don't know," I complained. "I didn't give it any thought, it's a load of bollocks isn't it? What is there to say? *You* come up with something!"

His laughing had thrown me a bit, but if the roles had been reversed, I'd have been having hysterics, too. I don't suppose Beth would be bothering me about it at the dinner tomorrow, but it would have been nice to have an idea of how to handle her request. We were outside the bar again.

"You know, maybe there's some way you can make a buck or two on this," said Troy.

"Me?" I said.

"Hell, yeah. They gotta pay you for the information, right? Tell 'em all kinds. I'll make up a story for you. You can string it along for weeks, months even."

This was all suddenly starting to sound like *Our Man in Havana*.

"Leave it out, Troy. Bloody hell. I wish I hadn't told you now."

I didn't fancy the bar again and decided to cut loose and leave Troy to his visitor.

"So, anyway, just to get everything clear, you're not involved in any espionage right now?"

"Get out of here. You know when someone's pulling your chain, don't you?"

He went in and I didn't. I walked to the S-Bahn, as confused as ever. Troy said no, but he couldn't help but scratch an itch on his nose while he did so.

That's what people do when they are lying, isn't it? Scratch about on the proboscis?

Wednesday, October 28th

The trees outside the Hardenbergstrasse offices of the British Council seemed almost mocking. Joanna's mother had kept the newspapers from the days following the storm, and some of the photos had been eerie. Having herself seen so many uprooted trees during her short stay in England, Joanna found those she could see from her window almost smugly rooted, as if Germany's legendary efficiency spread even to the roots of its trees. She gathered the file for the Consulate and debated alone whether to go now or after lunch.

Her desk phone was chirping.

"Hello," she said brightly.

"Jo, there's a Charlie Spokes to see you, he doesn't have an appointment. What? Oh. Stokes."

"Charlie? No that's all right, I'll come down."

Charlie Stokes, wearing black Levis and matching All Stars, was standing in the reception area reading a poster about someone in ceramics. He had his back to the room when Joanna entered.

"Hello Charlie," she said, having scoured all traces of surprise out of her voice. "What are you doing here?"

He spun round and smiled, if not altogether convincingly.

"Hi. How are you? I was just passing by, noticed the sign and remembered this was where you worked. Thought I'd just pop in and say hello."

"That's nice. Where are you off to, then?"

"The Ground Zero. It's a club. We've got a gig there, end of next month. I have to sign a contract to confirm."

The receptionist, who had since returned to typing on large, brown envelopes, looked up quizzically.

"The Ground Zero is nowhere near here," she said. And then, turning specifically to Joanna, added "Horrible little place, Jo, full of punks and Turks."

Joanna tried to visualise a scenario where punks and Turks provided the main ingredients.

"I was taking a scenic route," said Charlie defensively.

And he didn't need disparaging comments about the Ground Zero from Miss Starchy Pants, either. He intended to make a very strong impression on Joanna at that club, and he didn't want her frightened away a month early. In an effort to cut the third party out of the conversation, Charlie pointedly looked only at Joanna and skimmed a few decibels off the top of his voice. The receptionist began to type again.

"Have you got time for a coffee?" Charlie asked, gently.

"Pardon?" said Joanna.

"Don't you just hate it when they mumble?" said the receptionist.

Charlie counted to five.

E Minor

I would have preferred to be sat down quietly with a coffee or something, but it was close to lunchtime and the small places wouldn't have taken kindly to it. And as Joanna needed to transfer some paperwork to the consulate, she suggested I tag along. There hadn't been any idle chitchat, we just stepped onto the street, turned left, and she began.

"So, what is it you wanted to tell me about your father, Charlie?"

Bright and breezy she was, more so than suited her. But there was no point slowing the mood, unless I was prepared to talk to myself, that is.

"Well, that was a bit of a false hope in the end. There was an envelope of my Grandad's letters and papers and stuff. I found out that my Dad was shot in an Army exercise. Shot, and wounded only. I got excited thinking that he wasn't dead, you know. I thought my Mum's family had been hiding something from me all this time."

"Shot!" She sounded suitably shocked, as I had been. "What about the car crash? Isn't that what you said had happened?"

"Well, that's what I thought. Exactly. I was telling Troy all this, and he kind of brought me down to earth a bit."

"Troy?"

"Troy." She didn't know who Troy was. "He plays with us sometimes, a bit ad hoc, when he can. He's a sax player. I told him first, because there was a letter that had been written to my Mum from a friend of my Dad's in the Army. The guy's name was Chad Cafarella. Troy's surname is Cafarella, and I just thought it was, I don't know, hell of a coincidence."

"In what way?"

And as instantaneously as a flicked switch, her face changed.

"In what way?" I repeated, surprised. "In the coincidence way. It's not Smith, or Brown, or Jones, or Williams, it's Cafa-bloody-rella. How many of them have you ever heard of?"

"Cafa-bloody-rellas? None, to be honest."

She forced a smile, just in case there was any remote possibility that I didn't know she was teasing, but I didn't want jokes today. I wanted warm understanding. Or something.

"What kind of letter?"

"Just a letter saying that my Dad was being taken to Berlin of all places, to a hospital, I assumed. I mean, there was a page missing, so I've had to fill in the blanks, really."

"He was in Berlin, then? Doing his national service? How funny."

"Yeah." I replied. "There again, not really. Back in the sixties, practically the entire British Army was in Germany, wasn't it?"

"I don't know."

It didn't matter to me that she didn't know, it was a rhetorical question. What did matter to me was that she had gone a bit distant. We walked on without speaking, and I was about to reignite the flame when she stopped at a doorway. It seemed we were there already. I had never been to the Consulate, nor had the foggiest where it was, as I avoided officialdom, by whatever flag, as an alcoholic would a brewery.

"Here we are," she said. "I'll only be a minute. It's just in and out."

"Are you going to see Beth?" I asked.

"No, I never deal with her office."

She was gone and I waited. After a minute, she was still gone. I then used fifteen minutes of my life pacing up and down the spectacularly dull façade of the Consulate. I couldn't help wondering why we hadn't something altogether grander to welcome any defectors, as this utilitarian edifice would be their first port of call. Then again, it was just the Consulate. The British Embassy itself was in Bonn. I knew the Embassy over the other side of the Wall had a bit more oomph about it. Who knows, perhaps one day I'd get the chance to pace aimlessly up and down in front of that?

When Joanna re-emerged into the thin midday light, she did so with an attachment. He was a tall, overtly Aryan specimen with a dark suit and a look of such self-assuredness that your first instinct would be to slap him round the chops or, better still, get someone else to do it, as he was a bit on the large side. He was not a fit young scamp like me but, for some reason, he had his arm around Jo as he guided her onto the pavement in one of those public displays of chivalry that break out when middle-aged men collide with pretty young girls. But when Joanna turned right, and meandered away with said man close to heel, without so much as a flicker of a glance in search of Charlie Stokes, I felt a twinge that had nothing to do with it being lunchtime.

I set off in hot pursuit, or lukewarm at least.

"All right?" I said as I drew up alongside. I had intervened mid-sentence, but I can't remember whose. The man seemed diplomatically ruffled, so I assume it had been his. Joanna seemed surprised to see me.

"Charlie! I thought you'd gone to the club?" She had clearly forgotten her last words, then. "This is Günther. He's going to be liaising for the Staatsoper in connection with the gala. We finally met. This is Charlie."

The last three words were tossed across in his direction. He looked at me both briefly and intently, difficult to pull off without years of experience at something unpleasant.

"Hi," I said.

"Günther Reisz," he replied.

I imagined that if I offered him my hand, he'd have taken it, gripped it enough to make a statement, and let go when he was good and ready. So I smiled a harmless smile instead, and that clearly threw him off balance.

"Look, I'll see you tonight, Charlie, okay?"

Joanna was in a bit of a rush it seemed, and they set off again, him with a parting nod and curt smile. I watched them go. I imagined he did a lot of curt smiling, he looked the type.

For some reason, and I just couldn't put my finger on it, it didn't feel right.

Joanna was seated on the window sill, as was her wont when on the phone, looking down at the street. Martina had left a mug of peppermint tea and gone back to the kitchen. From the doorway, she stood in silhouette, her short-cropped blonde hair worn like a cap over her freckled face. She waited for the conversation to start, then melted away to wash vegetables. But she was listening.

"Mum?" Joanna frowned slightly as the connection was not as good as usual.

"Hello, darling."

"All right?"

"I was putting something in the oven."

"What are you having?"

"I made lasagne. The Martins are coming to dinner, remember?"

"Oh. Yes."

"I wasn't expecting you to call already. It's only been a day."

Joanna heard her mother laugh lightly.

"No. I'm going out with the girls later."

There was too much silence.

"Is something the matter?"

Of course there was something the matter. But how to start?

"No. I'm fine, it's nothing. No, it doesn't matter. You're cooking."

"I've finished now, it's in the oven. Go on."

"I need to ask you about my brother."

She didn't actually hear it, but Joanna felt an impatient sigh from the other end of the line.

"Joanna."

"You said my brother, my twin brother, died at birth. That's... that's what you said. That's what you've always said. But once Brian said something to me that was strange, and as soon as he said it, he tried to make it sound like he said something else."

"Joanna, stop. Please."

"He made it sound like he was alive, but somewhere else. It was... it was something like that, I can't remember. I didn't think anything about it. It was years ago. And then there was Brian's friend, the American he sometimes talked about, remember? Chad Cafarella. Cafarella gave you that record, didn't he? The one you always played, with the old-fashioned songs."

"Why are you doing this, Joanna?" Her mother sounded hurt.

"I met someone, Mum. He knows that record. His mother died just after he was born - or so he was told - his mother knew Chad Cafarella. I've seen his passport. He was born on the same day as me. I don't know what he's doing in Berlin, and he certainly doesn't know anything about this but... When were you going to tell me, Mum? *Why* didn't you tell me? Is my brother alive? Could my brother be here in Berlin? Mum?"

She gulped in some air, because she had barely used two breaths. While she waited for an answer, the tension and sense of confusion she had been carrying around all afternoon subsided. And in its place came guilt. She knew her mother was upset.

She also suspected, having said the words out loud, that she was utterly wrong. Her mother's voice was quiet.

"You told me you needed to take this Berlin job because you wanted to try something new in your life. You needed some space of your own. If it's all been about your father, or your brother, or the past... then it's all going to be a terrible waste, darling. Your brother died. Why would I lie? Why would I give him away? There were no more children. I couldn't have more children. Look ahead, Joanna. Please. There are no surprises or secrets. Your father just left. It was a long, long time ago. Your life is all in front of you. I'm going to call Brian tomorrow and ask him to stop encouraging you. There's nothing to be gained from it. Let's just live our lives, as they actually are now, not the way you wish they should have been."

"And Cafarella?"

"Nothing. It's just a coincidence. I can't keep talking about it, darling, really I'm done with it."

"Okay."

"Sweetheart, I know it's hard, but really, I don't think about it anymore. Not ever. Only when you start it up."

Her mother's voice had regained some strength, and Joanna looked over towards the kitchen, noticing that Martina had been listening. She smiled apologetically.

"All right, Mum. That's fine. I just..."

"I know."

"So, you don't eat meat, Charlie?" asked Alex.

"Everyone's a vegetarian these days, Charlie." That was Beth.

"Does an egg count, darling? Isn't that just a pre-chicken?" Isabelle.

"Why don't you just have a great big mixed salad with feta cheese, and loads of bread?" Joanna.

Charlie regretted mentioning his dietary fads the very moment the words "I don't eat meat, actually, so I'm going to have something different" left his mouth. Despite all attempts to the contrary, Charlie had arrived conventionally late and missed the original round of ordering. He was sitting at the head of the table, perched at the edge of a maelstrom of feminine chatter that made his brain hurt.

"I'm not a vegetarian," he protested, aware of the current faddish popularity of the affliction, and not wanting to be considered an arriviste. "I stopped eating meat ten years ago, actually. Definitely wasn't trendy then, particularly as I was living in Argentina at the time, where it's practically against the law not to eat an entire cow every single day of your life."

"You lived in Argentina? Sounds exciting."

Charlie had never lived in Argentina. He had never been to Argentina.

"I think a huge feta salad will do the job," he said. "And then some… bread."

Charlie Stokes released a smile onto the table to frolic and distract. Beth was looking at him keenly through slightly narrowed eyes. Charlie assumed she was either paying him a lot more attention now, or she had wind. Isabelle was as Isabelle is, though he noticed that she wouldn't look him in the face, which must have taken some effort. Alex glowed. Charlie hadn't noticed her much on the previous occasion, because she had been so understated. Tonight she wore a midnight blue ensemble, big hair and party make-up. Joanna radiated and twinkled, but appeared to avert her eyes from Charlie's now and again.

"Jo was telling us about your trip, Charlie," began Alex, now for the first time coming across as the natural head of the flock. Joanna had already had the gossip extracted from her, prior to Charlie's arrival, and he wondered what she'd said.

"Well, the parts I can remember were generally awful." He said.

"Charming," said Jo in a mock-insulted voice, but smiling.

"No. Obviously had you not been there it would have been more awful. Unbearable, in fact."

"That's sweet," said Isabelle to Joanna.

"Very sweet," said Beth to Alex.

"You're a sweet boy," said Alex, "it must have been a horrible day."

"Well no, it was a mixture. I mean, there were some special moments, too. Obviously." Charlie stopped himself gazing at Joanna while he said this, but it was difficult.

"Obviously," they agreed.

What did that mean? Was he saying *obviously* a lot? Was he saying it too much?

"A toast to Jo, for being there for Charlie." Alex raised her glass.

They were all drinking beer. Isabelle slopped a couple of inches' worth into an empty glass in front of Charlie and he raised it to his lips. Jo just smiled.

"Yeah," agreed Charlie. "To Jo."

The beer only needed to enter his mouth for him to feel the slight wave of nausea. He couldn't even take a sip. His body wasn't going to take any of that poison for a while. He looked across at Jo and raised his eyebrows.

"I think it's back on the soft drinks for me," he said.

Suddenly everyone laughed and the ice had broken. Charlie had no idea what Jo had told them, but he suspected she hadn't held back. It was tough being the solitary new male friend in a tight-knit pack of girls.

"I don't think you should be allowed to eat anything you can't prepare yourself from scratch," he suddenly announced, by way of an opening gambit.

"You're going to starve to death then, Izzy," said Beth. She looked at Charlie. "She doesn't cook. She can't cook."

"Why do you say that, Charlie?" asked Alex.

"I'm not a vegetarian. I don't eat meat, but I do sometimes eat chicken."

There was uproar.

"Chicken is meat, isn't it? Yes. I'd say so. It's an animal. Chicken meat. Don't we sometimes use the term chicken meat?" said Alex.

"And I eat fish, of course."

"Fish, too? Really, Charlie, you're a hopeless vegetarian. I can't even believe you bothered bringing it up."

"I didn't say I was a vegetarian. I said I didn't eat meat. I don't eat mammals. Nothing with hair, you know?"

He popped an olive instead. He hated olives.

"That's really interesting," said Alex. She had to saturate her mind with other people's lives, gossip and stories. So everything was interesting to her tonight.

"Nothing with hair? That's how you work it out, is it, Charlie?"

Isabelle did look at him in the eye this time. Charlie, of course, already knew what she was going to say next.

"So you'd eat a snake, then?"

"All I'm saying is that if you can't watch a cow being slaughtered, I'm not sure you have the right to cook its meat. That's all. I'm trying only to eat what I'm prepared to kill myself. That's my theory. But weren't we talking about ballet, just now?"

"So, you can kill a fish?" asked Isabelle.

"I can kill a fish, yes. I have killed a fish. I killed a fish as a child, too. I can do that."

"And you can kill a chicken?"

"I have killed a chicken, yes." Charlie paused. "I ran over it in the car. I know it's not the same thing. I'm still working on the chicken bit."

"His name was Herbert, actually, and he was so big it hurt." Squeals of laughter. Isabelle, of course. "Herbie I called him, obviously."

"If you don't give us a proper measurement, you're out of the competition." Alex was keeping score and was being fastidious. "So is that well hung, very well hung or painful?"

"Painful. Definitely painful," said Isabelle.

"Charlie?" Someone asked.

"I must be exempt, surely?"

"Just checking, sweetie."

"Five times? You? With Derek? That's not true, you're disqualified. If you lie you're disqualified, isn't that right Alex?"

"I was eighteen, at University. In a bed."

"Ditto, ditto and ditto."

"Sixteen, at Caroline's house. Sofa and the carpet."

A barrage of protests.

"No showing off. Just the first time, we said."

"That was the first time. On the sofa, but we fell off before the finish!"

More hysteria. It was Alex's turn. She was tipsy and wistful. All the girls were tipsy, but only Alex was wistful.

"Fifteen. Rimini. On the beach." Gasps of admonishment. "I was sixteen when we did it the second time. It was the night before my birthday. Once before, and once after midnight."

"An Italian, eh?" Joanna made it sound like a dream. Charlie squirmed.

"French, actually."

The disappointment was palpable.

"Nineteen. Front seat of a Cortina. The car park of the Rover's Arms in High Wycombe."

Silence.

"Oh Charlie," said Joanna, blissfully. "That's tragic."

"Yes it is," he said. "And thank you."

"No, all drummers are space cadets," Charlie was now saying. "It's the law, trust me. And Jake's a typical one. So, he does and says things like that practically all the time."

He had finally managed to wrench control of the conversation from the girls and had returned to the theme of Jake's theft of the guitar from the restaurant.

"He can't help it," he went on. "If you want cerebral introversion, you need to get in with the bass players."

"What about harpists?"

"We're still talking about rock and roll, aren't we? Do you know any rock and roll harpists? Seriously?"

"I think once a man gets married," said Isabelle, "it takes his wife a maximum of eighteen months to put an extra two stone on him, darling. As long as I don't learn to cook, there's no way my man will blob up into something I couldn't possible share a bed with."

"I thought the way to a man's heart was through his stomach?"

"Charlie, you're so naïve."

"Not true, then?"

"If I undid two more buttons on my blouse would you notice, or are you more interested in the tiramisu on my plate?"

Charlie pointedly turned his face away from Isabelle, but found himself instead staring at Joanna's top.

"You see?"

"Alex, Tony's lost weight, I'd say." said Beth, "We were only saying that on the way here, weren't we Izzy?"

"Yes. I said you must have been neglecting the kitchen for the bedroom."

"That's right, she did."

Alex laughed. It was the first time Tony's name had come up all evening, and she didn't want that to spoil things now, right at the end.

"Well, I'll be sure to tell him when I get home. I hope you didn't mention anything to him. He's still sniffy about his weight."

"No, we didn't talk to him. He didn't see us. He was in a taxi that stopped at the lights. I was going to wave, and then it pulled away. We were in a hurry on Monday, because a creepy man was following us from work, remember, Beth?"

"How do you remember which day of the week it was?" asked Alex, the words tripping out like a row of innocent children leaving kindergarten. "Anything more than a week or two ago, and the best I can do is whether it was a weekday or a weekend."

"Monday was only the day before yesterday, darling," said Isabelle, almost sounding put out. "I haven't had that much to drink. Are you okay, Jo? You're looking a bit pale."

But it was from Alex's face, under the lovingly applied make-up, that the colour had all but drained.

Charlie Stokes was in the toilet of the Athena. As he had done on the previous occasion, he stood in admiration of the sheer fragrant loveliness of the room. If there was a bathroom in a house somewhere that could boast such a pristine convenience he, for sure, had never been a guest. Considering it was in a restaurant and for public use was nothing short of astonishing. If there was one fault, and he hated to quibble, it was that the pressure not to besmirch its show house perfection was so great, he had felt obliged to sit down to take a piss. Sitting down gave him time to think.

So, he thought for a while.

E Minor

When I returned to the dining area, or more specifically table seven, the silence that greeted me was overwhelming and total. That's because there was nobody there.

Which was odd, I thought.

I had left behind me a dinner party, and returned to the washing up, all in the space of, what, how long had I been in there for? The restaurant was so small, however, that it used up half an eye's effort to pick out the figure of Alex huddled in conference with Dimitrios in the shadow of his gigantic cash register. I was just thinking of joining them to create a far grander occasion, when Dimitrios's laughable attempt at whispering announced to anyone interested that there was some awkwardness regarding a failed credit card payment. So I sat down and wondered where the others were, or rather where Jo was. They couldn't just have upped and legged it, surely? But there were no handbags at the table.

And, where there are no handbags, there are no women.

So, they'd gone all right.

I watched with interest while Dimitrios rubbed his avuncular features with his big hands, as if he were trying to install a better fitting expression. Alex turned and noticed I was back in my seat like a dutiful Labrador, and teased open that poker smile of hers. She was quite big on wistful, was Alex. She hummed a couple more words to the big man, and then floated over.

"Oh dear," she said, sitting down, "this is a bit awkward."

Alex pulled out a pack of Dunhill from her handbag and did the necessary. She tipped her head back and blew a thin trail of smoke in a nor-easterly direction, then offered me the pack. I shook my head.

"I thought all musicians smoked, Charlie?"

"It's a rumour spread by librarians."

"You're funny." She narrowed her eyes and looked into my soul, perhaps to check for litter. "She's a lovely girl," she said.

I'd have said yes if I'd known what she was talking about. Dimitrios had cut off the zither music. It had only been there in the watery background, but the sudden silence left me feeling a bit exposed for some reason. And then he put on some of that bloody awful Kenny G! Why had Dimitrios put on Kenny G? My toes were curling. What the scene needed was a bit of dialogue.

"Where did they everyone go?" I asked.

"They went home."

"Home? Just like that? Without saying goodbye?"

"Well, it was Joanna. She suddenly looked a bit peaky and said she didn't feel well, so the girls took her. They would have waited, but you were gone such a long time."

"Ah."

"It's been a lovely evening, hasn't it, Charlie?"

"Yes. Yes it has. How much am I in for?"

"Ah."

I may have said the exact same word just a few seconds before, but her 'ah' carried a lot more adventure than mine. She smiled again, an apologetic one this time, with all the cracks showing. I sensed time and mascara was weighing heavily on her lashes.

"Can you keep a secret, Charlie?"

Bloody hell, I thought. Not again, surely?

"Yes."

"I thought so."

She stopped looking at me and allowed her eyes to float around the room, probably to give her time to think how to begin. I've found that's usually the hardest part, the beginning.

"It's just that it would be nice to be able to tell someone. The girls mustn't know about this, Charlie. Do you understand?"

She leaned forward, resting on her elbows.

"It's a secret." I said, "I know how it works."

I relaxed as much as I could with Kenny G's squealing execration in support, and listened.

"The first thing, Charlie, have you got any money on you?"

"Yes," I said.

"A lot, or a little?"

"Much less than a lot, a bit more than a little."

I had nearly two hundred Deutschmarks on me, which I considered a small fortune, mostly earmarked for the rent. I knew what was coming, and was grateful it came quickly.

"Would you mind paying for the bill? I'll explain in a minute. And for the other week, too. I know you weren't even with us then, but... I'll explain outside."

"Outside?" That suited me fine.

"I thought we could just go for a walk, maybe towards the Zoo."

"Okay."

"Once we've settled up here?"

I got the picture. I paid the bill. Both of them.

They walked straight down Kantstrasse towards the Tiergarten area. In the dark, this part of West Berlin practically screamed itself hoarse with its neon celebration of consumerism, taunting its neighbours on the East with a flashing, flickering, multi-coloured assault of pointless subsidised excess. Alex had never been interested in politics or sociology and she spent no time pondering life's iniquities, having far too many of her own. She considered another cigarette, but stopped herself. She'd already had more than she'd have liked. Charlie was light on his feet, she noticed, he didn't walk like the average man. There was no swagger or attempt to appear wider or taller. She waited for a group of American army officers to pass.

"You know I'm married, Charlie, yes?"

Charlie hadn't attached any importance to it one way or the other, but his radar began to stutter. He nodded.

"He went to Milan the other day, just for a quick meeting, and hasn't been back. It's not the first time, don't worry."

Charlie acknowledged with a pursed smile and raised eyebrows. He wouldn't worry.

"In the time he's been away, less than a fortnight, the money left my account and the card I use for work expenses wasn't paid off, and it seems the card didn't clear for lunch the other day."

They had to stop, to cross Hardenbergstrasse, but Alex turned left and walked up it, so as not to lose her flow. Charlie noticed they were about to pass by the office of the British Council. He took it as an omen. He was weird like that.

"The thing is, Charlie, my husband Tony, he's not very straight. He takes risks, he bends rules, he… *really* bends rules, you know?"

Charlie didn't, but guessed.

"My father was an accountant with the Mob. Or, rather he was an accountant and he did a couple of little bits for them. Of course, he got caught straight away and, somehow, ran off to Canada. He met Tony there and they became business partners. They were two of a kind, I suppose. That's how I met Tony. I fell for his self-belief, I think."

Charlie smiled knowingly, but carried on walking in silence, wondering why he'd smiled. Alex relaxed into her monologue. She found Charlie easy.

"I've got a good job, at a magazine. I'm only the advertising manager, but it's a fashion magazine and there are perks. Once you get into a lifestyle, it's hard to get out. I invite the girls out practically every week, I've got an expense account, you see. I like the image I have. I like my life. Watch out."

A man pushing a bike, but looking at another man's wife, nearly collided with Charlie. It was louder here. They were at the Zoo Station and all life had been switched on and turned up to full. Charlie had to concentrate to hear what Alexandra was saying.

"My husband has companies and no end of complicated rigmarole that I don't understand, and am not supposed to understand. But I've known for a while that a lot was tied up in shares in two companies that were going to make us rich. Instead, they went down, down and down." She considered whether three times were enough. "And down some more. Then letters arrived, strange demands, you name it. And all this rubbish was in my name. My name, Charlie!"

She stopped walking.

"I found out that Tony's in jail in Toronto, also that he's not in jail in Toronto, also that he's in Berlin and not telling me. Take your pick."

She stood looking to left and right. Charlie noticed that she had the hunted look about her eyes. She opted for that cigarette after all. Charlie waited while she lit it. It meant waiting a while as she was not doing a very good job at it. He decided to contribute to the dialogue, but he was too slow off the mark.

"And what I mean by that, Charlie, is that I don't know where he is, or what to believe. The only thing that is clear as a bell and black and white in front of my eyes," she said, in a sudden smorgasbord of clichés, is that I am effectively bankrupt. If I can get them to stop my salary going into the bank on Friday, and get it in cash, I'll pay you back really soon."

Charlie, not unreasonably, was expecting to hear about the option available if they didn't pay her in cash. It seemed, however, that there was no plan B. Alex was inhaling on her cigarette with such force by now, that Charlie feared for her life.

"Can you get any legal help first?"

"Legal help? That's a laugh."

"I'm sorry."

"No, *I'm* sorry. Look, I'm going this way. Thanks for taking care of that, Charlie, but please don't tell anyone."

"I won't tell anyone. You know I won't."

They went in opposite directions, Charlie with a grateful peck on the cheek as a parting gift. But it wasn't Alex's problems that he was mulling over as he headed East. It was the realization that Joanna was the only one of the group that hadn't unloaded a big secret on him, and he was just wondering whether that was too good to be true.

Thursday, November 5th

We were all at the little *Kneipe* on Kopenickstrasse. The tiny bar no longer had its name on show, we all called it *Downstairs* on account of its proximity to the apartment. We were goofing about with the set list for the Ground Zero gig, and Ritchie and Dan tried to squeeze some juice out of the enigma that was the waitress. Her name was Irina and she was Czechoslovakian, but only in Jake's imagination because in truth she almost never actually spoke and certainly never gave anyone her name or nationality. She was, however, the most ungratefully beautiful girl in the world, and not one of us had ever come across another human less comfortable in her own skin. She had startlingly pale blue eyes like fragments of arctic ice gouged from the depths of her soul, but seemed so distressed by her utterly perfect face that she attired her entire being with layers of gruesome black clothing mined from the vintage clothing shops in West Berlin. But neither her dress sense, nor her purple hair, nor her blue lipstick, nor her nose rings could fully eradicate her drop-dead gorgeousness. For all of us, it was a painful waste of a masterpiece, mindless sexist pigs that we were. She also had legs that could melt rock and in summer you could almost hear the moans of despair of the patrons. It was a relief, really, that she only worked there occasionally.

Troy was dropping by with my ticket at four, so I left and made the short journey to our apartment building. I was surprised to see him already hanging around the landing.

"Hey, dude, better late than never, eh?" That surprised me and I checked my watch, only two minutes past four. "Don't bother looking at that crock of shit. When are you going to buy a real watch, man?"

"Why, what's the time?"

"Twenty-past four. Your phone's ringing."

I hadn't heard a peep from Jo for a week, though Ritchie said she'd called on Monday. Hoping that it was her, I fumbled deliriously with the keys and burst in.

In my rush to reach the phone, I caught my foot on an upturned corner of the senile rug and pitched full into the bookcase, taking no prisoners. I had barely enough time to contemplate life's iniquities, when a copy of Herman Wouk's *The Caine Mutiny* escaped its moorings and landed flush on my left eye. Thicker books have been published, I'll admit, but not many. At least it was the paperback version.

Troy hadn't rushed in after me, so I was sitting up, rubbing my eye and clutching my ribs, by the time he pitched up at my side wearing four layers of amusement.

"Christ, dude, was it worth the rush? You okay?"

"Yeah, yeah," I lied, though I stopped short at pretending nothing had happened, because my ribs were really hurting when I breathed in, there was an odd, sticky sensation around my left eyelid, and my knee was also a bit achy. But, all in all, I was tickety-boo. "I fell."

"You think?" Troy was looking at me curiously. He sucked in some air through his teeth, like he'd just been asked to pull a drawing pin out of somebody's backside. "That's not going to look too good in a minute."

"What?" I said, not much liking the sound of that.

"Your eye's coming up. You should put something on it, dude, like a steak or something."

"What would I be doing with a steak?" I asked. "I've got smoked mackerel, will that do?"

"Some ice, then. You do have ice?"

"Course we've got ice, we're not bloody savages, you know?"

We walked down the stairs and back along the street to the *Kneipe* to get some ice, because it turned out we were savages after all. It may only have been my imagination, but I was sure that the waitress, having perhaps subliminally taken in my new eye, actually looked at me when I reappeared.

Perhaps she was jealous.

"What happened to your eye, Charlie?" Jake was the first to speak. I'm not sure the others even noticed for a while, as it was the kind of place where light was considered an unnecessary luxury.

"Ritchie," I said, "I think I may have cracked a rib."

"In your eye?"

"Seriously, have a look, will you?"

I stood with my elbows raised, pretty much in a carbon copy of the pose I once assumed when being measured for a suit. Ritchie got up and had a poke about. He still hadn't mentioned a thing about his plans to resurrect his medical career.

"Your eye's swelling up, get some ice on it," he said.

"I'll ask Irina," said Jake, bless. He got up and performed a ludicrous mime in front of her, as he spoke neither German nor fantasy Czech, and the only word he had ever uttered to her was *beer*, which he always presented with a German accent, rising diphthong and solitary raised index finger. Ritchie had finished hurting me.

"Well? What do you reckon?" I asked.

"You probably bruised a rib, maybe cracked it. Either way, it'll take care of itself. It'll probably hurt when you yawn, that kind of thing."

"Nothing I can do for it, then?"

"Go to bed early?"

"Funny. Ah."

Irina had returned with some ice cubes in a short squat tumbler. I sensed she was lusting after my eye. Ritchie took the tumbler.

"Need something to put them in, though. Anyone got a handkerchief?"

"A handkerchief?" Jake made it sound as if he'd been asked for a kidney. Ritchie turned to me.

"Just take a sock off, we'll use that."

So, I sat down, took off my left shoe and sock and watched Ritchie load the ice cubes into it. He then placed it on the table and gave it a going over with the base of a glass ashtray. Once he was satisfied, he handed the frozen, sodden mulch to me with a curt patrician nod.

"Put that on your eye for as long as you can stand."

I sat on the chair, semi barefoot and with a sock against my face. I can't say it was a cool look, but it was soothing. And then, suddenly, it came to me: a wolf! An Arctic wolf. That's what Irina reminded me of as she looked at me. Troy handed over a narrow white envelope with the ticket inside.

"You might need binoculars if you want to see the whites of her eyes." He said. "It's near the back."

"That's okay," I said. And it was. "It is kosher, right?"

"Yeah. It's a Colonel's. We traded."

"For what?"

"A favour."

"What's that then, Charlie?" asked Jake. "Whites of whose eyes?"

"Charlie's going to the ballet tonight, boys." Troy made no attempt to sound any less bewildered. "To the opera house over the Wall."

"You're not watching Laura Farey, are you, Charlie?" pleaded Ritchie with a less than subtle hint of envy.

Charlie Stokes nodded.

"You bastard."

"Who's Laura Farey?"

"Are you serious, Dan? 'Who's Laura Farey?'"

"All right, Ritchie, we didn't all go to Cambridge."

"She's only the one prima ballerina in the entire world who still has tits. And you don't need to have been to Cambridge to know that."

Ritchie lifted the tortoiseshell glasses off his aquiline nose and, using a cloth, gave them a rub. I had noticed he had taken to wearing his glasses more often. He was also combing his jet-black hair more regularly, as if he were preparing his return to academia from the outside in.

"A ballerina with tits, Charlie?" enquired Troy, sardonically. "Is that even possible?"

"Wow, you know it's such a shame she's not here," I said, blowing a drip of melting ice off my top lip, "to fully appreciate the high regard she's held in."

"Are they real?" asked Dan.

"Let's drop the tits now, yeah?"

"Okay, Charlie."

Friday, November 6th

Joanna's hair was falling over her left eye and nothing she did to dissuade it from doing so worked. Perhaps she was trying too hard. Hair could be like that, very self-aware. Best not to pay it too much attention and it would probably all settle down out of boredom. She put on her coat and wrapped one of Martina's long silk scarves loosely around her neck. She checked her handbag and made sure everything was there. She imagined Günther would not be late. Before she left she looked in the mirror.

"I should have told Charlie," she thought.

Beth had already ironed Derek's shirt twice, which was perhaps two times more often than she'd have liked. Derek liked white shirts. He had dozens of them. All of them the same. But he was wearing blue tonight. Before she left, she looked in the mirror.

"I do hope I don't fall asleep," she thought.

Alex had wanted her hair cut before the performance and she had sold one of her watches to raise some hard cash. Along with a softer cut, she'd come out of the salon with subtle highlights. She looked good. She ran her fingers through the ends and double-checked her lipstick. She decided, after all, to go with the black and not the brown handbag. No further news from Tony. Herr Reiseneder had vanished. It *was* all over, wasn't it? Before she opened the door, she looked in the mirror.

"So, now what?"

I sabelle had applied her new mascara with intensity.

Her hair cascaded wildly in newly created waves. Her dress, worn for the first time, may have been on the way to a gala night of high culture but, if it could speak, it would be saying:

"Oi, oi, lads, over here!"

She changed her shoes five times in the seven minutes before she left her flat. When she was satisfied, she gave herself a sly wink in the mirror.

"Let's see, then, shall we?"

C harlie Stokes looked at his reflection. With a full day to brew into a fuller, more rounded stain, his black eye was now the centrepiece of his face. He stood and wondered whether it lent him a certain insouciance.

"No," he decided.

East Berlin.

T here was a buzz around the foyer, typical of a gala night. Well-dressed elegance, well-intentioned sartorial misfires, and the inevitable mutton dressed as lamb mingled in harmony. Thin spirals of cigarette smoke wriggled upwards to dance amongst the chandeliers. The Party apparatchiks strutted around in effortless arrogance, while a flock of chinless Embassy staff cackled and howled for Empire.

Charlie Stokes had made it through the border control with a surprising lack of the unexpected. He had received his one-day visa after having been forced to exchange twenty-five Deutschmarks for the East German equivalent, at an exchange rate of one for one. That the real world value of the East German mark was a fraction of that was clear from the near weightlessness of the coinage, made from wafer-thin discs of lightweight aluminium. Charlie, the first time he'd had a handful of the stuff, had reminded himself not to leave it lying around, in case a breeze should waft past and lift it up into the heavens.

He'd taken a bus, and stood in the middle, by the doors. The bus was full. When a pair of stern soldiers entered, he was disturbed to see two middle-aged women automatically give up their seats for them - a wordless manoeuvre that elicited nothing by way of acknowledgment from the men, for whom such deeds were clearly expected and demanded. Charlie considered directing a pitiful condescending sneer in their direction and, in the interests of balance, he also considered not doing so.

When he alighted and walked to the Opera House, the two soldiers, in their olive uniforms, did the same. It was not black tie for everyone, then. Not, of course, that Charlie was in a tux. He had one, just not in Berlin. He wore the same set up he took to Luke's funeral. Charlie was not a superstitious man, though maybe he should have been, with hindsight.

The *Staatsoper* was lit up by a haze of orange light hovering over the building, too shy to actually touch it. Bullets, bombs, and shrapnel of every denomination had tried to bring the edifice to its knees without success. It then stood in pockmarked, roofless isolation, like the architectural equivalent of an orphaned leper, for ten years before it was resuscitated, and the city's opera buffs were welcomed back within its elegant Palladian exterior.

Of course, none of that meant a thing to Charlie Stokes, who'd gone down on record saying that, as far as opera or ballet was concerned, he could leave it or leave it. While admitting that a sighting of Laura Farey in the flesh had its merits, he was here to surprise Joanna. And for that he could endure far worse than an evening of ballet.

It was busy on the Unter Den Linden. The *Staatsoper* could hold over a thousand and it felt that they had all arrived at the same time. The steps leading into the opulent entrance suddenly welled up with a dark mass of humanity. It reminded Charlie, irrationally, of trying to get into White Hart Lane, just without the chants about going home in a big white ambulance. As Charlie blended into it, and began to shuffle up the steps, he bumped into a tall, athletic man. There was quite a bit of shoulder bumping breaking out, though nothing to cause an international incident.

"Sorry," said Charlie, instinctively.

"English?" replied the man, in a heavily-accented but pleasant voice.

"Guilty as charged."

"I hope you have a nice evening," said the man.

Polite smiles were exchanged during a perceptible slowing in the pace before Charlie became aware of a second man who was keener to move things along. He whispered something under his breath that may have been *Komm Christian*, or may not have been. Charlie thought the shorter man had looked almost nervous. The tall man acknowledged the words, with the faintest of impatient nods, and off they strode. The taller man strode well. Unfeasibly long legs did that to a man. At the top of the steps, Charlie stepped to one side to look back across the street. By his relaxed standards, he felt both overdressed and out of place. It was clear, by the sartorial heavy weaponry rolling up the Unter Den Linden, that he could safely scrap the former and reiterate the latter. Joanna could see through the packaging, at least.

Christian and Max were mingling in the foyer, taking in the atmosphere along with the scents of expensive mistresses. Max should have been looking forward to the evening more than he was, but his head was still reeling from the impact of Christian's escape plan. What annoyed him the most was not that it was the kind of plan a six-year old might have thought up as a joke, but that it could quite conceivably work. They had walked to the *Staatsoper*, specifically so that Christian could outline his ideas without any danger of being overheard. Max knew that Christian would not even have told his own girlfriend, though she was an ex-girlfriend now. They had been walking briskly - Christian barely knew how to walk any other way - and when the essence of the escape route had been outlined, Max had been so shocked, his legs had stiffened as surely as if he'd been chinned by a gorilla.

"A trampoline?"

"Come, Maxie, keep moving."

"A trampoline? You want us to *bounce* over the Wall, Christian? On a *trampoline*? Are you completely and utterly insane?"

Max felt a leaden sickness in the pit of his stomach. He couldn't decide whether the crushing disappointment was a result of the plan itself or the knowledge that his best friend, and the brightest man he knew, had come up with it.

"I felt the same when the idea came to me the first time. But, you know, the more I tried to think about other ways, the more I kept coming back to the trampoline."

"You mean you had other plans, Christian, that were worse than this one?"

The next four minutes passed by without words. Max used the time to give the trampoline idea some gestation time. Once the initial surprise had subsided, the true worth of the scheme would undoubtedly make itself known and all would be happiness and light again.

"Jesus Christ, Christian, but what other plans did you have that could possibly have been worse?"

"We're teachers, but we're sportsmen at heart. We're fit, strong, determined, competitive. We don't need a plan that involves false papers, and a clever story, and a complicated plot and lots of interlinked episodes that all have to come off perfectly at the right time. No. We must find something new, something quick, sudden. One, two, three, gone!"

There was a glint in his eyes, whether of joy or madness Max didn't like to guess. "It's always the element of surprise that brings the prize, Max."

"Well, you're right about the element of surprise."

"We can go in June. No rush. We have to train and practice and rehearse."

"Where?"

"In the gymnasium of course. That's where all the equipment is. And that's where no one will ever be surprised to see us. It'll work."

Christian felt good. He knew Max would react this way. They had been practically inseparable for over twenty years. But that wasn't why he felt good. He felt good because now that he had articulated the plan, it had become real. The countdown had begun.

"Give me a cigarette, Christian."

Max wanted to look more arty and tortured, like others in the foyer. He even wished he had thrown more cologne over himself. He stood there, absorbing some more of the atmosphere.

"Hey, have you noticed that woman who keeps looking at you?"

"Yes."

Alexandra looked up, her eyes falling on the man's profile across the crowded foyer. She hadn't meant it to be anything more than a passing glance, but she caught herself looking over several times. Luckily the tall, straight-backed man with the close crop of fair hair hadn't noticed.

Alex was with Beth and Derek. Beth was wearing what she called her captain-of-the-bowls team ensemble of a white blouse under a navy silk jacket, but she could not have cared less. Derek was resplendent in a wide-lapelled mahogany suit that had drawn an involuntary twitch from Isabelle's eyelids. Isabelle, in turn, had launched herself into the crowd in search of mischief, like a heat-seeking missile. That Charlie Stokes had just stepped into her line of fire was his misfortune.

E Minor

I stood about a yard inside the opera house, being buffeted by a constant swell of passing handbags and shoulders, very much like a small trawler that had run out of fuel. What I should have done was keep moving and jostling. I should have taken a lap or two of the foyer until I got a feel for the smell and the clothes and the hubbub. By stopping, a single stride in, I had inadvertently made a statement. *Here I am*, I was saying. *Charlie Stokes has entered the room, please be upstanding.* But I was out of place. I had lost confidence in my clothes, possibly my hair was dishevelled. And I was definitely ten years too old to seriously believe that having intentionally non-matching socks was a statement of youthful originality.

Most of all, I had a black eye.

I couldn't see Joanna anywhere, though I wasn't sure whether she would be out here in the open, or beavering away behind the scenes, as I didn't exactly know what it was she actually did. I imagined that she'd either be hustling about with a harassed clipboard for comfort, or dressed to the nines as just another member of the congregation. I had just decided that the best way to find her would be to launch myself into the human undergrowth, when I was accosted.

"Ooh," squealed the voice, "what a lovely eye, Charlie! It really sets off your hair."

Even Isabelle was better than being alone.

"Yeah, thanks," I said, inadequately.

"Very sexy look, I might add," she said, taking me by the elbow and leading me away from the entrance. "The cloakroom's over here. A bit of a scrum, darling. Does it hurt? The eye."

"No," I said. "Bit itchy now and then."

She laughed and bit her lower lip at this, which I assumed meant there was more to what I had said than mere words. There wasn't. Isabelle was not very tall, even perched as she was atop a pair of quite ludicrously high heels. What I had never noticed about her, because she had never worn such a revealing dress before, was just how generous the breast fairy had been to her. To paraphrase someone or other, she had fallen off the cleavage tree and hit every branch on the way down. None of which would have mattered, were it not that I seemed always to be looking at them when turning to try and hear what she was saying. And Isabelle always seemed to be noticing that I was looking at them.

And, obviously, I was looking at them when Joanna prodded me in the sore ribs with the edge of her handbag.

"Charlie?"

"Jo."

"I didn't know you were coming. Why didn't you say?"

She wasn't talking to me. She was talking to my black eye. The smile was there, and the deep brown eyes, and the impenetrable expression. Oh, and a man was there. She had a man with her.

"Well, you did recommend it," I said to Jo. "The ticket was hard to come by. Luckily I'm well hung." *What?* "I mean, connected."

"I'm sure you'll love it."

"Yes."

It was the man from outside the Consulate. Obviously I couldn't remember his name, why on earth would I? He and Joanna were too close to each other, weren't they?

"Jo, you have to see what Derek threw on," said Isabelle. "I can't believe Beth is that desperate. You wouldn't wear a suit like that, would you Günther?"

Günther. That was it. I couldn't have cared less whether he would have worn a suit like that or not.

"Good evening, Charlie. I've been hearing about you."

He held out his hand as he did outside the Consulate, and I took it. If I were a connoisseur of handshakes, I'd have put his in the diplomatically perfect category. It was dry, firm but not aggressive, brief but not perfunctory, well-practised, harmless yet unmistakable. I spent too much time thinking about the handshake.

"Hello," I said. I had to say something, and that seemed to cover it.

Günther Reisz was an interesting piece of work. I suppose he was handsome enough in a Paul Newman sort of way, if that was your thing. He was around fifty years old, with an ease about him that I found disconcerting: a man for whom the word unfazed fitted as snugly as his suit. Without any doubt, he was planning something, and if he'd heard about me, then he must have been aware that I was too. It should have been awkward, but he just stood there. I'd seen more concern on the face of a man being asked if he'd like his tea stirred clockwise or counter-clockwise.

"What happened with your eye, Charlie?" asked Joanna. "Does it hurt?"

"No, but he says it itches," said Isabelle, ever helpful.

"I fell," I said.

"You're coming to the party after, Charlie?" Joanna said.

"Of course." *What party?* "It's the only reason I'm here." I wondered whether anyone else thought my voice sounded nervous and artificial.

"Oh, there's Andrew, I need to talk to him," said Jo - not to me, to the Günther man. "Be with you in a minute." That part she said to me. They walked away, he and mine. I turned to Isabelle's breasts.

"So," I asked them, "Günther is…"

"Debonair. Come on, let's find a programme. You can use it to fan yourself down."

"Have they been out before this evening?"

"Joanna dates lots of older men, Charlie. Some girls just prefer it. Looking for a father figure, that's all. Harmless enough. I do it myself sometimes. Not always, mind, because young men have so much energy, don't they Charlie? And show me a girl who doesn't need a bit of energy now and then."

I allowed Isabelle to manhandle me through a small phalanx of Party officials, each hopelessly inadequate at not staring at her cleavage, and tried unsuccessfully not to turn round to see what Jo was up to. It was only then, while fidgeting around in my trouser pockets out of stress or nerves, that I noticed my flies were open. I'm always ready to entertain.

"You're not going to flash everyone, are you Charlie?" Isabelle never missed a trick.

"No, you're all right," I said, "I'll wait until the interval."

As the bell sounded, and the masses shuffled eagerly into the auditorium itself, Alex was drawn towards the tall man. He was talking to the friend he had come in with. An usher was checking their tickets and redirecting them to a more suitable entrance. He looked up and their eyes met again. He smiled at her, self-consciously, and Alex smiled back. When Alex was shown to her seat, she was not at all surprised to find him next to her. In a theatre with a capacity in excess of one thousand hearts, she took it as a sign. A good sign. The man stood up and gave a curt nod. Alex was always a sucker for good manners and chivalry.

"Alexandra," she said, by way of introduction. "What a lovely theatre."

"Yes. It's your first time here?"

"Yes."

"You're English?" They were speaking in German. Her accent wasn't up to much.

"Yes. I work in West Berlin."

"Really?"

"I'm looking forward to the performance."

"Yes," he said, "my friend also. He adores the ballet, but he's never seen an English prima ballerina. Max is a fan of the Bolshoi."

Alex had to look round the tall man to get a view of his friend who seemed mildly ill at ease.

"My name is Christian," he said.

Alex took the proffered hand. Strong fingers. He had sort of greyish blue eyes, she thought. It was hard to tell without staring. It was too soon for staring. She looked ahead, her hands crossed on her lap, as the empty seats quickly filled and the rhubarb-rhubarb babel of the masses floated up and across her consciousness. She drifted into a soft, dream-like state. The orchestra tuned up, and the sound washed over her. Bliss, at last.

"Have you seen Laura Farey dance many times before?" asked Christian.

"Just once," Alex replied, with a start. "In London. At the Royal Opera House, it was lovely."

"London. One day I would like to go."

"You've never been yet?"

"No." He leaned forward to whisper theatrically. "There's a wall between us."

Alex had not given an iota of thought to the possibility that anyone not dressed in army fatigues or wearing those Party-approved charcoal suits, might have been a normal regular Ossi. But the news seemed only to further swaddle her emerging new view on life.

"Well," she said, "not right now there isn't."

Beth and Derek had adjacent seats, of course, Isabelle had seen to that. Beth thought it hysterical that she was sitting three rows in front of her Soviet opposite number. Beth had a file on her as thick as a Jeffrey Archer novel and twice as interesting. Evgenia Petrovna Vladimirova was forty-two years old and if that was her genuine hair colour, then Beth was a custard slice. Beth knew everything there was to know about Evgenia, including that she was a lot better-looking in the flesh than in her photos, the bitch. That everything she knew of Evgenia, Evgenia knew about her, bothered her not one bit. It was all just a silly game, anyway.

As the orchestra warmed up and the house lights began to dim, the air of expectancy was palpable. Charlie Stokes couldn't help but wish that it were Elvis Presley who was standing on the other side of the heavy curtain when it opened. He wondered, as he took one final sweep of the theatre before it fell into darkness, how many of the other shadowy figures might have felt the same. There was a tightness in his chest and stomach. His mood was taking a dip. His crush on Joanna was deep and painful. Perhaps the sight of Laura Farey's thighs would help.

Isabelle smiled and gave a girly wave to the company's marketing manager, Andrew Tait, known to his friends as Fat Steve. She had worked hard to make this event run smoothly, and was feeling just a tiny bit smug that, so far, things couldn't have gone more smoothly.

And that was exactly how Joanna was feeling, having been a pillar of support to Isabelle since the project began when, with a distant echoing bang, all the lights went out.

During the intermission, trade at the bar roared, with an acceptable level of mildly polite jostling. The electrical shut-down had moved quickly from catastrophe to mere inconvenience thanks to the rapid response of the Staatsoper's technical team who, luckily, had been in the basement at the time, having themselves been the cause of the bang. Certain unidentified members of the audience had lived through a painful second or two in anticipation of a stray bullet to the forehead, but it quickly passed. The inevitable brief delay had acted as a perfect warm-up for the main event. So, by the time the curtain rose for the second time and the orchestra launched themselves with flagrant abandon at the score, the audience had to be held back, metaphorically, from leaping to their feet and whooping.

Laura Farey had been stunning. Charlie Stokes knew effectively nothing about ballet, but that was more than enough to appreciate the astonishing artistry on show. By the end of the first half, he had begun to mull over Luke's clichéd premise that you could always tell how good a girl was in bed by the way she danced. Mr Farey was a lucky bastard. With the sap rising, Charlie's thoughts had turned to Joanna.

He saw her, amongst the animated throng, smiling and mingling. She was adept at both. He hadn't minded sitting alone in the auditorium, in the dark and without need for social distraction. But out in the open, so to speak, he was relieved to see Isabelle's breasts coming towards him carrying two glasses of orange juice.

"Charlie, darling, you look parched. Take one."

E Minor

I *was* parched, as it happened. I sent the contents down the hatch in a single throw. Cool, refreshing and, of course, not orange juice at all. I was glad I'd had the foresight to line my stomach with a decent dollop of macaroni cheese before I'd headed out East.

"Steady on, Charlie, you're allowed to sip it, you know."

"What was it?"

"Vodka and orange, darling."

"Vodka with orange, more like."

"You don't have to drink it."

"Too late."

"Another one?"

"Go on then."

It was the wrong thing to have said of course, and not for the first time in my life. A convivial atmosphere flexed its muscles in amongst the dense smoke. The first act had been well received, though it would have been hard to imagine a scenario where it wouldn't have been. Laura Farey had an absolute belter, and the rest of the cast supported her impeccably. The orchestra had gnawed through the senses at every opportunity, and the expectation was that there would be more of the same to come, with encores and bouquets. My mind was already on the party afterwards. And so was Isabelle's.

It was surprising just how many vodka and oranges one can fit in during a single intermission.

A lex and Christian had moved to the far left side of the bar. Max stood alongside them, there but not there. If life were a bowl of cherries, he'd come out smelling of gooseberry. He had been almost as engrossed in the performance as he had expected to be. Almost, because at every lull and pause in the hour's ebb and flow, he could hear Christian and Alex exchange a relentless flow of light but probing conversation, in the kind of hushed velvety tones that made the hairs in Max's nostrils squirm. He was a man who took life seriously and was not fond of surprises or acts of irrationality. Women, in his experience, were harbingers of both. The English lady was far too attractive to be brushed off like an errant strand of sauerkraut, and considerably more fragrant.

For her part, Alex had been caught by a sucker punch. From the moment she had first seen him, she had inexplicably been drawn to Christian's upright, almost aristocratic stance. She had known immediately, from that first cursory glance into his eyes, that he was a man of intelligence and honesty. There was also something indisputably down-to-earth about him. Here was a man who would tell it how it is, and expect no less in return.

Beth smiled. Poor old Charlie, she thought. Isabelle is infusing him with a third vodka and orange. It will all end in tears, or a second black eye.

"What's that you say?" asked Derek.

"I say it will all end in tears."

"Yes."

The second act was inspirational. Farey's finale with Oleg Smirnoff flew off the stage and into legend on an orchestral flourish so overwhelming that there was slack-jawed silence from the audience while it pieced itself back together and exploded into applause.

Alex had been holding Christian's hand. She couldn't remember for how long, but she knew she couldn't clap with just the one, so she let it go and stood up with the rest. She caught a glimpse of Max while she did so. It was obvious that he didn't approve. She wondered why, but not for long. There could have been a hundred reasons. She didn't care about any of them.

Charlie Stokes, decorum having been erased by the vodka, stood up and yawned with such violence that he winced from his rib injury. He was far too young to be thinking the thoughts he was thinking, but he thought them nevertheless. Nice comfy bed, please, here and now and let's be quick about it. There was a deal more applauding and standing to be got through first, and by the time the bouquets had been shared around and people finally began to shuffle along towards the aisles, power had returned to his legs. He made it to the foyer and stood in forlorn hope of being scooped up by Joanna, although he had worked out by now that this might not have been the best occasion for a quiet chat. Alex waved at him pleasantly. She'd been avoiding him, he thought, or was that some bloke she was chatting up? Good for her, let's hope he's loaded.

The general scene appeared to be one of rapid exit. In the same surprising way that a football stadium discharged its cargo in the seeming blink of an eye, the *Staatsoper* emptied like a bath with seven plugholes, and almost as loudly.

A hand ran across his bottom before clinging onto his left arm. Isabelle.

"Which way did you come through, Charlie?"

"Checkpoint Charlie."

"Of course!"

"Where's the party, then?"

"Stay here. You're coming with me."

E Minor

At that point I already knew what was going to happen. It's just a sensation you get deep down.

So, there wouldn't have been any point fighting it, would there?

The Berlin Wall was three and a half metres high, probably a metre or so wide. That was just the first one. They could take it by the Spree. A swim after the jump. It was possible. Surprise factor alone would give them a huge advantage. But what a jump!

It could work. It would take a lot of practice and trial and error. But they had the perfect cover for that at the gymnasium. It would take months to be sure they had it right. But what would a few months matter?

Max had given Christian's plan plenty of thought during the interval, as Christian had deserted him to chat up the English woman. What was the man thinking, anyway? His girlfriend had just left him. Even now they were inseparable, idly chattering about Leipzig of all things. The foyer was quiet, though not at all empty. As Max watched Christian and the woman attentively, he sensed movement behind him and saw the woman acknowledge someone with a bright smile. From behind him Max heard another English voice say:

"Alex, here's someone I'd like you to meet."

It was Joanna, her face a picture of serenity and relief at a job well done. Alongside her, still in costume and with full stage make-up, stood Laura Farey. She had an over-sized faux-fur coat over her shoulders. Evidently, they were about to nip outside.

"They want a couple of photos outside."

Alex extended a gracious hand.

"It was quite, quite lovely," she said, nodding blissfully. "Really, words are not enough, utterly beautiful."

"Thank you. I'm glad you enjoyed it."

Laura Farey dazzled them with a flashing white smile, and Max caught the full brunt of it. He practically wet his pants in excitement. He tried desperately to close his mouth. Ravishing was the word he would have used to describe her, had his brain not frozen. Joanna led Laura Farey towards the door, snatches of conversation trailing in their wake.

"You are certain this is not real fur?"

"It's fake, really."

"People might think it's real."

"It won't be in the photos. It'll be cold outside, between shots."

In the ensuing silence, Christian thought he could hear the hinges squeaking on Max's jaw as it swung slowly from side to side. He bent down and whispered in his friend's ear.

"Max?"

"Not now, Christian. I'm not completely here."

West Berlin

The party was in a club on Pariser Strasse, a few doors down from Madow but smaller and with safer, blander pop aimed at discouraging the underground crowd. Duran Duran and Wham seemed to be battling for supremacy, but it was hearing the Bee Gees' *You Win Again* that drove Charlie Stokes to the pavement outside. He wasn't there long before Joanna, who had been waiting for the opportunity, hunted him down alone.

"Hello, Charlie."

"Oh. Hello."

"Are you here to get the smoke out of your eyes, like me?"

"No. To get the Bee Gees out of my ears."

Joanna hugged herself against the change in temperature. "How are you feeling?"

It was a vague question that worked on a number of depths. Charlie took it on at the shallowest. "Me? Good. Yeah. Never better. Why?"

Joanna knew Charlie had been drinking again, but couldn't tell what level of damage had been inflicted so far, or whether there would be any point in trying to talk to him.

"I rang you the other day. You were out. Did anyone say?"

"Yes I know. I didn't ring back because…"

"You don't have my number. Yes."

"Nothing urgent then, obviously?"

Now that he was outside, Charlie realised that he had already drunk more than he could handle. Perhaps the chill night air was making the blood try too hard to pump some warmth into his body, but he could almost feel the alcohol sloshing against his secret hoard of private words, threatening to flush them out completely through his mouth to cause who knows what kind of trouble.

Joanna smiled and shook her head.

"You're coming to the Ground Zero gig next month, right? You're my guest of honour."

"Of course," said Joanna. "It's only fair now that you came to mine tonight."

"Indeed," said Charlie. "Good point. Although I was not," he said, "guest of honour. Not even guest *ordinaire*, really."

Joanna ignored the remark by looking down Pariser Strasse at a red Wartburg that had coughed to a standstill.

"Is Isabelle waiting for you?"

"Isabelle?" Charlie felt a jolt of adrenaline as he assumed a defensive position. "Why would she be waiting for me? Is Gerhard waiting for you?" And so what if it smarted, he thought.

"Who's Gerhard?"

"Who indeed? He certainly came from out of nowhere, that one, eh?"

"Do you mean Günther?"

"I might do."

"Shall we stretch our legs a bit, Charlie?"

She didn't wait for an answer and Charlie was caught by surprise, bounding after her unevenly with his hands thrust deeply into his pockets. As he appeared alongside her, she slid an arm through his, in search for some shared warmth. Charlie could smell the club's cigarette smoke escaping from her hair.

"Did you ever miss not having a Mum and Dad? I know you can't miss what you never had but..."

"You can't miss what you never had."

"Did you ever hate any of your friends for having them, when you visited them after school?"

"I was told never to hate anything."

"You said you hated Kenny G."

"Obviously, that's allowed."

They passed the red Wartburg and both failed to notice that Troy Cafarella was in the front seat, carefully folding a fresh stick of chewing gum into his mouth.

"I hated my friends for having Dads, sometimes," said Joanna. "Especially when I was a teenager and they were all arguing with theirs. I thought 'at least you've got one to argue with.'"

"My Grandad did his best, I suppose," said Charlie, thinking back as best he could. "But it's a generation jump, isn't it?"

"What is?"

"I don't know."

"I had a twin brother. He died at birth. I wasn't told until I found out. The other day, when you were speaking about Chad Cafarella, I got it into my head that you might have been him. That he hadn't died. That he had to be sent away for some reason."

"So he could end up broke in West Berlin?"

"Shut up, Charlie."

She was tired, and it showed, though not clearly enough to Charlie. He was drunk and decided not to shut up.

"Why on earth would you think I was your brother?"

"You know nothing about your mother, just whatever someone has wanted to tell you. You knew that song, your parents knew Cafarella, you were born on the same day. It's not such a stupid thing to think."

"It's completely stupid. Did you say anything to your Mum about it?"

"Obviously. And of course you're not my brother."

"I could have told you that. You look beautiful when you're angry."

"I'm not angry."

"Trust me, I know a Doctor, you're angry."

"Stop it, Charlie, I'm trying to tell you something."

"There's more? Fire away."

But it had passed now, that moment where she could have said what she had wanted to say. Joanna stood, feeling cold, glancing first up, then down the street. And that's when Charlie took her by the waist and kissed her on the lips. She almost slipped on the damp pavement as she backed away.

"Charlie, what are you doing?"

A strange question, Charlie thought, under the circumstances.

"I was just kissing you, Jo." He sounded like a small, confused child.

Joanna had pressed herself against the window of a jeweller's. In a bizarre act of self-defence she had grabbed Charlie's hands and was still holding them, comforted to know where they were.

"Why?"

Charlie's confusion wasn't wearing off.

"Why? Because I want to, that's why. Because..." he paused to confirm he had the words lined up in the right order and ready for launch. "Because I love you."

Joanna tensed, and lifted Charlie's hands to her face. She held them there for a second, with her eyes closed, then lowered them again. This wasn't going very well.

"Now can I kiss you?"

"You're drunk."

"I don't mind."

Joanna frowned and began to breathe quickly. The best thing was to get back to the party. But she didn't know how to start.

"What?" said Charlie. "You don't like me, is that it?" He thought he sounded like a ten-year-old in a playground.

"Of course I like you, Charlie," she said through clenched teeth. "Why would you ask such a thing? Come here."

She stepped forward and hugged Charlie. He held her, but lightly because he couldn't read the signals she was giving off. She spoke into his ear, to avoid eye contact.

"I love you too, Charlie. But it's complicated." Charlie lost the second sentence on account of the first. "We could be such great friends, Charlie, really special friends."

"I don't want to be great, special friends. I want to be… I love you."

"I can't, Charlie."

"Why not?"

Joanna pulled out of the embrace and stared at Charlie with a hint of desperation in her eyes.

"Isn't it obvious, Charlie? Can't you just guess?"

Charlie didn't have to guess. He had seen it coming over a week ago. He always knew that money talked and women listened.

"You've got someone else."

It was a question but it came out as a statement. Joanna did not answer. She did not need to answer. She could not answer. Charlie bit his lip, turned sharply on his heels and headed back to the party with Joanna's voice ringing in his head.

"Charlie. Wait. Let me explain."

But Charlie was already stumbling back down the stairs. He was greeted by a bouncing Isabelle, two Rum and Cokes, and the second verse of Rick Astley's *Never Gonna Give You Up*. There was enough promise in the first two to forgive the third.

"Cheers, Charlie!" She thrust the glass towards Charlie while simultaneously draining a generous slug from her own. Charlie followed suit.

"Cheers!" he shouted.

"Let's dance!"

"To this? I'd rather you poked my eye with a toothpick."

"Hang on, I'll go and get one."

She turned and shimmied towards the bar as a joke. Halfway there, she turned to face Charlie. He wasn't sure if she was dancing or having a seizure. He blinked and drained his glass. She was dancing.

A lex touched up her lipstick, and made a few unnecessary adjustments to her hair, which was still perfect. It crossed her mind to stay home and think. She felt she had plenty to think about. But she had promised to attend the party and had to maintain some semblance of normality.

What a strange evening, she thought. He was just some chap at the ballet, and she could seriously not imagine that meeting someone could be so effortless. Not even as a child, when friendships are forged on the briefest and flimsiest of premises, had conversation been so fluid and painless and utterly relaxing.

Perhaps it had been so long since she felt any sense of togetherness with Tony that she read too much into this man. Well, she would see on Tuesday. He had asked to see her again and they had arranged it for Tuesday. She giggled at her reflection.

"It's just a harmless crush, Alex. Don't make a fool of yourself, eh?"

E Minor

B eing drunk was growing on me. All over me, in fact. Everything was so funny, and everyone was so beautiful. Or ugly. I had given myself some rules, and they were working like a dream. Drink stuff with fruit juice or a soft drink: nice taste. Then, and this was the important bit that Troy had forced me to sign up to, a glass of water once an hour. Also, keep moving - dancing counted.

I forgot to drink water, or move, but no one's perfect. I had managed to avoid Beth, if not her quizzical looks whenever Isabelle groped me. And Joanna? I had put her to one side for the moment. Tomorrow I would let that thought do what it had to. Right now, I didn't need thoughts.

"Tequila!"

Well, that made me jump. Isabelle had a tray with four measures of tequila and two small saucers, one with lime quarters, the other a small heap of salt. I may not have been a drinker, but I knew what was coming. The best way to handle a Tequila Slammer is to be in a different town from where they're being served. On the other hand, when you're in the company of a good-time girl with plenty of exposed skin, alcoholic apocalypse is a price you might be willing to pay for the entertainment value. Suddenly, the soundtrack changed, and out of the mire of pop came the unmistakeable opening chords of The Champs' *Tequila*. Isabelle had even nobbled the DJ.

A small crowd of lunatics immediately gathered, like vultures round a terminally sick antelope. Isabelle handed the tray to one of them, a goofy-looking man with a toupee in the same shade as his tie. She picked up a piece of lime, and looking me straight in the eye, rubbed it against her left breast. She took a large pinch of salt and sprinkled it onto the wet skin, and placed the lime between her lips. Now it was my turn. I took one of the shots of tequila and bent down to lick the salt off her breast. Not too bad. I drank the tequila in one go and sucked on the lime that Isabelle was holding within her lips. There was inevitable lip-on-lip contact.

There are worse ways to spend seven seconds. The little entourage cheered. Isabelle took another slice of lime and tugged at my shirt until it came out of my waistband. She lifted it up and rubbed the lime into my abdomen. She added the salt. She took a shot of tequila and finally gently placed the lime in my mouth. Then she went through the same procedure as I had, only she took a lot longer than seven seconds over it. Once again, our little audience cheered. The show went on, taking longer each time, until all four shots were gone and I was kissing Isabelle wildly because she had taken her lime into her mouth and I was just looking round for it.

That was when she had whispered hotly in my ear:

"Let's go."

Three minutes later I was in the back seat of a taxi, rubbing the inside of Isabelle's thigh for something to do, before it hit me that I had indeed forgotten to think about Joanna. No, that wasn't what hit me. What hit me was that I was in the back seat of a taxi rubbing the inside of Isabelle's thigh for something to do.

"Have I missed it all?" said Alex breathlessly. "Alex. Lovely to see you," said Joanna. "Beth's at a corner table. She's grumpy."

"What's she grumpy about?"

"Isabelle got a bit crazy, that's all. You know how embarrassed Beth gets."

"Where is Izzy?"

"She left."

"Shame."

"With Charlie."

"Oh?"

"I'm so tired, Alex, I didn't realise how nervous I'd been until it was all over. My God, when the lights went out I could have died." She laughed.

"It was a lovely evening, Joanna, you and Izzy should be very proud. And Charlie? Before he left, was he himself at all?"

"That's a very good question, Alex. It's always so hard to tell."

"Have you spoken to him tonight?"

"Yes, but he's a bit drunk again, unfortunately. He doesn't know exactly what he's saying."

Alex tensed. She wondered what Charlie had not exactly been saying. Instead, she chose to think about Christian and this evening and next Tuesday, so Charlie didn't seem to matter. She went off in search of Beth, who certainly appeared in need of a shot of something enervating, and left Joanna alone.

Joanna would have been happier to still have Günther there to talk to. He was so calm and unperturbed. Perhaps her mother was right, after all, and mature men were the future. That made her smile. It also made her think about Charlie. The longer she knew him, the more complicated he seemed to become. Boys weren't supposed to be like that, were they?

"If only you were a girl, Charlie," she said under her breath, "I think you'd make a really good one." There was no doubt in her mind that Isabelle was going to have him on toast. The idea saddened her. And that confused her.

East Berlin

The contrast could not have been greater, and it was not lost on Christian as he watched his neighbour make heavy weather of saying goodbye to her boyfriend: Alexandra had artfully cut hair, his neighbour a sad, self-inflicted perm. It was East and West Berlin encapsulated in one superficial observation.

Christian and Max flopped onto the two remaining armchairs and sat in silence. Max had made up his mind not to say a word about the woman. He was prepared to believe that Christian was just trying to show that he still had it, now that Helga had left him. He lit a cigarette, like he had always done in this room, and waited for Christian to start speaking, like he had always done in this room. But the silence continued past the point of comfort, so Max broke it first.

"When do you want to do it?"

He spoke in that low-pitched mumble favoured by plotters. From now on, they would be living a lie. Not a single one of their friends or family could know what they were up to. Even a single confidant was like a hole in a bucket - sooner or later, your secret is a big pool of piss on the ground.

We're going to need three months of training. Let's double it for safety and call it six, or thereabouts. We'll go over in May, what do you say?"

Nothing. That's what Christian had to say.

"It's three, four metres we're looking at. It's going to take a lot of practice, Christian, but it's possible. I'll give you that much, you bastard, it's possible. And definitely unexpected. So, yes. Okay? I'm in. Now let's have something to drink. And say something, for God's sake!"

Max got up and went into the kitchen. It always amazed him how much a kitchen died once a woman bequeathed it to a man. There was nothing left to drink, of course, not anywhere, as he should have known since he had finished the last of it.

"Don't just smile in that way, Christian, please. This is a serious business now. Smiling is over."

But for Christian the smiling was only just beginning. Max was on board and already overexcited about the escape and the training required. That made him smile, of course. Good old Max and his faux-grumpy pessimistic front on life! And there was Alexandra. How about that, then? Too good to be true? A trap? Christian smiled again, but this time at his own paranoia. No, Alex was just one of those beautiful moments in life that Fate occasionally drops onto the floor. He was very much looking forward to seeing her again.

It would be no bad thing to have an ally on the other side, too, but no need to tell Max about that. Max wouldn't understand.

West Berlin

So much in life is judged according to context. You happily go to the theatre to watch a couple of hours of well-presented hoo-hah by an actress you really like, but cringe with embarrassment if the same girl trots out at half-time at the football to draw the raffle. You happily stand, tongue lolling, in front of a Mk II Golf GTI glistening indoors on a plinth made of lightly brushed aluminium, yet walk past the same model sitting outside on the kerb where it belongs, without a second glance. You happily stand, ankle deep in mud, eating an unspeakable mound of compressed flaccid chips covered in a steaming gruel of brown sludge that the poster described as gravy, but would frankly eat any waiter who delivered such an affliction to you at an actual restaurant. The same applies to smells: freshly mown grass is a universally admired scent that is out of place in a bedroom.

With the lights switched on and normal brain function, a girl might flinch at the approach of a cotton shirt heavy with the sweat of a man. She might stiffen if caught off guard by anything unpleasant emanating from an unwashed mouth. She might curl a lip at the sight of an uninvited undergarment in public view.

But in that surreal nether region of the mind whence darkness, lust and alcohol combine to live on marshy ground, there is no context. There is no ability to balance an opinion or a thought, no comprehension of consequences, or any wish for it. All that remains is carnal.

If Charlie Stokes were a firework, then his blue touchpaper had already been lit, and it was up to Isabelle to take care she was not standing too close. Isabelle was certainly no tart, but she was game, and she knew well enough that a man lived for the chase. Take away the chase and therein lay the boredom. And boredom wasn't something she bothered with. She'd never met a woman yet who could out-flirt her.

She closed the door of the apartment and wasted no time in deciding not to switch a light on. She reached out for Charlie, pulled him towards her and they collided in a hot, sweaty, primal kiss. They hadn't said a word in the taxi. Charlie had lolled about loosely and had gone from caressing her thigh to touching her, rubbing gently against the material of her Agent Provocateur briefs. She hadn't minded, it was why she put them on in the first place. She had squirmed a little and he had looked at her goofily. He had such a loveable face, she had always thought. The black eye simply added

189

some filth. She already knew that sex with him would be a compromised affair. He was too drunk to be anything other than clumsy, and she knew that he was doomed to love Joanna and would wake up guilty. She imagined there would be some kind of morning-after silent anguish that a wordless aspirin would do little to salve. She expected some vomit.

It simply didn't matter. She wanted him and wanted him so badly she was twitching. And so they kissed. They kept kissing while taking off their coats. Isabelle kicked off her heels and pushed Charlie against the wall. She expected awkwardness from him, but she was the one doing all the fumbling. Charlie's shirt had poppers. Perfect. She stepped back and ripped open his shirt in a tac-a-tac-tac of button popping. He looked down at his chest, damp with perspiration and exposed in the eerie light that came in through the windows. He took Isabelle by the waist and pulled her against him, running his hands up her back and holding her tighter. He bent down and kissed her neck and behind her ears and then again into her mouth. She could barely breathe. He was sweating. She was sweating. Sweat. Smoke. Tequila. Salt n vinegar crisps. Appalling, rancid odours completely masked by the sheer power of the sex drive. She drove her knee between his and clasped his thigh between hers. She rubbed against him. Her hands were everywhere.

Suddenly, she had no idea how, he had swung her full circle and she was the one against the wall. She pushed him away, panting. She felt like she was going to explode. But Charlie was on her again, kissing wildly. Then, perhaps imagining he was playing the part of some Victorian cad in a romantic cad novel, he put both hands to her cleavage and ripped Isabelle's dress open. Her breasts almost lashed out at him. He could hear Isabelle gasp. He was too drunk to comprehend, in pounds sterling or Deutschmarks, the exact cost of the damage.

"Charlie, you naughty, naughty boy."

She bit her lower lip and drew him into her breasts. She started muttering under her breath as he kissed them. With some heavy hip action and the use of her right hand, she was out of her dress and getting Charlie out of his trousers. They were still in the hallway. What happens when two people go about the same task simultaneously, and do so with the sole intention of being first, is that there is a certain amount of getting in the way and duplication of energy. In the rational cold light of a Tuesday mid-morning, two consenting adults could probably undress themselves quite adequately in a matter of seconds. Under the full force of a Saturday night fever, it took three and a half minutes and a broken vase.

Having sex standing up against a wall is not as fluid as in the movies. Isabelle grabbed Charlie round the back of the neck with both hands for support and wrapped her legs around his waist. The rest was up to him to sort out. Although it meant having to open his eyes, and hampered by having his trousers round his ankles and thus, technically, still on, he semi-hopped to a small bureau and, after first sweeping the surface clear of phone and accoutrements, he placed Isabelle on top of it. They continued to kiss each other. Charlie, like a child in a sweet shop, was too overcome to know what to do with Isabelle's breasts and ended up neglecting them to such an extent that she helped herself a bit on that front. When resistance became futile, she guided him in, and for a second or two everything went still and quiet but for the sound of their breathlessness.

"Oh God! Yes."

It's always yes, once they bring God into it.

"Fuck me, Charlie!"

E Minor

So I did. It would have been rude not to.

And here's a funny thing. I was thinking back to Woking, wasn't I? I don't know whether being more careful with what I drank had helped, or whether you can never be as drunk the second time. Maybe I was equally drunk. But the moment I felt myself inside her, the sensation of skin on sticky skin, the writhing and moaning, the kissing, the smells, the hair falling into eyes, the darkness swirling uncomfortably, there was only one conclusion I could come to: there's no way I could have had sex with Jo. I would have remembered.

I wouldn't forget this with Isabelle as long as I lived, and I wanted to. So that was a bit of a bombshell to me. Joanna can't be my girl, can she? Which is good, because I'm with someone else right now, aren't I? Poor Isabelle. Poor Isabelle? What was I saying? She had it coming. Talking of which.

"Oh shit. Charlie! Charlie? Oh, yes."

The table was banging against the wall and I think we cracked a mirror. I lifted her ankles up to my shoulders. It looked uncomfortable for her, but it was hard to tell what was good scream and what was bad scream. I paused, just in case.

"No! Don't stop."

Okay then.

In racy paperbacks, couples are endlessly climaxing simultaneously and the like, but it had never happened to me before. Just as the bureau's legs were about to give way, she came. And so did I, or maybe it was the other way round. Luckily, she was louder than me and didn't hear me shout: "Oh, Jo, yes!"

And that was that. My eyes had become accustomed to the dark and I noticed our reflection in the mirror. We looked like two porn fiends. All I could hear above the banging of my heart was Isabelle panting.

"Wow," she sighed.

And then, with a snap of the lock, the front door opened and Derek switched the light on.

And he did have very red hair, you know.

Alex woke with a start. She was confused initially and then, as a headache threatened to break out, she remembered where she'd been, and what she'd done, and whom she'd met. So, within five blissful minutes she was asleep again.

Isabelle was luxuriating in a bath of warm scented water, washing away at the ferocity of her encounter with Charlie and mulling over whether it was time to find her own place to live. I mean, Jesus Christ, even Derek has a key?

Joanna couldn't sleep. Two things played out in her mind. One was Charlie, of course. But the other was Brian Levine. Brian Levine had been at the Gala. He had hidden in the shadows, and hadn't acknowledged her. She had been surprised to see him there, shocked even. He hadn't asked her for a ticket. Every time she saw him, or spoke of him, or thought about him, she could only wonder about her father. It was destructive and pointless, just like her mother had warned her it would be.

She was alone this weekend. Perhaps that was a good thing. She would spend it doing nothing.

Beth was chilled to the bone and cursed the Audi's broken heating. Sid, grim-jawed under the flat misshapen nose, took the malfunction personally. Beth disliked emergency call outs at the best of times, but truly detested them when they impinged on a night out. And where were Derek and his non-materialising flask of bloody mulligatawny soup?

"What time is it, Sid?"

"Just gone twenty to four, Ma'am."

"Do you think you could find something hot to drink?"

"No, Ma'am."

Why does he insist on calling me 'Ma'am?' thought Beth.

Charlie Stokes had walked and walked, finally coming to rest in the salubrious pastures of East Kreuzberg, where his untidiness stuck out not one bit. Just before he reached his apartment, he stared for a while at the Wall and wondered, as he did practically every time he returned home in darkness, whether it would not be a laugh one day to shin up and escape to the *East* side. Just for a change. Would the border guards shoot him for trying to get *in*? Try and do one thing every day that scares you, said Eleanor Roosevelt, apparently. Scaling the Wall was on Charlie's list. It wasn't a long list. He didn't see the point in actively scaring himself.

"Jake! It's me, Troy nicked my keys." He had been holding a finger to the buzzer and could have done with a bit more hurry and go about the door-opening side of things.

"All right, Charlie?" croaked a metallic voice. "Had a nice time?"

"Just open the door!"

There was a sustained buzz, and Charlie heaved himself through. The sudden warmth of the staircase weighed heavily on him. Jake had left the apartment door open for him and Charlie Stokes plodded in, making straight for Jake's room.

"All right, Charlie?"

"Said that already, Jake," slurred Charlie.

He sat on the bed and flopped backwards.

"Good time?"

"Yes. Also no."

"Did you shag her, then?"

"Yes. And also no."

"Take a shower, Charlie, you stink." That was saying something, coming from Jake. "And you had a visitor this afternoon."

"Who was it?" Charlie was falling asleep finally.

"Didn't tell me."

"Must have said something."

"He said we should get a Hoover."

"What did you say?"

"I said 'that's what Charlie keeps saying."
"Goodnight, Jake."
"Goodnight, Charlie."
There was an altercation outside, the sound drifting up past the windows. It was never what anyone would call peaceful, but it was home for now.
"Charlie?"
"Hmm?"
"Can't you go and sleep in your own bed?"
"Yeah."

In another part of the city, Derek was floundering in a shallow, painful sleep. He was having a nightmare, being chased down a long dark hallway by two engorged nipples and Charlie's rampant todger.

Tuesday, November 10th

Alex and Beth were sitting on a bench in the Tiergarten. It was unseasonably mild and, without even the weakest breath of wind to move the air around, the watery, late autumn sunshine could easily be felt against the skin. Alex raised her face skywards and closed her eyes with a smile. November was an awful month. The clocks have not long changed and everyone is still coming to terms with the early darkness. The leaves have mostly given up on their trees and any idea of spring is a miserable and bone-chilling winter away.

"Have you decided what you'll be doing for Christmas?" asked Alex, her eyes still closed.

"My father has invited us to Zurich again. Well, not Zurich itself, he's been given the use of a friend's chalet up in the mountains."

"That would be lovely," said Alex, opening her eyes and turning towards Beth. "You'll have snow and a white Christmas. There will be snow, won't there?"

"Oh, there'll be snow," Beth said, as if confirming a diagnosis for a terminal illness. She didn't like snow much. It was disruptive, made everything look the same and was bloody cold. "I don't know yet. Isabelle's not keen, but the offer's there. What about you?"

Alex had no idea what was going to happen next week, never mind Christmas. It was one thing to speak lightly of taking control of your own life at last, but quite another to actually do so. She was still married to Tony and she still believed, though she could only admit to it with some shame, that he would yet cultivate some hare-brained scheme that would extricate her from his mess.

"We haven't decided yet," she lied. "Why isn't Isabelle keen to go?"

"Because my father has also invited my mother. Meaning it will be Christmas with my mother, Isabelle's mother and our father, and doesn't that sound like a recipe for disaster?"

Alex thought it sounded like a recipe for disaster.

"Not at all," she said. "He wouldn't have suggested it otherwise."

"You don't know my father," Beth laughed.

Alex smiled and soaked up the sun's positive energy before getting to the point of the get-together.

"Beth, you must know this, or better than I do, anyway."

"What's that?"

"Is there any kind of, you know, limit on the number of times you can go into East Berlin? Is there anything you're not allowed to do, or anyone you're not allowed to see?"

"Like going to the opera, or something? No. It's just the same process every time. Exchange your twenty-five Deutschmarks for a one-day visa and come back out the way you went in. That's it. I don't know how many times you'd go over before you'd pretty much seen everything you could possibly want to see. As for what you're allowed to do? Everything law-abiding. No different to here, really. Apart from that, it's all a lot stricter and less fun. Why do you ask?"

"Oh, no reason. I was thinking the other night how I'd only ever been across once before since I've been here. In some ways, it's quite interesting. Also, I had some friends ask me. They were thinking of coming for a month, but wanted to see plenty of East Berlin, try and get an idea of how everyday people live."

"Journalist friends? You know they're paranoid about everything over there, so you just need to be aware and respectful."

"Do you cross often?"

"Hardly ever. But every time someone visits, at some point they want to go and see. You know, buy a flag."

Beth had smiled and Alex had nodded and both had lied. Alex wasn't expecting any visitors, and Beth had been over countless times.

East Berlin

Christian Bauer rubbed the small of his back to ease away some stiffness. The evening before, he had fallen asleep on the sofa while being anaesthetised by a programme on DDR1, and awoke having aggravated an old sporting injury. He was relieved it wasn't a damp day at least.

He watched the exit from the S-Bahnhof in Alexanderplatz and, though he worried irrationally that he might not remember what she looked like, immediately recognised Alex as she stepped out into the street and stood blinking at the massive impersonality of her surroundings. She could not have appeared more like a Westerner if the students at his school had dressed her with the intention of creating a stereotype. He forgave her the sunglasses, because it was at least sunny. As soon as she saw him, she removed them.

And then she smiled.

"Hello, Alexandra."

"Hello, Christian."

They stood, about two metres apart, each displaying a self-conscious grin to the other. It was Christian who blinked first, and they advanced to exchange polite but relaxed kisses before laughing away any remaining awkwardness.

"Welcome to Alexanderplatz," he said, spreading his long arms.

"How very apt," she replied. "And how very big."

"We like big in the GDR," he said with a smile. "Come, let us find somewhere to sit and have a drink. Do you enjoy walking? It's still a beautiful afternoon. Let's walk towards the river."

Alex didn't mind where they walked, she didn't mind anything at all.

West Berlin

E Minor

There's always a moment just after you wake up, it can last a few seconds at most, when your life is a blank page. Not any blank page, but the first blank page in a book of blank pages. You are a vacuum of purity.

And then you wake up properly.

On the Saturday lunchtime or whatever time it was but Saturday for sure, this blank page moment lasted a full four seconds. It was time spent gazing at the wall of my bedroom. Faint unrecognisable sounds drifted rootlessly, a new life was beginning, and I was it. On the fifth second, by what means I couldn't say, something took hold of the cable inside my head that interconnected my ears, and began to twist it until the point just before the eyes popped out. I couldn't leave such a pain unquestioned and, layer-by-layer, my previous life emerged, with most of the headlines dominated by the previous evening. The sharp headache and the rasping throat were nothing compared to the heart-thumping, pulse-raising despair of remembering Joanna confirm she had gone for Günther with his undoubted financial stability, and the vague, but not vague enough to forget, memory of Isabelle and her heaving… The guilt. How could I forget the guilt?

Wait, wasn't there a Derek somewhere in this, too?

I must have groaned then, out loud, maybe even whimpered like a whipped greyhound, because I sensed a shadow in the room a few minutes later and I opened my eyes to see Jake with a small wooden tray and something steaming on it.

"Cuppa, Charlie?"

"I love you, Jake, will you marry me?"

"I can't, Charlie, I've got to buy some more milk."

By early evening I had started to feel a bit rough in a different way, and I spent all of Sunday in bed with some kind of bug. It wasn't a cold or a slice of 'flu, it was neck and head pains, off-and-on fever and pulses of semi-retching. I milked it for all it was worth, but was back up and eating on Monday evening and more or less fit for duty in the morning.

I'd been giving Joanna and Isabelle plenty of attention, particularly Joanna's admission that she'd taken up with Günther, so to speak. Having scraped all the fudge from inside my head and done what I could to focus on the facts, I concluded I might have been a bit on the rash side of premature. I mean, setting aside the wrinkles aspect of the issue, could Günther have captivated Joanna in such a short space of time? Was she that sort of a girl? She hadn't known me very long, but that was different. That was different, different, different.

Wasn't it?

Yes.

And then I decided to do the obvious thing, which was to go and talk to her. Sober. And that's what I did. I had no idea where she lived, and I didn't have her phone number either. But I had Beth's, and I reckoned I might be able to wangle an address out of her, in exchange for some made-up bollocks about Troy.

East Berlin

"And how does it make you feel?"

It was a good question.

Alex, rather than look at Christian's face, gazed around the inside of the little bar with its mix of intense young academia and slightly pungent renegades, and wondered. She had been here, sitting comfortably far away from her comfort zone, for more than an hour, and had willingly told Christian that her life was in the toilet and that her own husband had pulled the chain. It was different to telling Charlie Stokes. Charlie Stokes hadn't asked to know. Christian had.

"It's frightening, isn't it?" Alex said.

"Is it?"

Alex pulled a face.

"Well, yes. Of course."

"You still have two things that no one else in this room has. Freedom and choice." He noted her scepticism. "You think I'm being a revolutionary hippy?"

He smiled his big wide smile, and Alex was caught in the dazzle of his eyes. She had been wrong that first time. His eyes were not blue, they were green.

"You can fight against what your husband has done, or you can ignore it altogether, or you can find a small fortune from somewhere to pay off the debts but, whatever you do, it's your choice. You still have control, even though it probably doesn't seem like it right now."

And then he said it:

"It's only money."

She looked at him and caught some reflection in the corner of his eye, perhaps, who knows what it was, but without warning she burst out laughing. She caught herself immediately and stared at the dark brown, deeply polished table for a few seconds while she recovered her composure.

But when she looked up again, Christian had a silly grin on his face and was halfway through a laconic shrug of his wide shoulders. She started to laugh again, and he nodded. And that made her laugh even more. She laughed as if she were sobbing, and one or two amongst the huddled clientele looked up, so rare was the sound in that little bar. Alex put a hand to her mouth and tried to stop herself, while Christian beamed and slowly shook his head in approval.

"Sorry, but I…"

And again she snorted and giggled and finally began to cry, her eyes closed, her face scrunched up and her shoulders heaving rhythmically to her now silent sobs.

Christian leaned forward just enough to take Alex's hands and held them. In turn, she lifted his hands to her face and kissed them. She must be looking awful. She calmed down and let go of his hands in order to dig out a pack of tissues from her handbag. Oh dear. She looked around.

"I need a bathroom, Christian. Oh Lord, I must look a mess, I'm so sorry."

But she still smiled. She may have looked a mess, but she hadn't felt so good in years.

West Berlin

The apartment Joanna shared in West Berlin was on the third floor of a nondescript but well-maintained block in Charlottenburg, off the Otto-Suhr-Alle, and just a few stops on the U-Bahn from Ernst Reuter Platz. From there, it was a short walk to the office. She wasn't working today, that much Charlie had remembered from snatches of dialogue that had infiltrated him on Friday night. Whether or not she was home, he would find out soon enough.

Charlie Stokes stood with the scrap of paper in his hand, looking at the address and the array of name cards on the wall. Of course, Joanna would not officially have been there, and her name was not on the slot for the apartment on the third floor, left side. He pressed the button, long and hard, and waited. A click, then a female voice so muffled it was impossible to distinguish in the brief time it takes for the word, *"hallo?"*

"Joanna? It's Charlie. Charlie Stokes. Can I…"

There was a buzzing rattle and he pushed at the heavy door and stepped into the building. There was nothing grand or ostentatious, and yet it clearly housed a separate life form than his place. Perhaps it was the smell. There wasn't one.

The power seeped out of his legs with every step as he went up the stairs, the nerves building with every floor climbed, until he was on the landing outside the two apartments that flanked the staircase. Knowing that if he didn't just bang on the door without delay he was likely to turn round and head home, he gave it his signature knock, a syncopated affair with a sound for all tastes.

When the door opened, Charlie saw immediately that he was at the wrong apartment. A striking girl with high cheekbones and short, probably dyed blonde hair and something metallic on the side of her nose, stood scrutinising him intently, as if looking alone would have polished his shoes.

Martina had an image of Charlie Stokes in her mind, collated from the various conversations she'd had with Joanna. The reality on her doorstep was disappointingly accurate, but for the colourful residue of a blackened eye. She wasn't sure whether Joanna wanted him in her apartment, but neither was she sure that she hadn't invited him and not told her. Perhaps she should wait until he at least said something.

So she waited.

And he said something.

"Um. Er."

It was a start, she thought. She tilted her head a little to the side and waited some more.

"Joanna?" Charlie, by judicious manipulation of his eyebrows, had invested into that one word a full sentence of meaning without having to dip into his empty bag of German vocabulary.

"Joanna is out." It was not a German accent, but it was an accent.

"Ah right, okay," said Charlie. "But Joanna lives here? It's just when you opened the door."

"Yes?"

"Nothing. Well, fine. I was just passing," he said, "Do you think she'll be back soon?"

"Yes. I thought maybe this was her now. But it was you."

"Yes."

"She wouldn't knock like that. We have a bell."

"And probably a key."

"Yes. Please, come in."

Charlie walked in, wiping his feet on a non-existent mat. The apartment almost immediately opened up into a large living-room area that was bright and artfully feminine. He stood next to a tan-coloured leather sofa that was part of an impressive three-piece suite. He considered sitting, but decided to remain resolute and upright instead, and also fidgety.

"My name is Martina."

"Hello. I'm Charlie."

"Yes. I've just made coffee. Would you like some?"

He didn't know. Would he like some? Yes? No?

"Sure, thanks," he said. "Yes."

She moved, in a feline swagger, to the kitchen. Charlie left it a few seconds before following her. There were two more doors off the passageway and that was that, compact but homely. The first door was open to show a bedroom, while the second was closed. He arranged himself around the entrance to the kitchen and marvelled, as he always did, at how a kitchen should look like, and how it would take killing the three other men who lived with him, and employing a maid, to get the one at his place to come anywhere close.

"Do you take sugar?"

Martina clearly expected the answer to be no, as she presented Charlie with his cup. Charlie did, but would go without. He had to sort the accent out because, as far as he knew, she was Russian.

"So, where are you from, Martina, your accent is different."

"Warsaw."

Not Russia, really.

Martina gazed at Charlie again and floated past him.

"Have you been to Warsaw, Charlie?"

It would be many years before he discovered that the city groaned with beautiful women, but at that moment Charlie could hardly imagine any reason why anyone could think he'd been there before. He assumed it was a rhetorical question, but to be safe he said:

"No."

There was no follow up question from Martina, so Charlie spoke about the apartment.

"Nice flat, by the way. Been here long?"

They were back in the living room, and Martina had sat down on the armchair. She looked at Charlie and noted the way his eyes flitted about the room, processing tiny pieces of information. He was standing by the television cabinet now, looking at the photo frames. She wondered whether he was a spy. He behaved very much like a not very good one.

"Six months or so. We moved in beginning of March. Please sit down, Charlie. The sofa is very comfortable."

She didn't smile, Charlie noticed, it probably didn't suit her. He needed to think.

"Actually, sorry but can I just use the bathroom, please?"

"Yes. Sure. It's the last door."

Charlie set his cup down on one of the coasters on the coffee table and left for the bathroom. As he drew level with the open door of the bedroom, he poked his head in again and caught sight of a photo of Joanna and her mother. The red top she had been wearing when he first saw her was folded neatly at the top of a freshly ironed pile of clothing at the foot of the double bed. He moved on. There was only the door at the end and, sure enough, it was the bathroom. He locked himself in and washed his face with cold water. Dabbing it dry, the feeling hadn't gone away, so he washed his face some more. That's why he didn't hear the front door being opened, and Joanna returning. Charlie dried his face a second time and gave it a rub with his hands for good measure.

There was only one bedroom.

When he opened the door, therefore, he was already a little less surprised than he would have been to see Martina giving Joanna a kiss on the lips and a gentle caress of her left cheek with her fingers. Joanna had no more expected to see Charlie in her apartment than a herd of zebra, and Charlie would probably take the look of shock and surprise on her face to his grave, be it cremation or burial.

East Berlin

The bar was almost a pastiche of some slightly dodgy living room from a mid-seventies sitcom. The ambience was unique and such was the scrum inside, that there were now two strangers at their little table - the custom being to squeeze every last available seat from a bar at the expense of what the British would almost certainly consider their personal space. The couple alongside them wore wire-rimmed glasses, fashion-free hair, and University scarves. After some polite exchanges with Alex and Christian, the students had returned to the argument with which they had arrived.

Alex and Christian had barely paused for breath since they arrived, even talking about fashion at one stage. After the two students had settled at their table, however, Christian had leaned more to the monosyllabic and inane. He had placed his newspaper unread on the table when they arrived, and surprised Alex by taking a sudden interest in the crossword.

"Let's see how I am today," he said in a faraway voice.

"I'm not very good. Don't ask me for help."

Alex watched as, with a pencil he had extracted from who knows where, Christian gave the clues some thought and quickly completed four or five. She couldn't tell exactly, as he held the now folded paper up in front of him as if he were reading a paperback. He turned the paper and showed it up close to Alex.

"I think these are right, though, don't you?"

In the boxes he had written: Say *"it's been nice meeting you. I have to go now". Leave. Wait for me at station."* Alex felt uncomfortable and wondered whether she was being teased.

"Like I said, I'm not one for crosswords."

"I think I'm right," said Christian.

And he returned to the clues, with the paper up close to his face again. Alex gathered up her handbag, and pushed back her chair.

"It's been nice meeting you. I have to go now."

She smiled and Christian lowered his paper and gave a friendly nod.

"Goodbye," he said in a level voice and, with a short smile of his own, lifted the paper again.

Alex wove her way out onto Friedrichstasse, where she buttoned up her coat, and checked her bearings. The Bahnhof was within sight, so there was no danger of her getting lost, but for a few moments she stood motionless, absorbing the atmosphere and thinking about how much darker the dark was on this side of the Wall.

She had no concerns that Christian would not show up, and soon, and hadn't for a second questioned what had just happened. If it had been Tony being cryptic, that would have been an entirely different recipe. She seemed barely to have arrived at the station before Christian's long legs catapulted him to her side.

"Christian," she said, "what was that all about?"

"I think our table guests may have been taking too much interest in you. Or me, I should say. It's better that they think we were just sitting together as strangers."

"What?"

"Really, it's nothing to worry about. Some years ago, I was able to travel abroad. I was a good sportsman. I once went to Norway and also to Finland with my club. I was looking forward to a trip to Edinburgh when my Uncle was involved in an argument with a Stasi officer and there was a fight. My Uncle was a wrestler and it didn't end well for the Stasi officer. They put him in prison and made sure I paid for it, too. I never went to Edinburgh and I have never been allowed to travel again."

"I'm sorry."

"I was followed for a long time. There are always plenty of people here who are willing to follow you, I'm afraid. That all gradually went quieter, but I am always very aware. Especially with you being here. You look very much like a *Wessie*. They'll think I'm planning to escape."

And he laughed to show what a big joke that would be. It was the only time since she'd met him that Alex had ever heard him sound false.

Alex looked down at her shoes, coat, and expensive handbag and could see the issue. She would go shopping for some anonymous clothing, so that she was less obvious the next time. The next time?

"When can I see you again? Can you meet me here, or tell me where to go? What about Saturday, won't a Saturday be easier for you?"

Christian bent down and kissed her on the mouth, firmly but hesitantly. Alex went blank.

"Saturday, at eleven. I'll be here, waiting." Christian said.

And those were the words Alex took with her back across to the shiny, shouty side of the Wall.

West Berlin

E Minor

Joanna's face, for the split-second it took for me to record it as an image for life, was a picture that told a thousand words, because I guessed that was how many she'd tried to use before settling just on saying my name.

She untangled herself from the Polish girl, whose name now escaped me along with much else, and stood there ashen-faced and gutted. I hated that she looked so distressed and that I, with my uninvited presence, was the reason. Perhaps, had we been alone, it could have been handled better. But we weren't. Once I decided to move, only a detour to sweep up my coat from the living-room prevented me from breaking whatever the record was for exiting that particular apartment from a standing start in the bathroom.

I didn't look at either of them, but Joanna made a grab at my sleeve as I left her in my wake, and I heard my name under her breath. Once I reached the second floor, I was aware of the footsteps behind me but I only stopped at the ground floor hallway. I turned, clasped my hands on the back of my head, and waited for her.

Joanna took the final six steps increasingly slowly, as if suspecting one of them contained a hidden hand grenade. She looked at me straight in the eyes, I'll give her that, but she didn't know what to do with her hands, so she buried them into the pockets of her stonewashed Levi's. So, after all the descending, we just looked at each other calmly.

"Say something, Charlie."

"You say something."

"I wanted to tell you. I was trying to tell you, on Friday. I just couldn't."

"Oh, well that's all right, then."

It was difficult to know how to react. I felt all manner of things, and all at once, but if I had to pick just one, I'd say confused.

"How long have you and her been together? I mean, okay, just to settle everything, you're a couple. That's it, isn't it? You're, you know."

I realised I was nodding in that stupid way gormless people nod when they're trying to shake words out of their head that weren't fitting through the mouth.

"I'm not a lesbian, Charlie," she said.

"I think you'll find you are."

I hadn't asked for an explanation, and certainly wasn't in the mood for one, but it came anyway.

"I've been with boys before."

She made it sound as if that made everything all right.

"And will you again?" I asked.

She looked down at her feet, answering with her silence. I turned and took hold of the door handle.

"Charlie, don't. Wait."

For what? I thought. But I waited.

"When I was fifteen or sixteen, practically the only thing my friends were talking about was boys, and snogging, and groping and who'd touched what… it was supposed to be so exciting and naughty and I just didn't feel anything. Inside, I mean. I wasn't twitching in anticipation, like they all seemed to be. I daydreamed about where my father might be, and what he might be doing. There were never any men in our house, nothing masculine around at all. I wasn't interested in Donny Osmond and I never fancied David Cassidy."

"Nor did I," I said.

"When I went out to the cinema with a boy, sooner or later he'd try and put his arm round me but…I can't explain. It was more the feeling I'd imagine if your brother put his arm round you, to look after you. That kind of arm around the shoulder."

She stopped for a bit of wistful thinking. It suited her.

"I got tired of everyone's obsession with sex and gossip and giggling. Just the idea of boys…I was so bored with it. Then it crossed my mind to become a nun."

"A nun? Jesus!"

"I didn't tell anyone, and obviously it was never going to happen, was it? But it took my mind off things."

"Bit drastic, though. Couldn't you have had a cup of tea and a biscuit?"

It's like a disease, this problem I have of occasionally coming out with ill-conceived facetious comments. She ignored me anyway.

"One day, I went to the hairdressers. Not the usual place I went to. There was a girl who washed my hair. I don't know what she did differently, or whether she thought she saw something in me, but it made the hairs on my arms stand up. From my head to my back, and arms, and even my legs, everything sort of tingled. I kept my eyes closed the whole time because I felt embarrassed. I went back two weeks later, and from then on every two weeks. I didn't even pretend I wanted a tiny hair cut, I just asked for a shampoo. I don't know if the girl knew what she was doing, or not. Sometimes I dreamed about her, about her hands.

"I wanted her to kiss me. Just to find out what it was like. I had kissed a boy by then and I wanted to feel the difference. Soft lips, soft skin, soft hands. But she didn't kiss me. I never even spoke to her. Did that make me a lesbian, Charlie, having thoughts and dreams like that?"

"I guess so," I said. "Can I go now?"

Joanna looked a bit wounded and some of the brown in her eyes quivered. I rubbed at my hair and face with both hands, thus transferring all the leaden bacteria from the stained brass doorknob. I was finding it difficult.

"I carried on for two years like that. Going out with boys, dreaming about girls. By the time I left school, I had a reputation as a tease. But as soon as any of them put their hands on me, I just froze. When I went up to

University, I started afresh. I had sex before the end of the first week. It was awful. That was the only time I slept with a man."

Joanna stopped, and looked right through me. She opened her mouth to speak again, then thought better of it. Perhaps she had given me the floor. I thought carefully about what to say, then discarded it for the more obvious.

"You don't become a lesbian because your first shag was crap! Otherwise, all the lads and I would have ended up as gay as coots, trust me!"

"Don't be silly, Charlie."

"Well."

"Just before Christmas, when all the parties started, it happened. I didn't plan it. It just happened. There were five or six girls. We had too much to drink, of course, and the conversation, as usual, turned to boys, and relationships, and sex, and fantasies, and… You're not listening, are you, Charlie?"

She had me there.

"You just want a simple answer. There isn't a simple answer. All right?"

She turned and stomped up the stairs, before stomping back down again, her eyes blazing.

"It's easy for you, isn't it? Everything's wired up properly, all you need is a nice girl in a tight top in front of you, and you're away."

In a handful of cavalier words she had painted me as a caveman. I'd have taken offence were it not true.

"One of the girls kissed me. I kissed her back, and that was that. I didn't know what I was doing, but she certainly did. The others just laughed, or something, and carried on with what they were doing whilst this girl and I made love in a bedroom. It was everything sex with the boy hadn't been. I thought that was that. I had found what I wanted."

You could have fed the silence to a pig, so loaded was it with sauce.

"It wasn't," she said. After a week, it was clear this girl was going to laugh it off as one of those drunken experiments. She said she wasn't a lesbian, of course. I told her she must have done it before. The things she did, the things she knew. She just snorted. What if she had? That didn't make her a lesbian. She made it perfectly clear that she wouldn't be happy if I started spreading lies. So I avoided her, and the other girls from that evening, and got on with it. There is more to life than sex, Charlie."

She didn't need to tell me.

"When Martina arrived in the office where I worked, she was the first openly, proud lesbian I had ever met. She signed petitions, and went on marches, and subscribed to magazines, and went to the right bars and clubs. I never had any interest in that. Not then, not now. She knew exactly what she was. I never did. I didn't know what to do, where to go. So I let her seduce me. It was fun. And she really wanted me. She was in complete control of everything, and I loved that. She took care of that part of my life, and all I asked in return was that she told no one."

Now she looked at me again, but this time her eyes got to me. Her eyes were like those of a helpless puppy. I wanted to cry. I wanted her so badly. She gave the slightest of shrugs.

"And that's it, really," she said.

I tried to take it all in.

"I came to Berlin because I wanted to live my life this way, somewhere that wasn't home. Away from my Mum, my friends."

"She doesn't know?" I asked.

"Nobody knows, Charlie. Just Martina, and now you."

And one other person, it turned out.

"Oh, and Brian Levine."

"Who?"

"You met him at the funeral. The little man in the funny suit?"

"And he would know because…?"

"Sometimes I can talk to him. He arranged my transfer here. He has connections and used them to help me. He said it was important for me to live my life how I wanted to live it. Or at least find out if it was how I wanted to live it."

"And is it?"

"Sure. I think so. Yes."

"I had absolutely no idea," I said.

"I just thought…" she said, and she seemed so sad and small and innocent that I felt guilty. "You were sweet, and different, I thought you would be a fun person to get to know. I didn't know you'd be interested in me in that way, so none of this would matter."

"Well, it does matter."

I convinced myself that I could mould a collection of thoughts and emotions into something manageable like a speech, but it was a struggle to get it going. It felt like trying to jump-start a car without help. It's a huge struggle and strain just to get the bloody thing to move at all, but once it does - and you get a bit of rhythm and speed, the main concern is not to get carried away because, if you're not careful and push too hard, instead of leaping into the driving seat, you end up watching the car hurtle down the High Street and through the windows of WH Smith.

"You are so…lovely." It wasn't going to be a deeply memorable speech, it was going to end up more of a statement. "You are so lovely. The second I first saw you, it's like I fell into a hole, something went inside me and I haven't been able to think about anything the same again. My best friend died. He was killed, and I still thought about you and your mysterious eyes, and your face, and your skin and you smile all the time, and you always understand what I'm saying, even when I was drunk in Woking. And you came to Woking. You came to be with me, so I wouldn't be alone, so… so I wouldn't be alone. And I thought maybe you felt something for me, or why else would you… would you have looked at me, the way you looked at me that day? So, I thought that maybe you and I could, you know, I mean…I thought we had actually slept together anyway! It was only the other night that I realised that we hadn't done anything. Ha!"

"You could have said *something* to me. I went to the ballet to surprise you, to be with you, and show you how cultured I was, and how witty I was with my red sock and my blue sock. And we would laugh in the interval holding a glass of champagne with our little fingers sticking in the air, and you would tell me – no, you would whisper in my ear- that there was a party and that please would I go, and I would go. And, eventually, when it was late and everyone had gone home, the only two people still standing would be you and me and we would be dancing in the middle of the room and…"

"Please don't tell anyone, Charlie." She just cut me off. "Please?"

"I won't tell anyone. But this is 1987, you know. I don't think it's a crime anymore." I turned for the door and the promise of some air.

"I just don't want people to know, Charlie."

I nodded as I left. I heard her call out as the door closed behind me.

"We'll all come and see you at the club!"

I walked to the station like a man whose legs had been filled with blancmange, and insides replaced with acid. It's a terrible thing, self-pity.

East Berlin, Saturday, November 14th

Christian and Max argued mildly for almost an hour. Christian had told Max he was too busy to see him, and Max had hounded him relentlessly until Christian could take it no more and said, simply, that he had a date with a girl.

"A girl?"

"Yes. So let's just meet up this evening instead. That's not a problem, is it?"

"What girl, Christian? When did you have time to meet a girl? Oh, my God, not the American?" It was as if the life source had been sucked from his very soul. "Dear mother of God no, Christian!"

"She's not American, Max."

"Are you insane?"

"Are you not?"

"Then I'm out, my friend."

"Out of what?"

"You know what."

Christian laughed.

"Max, did you think I was going to tell *her*? Now who's the one being insane?"

"Of course you will tell her. Not today, maybe not next time, but soon enough. Why don't you just walk around with a poster telling everyone your plans? That's what you're doing anyway, letting yourself be seen with an English woman. What do you think people will think? Do you think they will not suspect? Are you willing to take that risk? I'm not. I am not, Christian. No."

And so they had gone on, extemporising on the same theme like an old married couple stretching what little they had left to say to one another for the entire day.

"This is why I didn't tell you, Max. Because I knew it would be like this over and over."

West Berlin, Monday, November 16th

The first Monday after publication was a slow day at the West Berlin offices of Cavalcade Print & Media, publishers of *My Style* magazine. Alex was nonetheless surprised to find the entire ground floor's office desks empty. It was only as she reached the first floor landing, and saw the conference room full of chattering people, that she realised there was going to be a staff meeting, though she had no recollection of having been told about it. Dagmar saw her and stuck her face out.

"Alex, we're all in here."

"Is there a meeting? I had no idea, I can't believe I forgot."

"No, we've just been told."

"Nothing serious, I hope?"

"Someone thinks we're been bought up."

"Really? Wait. Let me leave my stuff at my desk. I'll be back in a second."

She skipped up to her office on the third floor and left her coat and case by her desk. She noticed the A4 internal memo laid on the keyboard of her computer informing everyone about an Extraordinary Meeting. She was wondering whether anyone had put the coffee on and, if they had, should she quickly pour herself a shot, when her boss, and a man she had never seen before, appeared in front of her as if by magic.

"Oh Alexandra," said her boss, appearing relieved to catch her alone, "perfect. Let me just have a word before we go downstairs. Why don't we all just sit... over there?" And he indicated towards his office in the corner, the only one in the open plan layout with a door.

"Coffee first?" Alex really fancied one now.

"Maybe in a moment, yes. Let's just have a quick chat about our big news."

Alex was excited. Who wouldn't be excited at the words *big news*? Excitement only made her crave coffee more, but she followed him to the corner office and sat down, as it happened for the last time, as an employee of Cavalcade Print & Media.

Thursday, November 19th

Beth sighed, and shrugged, and puffed out her cheeks, three actions for which she was known and admired by all her colleagues at or connected to the Consulate. She sat in an uncomfortable, high-backed leather armchair she felt sure had been round the world twice. The Attaché and Assistant Attaché were over from the Embassy in East Berlin and they were sitting in a small room adjoining the Consul's office, each trying not to bore the other to sleep. The radiators were set those few degrees warmer than the ideal that can so easily bring a drifting mind to narcolepsy. Lewis, one of Beth's team, was also at the meeting.

"We're smoking too much, aren't we? Is this too much for you, Beth? Christ, we're both on the cigars now. Should one of us stub out?"

The Attaché looked around the room and focused on the Assistant Attaché.

"Do you want to put yours out? Or shall we open a window?"

"Open a window would be better, eh?" That was what the Assistant Attaché thought to that.

"Really, it's fine, it doesn't matter," said Beth. "We're about done, aren't we?"

"I suppose we are. What about lunch? Join us for lunch, Beth, or do you have plans?" Beth knew that the boys didn't want to have their lunch compromised by a woman, but appreciated, as she always did, the invitation. It was almost a ritual.

"That would be lovely thank you, but I can't today."

"Shame. Next time, perhaps."

"For sure."

"Oh, wait, there's that one last little thing, Beth."

"Oh?"

"The young American chap." The Attaché rubbed his thumb and index finger together in a feigned pantomime of forgetfulness.

"Cafarella?"

"Yes. Pull him in, would you?"

"Yes?"

"Yes. We think we know who's running him. Pretty big fish, actually. So, if you could sweep him up by the weekend it would be nice. See if you can fix something up with the police, like that other time. That was neater, for all of us anyway."

Beth gave it some thought, which is when she had sighed, shrugged and puffed out her cheeks. It meant another weekend interfered with, but Charlie Stokes' gig was perfect.

"We can do it on Saturday night."

"Tomorrow would make me feel more comfy, or even tonight," said the Attaché. "Don't you think?" He had directed this to the Assistant Attaché, who nodded once by way of letting his colleague know what he thought.

"Saturday will be neater," said Beth. "And if you want the police involved, then Saturday would be perfect."

"Saturday it is, then. Goodness me, I think I'll open a window myself, eh?"

Charlie Stokes fed the last string through the bridge and up into the machine head. After a few perfunctory turns, he tuned it to E and set the guitar down on the bed. He collected the empty packets, coiled up the old strings, and stuffed everything back into the plastic pack the new ones had come in. He went into the kitchen and made a mug of tea without bothering to ask if anyone else wanted one. Apparently, Ritchie had gone to the library but the rest of the lads were in, just loafing about. From out of the window, the Wall looked like a piece of childishly vandalised theatrical decoration. It was often at this time of the day, not the time itself but the period just as darkness was falling, that the Wall looked at its worst. It brooded like a street yob, barring the path to lightness and joy. With a hint of autumnal mist and murk, it was a fiendishly unwelcome sight. Dan was gazing out onto the street below, planning his evening. He was aware of Charlie's reflection.

"It's so depressing, that thing. It's like we're stuck in a big playground, and all we're supposed to do is have fun, all the time," said Dan, not knowingly considering himself much of a philosopher.

"Well, you do know that we can get out any time we like, don't you?"

"Yes, but that's the weirdest part," said Dan in agreement. "Why does it always seem like *we're* the ones that are trapped?"

"Too much philosophising for me, Dan," said Charlie. "The water's just boiled."

He walked to his room and, after setting the tea down on the small bedside table, he propped himself up in his bed and picked up the guitar.

E Minor

It's hard to describe exactly, it's unique. And it's not just about the sound. It's a feeling you get when you first strum a guitar with fresh new steel strings that have never been touched before. There's nothing quite like it. It's as if thousands of invisible choral fairies are sitting along each string, like sparrows on a telegraph line, and once the strings vibrate they scatter into the air and tickle the sound waves with their magic wings. You only get it for a minute or two before the strings bed in. I love that moment. It can lift any spirit, even one that's been squashed into the lino like an over-ripe grape.

So, I settled on the bed with the guitar on my lap, gave all the strings a final tune and gazed into the middle distance, a favoured spot of mine. What you need to do, when your new strings are ready to sing like they are, is choose a nice big open chord like G major, something that will fill the room with high-flying optimism. Or a C major perhaps. Well, any major chord, really.

So, it was odd to find myself playing an E minor instead, and hearing its melancholic tone whining around the bedroom, looking for somewhere to hide. I tried to remedy things by chasing after a D major. But that just gave me the seed of a melody, so I went back to the E minor and then, rather dramatically, to F sharp minor. From there I nudged it up to G, and over the next few minutes, or half an hour, or whatever it was, I wrote a song.

It was a song for Joanna, or because of her.

"New song, Charlie?" Jake appeared in the room with a fresh brew. I hadn't touched mine.

"Yeah."

"What's it called?"

"Charlie's Lament in E minor."

"Cool."

West Berlin, Saturday, November 21st

Ground Zero, from the décor to the staff, was pre-grunge alternative, with an eclectic range of beers to go with the barbaric and often anarchic cocktails. Like so many venues, it had a following and a reputation, so bands liked to play there. This was the first time *Rolled Oatz* had been booked and Charlie knew it was probably going to be the last.

Like so many nightspots whose success relied upon the character of its clientele, Ground Zero was a poor, shabby specimen during the hollow vacuum of daytime. Tatty and reeking of stale life, it would be hard to imagine anything uplifting of note ever happening there.

The gear was spread around the tiny raised stage, with coils of black cable laid out strategically to designate who would be where. The floor was painted in a thick matt black paint that bore the scratches and scrapes of Berlin's itinerant rockers. And over it all, the unique, nicotine-infused rubbery aroma that hangs over a performance space like a cloying fog of unleashed mayhem. It ought to have been exciting setting up at such a sought-after venue, but Charlie had spent the past fortnight in a prolonged fog of morose indifference, and the virus had spread like a deadly plague of apathy. They all went about their little pieces of personal business, with only rare nuggets of banter mined out of the silence.

"Why doesn't Dan take the left hand side then, Charlie?"

"I don't know, Jake. Why don't you ask him why he doesn't take the left hand side?"

"All right, Charlie. Dan, why don't you take the left hand side?"

"Jake, don't keep tightening it, you'll just break it again."

"Eh, watch the fucking hair, pea-brain. Sorry, Charlie I thought it was Ritchie."

Although the club wouldn't open to the public for some time yet, a girl with dyed blue-black hair, cut into a retro Mary Quant bob, had already started work and Ritchie had tried to make a pass at her twice by way of a warm-up. He always thought he had more chance if he started early. When he saw Charlie go into the storage room behind the stage, Ritchie followed him. As Charlie was bent over a holdall stuffed with miscellaneous extension cables, plugs and adapters, Ritchie decided to announce his plans regarding his return to medicine.

"Listen, Charlie, I need to tell you something. Should have told you before, but, I don't know… Then there was Luke."

"It's all right, Ritchie, I know." Charlie found what he was looking for and stood up gingerly before turning round. "Troy told me already. You're going back to school."

"Yeah."

"If it's what you want. This is over for all of us, isn't it?"

"It's been fun. Really."

Ritchie, like the rest of the lads, had sensed that the Berlin adventure might not last until Christmas.

"Let's blow them out of the water tonight," he said.

"Yes," said Charlie, "let's."

He ran a hand across his nose and thought of something interesting to say.

"Do you have any gay friends? I mean, you were at Cambridge, probably a hotbed." If Charlie had expected any kind of reaction, he didn't get one - just an unexpected answer.

"My brother's gay. None of my friends, though, that I'm aware of."

"No, seriously."

"I am serious, Charlie. My brother's gay."

"Chris?"

"My older brother, Josh." Charlie had to think hard to dredge up any recollection of an older brother.

"You've got a brother who's gay?" Charlie didn't try too hard to hide his surprise. "When did you know? I mean, when did he tell everyone?"

"It was after I left home. Actually, while I was at Cambridge. Can't remember exactly. Why?"

"How come you never said?"

Ritchie shrugged. "Would you have?"

It was Charlie's turn to shrug now, but a different kind of shrug. Charlie was not aware of any of his friends being gay. Was that because he didn't have any gay friends, or might there have been one or two who simply kept it quiet?

"How does it start? I mean, how do you decide you're gay? Do you just try it out?" Clearly, Charlie was struggling to grasp the concept.

"It's not a hobby, Charlie. You don't just bloody take it up."

"Well, you'd have to, wouldn't you? To know it was really what you wanted. What if you announced you were gay, and then five years later decided you weren't?"

Ritchie had no idea where Charlie was going with this and wished he hadn't said anything about his brother. He picked up a cable he didn't need, so he had something to do with his hands.

"Then, I suppose, you'd stop being gay, Charlie. Although, as I think I said earlier, it's my brother who's gay, not me. You should be asking him."

"Was he glad when people knew?"

"Well," said Ritchie, "I think for a good while he probably wished he hadn't told anyone, let's put it that way." He took off his glasses and rubbed the lenses with his shirt. "Are you on the turn or something, Charlie, and want some advice?"

"Nah. I was just wondering about someone else, that's all."

"Daniel, right?"

"No, not bloody Daniel, it's nothing to do with us. Forget I said anything. Jesus!"

"What's the time, Charlie?" It was Jake, for whom constantly asking for a second opinion on the time, despite having his own watch, was a personality disorder.

"Nearly seven," said Charlie.

"I make it half-past."

"It's nearly seven."

"That's strange."

"Still nearly seven, though."

"Burger shit, or pizza crap tonight?"

It was band etiquette that the pre-gig meal had to be fast food takeaway. This tradition was immutable, even if they ever ended up doing a show next door. The phone was ringing, so the decision was put on hold. Jake reached it first.

"Charlie, it's Troy," he said, handing over the receiver. Charlie took it and listened without a word, though he glanced at his watch. It was a short message.

"Okay, yeah." Charlie replaced the phone. "What's the number for the place that delivers?"

They were not scheduled to start until ten o'clock. In the time it took for the food to arrive, they could all fight and quarrel over the bathroom, though in truth only Charlie and Dan ever got stressed about being fragrant enough when they would all be soiled to the core within fifteen minutes of launching their set.

When the food arrived, it was Jake who came to the trough late.

"What's that, then, Charlie?"

"It's a pizza, Jake."

"Did you drop it in the garden, Charlie?"

"It's called rucola. It's good for you, Jake, helps keep you regular or, in your case, in time."

"Nice one, Charlie."

"Piss off, Dan."

"Keeps you in time…"

"There's a queue to get in, darling, I don't much fancy that. How late are we, anyway? Didn't Charlie tell us not to bother coming before ten?"

"That's good, isn't it Izzy? It means it should be busy. Charlie would want it busy, wouldn't he?"

"Yes, but queuing up!" Isabelle did not really go in for that.

Beth rolled her eyes and Alex nudged her with her elbow.

"You can always just flirt your way in," said Beth. "Look, Joanna and Günther have beaten us and they're right at the front." She acknowledged Joanna's wave and smile.

"Quick, quick," said Isabelle, "we'll crash in with them. Come on!"

"I say," said Alex, self-consciously appraising her clothes, "it's quite alternative, this crowd, isn't it? But that's what's so great about Berlin, eh Beth?"

Beth shrugged. She was not expecting a relaxing Saturday night, but it had nothing to do with the alternative nature of the crowd.

E Minor

I didn't look at my watch, obviously, because I was playing and singing, but judging by where we were in the set list and that we had kicked off a fashionable half-hour late, I'd say about quarter to eleven. That was the time when we reached a moment of apotheosis, as I believe it's called.

Ground Zero was not one of those cavernous venues that required five hundred ravers to take the echo out of a room, but it was an odd-shaped place and it didn't take too many bopping in front of the little stage we were on to fire up an atmosphere. We had everything pretty cranked up and the acoustics in there were great. Troy took on a sax solo as if someone had questioned his manhood, surfing on top of a stomach-chunking beat that Jake and Ritchie laid down. Dan, for once, underplayed his lead guitar, leaving little diamonds on top of the cake, and I made sure there weren't any holes anywhere else. The energy hit the crowd and came back with interest, and so the monster grew.

We were absolutely rocking the fingerprints out of our skin, man.

That's when I saw Joanna.

That brought a mixture of emotions. There was relief that the band could not have sounded better, assuming she liked that kind of thing. That was followed, abruptly, by the realisation that it probably no longer mattered whether or not she liked what the band was cooking. Then, with barely time for a breath, came the third and oddly most potent sensation, one of irritation and jealousy that she had brought Günther, of all people, with her. Was she still going to accept dates? Why not, I thought. That's what Isabelle was saying, wasn't it, all these men flocking around her?

I probably lost my concentration there, because I almost missed the lads doing a key change, so I put away the thoughts and plugged myself back into the music. I gazed into the front rows of the club and singled out the better-looking girls. This was the tune Troy had played me in the car with the solo he assured would blow the dress clean off a girl. No luck yet, but I had my eyes peeled.

It wasn't as busy inside as the queue outside had led them to believe. The club had a long bar, in front of which were scattered small tables and chairs. It was one of those places with concrete support columns, and these had all been adapted with shelving that acted as a place for resting a glass or seven. There was a dark enclave at one end, as appetising as the bruise on an apple. The stage was at the opposite end, again tucked into an enclave, barely a yard in front of a small, circular wooden dance floor on which fifty or sixty people were absorbing the full force of *Rolled Oatz*.

The girls were in a tight huddle, looking like they had been superimposed onto the scene from somewhere altogether more civilised. Günther, somehow, appeared no less out of place here than at the Staatsoper. He fitted in everywhere, and with anyone. It was a gift. Beth blinked several times, an involuntary action that did nothing to hide the impression that she was a square. She'd been in louder places, but Troy could wring some murderously high notes out of his saxophone, and sometimes they leaped out unexpectedly. She grabbed at Alex's arm in mock apprehension.

"Don't let them get me, Alex."

"Looks like a wild party," said Alex, smiling. She was smiling loudly.

"What?"

Isabelle, her eyes shining like a cat's in an alleyway, pulled at Joanna's hand.

"Come on, darling, let's get a better view of Charlie. There's a bit of space back over there. No, Günther, you go and make a bit of space, I'll see what I can get out of the barman. Oh, all right, Joanna, go with him."

Joanna and Günther made their way to an empty column and, while Joanna waited, Günther made a quick foray into the gloomy recesses for the last three remaining unaccounted-for bar stools. Although she was happy to stand, Joanna felt obligated to sit on a stool. She looked over to the stage. They were all wearing black roll-neck cotton shirts and black denim trousers. The second guitar player was still wearing a black leather jacket. She imagined it would start to feel hot in that. Charlie was lost in some other world, she thought, though not so lost as to forget about ogling all the girls. The saxophone player was pouring himself into his instrument and the drummer was flailing at his drum kit, his unruly curls bouncing off his head and the lights glinting off his glasses.

"They've got a cocktail here with only numbers in its name, darling. Do you dare?" Isabelle had burst into view, still laughing about it. "Loud, energetic and sweaty," she said, raising her voice. "Like all the best things in life, eh?"

Joanna smiled. Günther simply observed.

"They look like they're enjoying it," she said.

"You can't be in a band here and not enjoy it, darling. Which one is the American, do you know?"

"The one playing the saxophone," said Joanna.

Charlie had mentioned them all by name, during his many stories, but she had forgotten some of them. She wondered how they felt, playing without Luke and knowing that they would never do so again.

Beth and Alex joined them as the song ended in a tight flourish of cymbals followed by beery whooping, whistling, and applause. From one of the boys, no one knew which, came a cheeky shout of "thank you, Berlin" before a click, click, click-click-click of drumstick against drumstick counted in the next number.

"I bet this is not your normal scene," said Isabelle, chipping away at Günther.

"One should be open to everything," he said calmly.

"And everyone," said Isabelle, and she elbowed Beth in the ribs to be sure the double-entendre had been registered.

Beth didn't mind this time. She was watching Troy. She couldn't be completely certain, but she thought Günther was giving her the eye - or was watching her, if nothing else. Or maybe she was being wishful, which would be a first.

Alex was thinking about Christian, her life, and Tony. It was a lot to take in on a night out. She was glad of the distraction that Charlie taking the microphone provided. She lit up, because it was fun to see this side of a person you only ever knew in a certain way.

"Whoo-hoo, go on Charlie!"

It was completely out of character to behave like that, and she could see Beth was taken aback, but in a nice way.

"Get in there, Charlie," said Isabelle, as proud as a parent seeing a delinquent son finally make good. "Anyone know what he's singing? He doesn't know the words, does he?"

The band were playing *Louie Louie*, a song to which no one knew all the words, not even the FBI.

"Beth, could you make lunch next week? I've got a bit of news," said Alex.

"All right. Thursday is always the best day for me. What news?"

"Oh, nothing like that, there isn't a baby coming."

"That's a shame. I had you down as the first of us to deliver. Or me, I am the oldest, after all." She shrugged, of course.

Joanna noticed some American soldiers had turned up, loud but cheerful and with girls already picked up. They headed straight for the bar without a sideways glance. It had become slightly more crowded quickly. Behind her, raised almost to the ceiling and reached by a narrow flight of stairs of barely believable steepness, was an enclosed DJ's booth where the DJ was preparing for the band's breaks. She wondered when there would be a break and whether Charlie would even come out and speak to her, or the others. She wanted him to know she had come, as promised, before considering going home. It had already been a long evening. Günther's invitation had come late.

Something made her look up. The band had stopped. No, they hadn't, it had just got much quieter. There was just the sound of a single guitar whispering a collection of sad but beautiful notes that seemed to stagger over the heads of the crowd in front and flutter about her hair and face like butterflies. It was a jarring change of tone and mood that left the club in a state of expectant limbo, on edge, waiting for a searing squeal from the saxophone to signal a new assault from the drummer.

It did not come.

What came was a light emotive voice, singing about love. It was Charlie's voice. And it was Charlie's love. And Joanna no longer needed to wonder whether Charlie knew she had come. Through the restless crowd, who talked and fidgeted in the unwanted quiet, Joanna saw Charlie looking at her. For a brief moment she was reminded of the way he had stared at her that first time at the restaurant, and how she had stared back. He wasn't staring now, at least half the time he had his eyes closed. But when he did open them, it was to look at her. She found it unbearable.

"Charlie," she said in a whisper that wouldn't have disturbed a soufflé, "don't. Please don't."

Her eyes welled up out of sadness, and anger too. She didn't ask him to fall in love with her. It's not compulsory for a good-looking man to fall in love with a good-looking woman. It's not the law. But she did not want to feel anger, not at Charlie.

It wasn't Charlie's fault.

Troy's saxophone began to decorate the song, then Ritchie on the bass guitar, and a few riffs from Dan on guitar. Jake added nothing, it was not that kind of tune. None of the others knew Charlie was going to pull that little surprise, and each had to wait to get an idea of the tune, and pick up the chords. They'd have left Charlie to it, if it were not for the groundswell of boredom that was threatening to derail their performance.

There was a lot of movement in the club, particularly in front of the stage. Once the lads had decided to jump in, Charlie lost his reverie and became aware that he'd lost the crowd. As he sang and played his beautiful song, he was hit hard by an awful realisation that he was wasting his life. No one gave a shit about his music. They wanted something they knew already, played loudly enough to mulch the brain. Fine, they could have that next. He saw Troy bending down, listening to an American soldier. The requests were starting already, then.

E Minor

That was when our amp blew. It didn't go bang, it just died. The only sound anyone could hear was my heart sinking. Troy looked at me. Jake looked at me. Ritchie looked at the amp and went at it with a screwdriver immediately.

"Charlie?" Dan always assumed I had a plan for everything.

Only I didn't. It's not like I keep spare power amps in my bloody pocket, is it?

"It's fucked, Charlie," said Ritchie, staring at the amp's innards. "What we gonna do?"

"What about Hermann?" said Dan, remembering the guy from that blues band we once played with. "He's got that big old monster in his basement."

"It's only 400 watts," said Ritchie, immediately kicking that one into touch.

"Better than nothing, surely."

"Debatable, actually."

"Shall we debate it?"

"Piss off, Dan."

"What's the point? It'll take too long," I said. "What time is it?"

"Five to eleven."

"I make it half past."

"Don't care what you make it, Jake, I just want to know what time it is."

We hadn't been playing long enough for the first break but I got the DJ's attention up in his booth and, with the miracle of hand gestures, I gave him the all clear to fire up the jukebox. Once the music blasted the club back into life, I tried to make a plan. Troy was first to my side.

"It's not great timing, Dude," he drawled, "but I need ten of your English minutes."

"Not now, surely?"

Unless he knew where to find a spare power amp at short notice, I didn't have ten minutes for him. But then as Troy was exactly the sort of person who would know where to find a spare power amp at short notice, I followed him. He drifted towards the emergency exit doors behind the stage, and surprised me by opening them and slipping out into the street.

"Where are you going, Troy?"

"Anywhere, as long as it's by eleven."

"Eh?"

Without doubt, Troy was the most laid-back person I'd ever met, and I'd met a few. And while I wouldn't go so far as to say he was stressed, for the first time since I'd known him I noticed a degree of urgency in his eyes. I was already on edge, so it didn't make much difference to my mood, unless what he wanted to tell me was particularly unusual.

It was.

Isabelle was a committed people watcher, though it was beyond her not to articulate thoughts and judgments that were better left unsaid. She was flustered that Beth wasn't paying attention.

"Well, you wouldn't, would you, Beth? Pay attention."

"Hmm? No, not with the red shoes, no."

Beth had lost sight of the boys in the band. There was a lot of dancing and gyrating taking place in her field of vision. The DJ had pumped up the volume and clubbers were putting themselves about to music that stretched the bounds of the term. It was at times like these that she realised there were at least two parallel worlds in existence, only one of which generally received her patronage. She had the idea that the boy who drummed had gone to the toilet, while the long-nosed one in horn-rimmed glasses was leaning against the doorjamb of a storeroom to the side of the stage. He was sipping from a small bottle of beer. She considered a breath of air outside but, as she had barely been inside a quarter of an hour, decided to tough it out. It really was an appalling place.

"Do you come to this kind of place ever, Izzy?"

"Of course, Beth, all the time." Isabelle laughed and Beth knew that even her half-sister had her limits.

Alex had overheard.

"Do you think this is the kind of music the club usually plays?"

"Why? Don't tell me you don't like it!"

There was some good-natured hysterical laughter, toned down just enough to respect Charlie's decision to play the venue.

"Not sure it's the sort of crowd for Charlie's band, do you?"

"Oh, I don't know," said Isabelle, "sometimes this is all an act. I bet underneath the clothes and the make-up, they're all just the same as us. Shall we go and tease Charlie a bit?"

E Minor

He had my full, and what might be called undi-fucking-vided, attention. "Sorry. What? You're what? What?"

I stopped speaking because I know when I'm beaten. Troy had just told me that the police were going to show up any minute and he would be picked up. He would be picked up by them, but on Beth's behalf. What absolute tosh and bollocks.

"You gotta listen, and quick, this is all to do with you."

"What?"

My dialogue had shrivelled up, I could see that. What I couldn't see was what it all had to do with me. I decided to stop interrupting. He spoke and fast.

"Chad Cafarella was my cousin, Pa's eldest brother's boy. Joined the Army, ended up in Germany for a while. Good piano player. Based in Hamburg. He did a lot of extras, met up with a bunch of guys doing stuff, this and that. He fixed it for singers, bands, and musicians to play at the bases. Some big names, but mainly unknown or little-known entertainers, mostly from England, looking for some adventure and experience. I'm talking nineteen-sixty kind of time, you understand?"

I understood. But I understood silently. He went on.

"He had a Brit pal, a Jewish kid whose parents escaped the Nazis years before, you know the score. He had an agency in London. He sent people over for the British bases, working with a German guy called Manfred, and a British soldier." Troy appeared restless now, and looked ready to take flight. "Are you ready for this?"

I shook my head, or it shook itself. Not to indicate I wasn't ready for this, more to confirm that I was not following, or not yet anyway.

"The British soldier was Private Harry Winston Stokes."

He stopped.

He waited.

I froze.

And all in all, valuable time ebbed away.

Troy took my sleeve and literally dragged me along the street. At the corner of Lausitzer Platz he looked down towards the train track, and I assumed he was calculating how long it would take him to reach Görlitzer Bahnhof. I stopped because I'd forgotten to breathe, and there are some things in life you can't forget.

"That's your old man, dude. Okay? Harry Stokes."

I nodded.

"In 1961, before you were even born, there was trouble, and a fight, and two people died. One of them was your Dad. He took a bullet from a fight between the German, Manfred, and a politician's son who was a corrupt sonofabitch. Your old man took the rap for it, but he died a few days later, and Manfred disappeared."

"I told you he was shot," I said. "But he didn't die."

"Oh, he died. I'm sorry, man, but you've known all your life he was dead. Your people lied to you for sure, but not about him being dead, just how he died."

There was plenty of traffic moving outside, but only one car pulled over and partly mounted the kerb.

"Come on, get in," he said.

"Get in? Shit, I'm in the middle of a gig. We're in the middle of a gig. Hang on, you're not going back, are you?"

I got in the car. The driver was a soldier. I thought I recognised him as the man who was asking Troy for a request, but I couldn't be sure.

"I'll drop you back off in two minutes, Dude, we'll take a circuit of Görlitzer Park here, and we'll be done."

I began to feel hot in the head again, as I always do under stress, and I wound down a window. Incredibly, I had forgotten about the gig, and the broken amp, and Joanna, because of my Dad.

"Sorry, Troy, I'm lost again. Why is Beth after you?"

"Chad kept a diary. Not like a chick, with crap in every day, but he wrote stuff down, and collected memories. He married a Scottish girl and they lived in Edinburgh. He was killed in a car crash about three years ago. At the funeral, I met the Jewish kid, the guy your Dad and Chad knew. Not a kid any more. We talked for hours, about music and about Chad. And that's the end of it."

"That's not even the beginning, mate." I pointed out.

"Last year, after your Grandpa died, this guy turns up on my door with a package. A package and a plan. He tells me to open the package and read everything. He comes back the next day and tells me that the guy Manfred is sick and dying and wants to ease his conscience. He knows that, officially, your Dad died a murderer. He wasn't a murderer."

"What? My Dad officially died a murderer? That's news to me."

"I know. Manfred went East and, get this, became a spy or some shit or other. Okay, I need to split. It wasn't supposed to be me that was telling you this, and now I've got to rush it all."

At that point we had driven half way round the perimeter of the park, and it had become a bit too Len Deighton for my taste.

"Manfred wanted to look you in the eyes, and tell you the truth. He was dying. He needed you to be here in Berlin. That's how I came into it"

"So, you specifically persuaded me to play in Berlin instead of Hamburg?" Troy nodded. "Just so that some guy can apologise to me about framing my Dad?"

"You're condensing it a bit, Dude, and missing some of the point, but yes. Hell, I love playing with you, though. It's been a blast."

"Troy, I've been here for months. Where is this bloke? Where's Manfred?"

"I don't know. I never saw him. I had messages here and there. When you arrived here, he got sick again. Then he had to go to Moscow, for Christ's sake. It kept going on like that. And that's why your goddamn pal Beth and her team flagged me up. Manfred must be important over there. Hell, I don't know, but I'm not sticking around to be set up for something. I ain't done anything wrong here, but I'm no saint and I can't have my life looked into like that, understand?"

"Why didn't you tell me?"

"I wanted to, Dude. But this was Manfred's gig. Then Hank here appears and tells me to get the hell away, because they're coming to get me in five. Thank god for security leaks, eh? Now get out of the car and get yourself back in there. Oh, and I need twenty clean minutes, Dude. Okay? "

"What do you me to do?" This was pressure, I thought.

"Hell, you'll think of something, Charlie," he said with a big, goofy redneck smile. "That's what you're good at."

He pushed me out of the car with hearty slaps on the back. As the car drove off, he stuck an upturned thumb out of the opened window.

And I never saw him again.

"Charlie, where have you been? I've got a drink for you. It's only sparkling water."

It was Isabelle carrying a large tumbler and a smile. Beth was four inches behind her. Charlie had come back through the main entrance, having been waved through by the doorman, and the music, loud and faux-psychedelic, and the juddering it caused in his head reminded him that the band were short of a power amp. He was aiming for the stage and had been intercepted barely three steps from the goal.

"Thanks."

Charlie took a huge gulp, because he had become parched with nerves and confusion. It was gin and tonic, of course, though Isabelle had got the sparkling bit more or less right.

"Yeah, cheers Isabelle. Very funny."

"What's up?" asked Isabelle.

"Where's Troy, Charlie?" asked Beth.

"The amp's blown," said Charlie. "We can't play without it. Troy and I went to a mate's house to borrow a spare. They're bringing it now."

Beth relaxed. She considered taking Charlie to one side, but immediately thought better of it. The steady throbbing behind her left ear was spreading, and she would have liked nothing more than to head off home now.

"Izzy, I'm not really feeling one hundred percent. I might shoot off in a minute."

Joanna overheard, having also joined them.

"Already, Beth?" she asked. "Are you okay?"

"My head's banging, Jo. I wasn't in the mood, to be honest, but I thought it was right to come and cheer Charlie on. This is really not my kind of place."

"Why don't you let Günther go with you, he's had enough I think. He only came out for the dinner after all, poor lamb. I don't think he knows what's hit him."

"Where's Alex," asked Beth, looking around.

"She's talking with the bass player. He's told her he's a medical student apparently."

"No, really? And she's not swallowing that, is she? Is he asking her if she needs a check-up?"

They laughed at the childish desperation of men and the immature fantasy lives they dreamed up in search of new chat-up routines. Unfortunately,

Ritchie *was* actually asking Alex whether she would like a check-up.

Charlie hid in the side room, still grappling with the gin and tonic, or at least trying to find somewhere to put it. He was trying to think of what to do next and considering simply closing the door, stacking all the crates up against it, and waiting for as many hours as he could, to be sure that everyone had given up and gone home. That was assuming the people in the club were the type to have homes. Many of them barely appeared human.

"Shall I take that, Charlie?"

Joanna. He would know that voice from now until eternity. He turned around. She wore red again, and red lipstick, and the fingernails were red. It was all very red tonight. She took the offered drink.

"Did she say it was water?"

"Yes she did. It's not."

"I know. She thought it would be funny. I think she fancies you, Charlie."

"She fancies everyone."

"No, she doesn't."

"Okay."

Joanna felt slightly at a loss, as nothing she said seemed to be hitting the spot or, if it was, it wasn't the right spot. Dan offered her a bottle of beer, which she turned down politely. Beth, teasing a thread away from her blue blouse, sidled up.

"Nice top," Dan said to her. "My Mum's got one almost exactly the same."

"That's nice," said Beth, lying.

Charlie rubbed the back of his neck to ease away the tightness, because nobody else was going to. He sensed, rather than saw, Jake enter the room, and was reminded of the scene in a Marx Brothers film where lots of people keep entering a tiny cabin. Or some room or other. Or something.

"Charlie, the manager's wondering what's going to happen?" Jake asked. "Seems to think it's our business to have a working amp, not theirs."

Charlie could not argue with the logic and, for a change, he did not argue with it. He did not want to mention Troy's name, with Beth right next to him, for fear of activating her antennae, but what he now felt he wanted was to tell Joanna about his father. It may ultimately not have changed a thing, and the man was still someone who died over twenty-five years before, but it was a subject they had spoken around and it did not feel right not to tell her. Still, perhaps he would wait for another time.

"Let's wait and see what happens with getting another amp."

They waited twenty minutes.

Twenty minutes which hung more heavily on the shoulders of some than others. The trigger for Charlie's actions was an American soldier wordlessly packing Troy's saxophone in its case, something that caught Ritchie and Dan off guard. Ritchie was a tall man, but there was something disconcerting about a soldier's uniform that prevented him from steaming in to ask what was going on. That, and the calm untroubled nature of the theft.

It was no theft. It was another of Troy's friends, and once he had placed the instrument in its case and lifted it off the floor, he nodded at Charlie and left. Charlie took that to mean that Troy was clear, so he went looking for Beth, to sort things out.

E Minor

I knew the gig was over. The club was hammering along nicely without us anyway, and I supposed the reaction of the crowd to our cancellation would dictate the management's willingness to cough up the fee for a thirty-minute cameo. To beat Beth to the opening line and thus be in control of the dialogue, I began talking long before there was any hope of her being able to hear anything I said.

"Sorry, I didn't hear," she said.

She strained to hear and I strained to speak.

"I've got some information about Troy."

"Oh, that's all right. I'm afraid it's out of my hands now, anyway."

"No, you need to listen, because it's actually about me."

"What is?"

This was one of those conversations that wouldn't work in shouting mode, so I guided her into the little room again and explained, as quickly as I could, what Troy had told me. It didn't seem to be going down smooth as silk, but it's not my fault it was a dull tale of misunderstanding about nothing much at all. Sometimes life is boring, even in West Berlin. She made a lot of puzzled interruptions, delivered in hunched bewilderment and, if I had to lay a bet, I'd have put a tenner down that she didn't believe me. I was wondering whether this was an angle I hadn't given enough attention to, when Dan burst in, surfing a wave of chaos.

"Charlie, there's a fight!"

Ground Zero was not a venue that attracted testosterone, and my first reaction was to assume Dan was tripping. I was wrong. Someone's milk of human kindness had clearly been spilled, because I heard some high-pitched screaming from somewhere not far enough away for my liking, along with breaking glass and splintering wood. And through the doorway I saw glimpses of frightened people scurrying. I heard all this because, unusually, the DJ had switched off the music to make impassioned pleas for restraint, calm and peace and love, man.

But nobody listens to a DJ.

Also, through the doorway I saw Joanna. She looked uncomfortable and frightened, but was being expertly shepherded by Günther, who had his left arm over and around her while using his right to move people out of the way. And he did so without a hint of politeness. That should have been me, I thought, squirming with jealousy. If Joanna had any requirement of a White Knight, then I wanted the part. Why didn't she tell *him* she was a lesbian, and put him out of his misery? They passed out of my view and I stood there, staring.

I think I might have remained standing there, like a blind, slowly melting snowman, for all eternity.

But someone fired a gun. Twice.

"Bloody hell, someone's shooting! Everybody hide! Somewhere. Anywhere… Charlie. Charlie?" That was Jake, wide-eyed, wild-haired, and stammering. He was at the vanguard of a tidal wave of panic-stricken youth that was pouring into our little room, in what I would have to admit was an impressive but uncoordinated display of the human herd instinct.

In the *mêlée* I got an elbow in the eye, the other eye. There was a crash from the back of the room as someone fell against a tower of beer crates. More people piled in. I could see this could get ugly.

"Stop!" I tried to say, but nothing came out.

I saw Joanna, looking around her. Not for me, not this time. She was just inside by the door, against the wall, watching the people stumble in. Christ, someone was going to get crushed! I tried to get to her, but I was moving inexorably backwards in the crush, like lazy lava. Günther was there, though, and she huddled against his back while he dealt with any unnecessary hysteria with what I believe is called justifiable force.

After a metallic sound, there was a sudden icy blast about my neck and it was then that I realised that there had been an emergency exit in the room all along. I allowed myself to be sucked out into a courtyard where chaotic jostling had taken over seamlessly from the dancing. When someone suddenly grabbed me from behind in a forcible ejection, something inside me finally snapped. I twisted round and swung a punch.

And hit a policeman on the jaw.

There were a number of them there, helping to pull people out in the open and clearing space for those behind, but mine was the only one that anyone had punched. He didn't look happy. Affronted, I'd say. But definitely not in the least bit hurt. It wasn't all flowers and harp music though, because my hand brought tears to my eyes. It hurt a lot. My Grandad always said that I would probably punch like a girl.

Without much in the way of social chitchat, I was frogmarched to a police car and made to stand with my hands on top of the roof, and legs slightly spread on the ground. And as I stood there being searched and jabbed about, I couldn't help but think of Troy, because these blokes sure as hell hadn't just happened to be outside on the off chance that someone would fire a gun and cause a disorganised evacuation. I smiled at the comfy feeling that he got away.

Smiling didn't go down well. They asked me several questions, which I couldn't answer, and was posted into their warm car and driven to the City's main police station on Platz der Luftbrücke. Which was nice.

Beth sprung me just after one o'clock.

I had an hour in a holding cell but, unfortunately, not solitary confinement. There were two squaddies in there, about as rat-arsed as it was possible to get while still conscious, and an enormous round Turk with a frankly ludicrous moustache. Under different circumstances I'd have felt obliged to test it for authenticity. Two police officers took me out of the cell and up to a ground floor interrogation room. They sat me down behind a plain square table that was bolted to the floor and then left. I'd be lying if I said I sat around taking in the view, because there was absolutely nothing to look at. The walls were bare, there wasn't even an ashtray on the table and the carpet had no stains or rips that I could try and use for a quick self-administered Rorschach inkblot test.

What the lack of visual stimulus did ensure was full focus on the pain in my hand. I even wondered whether I'd broken it. I was rubbing the sore part yet again when the door opened and a plain-clothes detective came in. He may well have been some little girl's Daddy, but he looked like someone had been following him around all day waving a bowl of shit under his nose. He had a manila folder in his hand. I hoped it wasn't a file on me, because it looked empty and who wants to be insignificant? He sat down, and looked at me as if I was the one holding the bowl of shit.

"Charles Stokes. Englishman." he said. He knew his stuff, this one, I thought. "And yet, you are the invisible man."

Obviously, I never got round to the tedium of registering with the *Ausländeramt* nor applying for an *Aufenthaltserlaubnis*, so I imagined they could throw a bit more at me, if assaulting a police officer wasn't enough, regardless of whether it was with a girl's punch or not. Whatever angle the detective was going for, he never got the chance to start. A uniformed officer came in, bent down and exchanged whispers. Without a word to me, the detective left the room. The uniformed one simply said: *"Komm!"* and I followed him out to the front desk.

"Hello, Charlie. What the bloody hell have you been doing?"

It was Lewis, and his overcoat.

I did not want for company during my last few hours in West Berlin. There was a little more of Beth's entourage waiting outside, along with the Audi and Sid at the wheel. Other than those first few words, nothing was said until the car was moving.

"We've promised our friends that you'll be out of the country by the morning, Charlie." said Lewis. "We're taking you to your apartment. You can shower, sleep, and pack in the morning. Then you'll be taken to the airport. Don't expect to be welcomed back for a while. If you climb down a drainpipe and escape, we'll make up a story and the police will put you away. You can call whoever you want, and do whatever you like, but at 11 o'clock you'd better be packed and ready, understood?"

"Yes." I said. It seemed clear enough. I was worried about my hand. "My hand is really hurting."

"Take an aspirin."

"What if it's broken?"

Sid assured me it wasn't broken. Apparently he was an expert on the matter.

"Can you move your fingers?" he asked.

"Yes," I said.

"It's not broken."

It was. Not until I got back to England and had an x-ray did I find out I had broken the fifth metacarpal bone of my right hand. The plaster cast allowed some movement of my fingers, but I had to wipe my arse left-handed. So, six weeks of hell.

It was buzzing in the apartment when they dropped me off.

"Charlie!"

I couldn't help but laugh, despite everything. I suppose it was a release of tension, and not just from that evening.

"What happened? I saw you getting nicked." Jake's eyes were like saucers.

"Rock and roll, Charlie," said Dan. "But I think that's it for me. I'm going to work in a bookshop in Cheltenham."

There was a babble of different voices burning like candles dipped in adrenaline, and I flopped onto the sofa until they had settled into a hissing silence.

"Listen," I said, "I've had this great idea."

I'd never seen a room empty so fast. I had a phone call to make.

Joanna had not long gone to bed, but she could not sleep. The apartment was especially quiet, with Martina away. The phone's ring startled her, and she forced herself to take a calming breath before getting up. She had an idea of who it would probably be, and she was right.

"Charlie," she said. Her voice was dry and staccato. "What's the matter?" She wanted some water. "What happened?" She listened briefly. "Oh, no. Really? What time? Yes, all right. Yes, I know where it is. Okay, at half past. Goodnight, Charlie."

She looked at the bedside clock. There was time for six hours of sleep, if not the likelihood.

Sunday, November 22nd

E Minor

I sat at a window table, feeling so tired that I thought my forehead had melted and was falling over my eyes. I was already packed. I had selected what would accompany me on my deportation the night before, while fending off opinion and counter-opinion from the boys in the apartment, wallowing through the last vestiges of the night's excitement. Sleep, requiring painkillers, had been barely an hour before the alarm went off. A long shower had left me looking outwardly bright and respectable, like a freshly decorated house whose foundations were gone.

I was glad to be leaving West Berlin. It was sudden, the feeling. Almost from one moment to the next, it had lost all its purpose, charm and interest. That was not West Berlin's fault, it was mine. I had come for all the wrong reasons. I didn't even have reasons. It was nothing more than a hare-brained scheme whose only redeeming feature was its ability to convince others to take part. I would never have discovered the truth about my father's death had I not come but, in the general ebb and flow of my life, how my father died would have no bearing on anything. My father *not* dying would have been a story. Here I was in another little café, this time on Heinrich-Heine-Strasse within sight of the U-Bahn station of Moritzplatz, on another Sunday morning, feeling drained.

"All right, Charlie?"

I jumped, because I had missed her coming in somehow. She looked incredibly tired and puffy-eyed, but this only made her more attractive. She was smiling because I knew she had addressed me like the boys normally do.

"Hey," I said. "I was miles away. Well, I soon will be."

Joanna sat down and switched on her brown eyes. It was like being bathed in warm chocolate. But it made me feel hollow.

"So, what now, Charlie?"

"Off to Blighty," I said. "And probably just as well."

"Did they arrest you?"

"It's complicated," I said.

"You can come back, can't you? Who's to know, it's not like they really do anything at passport control."

"I think I'll lie low for a while, either way."

"Your hand is swollen, Charlie, does it hurt?"

"That would be yes."

I held my hand out in front of me and gave the little finger a bit of wiggle. She took it with both her hands and the cold fingers immediately felt soothing against the swollen skin.

"You should get it looked at, it might be broken."

She could have been talking about my heart.

"I will."

She wouldn't let go of my hand, but I wished she would. I just didn't say.

"Well, it turned out that my Dad died from a gunshot wound in Hamburg. It also turned out that Chad Cafarella was Troy's older cousin. He and Dad were friends over there, and with a couple of others they got up to mischief, I don't doubt. Troy knew all this. He knew before we even met."

"Knew what?"

Joanna had leaned forward. I gently pulled my hand out from hers on the pretence of dealing with an itch round the back of my right ear. And then I thought: what does it matter what Troy knew, or when? Nothing at all. It was time to move on. I pulled a slip of paper out of my pocket and slid it across the table.

"Oh, nothing. Doesn't matter. This is my address. I'll be there, or somewhere else. If you want to write, send it there. Eventually, I'll get it." I looked at her sweet, tired face. "If you want to write."

"Yes, Charlie," she said with a smile. "I think I'll want to write. Will you?"

She reached inside her navy woollen coat and handed me a small, unsealed envelope. I extracted from it a photograph, which I recognised immediately as the one I had taken that first day. I wasn't going to ask how Joanna came about it, perhaps Isabelle had made copies. I'd seen it before, once, but this time I knew something of what lay behind all the faces. Each of their smiles, forced or otherwise, no longer hid their secrets. Or not from me, anyway. To look at Joanna in the photo was like reliving the first time I'd seen her. Taking it out of the envelope I had noticed writing on the back, and when I flipped it over, Joanna's address was written in full.

"Yes," I said. "I will."

The plan was to say *Auf Wiedersehen* properly, because I didn't want my last memory of Joanna to be the sight of Günther protecting her from a riot I probably helped create. Now was the time to hug and go.

"I have to go. I just needed to see you."

I stood up, a powerful mental battle raging between wanting to get the goodbyes done quickly and wanting the goodbyes to stretch out until next Thursday. There were butterflies in my stomach, but dead ones.

We embraced with our coats on. I held her tightly and she squeezed me and at the exact right time, I gave her a big kiss on her cheek and let her go. At that point I would have cried, but I had put on the armour. I looked down at my feet, and had to clench my teeth for support.

"Take care, Charlie," she said.

I just nodded, more like a tic. And I didn't look up until I knew she wasn't there anymore. I was going to wait until I was sure she would be out of sight before leaving the café, but something changed my mind. I pressed my face against the window where I could see as far as the entrance to the U-Bahn on Moritzplatz. She walked steadily, but not fast. There were so few people around, that I never lost sight of her. I calculated how many seconds before she would reach the station and disappear. My chest began thumping. Please, Joanna. Go on. Do it. Just look back.

A white Mercedes van passed, and for a few seconds I couldn't see her. I almost felt sick. Come on, what? No, there she was. She was nearing the entrance. She would be out of view any second. Now.

She turned round and looked back and stopped and was gone.

And that's when I decided that all hope was not lost.

Monday, November 23rd

A lex knocked on the door of Herr Reiseneder's office to give him some news. She could have done it over the phone, but she wanted to be looking at him, in the flesh so to speak, just to be sure.

"Mrs Gagnon," he said, "I wasn't expecting you."

That much was true.

"I'm afraid I have no further news."

Here he was on less firm ground.

"I shall only be a moment, Herr Reiseneder," said Alex, practically fizzing with self- belief. "Would you inform my husband that I am moving out of the house?"

"Out of the house?"

"Out of the house."

"I should also be grateful if you would inform him that he is no longer required as a husband. And finally…"

"Mrs Gagnon, I am not in contact with your husband."

"And finally, I would like you to inform him that, if I can be bothered, I shall commence divorce proceedings against him."

"And if you cannot be bothered?"

"I shall simply leave him."

Alex had not sat down, so her departure was swift and silent. Herr Reiseneder stood looking at the door, as he had a premonition that it would be opening again. It did.

"What I mean to say, Herr Reiseneder, is that I have left him."

Beth had misplaced her tan brogues again. She knew Isabelle hadn't taken them because Isabelle had told her plainly that it was a curse beyond Satanism to have a sister with the same size feet and no taste in footwear.

She had a black pair. All was not lost.

An hour later she was ambling into the Tiergarten, crossing the Landwehrkanal on the Strasse des 17 Juni, in the presence of the Attaché from the Embassy and an unexplained Yorkshire terrier. Some of the ambling was down to the terrier's indecisive walking style, and some to the Attaché's conversational techniques, where a great deal of emphasis was placed on coming to a standstill at exciting moments.

These exciting moments were relative, of course.

Beth was the self-acknowledged Duchess of Ambivalence and had always been so. While this ensured she would never be a coruscating success in the cutthroat world of business, it also ensured she would never allow problems or defeats at work to trouble her unduly. That Troy had got away bothered her not a jot. In fact, she quickly accepted that Charlie's explanation was acceptable. Beth did have a gift for reading people, and she believed Charlie. She and the Attaché had discussed many mundane issues, and then he surprised her.

"We're going to have a bit of a shuffle around, don't you know?" he said.

"Oh."

"Yes."

Wordlessly, the Attaché paused while the terrier set about some ablution duties. Beth thought it might be nice to have a dog again, just a small one like this. Walks in the park might help in the battle for fitness.

"What sort of a shuffle around, then?" she asked.

"Well, it's London's decision, of course. They wanted to poach some people, move others around, close this and open that."

"That's nice," said Beth.

Terriers could be a bit of a handful, though, she seemed to remember from somewhere or other. A Labrador would be lovely, if not for all the hairs.

"We want you to come over to the Embassy. Twelve months, anyway, see how it goes. What do you say?"

"East Berlin?" Beth had not expected to catch that one. Still, it could be fun for a change. "I don't know. It's a bit out of the blue. But I suppose it could be fun," she said.

"Yes, indeed. It could be fun. It just won't be. Rest assured on that score. It's always good to accept these little changes, for the sake of your career, I mean."

"I know." Beth would have to talk to Isabelle.

The terrier, on cue, extruded an enormous turd onto the grass, quite disproportionate to the size of the dog, and any lingering ideas of a little canine companion were swiftly abandoned.

Thursday, November 26th

Dimitrios had absorbed all the gossip about the crazy Englishman's crazy gig at Ground Zero (he had no idea where or what that was) and the gunfire and the soldiers and the misunderstandings and the Police raid. There was only so much entertainment a heart could take these days, and he thanked god again for his restaurant and his simple life.

"Dimitrios, don't let it get cold. Hurry!"

And for his wife, Alikaki.

They were seated at table seven, which had become something of a humorous eccentricity, as it was by no means the best table in the restaurant. Alex was tapping the side of her wine glass with a fingernail to announce that she had something to say.

"Oh, she's going to give a speech," said Isabelle. "Quiet at the back, please."

"It's not a speech. Definitely not a speech," said Alex, "but it is an announcement of sorts."

"Will there be a toast?"

"I can put one in, if required."

"It is more than required, it's obligatory!"

Alex had to take a deep breath. It was when she placed a hand against her chest before exhaling, that the others settled into silence as they sensed it might be something serious, or at least uncomfortable.

"You girls are my best friends here. But I think that I may have been living a bit of a lie recently, and I want to break out from it. We all have certain things we like to keep to ourselves, things that are too private, but I don't want to anymore."

Alex took a sip of wine. Today they were all drinking wine, she had been adamant.

"I am broke. I have been broke for months, actually. I don't want to waste time on details, but Tony is almost as much of a criminal as my father was, and his investments collapsed. This affected my money. When the stock market crashed last month, I ended up in a lot of trouble. Tony had put stuff in my name and I've been chased for the money."

"Oh, Alex," said Joanna.

"I don't know why I didn't say anything. I've always been the one that splashed the cash. I've got an expense account and I wanted always to treat you all. I just didn't know what to say if I couldn't do this anymore."

"For God's sake, Alex," said Isabelle. "You're our friend, you're not our sponsor. Why didn't you say something?"

"What would I have said? No one wants to hear about another's money troubles. Really. Trust me, they don't."

"What's Tony doing about it?" asked Beth.

"I don't know where Tony is." That caused a stir. "I don't care where he is. I'm finished with Tony." That was her cue for a generous slug of the red. "I'm leaving him. I know there'll be a mess, and I suppose the banks or whatever will come after me, but I don't care. I have had enough. None of it is of my doing. I've been selling bits of jewellery to get by."

Isabelle shook her head in pained disbelief. Once jewellery was being sold off, life was becoming serious. Incredibly, she kept quiet.

"Tony is in jail, by the way."

"What?"

"Or maybe he's somewhere in Berlin."

"Alex?"

"Confusing, isn't it?"

"When did you last see him?"

"It was weeks and weeks ago, but he's alive. He rang me once. I don't want to talk about Tony. I've also lost my job."

"No?"

"When?"

"Why?"

Alex lifted her glass.

"Time for a toast, then?"

"Come on, Alex, what happened at work?" asked Joanna. "You loved that job."

"The company that owns the magazine were bought out and the buyers wanted some changes in management. But, there is a silver lining. I got quite a big pay-off, actually, and I was encouraged to go quietly." She laughed. "So, lunch is still on me." She lifted her glass. "That's the toast: Lunch is on me!"

They all giggled and that seemed to loosen the atmosphere. Alex smiled at each of them in turn, as if to assure them she was fine really, and everything would turn out for the best.

"But, darling, what will you do now for work? Are you leaving Berlin?"

"No, I'm staying. I'm going to find somewhere cheaper to live and a different job. Also, I've met someone else. I'm going to give it a go."

"Alex, what have you been drinking? Met somebody else? When did this happen? Who is it, anyone we know?"

Alex told them about Christian, and how they met at the Gala, and how she had been to visit him over the Wall. There followed a lot of excited chatter about what it must be like to live in East Berlin and, probably moved by Alex's honesty, Beth began to tap lightly at the rim of her wine glass with a fork. She smiled uncomfortably when the others turned to face her, and immediately regretted her moment of boldness.

"It's the day for announcements," said Joanna. "I wish I had one."

"I have also been asked to leave my job," said Beth, "although no money is involved. I'm being moved to the Embassy in East Berlin. Time for a move, it seems."

"East Berlin?"

Isabelle's face had drained of colour. Beth knew what was coming.

"What about me? What about us? Bloody hell, Beth. Can't you just leave and do something else? It's only an office job."

"It's steady and it's a civil service job, Izzy," said Alex, gently. "Beth needs that."

Beth cleared her throat.

"I don't do the job you think I do."

"Speak up, Beth, I can't hear you."

"I can't," she replied. She dropped her chin. "I work... I work in intelligence analysis."

The others would not have understood what she was talking about if she had said she knew how to 'dipsulate a cornicular'.

"No, you don't," said Isabelle. "I mean, I don't know what you're talking about, but whatever it is, you don't do it."

"It doesn't matter. I can't tell you about it. I'm just saying that I actually have quite an important job. And they want me to work over there, for a year at least anyway."

"When were you going to tell me?" Isabelle was hurt.

"Today. Today after work I was going to tell you. And we will talk about it tonight."

"Alex can move in with you, Izzy," Joanna said. "Why not? You need somewhere to stay Alex, and Izzy never likes to be alone at night. You'd be perfect together."

"You know, I could. Couldn't I? That might be fun, Izzy," said Alex.

Isabelle had clouded over like early summer in Brighton, with the face of a little lost girl who had wondered onto the street looking for her Mummy because she didn't like the playground. A part of Beth wished she hadn't said anything, and another part had been glad. And Joanna's suggestion might not be a bad little idea.

"You know I can't live by myself, Beth. I can't spend the night somewhere alone. You know what I'm like. And I can't live in bloody East Berlin, can I?" With a petulant sweep she drained her glass like a diva in mid-tantrum, but used the distraction to sprinkle a little thought onto the proceedings: "Alex," she said, "that's a great idea. I accept."

From that point, until the main courses were obliterated, it was all about Alex, and no detail of Christian Bauer's existence was considered too insignificant for discussion, dissection or dissemination. Joanna, who perhaps caught up in the mood of confession, or by feelings of guilt towards Charlie, or by the exuberance of the conviviality on show, felt a sudden almost irrational requirement to speak out about her sexuality. Why not tell them what she had not told Charlie until it was too late? Could she not trust them to keep it to themselves? And then again, why should they? It was nothing to be ashamed of. Tell and be damned, as someone or other once said. That was the kind of thing Charlie would say: *as someone or other once said*. She smiled, and she shook her head, and she cleared her throat.

But she didn't tell them she was having a lesbian relationship.

As for Isabelle, she'd no more likely tell Beth she was an escort than dip her head in a bucket of cold custard.

Then again, she was not an escort any more.

She was still a nuisance though, and it was she who planted the seed in Alex's head that maybe she should consider trying to smuggle Christian out of East Berlin, so that if they were to live happily ever after, it could at least be somewhere less scarred.

"Beth could fix it, couldn't you?" she said. "You'll be over there with all that diplomatic immunity."

Beth was horrified.

"Oh, God, no! Don't even think about it. I knew I shouldn't have said anything. Really, Izzy. The Embassy will not get involved in anything like that. Tell him to plan his own escape." But she couldn't help but laugh, too.

"Or he could wait until the Wall comes down," suggested Isabelle. "When will that be, Beth?"

Beth pulled a face and shrugged.

"Who knows. Never?"

East Berlin, Saturday, November 28th

Alex found the moment of stepping into the station at Friedrichstrasse oddly exciting. East Berlin was so incredibly unlike West Berlin, and its cavernous, dated concourse seemed the perfect buffer with which to warn the traveller that they were about to step out into a land where the volume had been turned off and the lights dimmed. Of course, her excitement would undoubtedly wear off along with the novelty of her trips.

She kissed Christian and slipped her arm through his. Carefree as teenagers, they made their way along Friedrichstrasse towards Unter Den Linden, there to take a leisurely stroll towards the desolate deprivation of the Brandenburg Gate as seen from the East side. For Christian this always seemed such a symbol of the disparity between the life he led and the one he could lead. He walked with an awkward gait, almost a limp occasionally, and Alex had noticed.

"Are you all right? Sometimes it feels like you're limping."

"My back is a little tight. It's an old sports injury. I have to manage it a little. The damp never helps." He smiled.

"Christian?"

"Yes?"

"Does it ever seem unbearable to stand somewhere like this and look at that Wall - I mean, it's not *that* big - and realise it's the only thing that's stopping you being over there?"

Christian laughed.

"That, and the dogs, and the soldiers, and the guns, you mean?"

Alex laughed with him, but it was not a proper laugh. They were holding hands and she squeezed tighter, gathering up a bit of courage. She took two quick breaths.

"Christian, why don't you try and escape?" She paused, gritted her teeth, and went on. "I want you to try and escape. I'll help you. Anything you need. Come across. Come across, and be with me."

She had been too nervous to look at him. When she finished, and was greeted only with silence, she stared blankly towards the West and wondered whether she had made a terrible misjudgement. Her mind scorched back to that awful moment when she had walked the entire length of the village hall, in full view of all the other nine-year olds, to ask Gary Grover for a dance. And he had looked away and snickered with his pal, Bill the Belly. It had not been easily forgotten.

"Come with me," said Christian.

They retraced their steps up the once-magnificent avenue of the Unter Den Linden. Tiny raindrops danced in the air, barely large enough to contain water, painting a glistening sheen on the dark, bullet-scarred buildings that could have been lifted straight out of a film set. Whose heart could sing living amongst all this? Alex thought. But maybe not everyone felt the same.

"Did I say the wrong thing?"

Alex might have been concerned she had said the wrong thing at the wrong time but Christian, though silent, appeared his usual self. When he did finally speak, his voice was every bit as calm and controlled as it had always been.

"My birthday was on November 8th. I was twenty-eight years old. This is where I work. I was born in Leipzig. East Germany has made me what I am today. I am someone you've just said you have feelings for. So it can't all be bad."

He was teasing her, but Alex had no idea. She felt mortified she had made such a crass assumption and cursed her arrogance. But where did she go from here? Maybe she should at least say something? That would be a start.

Too late. He hadn't finished talking.

"Do you know what I want for my thirtieth birthday?"

"A new watch?"

"I want to wake up not being here."

They continued, still slowly, with Alex not completely sure of what he meant, until it began to rain with more certainty and they picked up the pace. Alex was aware of being led.

"Let's have a hot drink," said Christian.

"That would be nice."

"And I'll tell you my escape plan afterwards. It's probably better than yours anyway."

Alex looked at him in open-mouthed surprise. Then she smiled and shook her head. And if her surroundings had been more conducive to it, she would have cartwheeled across the street and sung hallelujah.

"Not until next year in Spring time. And that's only if everything goes to plan. And it probably won't. Do you understand what I'm saying, Alexandra?"

"I have to be patient?"

"Yes," said Christian. "So you'll have to come and visit me here for quite some time yet."

And she did, for quite some time.

1988

Some people are wary of coincidence. The mere idea of some loose concurrence of events fills them with suspicion or doubt. They look for the hidden meaning behind the apparent meaning. For these people, coincidence is a myth they would no more believe in than the existence of Father Christmas or the tooth fairy. For others, coincidences are harmless examples of the magic and mystery of life itself, enjoyed for their own sake, depending on how great and extraordinary the coincidence. For the greater good of mankind, effort should be made to separate the one group from the other. Let the tax inspectors and the homicide detectives swim amongst their own kind.

If asked to choose the day when the single most important event of the year had occurred to them, Charlie Stokes, Joanna, Beth, Isabelle and Alex would each have thought long and hard. And they would almost certainly have chosen this one. Considering that not one of the events was connected to the other, this indeed qualified as a coincidence.

London, Thursday, May 26ᵗʰ

Charlie Stokes had never been to this part of Bayswater before, but he found Orme Court with little difficulty. Brian Levine was waiting for him, outside his neat offices on the second floor. He was beaming and some of his happiness spattered onto Charlie's shoes.

"Charlie Stokes. Dear boy. This way."

Brian Levine had a secretary called Edna and the pair of them had been in this same office for twenty-eight years. Edna could have worked the room blindfolded. She sat at her desk behind a wide-carriage Olympia typewriter. When Charlie walked in she stood up, and also beamed at him. It was a day for beam receipts.

Just after Christmas, four stitches in his fingers from when he had tried to trim the cast with a hacksaw so he could better strum a guitar, Charlie had decided to go away to the sun for what remained of the winter months, and to do this he would sell his guitars, except the ones he couldn't bear to part with. So, actually, he sold one guitar. He sold his car twice. He had already sold it once, before he left for Berlin. The friend who had bought it went to Australia for six months and left it in Charlie's care. So Charlie sold it again, but to a man from Guernsey. It was dog eat dog.

That was when Brian Levine had telephoned. He had wanted to know about a ballad Charlie had written, and Charlie had wanted to know why, and the two questions had tangoed. So Charlie had sent a little demo, and then flown south and forgotten all about it.

"How about a drink, Charlie? I have Coke in the fridge."

"Thanks."

Edna fetched the Coke.

"Well, Charlie. I've got some good news for you," said Brian. "Sit down, dear boy, sit down."

Charlie sat down.

"The Starrliners want your song on their new album."

"What?" Charlie stood up, shocked. "Why? They write their own stuff."

"Not always."

"That might be worth a bob or two," said Charlie.

"I do hope so, Charlie, because I thought I'd manage you for a while. Only ten percent across the board. It's only fair."

"Yes," said Charlie, laughing. "That's only fair."

"There's just one thing they mentioned."

"Oh?"

"There didn't seem to be a title."

"It's called *Charlie's Lament in E minor.*"

Edna arrived with a Coke for Charlie.

"Let's call it *Such Is Love*," said Levine. "They might not want to play it in E minor."

"They might not at that," said Charlie. "I'll call it *Such Is Life.*"

"We'll call it *Such Is Love (Such Is Life)*. I like a title with parentheses."

East Berlin

Christian Bauer knew the moment it happened that it was serious. He maintained what balance he could on his left leg, and collapsed onto the floor like a pair of discarded trousers in a teenager's bedroom.

Perhaps he had lost a little concentration in the run-up. He had allowed a conversation from months ago to filter into his consciousness.

"What I'd like to do first, when I leave here," he'd said, "is go to Italy."

"Italy?" Alex's face brightened. "Really?"

"Yes. I'd like to visit Naples and Sicily, and eat real pizzas. And speak Italian, of course."

"Of course. *Chiunque dovrebbe parlare un pò d' italiano prima di andare in Italia.*"

"You speak Italian?" Christian sounded impressed.

"My mother's Swiss-Italian. I adore Italy, and I love the South." She made no effort to tone down her childish excitement. "I promise you the first thing we'll do is go to Italy. By train. I'll reserve the seats now."

And they had laughed and walked on.

He rolled over onto his back and held his right knee with both hands. It was a deeply intense pain that told him the escape would not be going ahead next week, and it did not matter how much training had been put in, or how perfectly it had all been prepared, or how crushingly disappointed Alex would feel. He had just ruptured his cruciate ligament, and all bets were off.

The time for patience was upon them.

Again.

Beth and Isabelle were returning along the Unter den Linden from Marx-Engels Platz. Alex had asked them to go and watch the display of gymnastics and acrobatics that Christian's school were participating in as part of an outdoor health extravaganza. Christian appeared to have injured himself, and Alex had loitered for the opportunity to see how he was. Beth was hurrying back to the Embassy, but she would tell Isabelle the news now, on the hoof.

"Do you know what they asked me to do today?"

"Blow up a bouncy castle?"

"They want me to go to Budapest, to work. They want me to work in Budapest!"

"But Beth, why? Are they going to turn you into a communist?"

They were about to cross Friedrichstrasse. Isabelle would peel off here and walk to the station. She'd been walking far too much for her liking. They stopped at the kerb.

"I go where I'm told, I suppose."

"Why don't you do what you want to do?" asked Isabelle.

"How would I know what I want to do? I prefer it this way. I'll miss Berlin."

"Will you?"

"I'm not sure."

"Oh my God, Beth, you know what this means, don't you?" Isabelle's eyes sparked into life. "Goulash. You'll eat nothing but goulash and turn into a great fat blob."

"I have to be back, Izzy, that's where you have to go," said Beth, helpfully pointing the way to the station and crossing point. She gave Isabelle a kiss on the cheek. "I'll call you later."

Isabelle moped most of the way back into West Berlin, but when she stopped outside Zoo Station, to adjust the laces on the Reeboks she had worn for the trip East, she received a gentle pinch on her backside. The kind only a friend, or someone incredibly brave, would dare to attempt. She assumed it was Joanna, although she was today beginning a weeklong holiday. But when she turned around, Isabelle saw that it was a man, and not just any man.

It was the Belgian chocolate salesman. His name would perhaps come to her in a second, perhaps not. The man she allowed to take the naughty photos that Charlie had seen. His name was Anton. Of course it was. He was rather handsome, she thought.

Awkward.

"Isabelle," he said. "This is incredible. I was at the café across the street. I arrived this morning. I was just thinking about you, I look up, and there you are. It's unbelievable, eh?"

Isabelle had to admit it was unbelievable. And she didn't believe a word of it. But a handsome man in chocolate, sober let's not forget, seemed genuinely grateful to see her. She would just go along with it. See what happened.

What happened was that she fell a little bit in love.

And then a little bit more.

West Berlin

Joanna had packed lightly, by her standards, taking only a medium sized black Nike sports holdall for her trip. She was only going for a week and her Mum was not shy of using the washing machine. Joanna did not want to be lugging unnecessary weight to and from the train once she had arrived at Gatwick.

She had nevertheless treated herself to a taxi and stood at the window, ready for departure, looking down at the lime tree in front of the apartment block, thinking how beautiful it looked at this time of the year. She would go down in fifteen minutes. In the meantime she would look at the tree, and read Martina's short letter for the seventh time.

"*Dear Jo,*

I should be speaking to you now, instead of writing this, but I don't think I would be able to find the right words. I've never had any difficulty in telling you what I think before, not once, and you've always been the easiest person to talk to. But this time I can't face it.

I am leaving, sweet Joanna. I am going to Warsaw tomorrow.

Yes, I mean leaving in that way. I have decided it's time to move on. It's the right decision, I know it is, and that makes the pain more bearable.

I love you. Of course, I love you. And I have been so happy with you, you know that. But I need someone to love me too, and I know that you do not. Not now. I'm not sure you ever did. Before, it didn't really matter perhaps, but it does now.

I have always known who I am, from as long ago as I can remember. But you have never known, have you? Another confused girl! I didn't mind, not at first. But now I feel I shouldn't get in the way of you finding what it is you are looking for. My own father was a drunk and a thief, so maybe I find it harder to understand your need to find out more about your own. You told me you would come to Berlin to be with me. But you've become more and more distracted, if that's the right word. It's more and more about your father. And what about Charlie? Yes, I notice these things. Your eyes tell me!

Your journey is getting more complicated, and the time has come for you to continue it alone. Until you can stand in front of that mirror and know who you really are, you will never find peace. And neither will anyone else you are with.

Please remember this: I am not leaving you because I don't love you any more, or because I have found someone else. I am leaving because it's the right thing to do, for me and for you.

I will miss you, Joanna.

Be happy, my little brown-eyed girl.

Martina x"

1989

The Starrliners' fourth album, *Not Always What It Seems*, reached the top 10 in the UK's album charts on the third week of January and sold solidly throughout the spring. But it wasn't until the early autumn, when Joanna was back visiting her Mum, that she heard Charlie's song on the radio. She had the record, of course, and the song was the third track on side two. It was the only track she listened to. She was not a fan of The Starrliners. She smiled. It would be a few pounds more into Charlie's bank account. Her mother came into the kitchen holding the phone.

"It's for you, dear," she said. "Isabelle."

"Hi, Izzy, how are you?"

"Absolutely fine, darling. I'm in Antwerp."

"What are you doing there?"

"Getting proposed to!"

"No?"

"Yes!"

"Oh my God, Izzy. You're getting married?"

"Yes. Yes, I'm getting married. I said yes, so yes!"

Joanna pictured Isabelle jumping up and down and, possibly, squealing.

"And I'm moving to Belgium, darling. It's like heaven. They only eat chips and chocolate. I just spoke to Beth and she's so happy."

"Of course she is. Oh, I'm so pleased for you!"

Joanna heard the radio DJ list the dates of The Starrliners' 1989 tour: a week after playing at the Hammersmith Palais, they would be at the Deutschlandhalle in West Berlin, on November 11th. She wondered whether Charlie would consider making a trip back.

Joanna's mother overheard the talk of marriages and sniffed wistfully. She had wisely stopped making comments on the matter, though she would still sniff wistfully when the opportunity presented itself.

East Berlin, Monday, November 6th

They lay naked under the sheet, Alex on her left side with her right hand softly stroking his chest, shoulder and arm. Christian lay on his back, eyes partly opened, looking at the ceiling - or maybe at the stars and the heavenly constellations and the ceiling just got in the way. This would be the last time. The last time they would be together in this or any other room in East Berlin.

For Alex it was the end of nearly two years of countless day trips, hundreds of Deutschmarks in border currency exchanges, nervous journeys, secrets and lies, delays, disappointments, accidents, operations, arguments - for there had been arguments too. It would all be for nothing if Christian could not grant his own wish to be over the Wall before his thirtieth birthday. And that was now only two days away.

And Max, his best friend, had left him to it.

Alex would probably not have slept that night anyway. She had an hour before she would need to be at Checkpoint Charlie. That was half an hour for sure that she could stay here looking at his profile. Christian lay still and calm and relaxed, secure in his fate. But it wouldn't be Christian who'd wander the world bereft and empty if it all ended in tragedy, she thought. It would be her. The possibility was almost unbearable. All she could do was look at his face and try and wipe away the memory of this evening, and

Max's final words.

Nothing had survived of Christian's original and daring plan. His first knee reconstruction had needed a second within weeks of resuming the training. As she got to know him better, she accepted that if he had a fault, he could be stubborn. How Max despaired sometimes.

The unpleasantness took hold after Christian finally abandoned the trampoline idea one day as he punished himself in the pool, swimming endless chlorine-assisted lengths in a desperate push for rehabilitation. He had always been a decent swimmer, but it was becoming clearer how strong a swimmer he could become. And, as the time ticked by with his knee effectively destroyed, he announced that he would swim across the Spree.

Max refused.

Max said they should wait. In another two or three years, with all the reforms in the Soviet Union and other communist states, things would change for the better. Things would loosen up for sure.

"We're young, we have time. What's another two years? You started with this crazy business two years ago. We're still here. It's not so bad that we can't wait a while longer."

"Nothing will change, Max. I will not turn thirty here. I made a promise to myself. I am going over. Whatever it takes. I can make the swim. You can make the swim."

"Listen to yourself, Christian! 'I can make the swim'. It is not the water alone that is going to try to stop you. I am not doing it."

"Yes, you are," said Christian, and he had smiled.

Alex had been at one or two of these occasions where the two old friends had argued. She had felt uncomfortable, and responsible. She knew how Yoko Ono must have felt. But tonight the argument had a ring of finality to it that cut her to the marrow. She had brought over a miniature brass horseshoe "for luck". Christian had laughed, tossing it up and down in his hand.

"This is good, it will help my buoyancy."

Max had been apoplectic.

"Foolish woman! How will that help Christian? Lucky horseshoes? Do you think this is a game for children? Can you not see what is out there waiting for him?" The force of Max's venom shocked Alex.

"And you, Christian," Max went on, "please tell me that you have come to your senses. Tell me, dear mother of god, you will not be so stupid as to do this. Damn your stupid birthday. Why won't you just wait? Everything will sort itself out. Ha! Patience you used to say. You are a hypocrite, my friend, but worse than that, you are an idiot. You are a selfish, foolish idiot." Tears were welling up in his eyes.

He bit his lip and Alex saw his fingers form raging fists. Christian, shocked but no less committed, moved towards Max.

"No, don't touch me. Don't come near me."

Max stood at the doorway, panting and now aware of his raised voice and how someone may have heard him. He put his rage down, and kicked it across the floor. His voice was quiet, measured and calm.

"I will not be there tomorrow, Christian, to watch you die."

And with that, he was gone.

A lex and Christian lay in silence for a further fifteen minutes, which to Alex had felt like fifteen seconds. Their remaining time together was burning away like a rampant fuse, and no amount of half-arsed meditation on her part was going to eradicate the rising sense of impending disaster that was choking her every breath. She would not be making any melodramatic speeches. Christian had been quite clear on the matter. She could do that once they were in Italy. She had talked incessantly about Italy. She had already bought the train tickets, and memorised the seat reservations.

"Can you still go ahead without Max?" she asked.

"Max will be there," he replied.

"I don't think so."

Alex would comfortably have bet her house on Max not being there, but her house had been repossessed. It was Max's job to phone the Embassy in the morning, if anything went wrong.

"Don't worry," Christian said. "He will be there and he won't watch me die. I'll tell him to look the other way."

"That's not funny."

"Come, let's get dressed. Time for you to go."

As Alex numbly put on her clothes, she imagined this was how a death row inmate might feel after being woken up on execution day, wanting nothing more than a few more hours under the duvet. She pulled herself together and allowed Christian to walk her to the bus stop. She didn't kiss him or even look him in the eye. She would save it all for tomorrow night.

Tomorrow night would be the start of a whole new life.

West Berlin, Tuesday, November 7th

E Minor

To be honest, I lost track of the phone calls, and I struggled to remember the schedule, it had changed so many times. I was at the Hotel Heidelberg in Knesebeckstrasse. Now that I could afford to, I determined to cast away the grimy memories of straitened circumstances and labelled foodstuffs in a shared kitchen. However the trip went, it would be comfortable, and central. Brian Levine told me where to stay. He didn't pay for it, but I couldn't fault his recommendation.

Within an hour of checking in, I'd spoken to Beth, I'd spoken to Isabelle and I'd had a brief, practically surreal conversation with Alex, who sounded as if she were low on drugs. I'd even heard from Dimitrios at the restaurant. But I didn't speak to Joanna. It had been a long time. I wanted to be looking at her in person the next time I heard her voice. For Joanna I would wait until Thursday evening.

Save the best for last.

Although it was not Alex who would be skulking in the dark and trying to appear invisible, she had dressed entirely in black casual clothing, designed for ease of movement and stress-free soiling. Apart from the black canvas plimsolls that she had bought new, everything was from the second-hand shops. She had become far less fashion-relevant since meeting Christian, but not so much that she enjoyed dressing like an intellectual on hard times.

It was the poet John Keats who wrote of autumn's mists and mellow fruitfulness, but there was nothing either mellow or fruitful about Alex as she huddled in the front seat of Isabelle's car. There was no denying, however, that the mists were out and plentiful. It was a dank, heavy, miserable night with poor visibility. They couldn't have asked for anything better.

Alex had the window wound fully open, and when she heard it she jumped, but without moving. It was not like in the films. There was none of that musical ricochet or gentle reverb. It was just a flat crack. But she knew what it was. She had been to Bisley once, with her father. What she had taken from the day, more than anything else, was how different a rifle shot sounded in real life compared to the telly.

She heard shouts in the distance. Were they shouts? American voices? One shot only, or was it a car backfire? Confusion. She got out of the car. What was the time? Who just fired a gun? Where was Christian?

What?

Who?

Where?

It had taken an hour, moving a few sodden metres at a time, to almost reach the bank. He crawled along with the speed and grace of a slug, and waited, with the outer covering of normal clothes on top of his wetsuit giving him the appearance of a bloated seal. For the first time in over two years, Christian Bauer thought he was frankly the stupidest person East of the Brandenburg Gate. Having inserted himself through the tiny gap in the fence that Max had found, he was now as likely to be spotted if he tried to return from no-man's land, as he would be going ahead with the swim. If they saw him, it was jail. But there was no guarantee, even if they began shooting, that they would necessarily hit him. A lot of these guards in the *Grentztruppen der DDR* were still teenagers. They wouldn't try too hard to be accurate. Just as long as they could show their superiors that they'd made an effort.

With a silent prayer to an invisible god in whom he had long ago stopped believing, Christian Bauer raised himself to a crouch and made his move.

"*Halt!*"

Unbelievable. It was not possible. Where had that little bastard been hiding?

"*Halt!*"

Christian was up to his thighs in the dark, murderous flow of the Spree, but before deciding what to do he turned round. There was just the one guard. He looked about twelve-years-old. He was pointing a rifle in his general direction, the muzzle waving about like a tall-stemmed flower in a strong breeze. A nervous young soldier.

Christian had been thinking; which would be worse, capture and imprisonment, or escape and possible death. He raised his hands but kept inching backwards into the deeper water. He saw the flash and simultaneously felt the thump in the chest area as he was driven backwards. As a bullet travels faster than the speed of sound, he probably never actually heard the shot. The air filled with shouting voices on both sides of the river.

Heinrich Östler was nineteen and in his third day in the job. He had been taking a piss and had only just zipped up when the dark figure appeared from nowhere and advanced into the water. He had intended to shout "*Halt!*" for a third time when his cold, young fingers twitched and he unintentionally gunned another human being down. There was a commotion above the water as sleeping birds flapped and splashed around in the confusion. He tried to look for signs of a body but it was too dark and misty and his stupid, worthless torch had no battery life left.

The time was fourteen minutes past eleven on the seventh of November, nineteen eighty-nine. These details had to go into the incident report.

The definition of luck is generally accepted as *success or failure apparently brought by chance rather than through one's own actions*. There are those who believe that you create your own luck. There are those who believe that you get the luck you deserve. There are those who believe that some are born lucky. None is true. Luck is chance. What you do once you have been the beneficiary or victim of a piece of good or bad luck is most certainly down to you. Until the next time.

If there is a next time.

West Berlin, Thursday, November 9th

E Minor

I'm all for sex, drugs and rock and roll, more or less, but would substitute cheese or tea for the drugs. One of the guys in The Starrliners had given me some valium once, because I'd mentioned having difficulty sleeping the previous days. Now and again, I popped one. They took just enough off the edge of anxiety to be the difference between worrying needlessly about life until three in the morning, or nodding off for a kip. I had taken one the night before and, surprisingly, I had taken one before leaving the hotel.

With every day that I'd got closer to seeing her again, I'd felt more nervous. We were all meeting again at the Athena. It had been agreed for eight o'clock, brought forward from the previous nine, when I was handed a note from reception with the simple instruction to make it six-thirty. I had already walked there the day before, and again in the evening, and I knew, to the minute, how long it would take. I had bought myself a proper watch on my last birthday, one that told the time and did not stop randomly, so there would be no chance at all that I would arrive late.

I arrived late.

Alex wore no make-up, and her hair was drawn back severely and tied up in a ponytail of sorts. She had never in her adult life neglected her appearance, but that was of no importance to her. She wore the same recycled black clothing she had been wearing on the night.

She floated along the carriages on a cushion of disconnected emptiness, checking the seat numbers, stopping to let others pass, no longer bothering to smile even out of politeness. She dragged her case behind her as if she were taking a recalcitrant dog for a walk in the snow. She found her seats. She put her coat and handbag on the table then continued to the end of the carriage where there was still room for her case. She had no idea how she got her legs to move around at all. She had nibbled on small items of food almost constantly for the past thirty-six hours. She couldn't eat, but she knew she would become truly ill and unable to make the trip if she didn't ensure something was going into her system, besides pain and sorrow. She took the window seat and unpeeled a banana. She broke an inch off at a time and took an age to chew each piece as she stared blankly out of the window. She had boarded early. Berlin could not disappear quickly enough.

She took a sip out of a small bottle of water and she settled into her seat, pressing her head back and closing her eyes. She took one long breath in through her nose, held it, and exhaled through her mouth. She repeated this until a haze of semi-consciousness descended. She visualised a small stream, a grassy meadow, a tree in full bloom, the sky of clear pastel-blue. Not even the slight jolt, as the train pulled away from the station, took her away from this sanctuary. She would not open her eyes again until she was sure that she would not see Berlin again.

So it was with huge annoyance that someone dropped something metallic onto the table in front of her, shattering her idyll and making her start. She clenched her teeth and fought hard not to open her eyes. She took another long, long breath through her nose and started the process again.

"I'm sorry, madam, but you are sitting in my seat." It was a tired-sounding, raspy voice. A man.

Alex sighed, a tightening in her head. What kind of a fool interrupts a sleeping lady who looks like she's asleep, because of a bloody seat reservation? This was her seat, both of them were. Hers and...

She opened her eyes.

There was a collage of images, really. She was aware that a figure encroached on her left side and that there was a smell of, what was that, antiseptic? There was something on the table, several things. A clear plastic envelope with possibly a passport behind a seat reservation. An ugly crimson smear across it. Ink or ketchup or…blood? And the metal thing that had clanked onto the surface and jolted her? What was that? Something in brass?

A small novelty horseshoe, disfigured slightly on the right side. Alex leaned forward and groped at it with a trembling hand. Splattered like a baked bean that had been trodden on, and partly wedged in one of the horseshoe's holes was something in metal. A bullet.

She did not look to her left. Not yet. She closed her eyes.

It could be a soldier with a message.

It could be Max.

It could be Isabelle or Beth or even Charlie bloody Stokes.

Please, please, please. Don't do this to me, Alex thought to no one in particular, please don't make it someone else. Something, possibly a hand, was touching her shoulder.

She opened her eyes. They were instantly full of stinging tears. It was like looking through a windscreen in a rainstorm with the wipers broken.

His left arm was in a sling. There was a bandage wrapped around his right ear and across and round his temple and his face was full of scratches one or two of them deep.

She couldn't speak. But she could cry.

It was Christian. Alive. Maybe not well, but alive.

She reached out to him trembling and he offered her the tips of his fingers. She grasped them so as to be sure this was not all some sick mirage resulting from a dodgy banana.

It was not a mirage.

"I don't understand," she said.

"Well," he replied, "it's perfectly simple. You are sitting in my seat."

It broke the tension, the shock and the near-hysteria and Alex began to laugh through the tears. It was when her nose began to run and she fumbled for a tissue that she thought how unattractive she must have appeared. She dabbed at her face, blew her nose. She shook her head in disbelief, she stood up and they embraced.

"I look a mess, darling," she said. "But it's all right. You look worse."

She sat him down and then recoiled. Under an ill-fitting overcoat he seemed to be wearing pyjamas, sandals and… a hospital gown?

"Christian, what are you wearing?"

"They wouldn't discharge me," he said. "They think I'm in the bathroom.

An American soldier drove me to the station and opened the door as the train was about to leave."

"You can't go all the way to Milan like that."

"Yes, I can."

"No, you can't."

They were going to marry and spend the rest of their lives together, so they might just as well begin the journey with a long and pointless argument.

The door to the Athena restaurant was wedged open with a folded beer mat stolen from the new Irish pub that had replaced the Armenian bar four doors down. Fresh air was good for a restaurant. But there's no need for too much of a good thing. Dimitrios Fanariotis, as he had done on countless previous occasions, bent down and pulled the wedge out. He stepped outside, as the door swung closed, and took a habitual look up and down Kantstrasse. It was dark or he probably would have noticed the young man striding along, hunched against a cold breeze and looking at his watch.

E Minor

I wondered which of them I'd see first, and whether I'd be in before or after Joanna. It was quarter to seven when I got to the restaurant. I was on the opposite side of the street, intentionally, so that I could look across at the place for a few seconds. I have no idea why. During a suitable break in the traffic I skipped across the road, showing my usual flagrant disregard for the city's strict laws on jaywalking, and went in.

None of them was there. So I was glad I hadn't arrived on time. But then a man stood up, looking at me and gesturing with an open palm to a seat on his table.

Günther Reisz.

Now, what was that all about? And what was wrong with him? He looked like he'd been dead since last Tuesday and hadn't been told yet. It hadn't been any part of my plan for the evening, but of course I went over and took the hand that was offered me. The handshake hadn't changed. I removed my coat and draped it across my lap as I sat down.

"You're looking well, Charlie."

"You, too," I said. Why wouldn't I lie?

"That's all right. You don't have to say anything. You are shocked by my appearance. You should be. I'm sick. I'm dying. Maybe next month, maybe next week, maybe tomorrow." He looked at his watch and at first I thought he was going to give me another alternative time for his death, such as maybe at eight-thirty. "I asked you to come here earlier because I have something to say and then I must leave and this I must do before Joanna arrives."

It seemed impossible to arrive in Berlin and not immediately be immersed in a layer of uncalled-for mystery or confusion. So Günther changed the time I should go to the restaurant?

"Drink, Charlie?"

It was a question from Günther, but it was Dimitrios who made most of the noise. He hadn't recognised me when I slipped in, but he had now. He smiled and looked like he was unwinding to give me a big hug or a left hook, so I stayed seated and smiled. The big Greek bashed me around the shoulder blades a couple of times.

"Welcome back. You are well? Some more wine?"

It was one of those questions where you didn't answer, you just listened. He came back with a half-carafe of house red and while he was away I gave Günther's gaunt, grey-tinged skin and sunken eyes the once-over. It takes time to adjust to someone who has told you he is about to die soon. I felt uncomfortable and then hugely guilty for feeling uncomfortable. I mean, I wasn't the one who was about to die.

"It seems you are well now, Charlie. Any plans? Brian keeps me informed a little."

"This and that. Sorry, Brian?"

"Brian. Yes."

"Brian Levine?"

"Yes."

"So you met Brian on one of his trips here?" I wasn't expecting that one, either. Quite a coincidence I thought. And I pulled an appropriate face.

"I don't have time to have this kind of dialogue, Charlie. Perhaps it's best if you just listen."

Charming, I'm sure. Dimitrios had slopped some wine in a glass and I sent a mouthful scorching down my throat. I already couldn't remember whether red wine and valium were a good mix or not. Instinct told me not. I raised a glass to Günther and had a second, more conservative, sip and cleared the stage for him.

"I was born here in Berlin, Charlie. My father came from a family of industrialists, but my mother was Scottish. I was three years old when the War began. I had two sisters. My father of course was away, shooting at your grandfather, I daresay, and being shot at in return. Eventually my Mother was interned, and things got difficult until, through connections of my father, we were spirited away to Ireland, and after the War we moved to England. My father was killed somewhere or other, my mother never said, I think it was North Africa. We settled in Cambridgeshire first. I went to school, made friends. In nineteen fifty-four my mother was misdiagnosed and died from the polio epidemic. It hit me hard and, I have to admit, I turned a little against England, if not the English themselves. I decided to go back to Germany and went to University in Hamburg. That's where I met my wife."

There was a pause, but none of that glistening of the eyes that you might expect from one of those romantic stories.

"Are your feelings towards Joanna as strong as they ever were?"

Well, that came out of the blue, I didn't see it coming. Nor did I know what to do with it now that it had landed. But if there's one thing I never forget in situations such as this, it's how to buy some time.

"Sorry?"

"Come on, Charlie, I could be dead in an hour."

I thought that was a low blow, but I took the point regardless.

"Why does it matter?"

"Right now, it's the only thing that fucking matters to me. Now, are your feelings towards Joanna as strong as they ever were?"

Up until that point, I had listened simply because it was clear Günther had something to say to me. But I had not been interested. I was now more than interested. I was confused and yes, curious. Curious and confused. Welcome to Berlin. I was about to question his motives, but decided to answer instead.

"Yes."

"I shall leave here shortly, after I have told you a story. There is no happy ending. But there will be an ending, and that's all I ask for myself now. Ready?"

Was I ready? For what? I nodded.

"I killed your father."

Okay, I wasn't ready.

It had been on the news. Friends were calling each other to confirm whether they had heard. Strangers spoke on street corners. And people began to head in the direction of the Brandenburg Gate. If it were true, they wanted to be there and see it with their own eyes. Some were stuffing hammers into their pockets.

A world was coming to an end.

I stared at his face. This was the man? This was Troy's mysterious person? Günther bloody Reisz? And right under Beth's nose all those nights.

I was literally speechless.

He drank me in like a pro. I could sense he was weighing up each startled eyebrow and every furrow in the brow, calculating the mental cost of each new attempt to form a word. But he himself made no attempt to speak. He just fucking sat there like a sick man who had lost the pin from his grenade and was wondering whether you wouldn't mind terribly just hanging on to it for a second. Eventually, I settled again, like sediment in a pond, and dived right back in. Before I did, I drained my glass of house red. The valium could go to hell.

"Troy told me about my Dad. He didn't tell me it was you." I stooped to belch silently. "I think you'd better explain."

"I became friends with Brian Levine in '56. He had set up his management company, we shared a passion for the Arts. I played the piano. I stayed in Hamburg after my studies and got involved in everything. Rock and roll was big, clubs were opening everywhere, bands, musicians and singers were coming in from England all the time. Brian had a stable of artists. It was fun, there was money to be made, but it was rough and there were many crooks and corrupt officials. I became friends with two soldiers; your father Harry, and Troy's cousin Chad. Your father was trouble, Charlie. He wasn't a bad person, but he didn't think. I lost count of the number of times we had to get him out of a problem."

Why didn't that surprise me?

"I met Ingrid there, as I said, and we put a singing group together. She and three other girls recorded an album in an old-fashioned Beverley Sisters style and we got married. Nothing happened with the record. Your father, Chad, Brian and probably all of Ingrid's friends in Hamburg ended up with a copy, but…"

Just a little, I was edging towards the front of my seat.

"One of the girls foolishly got involved with the son of a local politician.

He was corrupt and stole with impunity, he was untouchable. One night this pig of a son beat Hanne, the girl from my wife's group. I went looking for him. Your father begged me not to get involved, that it would be too dangerous and that there would be terrible consequences. But I wasn't going to leave it. We found the son of a bitch easily enough and he was bragging about what he'd done to Hanne. I jumped him and hit him and kicked him and I put in too much fury and not enough accuracy. He was down on the floor and he pulled out a pistol. That was the kind of man he was. I went at him again and wrestled the gun off him easily enough, so he came at me with a knife."

Günther stopped and drank some water. I thought there was some colour to his cheeks, from the drama of his recollection, but it was just my imagination. He was still as grey as a slab of old fish.

"I fired the gun. It missed but he went stumbling over a low wall and onto a concrete walkway below and there was no doubt in my mind, even in the dark, that he was dead. I turned to run and there was your father, slumped against a doorway, holding his chest, blood coming through his fingers."

I didn't know how to handle this now. My Dad had never really been a real person before. He was someone I was told almost nothing about, and all of it bad. But this seemed altogether different.

"We had to think fast. Your father…" Günther stopped as if to correct himself, "Harry was conscious. He'd seen one of the son's friends in the shadows. We were in trouble. Harry told me to go. The police would arrive, they would call for an ambulance. This was West Germany, they would be quick! I remember him saying that and trying to laugh. He begged me to put the gun in his hand, to leave him to take responsibility. I left him. I rang for an ambulance from a phone box on the corner, and made plans quickly to save my wife from the consequences.

"If your father knew that your mother was pregnant with you, then he never told us. I had Ingrid out of our apartment in less than an hour and Chad helped get me to West Berlin. The plan had been to go to England once I had safely settled things here. Do you know what Ingrid said to me when I sent her away? That she was pregnant!"

He started to chuckle. He was the first man in my life I had ever seen chuckle and make it not seem like fun.

"I had been back here no more than three days when I was raided at four o'clock in the morning and that was the point my life went down a different road."

"Go on."

"I was put into the back of a car and driven into East Berlin. After that it was simple. Work for the rest of my life for the Stasi or life imprisonment in West Germany for murder. And it wouldn't have been life imprisonment. I would have had a fatal accident within six months, of that I was certain. So that was that. Now, let's talk about Joanna."

Pardon me?

"Sorry," I said. "That's it?"

Surely, there was more. Günther smiled and this time with feeling.

"I had to forget about Ingrid and the baby, and England, at least for a while. But I did not let go entirely of Brian. I still had quite a lot of money, and Brian also had money that was mine in a London bank. We were involved in lots of adventures, Charlie. It doesn't matter now, nobody cares. I became Günther Reisz and the old me vanished for ever."

"The old you?"

"My real name is Manfred Fassbinder."

"I see."

"Do you?"

"Is there something I should see?" Bloody hell, this was hard going.

"I found I had cancer a few years ago. It was a blow, of course, and a time for reflection. I recovered but, as you can see, once it gets you the first time… I only discovered that you existed at all then, after Chad was killed. And I don't know why, when you consider the life I've led, but I felt responsible and wanted you to know what I had done, and I also wanted to see my daughter just once."

I knew what Fassbinder meant in English.

It was the German word for a cooper.

That song from way back then. Chad Cafarella. Brian Levine.

Joanna Cooper.

I stood up so quickly that my chair tipped over backwards. I spoke rather rudely.

"Joanna! You're Joanna's father! And she doesn't know, does she? How could you have done that?"

"Sit down, Charlie," he said.

And I sat down.

"They are lifting travel restrictions from East to West Germany. That means it's over. The Wall will come down and quickly. People like me? We need to hide. I have met my daughter. I'm proud of her. I don't think she needs to see me like this, and I don't think it will make her world any better knowing what I have done with half of my life. I can't stop you telling her. That's a choice you have to make, Charlie."

He stood up. I couldn't believe he was going just like that.

"Wait. You can't just go. There's so much you haven't told me."

"I've told you everything you need to know."

"How do you know what I need to know?"

Günther, I still thought of him as Günther, was putting on his coat and it was hard work. He had a walking stick under the table, I hadn't noticed it. I bet he probably knew four ways to use it to kill a man. Buttoned up and with the stick safely in his hand, he made me open the door for him. I also hadn't noticed the car and driver outside, clearly for his use. He took hold of my arm and squeezed. Hard. It hurt.

"Don't think about this anymore, Charlie. Put it away. I don't want to spend another hour in a Greek restaurant going through every last detail of what I did to try and get Joanna here or to find out about you. I could, but then I'd have to kill you. And I hate Greek food. Tomorrow, or next Wednesday, a bus might knock you down, so don't waste time on it. Joanna will be here soon. You have another chance. It's your choice. Good bye, Charlie."

He turned and walked to the car. The driver was out quickly to open the door. Günther got in and, once the door closed, wound down the window.

"That song they bought from you, *Such Is Love*. I preferred your version."

They were his last words to me. Some sugar to sprinkle on top of the enormous stinking pile of unanswered questions he'd left steaming on the Kantstrasse pavement. The car pulled away and I watched it go. Without meaning to, I found myself walking after it. My coat and next appointment were both in the Athena. They could wait.

Charlie Stokes was in turmoil. As he reached and passed Savignyplatz, he folded his arms across his chest and held himself tightly. It was a gesture of defiance against the cold, and to keep his heart from jumping out of its moorings. He walked quickly, chin tucked down, shoulders hunched up, back slightly stooped. It was his cold weather gait. He reached the entrance to the Zoo and it was here that he became aware of a change in the atmosphere. It was no normal Thursday evening vibe.

Over the city a new layer of sound was being laid. Car horns were honking erratically, like a celebratory Morse code, and people were shouting at each other from across doorways and streets. An old lady, her head swathed in a crocheted scarf of red and black, tugged at Charlie's elbow and babbled imploringly at him in a torrent of incomprehension. He, of course, understood nothing, but there was no hiding the bewildered gleam in the old lady's eyes. She let go and approached an elderly couple. They huddled together, like a coven of witches, exchanging versions of the gossip.

Like New Year's Eve, Christmas Day or the night after Spurs beat City in the FA Cup replay in '82, there was an unmistakeable air of shared rising euphoria. Charlie stood watching, listening, thinking. When, finally, he began to shake from the cold, he hurried back towards Kantstrasse, swimming against a tide of excited young people heading in the opposite direction.

E Minor

I sat there, flipping the photograph around with my fingers. It seemed like a lifetime ago that I had taken it, and longer still that Joanna had given it to me as a memento. The four girls, sitting at this restaurant, smiling. More or less. I had looked at it often during the first few months, and then I'd put it away and tried to move on. I might normally have been amused that I was sitting at the same table this evening. But nothing felt normal.

I picked at some bread, trying to make my mind up. Round and round it went in my head, it still wasn't sinking in. What was I going to tell her? How do you pull that one out of the fire? How do you go out with the girl whose father killed yours? How ridiculous did that sound? Did I want to go out with her? That's what I'd come to find out, wasn't it?

Perhaps, after all, it was time to move on. I pulled a felt-tip pen out from a pocket and gazed at that funny little photograph again. Across the top I wrote 'a table in Berlin, October '87' and propped it up against my glass. I left a fifty Deutschmark note under a knife and put on my coat. As I buttoned it up, I saw her. She was outside, across the street, looking in.

My insides twisted and I thought I was going to be sick. Whatever that meant, it meant something.

Joanna was standing on the other side of the road, just as he had once been. She wore a navy trench coat and a scarf, but her head was bare and her hair was shining. Her hands were thrust deep into her pockets. Charlie waited, but she didn't move.

He did.

Charlie Stokes stepped out onto the street and they looked at each other like a pair of old gunslingers weighing up the odds. Charlie gazed at this girl who he had simply never seemed able to shrug off. Joanna smiled nervously. He took that as a good sign. His head was so exhausted from the battering it was receiving from his mind, that Charlie crossed the road without looking and was almost extinguished by a bus - just as Günther had warned. He stopped two feet away from her, still unable to speak.

Joanna didn't say anything either.

For more than thirty seconds they stood in a silent bubble of their own making, while people hurried past to gawp at the crowds congregating along the Wall.

Charlie had rehearsed what he was going to say. But that seemed irrelevant now. Whatever Joanna had intended to say had also frozen.

Joanna took her hands out of her pockets and they each took a step forward and embraced silently.

Inside the restaurant, Dimitrios stood in the doorway and watched them. Such is love, he thought. He had found the photograph and the money. He smiled.

Joanna put her arm through Charlie's and hugged it tight. She had no real idea what she was ready for, or how it would work out. It felt right, and that was all she asked for. They began to walk, slowly, back in the general direction of his hotel. Charlie was just thinking how life was not like an episode of Columbo: sometimes you just didn't get all the answers.

Each incapable of finding words considered worthy enough of breaking the silence, they continued. They didn't look at one another. They just walked. Charlie felt good. He had no idea whether this was the beginning, or the end, of something. But it was certainly something. He couldn't be sure if there would be a happy-ever-after, or just happy for as long as it lasted. But as long as there was some happy in it, somewhere, he would give it a go.

E Minor

Was now the time to tell her about her father? Should I *ever* tell her about her father?

Or about mine?

There was so much to talk about. Where would we even start? I wondered which of us would be the first to speak. I thought about whether it should be me.

On reflection, I decided that the best move would be to keep walking, and to shut the fuck up.

THE END

THE STORY BEHIND THE STORY

This book is a work of fiction of course, and intended as a piece of light entertainment. However, it would not have come about at all had it not been for a small, black and white photograph, which, in real life, was exactly as I have described in this story. A photograph of four young women, sitting at a restaurant table...in Berlin.

Writer Claire Elizabeth Terry, with whom I had contact on online social media, posted such a photograph and had written simply, 'Berlin. 1989.' When I saw the photograph, and the description, I immediately commented that it sounded like the opening of a novel. I had been to West and East Berlin in 1987 and it had left strong memories. As is often the case, two hours of banter ensued, with film producer Brian Levine also adding spices to the stew, and at the end of the evening I found that I had agreed to write a book! I think it was more of a dare than anything else. More glamour was added to the recipe with the lovely Michael L. Reiseneder and, between these three highly artistic and unspeakably gracious people, a slightly loopy idea became reality.

I can't show you the original photograph; it wouldn't be fair on the real people in it. But it's exactly the way I described it in the story, including the mystery elbow.

Although I will admit that Claire was one of the lovely ladies in the photograph, who she became in the book I couldn't possibly tell you.

What does this tell us? There's no such thing as a crazy idea.

What's yours?